THE LEGACY

Ann Markim

The Legacy
Copyright© 2019 Marge Knudsen *aka Ann Markim*
Cover Design Livia Reasoner
Prairie Rose Publications
www.prairierosepublications.com

Prairie Rose Publications

All rights reserved.
ISBN: 9781795037686

Chapter 1

October 23, 1874

Thankfully, I survived the Atlantic crossing and interminable train journey from New York to Cedar Falls. At times, I was so ill that I was not certain if I would live or die. On my eighteenth birthday, a downpour and constant jagged lightning kept me prisoner in my cabin. Throughout the day, squalls churned up colossal waves. The ship pitched from side to side, down and up with such force it flung me from my bed. I prayed that my death would be swift and painless when the vessel capsized.

Throughout my journey, memories of being with Jorn in Denmark last summer kept me going.

Despite the incessant sour smell of fermentation from Peder's brewery, I feel much better after my four days in Cedar Falls. I am lucky that my brother has willingly taken me in. He sent word to Jorn that I am here.

Peder says Jorn usually comes to town on Saturdays, so I expect he will call on me tomorrow. It seems like years since August, when he left me to return to America. I can hardly wait to see him, and I am sure he is eager to see me, too. I had so wanted to wear something pretty for him, but all my garments have been packed in trunks for so long that they are creased beyond help.

That is a small thing, as we have our wedding to plan, and I hope he will show me his vast farm, which he described so proudly when he told me of his life in Iowa. Many times, I have imagined what his house looks like, since I am soon to become its mistress. I wonder how many servants we shall have. Probably quite a few, since he has helped so many people emigrate from Denmark.

Oh, Jorn. Your Special Girl is here and ready to begin our life together.

The clock struck three. A boisterous din shook the floorboards. Rowdy men were gathering in the pub below. Not pub. Peder had called it a saloon. Was Jorn among the raucous group?

Anna Jorgesen studied her reflection in the small mirror hanging on the wall of Peder's room. Her hair, a bright blond when properly coifed, looked drab and disordered. Dark circles beneath her blue eyes added years to her gaunt face.

Footfalls, heavier and slower than Peder's, sounded on the stairs.

She tried to pat her limp hair into place.

A knock sounded.

Her stomach quivered. Smoothing a wrinkle in her brown satin skirt, she hurried across the room.

Smiling, she opened the door. "Hello, Jorn."

Eager to hold him close, she held out her arms.

Jorn Stryker backed down a couple of steps and stood there, wearing a gray flannel shirt and wool coat. A wide-brimmed leather hat rested atop his light brown hair, which curled slightly at his shoulders. The line of his mouth was grim.

She searched his face for a trace of his usual enthusiastic greeting.

"Anna." He removed his hat and held it at his side. His emerald eyes held no spark.

Her chest tightened.

"Please, come in and sit down," she said, forcing a cheerful note into her voice to cover her growing bewilderment. She led him into the barren parlor. Peder's only two armchairs stood facing each other with a small low table between them. His bed had been pushed against the wall.

Anna gestured for Jorn to take the nearest chair. He placed his hat on the table and sat. She seated herself opposite him.

"You're looking well," he said.

It sounded more like a perfunctory pleasantry than an observation, especially since she still bore the vestiges of her recent illness.

As she gazed at him now, anticipation of the warm sensations his whispered sweet words had conjured within her slipped away. His stern face mocked her memories of the swelling ache that had throbbed whenever they kissed. His distant manner crushed the residual desire that had burned so powerfully when he touched her, igniting the impulse to give herself to him over and over again.

Why didn't he say something? Anything?

Her mouth went dry.

Maybe he was waiting for her to start the conversation. She inhaled slowly. Might as well get right to the point. "I'm carrying your child."

"So your letter said." His gaze bored into her. "How do I know it's mine?"

She reeled. How could he even think that, let alone ask it?

Her stomach roiled as it had on the Atlantic crossing. She swallowed back the bile and straightened her spine. "Because the first time you took me, you found me to be a virgin. And there has been no one since you. I've been too ill for such things since I have been with your child."

He huffed and looked down at his hands, fisted in his lap. Opening his fingers, he unbuttoned his jacket. "Now you and your family expect me to marry you and make a respectable woman out of you."

"And an honorable man out of you," she said tersely.

"I have no room in my life for a wife and child. Farming my land and my trips to carry out my work in Denmark take all my time." He leaned forward, his tone irascibly patient. "There are many unmarried Danish men in the area, some I have brought over myself. Several of them are looking for young Danish women to marry. Cedar Falls has few eligible women of any age. Perhaps I could arrange—"

"You would allow another man to raise your child as his own? And your child to take another man's name?" She squeezed her shaking hands together. How could she have given herself so easily to a man capable of such a despicable proposition?

Jorn heaved a sigh and sat back in his chair. "And if I don't marry you?"

She inhaled a sharp breath. Tearing her gaze from him, she struggled to come to terms with the enormity of his question. She swallowed to quell the panic rising within her then looked up at him. "If I have this baby out of wedlock, my reputation will already be ruined," she snapped. "So, I will tell everyone in town that you are his father. Let them know what kind of a man you really are."

He watched her, steepling his hands and tapping the tips of his fingers together. "Your father has written that he will shoot me as a trespasser if I ever set foot on his land again." His jaw tightened. "And although I may be able to arrange another point of operation north of the occupied area, it will take at least a year to communicate the change to my compatriots behind the German border."

Since Peder had introduced Jorn to the family five years ago, they had done everything they could to support his efforts. Everyone considered him a hero, Anna most of all. Now, her father deemed him a criminal and her mother called him a devil.

"Fader disowned me and sent me out of the country," Anna said through clenched teeth. "I had to leave Moder and Bedstefa and all my friends behind."

"Speaking of your grandfather, he has written that, unless I marry you, he will no longer allow me to use his compound as a gathering point for those who wish me to lead them to America. I don't know anyone else in Copenhagen." He spoke as if Anna had orchestrated the letter. "I am without a location to bring the refugees from German occupation and meet up with the others who are to make a crossing with us."

An ache gripped her temples. "You should have thought of that before you seduced me."

"I seduced you?" he scoffed. "What about those pretty blue eyes fluttering at me? The close-fitting dresses that displayed your bosom? Your responsiveness to my kiss? You didn't tell your father about any of that. In his letter, he accused me of taking advantage of your innocence. You didn't tell him you came to me willingly."

Heat scorched her cheeks. "I was naïve. I didn't realize where my actions would lead." She swallowed. "I regret that I didn't keep a tighter rein on my behavior."

She closed her eyes and rubbed her temples for a moment. Blaming each other would get them nowhere. She clasped her hands together then looked at Jorn. "We are both at fault. But it's not fair to make our child suffer as a bastard because of our mistakes."

He covered his face with both work-roughened hands, then rubbed them downward hard enough to draw the skin with them, leaving a grotesque angularity to his features like a drawing of the devil she had seen in a book.

Again, he steepled his hands and tapped his fingers together. His eyes appeared unfocused, and the corners of his mouth sagged.

"I will come for you at eleven o'clock on Wednesday morning. The Justice of the Peace can marry us then." He stood abruptly, swept his hat from the table, and strode out the door.

Anna stared after him. Today she had seen a side of Jorn she had never expected. A sour taste burned in her throat. Trembling, she rose from the chair and staggered to the bed. She clutched a pillow as sobs wracked her body.

• ♥ •

Anna sat beside her new husband on the wagon seat, watching the countryside pass. The wheels bumped over the rutted trail. Brown, leafless trees and gray-black grass, weeds and crop residue, killed off by the frost, seemed even duller under the ashen sky. Incessant wind blew the chill right through her thick wool coat, numbing her fingers and causing her teeth to chatter. If only Jorn had brought an enclosed carriage instead of this open wagon. She sighed and rubbed her hands together to warm them.

Since leaving Cedar Falls, she and Jorn had said little to each other. The man beside her was no longer the kind, caring lover she had known last summer. She should not have forced him to marry her. Would he make their life together a torture?

It would be a high price to pay for her indiscretions, but surely, her father would relent and accept her back into the family now that she could legally give her baby Jorn's name. Once she settled into her new home, she would write to her parents about the marriage. The Justice of the Peace had united them in matrimony with few words and only her brother witnessing the occasion. No joy, no celebration, no wedding feast with friends and family. Moder would be disappointed to learn the ceremony had not taken place in the church, before God.

Jorn pulled back on the reins, rousing Anna out of her reverie. The horses slowed as they pulled the wagon around a curve in the trail, then resumed their steady pace. Again, Anna set her gaze on the bleak scenery and returned to her thoughts.

Filthy dust kicked up by the horses and the relentless wind caked on her brown satin traveling dress, which had been clean and pressed for her wedding. The rest of her things remained packed away, still creased and wrinkled.

The wagon lurched. The force nearly knocked Anna off the seat. Jorn reached over with one strong hand and clutched her coat. Her trunks thumped the box with such an impact she feared they might break through the floor. She grasped the iron rail that ran along the seat back until she was certain she had regained her balance. Without a word, Jorn released his hold and urged the horses to pick up the pace. A flurry of nausea churned in her stomach. Placing a protective hand on her abdomen, she turned to look back at the cargo. All was secure.

"My land starts here." Jorn pointed to a split-rail fence to her right. Then he moved his arm and pointed to a cluster of buildings off in the distance. "That is my homestead." He returned his hand to the reins. "There are three smaller homesteads on my property."

Last summer she had been impressed when he told her about his land. Today his boast only elicited a sigh. At least he was finally talking to her.

"The two not visible from here are occupied by greenhorns," he continued. "Each will be working on my farm for three years, to reimburse me for the money I paid toward their passage to America."

Anna stole a glance at Jorn's face. Its animation surprised her. She wanted to prolong this civil conversation. "Did they both cross with you this summer?"

"Yes." He gestured toward a small farm on the other side of the path. "The place up ahead on the left is my other homestead. My hired man, Morton Andreasen, lives there. He worked off his debt to me last year, and now I pay him a small wage to help me run the farms and train the new men. He is saving up to buy a place of his own one day."

The home appeared to be not much larger than her father's chicken house, and the out buildings were small. In the dooryard an ample stack of wood was piled near a solid fence, and two cows stood in the pen beside one of the sheds.

"How much land do you own?" Anna asked.

"Five hundred and sixty acres." His chest expanded as he spoke.

She stared at him. That more land than her father owned, and he was considered quite rich. Her husband might not be honorable, but he was ambitious. Anna would be sure to mention the impressive size of Jorn's farm in her letter to her mother. Her father might reconsider his decisions once he learned of her husband's wealth.

"What do you do with all that land?"

"Raise corn and wheat crops. And beef cattle to sell for meat. I am acquiring milk cows, but I will need more help before I can operate a dairy."

"Do you have a housekeeper?"

Jorn laughed derisively. "No. It would be an unnecessary expense." He looked at her, his face grim. "And, anyway, now I have you."

She worried her lower lip. He sounded as if he considered her a possession, a servant, not a wife. She closed her eyes. Had she made yet another horrible mistake?

• ♥ •

While Jorn hitched the horses to a nearby post, Anna scrutinized her new home. Constructed of hewn logs, the structure listed slightly to the left. Two windows flanked the coarse slab of wood that served as the front door.

Her chest tightened.

Jorn expected her to live in this hovel. For as big as he claimed his farm to be, his small cabin and the rough-built outbuildings exuded poverty. It was nothing like the splendid houses and granaries of successful farmers in Denmark. Nothing like the home where she had grown up.

Carrying a box of supplies from the general store, he approached her, hard-faced. "Open the door."

She hurried ahead of him and lifted the rusty latch. Instead of holding the door, she left it open and preceded him inside. She found herself in a dingy parlor that smelled of damp earth, only a slight improvement over the odor of fermentation that permeated Peder's home. Before the open fireplace two chairs were separated by a small table holding a kerosene lamp. A half-full woodbox sat in the corner nearest the hearth. Along the adjoining wall stood crate filled with books and papers. To her right was a bedroom, with a small chest of drawers adjacent to the head of a rope bed. No door, not even a curtain, screened it from view of the parlor.

A heaviness settled in her belly.

Haphazard patches in the chinking dotted the hewn-log walls. A ladder led to the second story, which spanned only the parlor and bedroom. The kitchen jutted out to the rear of the house, an apparent afterthought.

Jorn set the groceries on a bench in the kitchen. "I am going to unhitch the horses and put the wagon in the stable."

"What about my trunks?" Anna asked.

"They are too large for the bedroom. I will put them in the barn."

"You expect me to go outside to get a change of clothes or one of my personal belongings?" Pain throbbed in her temples. "I would wager you do not keep your clothes there."

"I do not own two large trunkfuls." His gaze skimmed over the meager space inside the cabin. "I suppose I could put the chests in the woodshed." His tone was as cold as the cabin.

Wary, Anna stared at him. "Where is that?"

"Out here." Jorn led her through the kitchen door.

Against the outside wall stood a lean-to, filled with wood splits in cookstove- and fireplace-sized pieces. A makeshift gate enclosed the open end. Anna peered into the darkness, allowing her eyes to adjust. Something moved. A rustle led her gaze to several small, dark figures with long tails scurrying among the stacks.

She shrieked.

Jorn laughed. "They are only mice."

Gritting her teeth, she turned to face him. "I will not have my things here where vermin will chew on them." She put her hands on her hips. "If you will not allow my trunks in the house, leave them in the wagon. I will return to Peder's now.

You may pick up your team tomorrow."

Anna did not know what choice Jorn would make, and she did not care. She could not live in this ramshackle house. Although she had taken her marriage vows with an honest intent to make them work, her resolve had faded over the course of the afternoon.

He studied her for many tense minutes. She held his gaze, saying nothing.

His eyes widened, and his smile disappeared. "Where do you want the trunks?"

Instead of triumph, fear swamped her. Jorn might find some cruel way to retaliate. She stepped back inside the house and pointed. "I suppose they will have to stand along that empty wall of the parlor."

It was the only space large enough to be able to walk around them. Although pawing through her belongings every time she wanted to retrieve something would be inconvenient, she would have no choice.

While shopping with Peder in Cedar Falls, she had seen a cabinet maker's shop. Enough currency remained in her satchel to purchase a small armoire or a plain chest of drawers, though the idea of setting a piece of fine furniture on this dirt floor galled her.

Jorn wrestled each of her trunks into the house. Grunting, he jostled them into the location she had designated. When he finished, he swiped the back of his hand across his sweaty forehead. "What do you have in these things? Bricks?"

Anna recalled the care and craftsmanship with which her generous grandfather had fashioned these trunks. "Bedstefa made them strong and heavy. To withstand the ocean crossing."

When Jorn had placed the trunks in the parlor, he turned to her. "I am going to change into my work clothes and do the chores. You can start supper."

His tone was gentler now, but it did not still the agitation churning inside her.

Last summer, she had reveled in his beautiful, strong body, but his demeanor in America had extinguished all traces of the desire she had felt only a few months ago.

As he headed toward the bedroom, she turned to check the foodstuffs in the cupboards and put away the groceries. Her fingers shook as she reached for the cabinet door. She scanned the cans and jars on the shelves, but could not focus. She buried her face in her hands, inhaled half-a-dozen deep breaths to stave off the sobs threatening to overtake her.

After a quick inventory of the provisions, she squinted to see the mantle clock. Ten past four, nearly time to begin making supper. She looked down at her dress, which needed to be cleaned, pressed, and put away for fine occasions. After Jorn went outside, she would change into a house frock.

A few minutes later, he appeared in coarse worn pants, a flannel shirt, and wooden shoes with knee-high leather tops. "I will bring you some eggs and milk."

"Eggs. Milk," she said in English, showing off some of what Peder had taught her.

Jorn raised an eyebrow. He reeled off some words she did not understand.

"Peder has been teaching me two or three words each day," Anna said, disappointed that she had to return to speaking Danish. "Perhaps you can teach me a few every morning, and I can practice my English with you at night."

"There is no reason for you to learn English." Jorn growled. "Most of our neighbors speak Danish, church services are in Danish, and many of the shops in town have at least one clerk who speaks Danish."

Anna nibbled her lower lip. Throughout her train trip from New York to Cedar Falls, communicating with people she met had been problematic. The Latin and French she spoke fluently had offered no help. A slightly sweet metallic taste met her tongue. She swallowed. "But English is the language of America. Since I am going to live here, I want to learn to speak it."

Jorn rolled his eyes and exhaled. "We will be retuning to Denmark when the Danes again control South Jutland."

Without even a glance in her direction, he snatched a tattered coat from a peg by the kitchen door, shrugged into it, and started out.

"Dinner will be ready at six o'clock," she called after him.

A smile tugged at the corners of her mouth. They would return to Denmark. She would see her grandfather again, and attempt to make peace with her father. When would King Frederick wage war for the occupied land? Not soon. The previous conflict had left the monarchy nearly destitute.

In the meantime, Jorn expected Anna to live as a pauper. At least they had enough food for tonight's meal. She had seen some canned beef for making gravy, and ingredients for dumplings. A few canning jars of vegetables and fruits stood in the cupboard. Surely, Jorn had not put them up himself. He obviously employed no servants. Then who?

She set out a mixing bowl and checked the crate near the cookstove. Few pieces of wood remained. After she changed, she would raid the supply by the hearth and start the fire. She could not bear to enter the lean-to, infested with mice and who knew what other vermin. She shuddered.

Some cats might reside in the outbuildings. If so, she could lure them to the woodshed with milk, in hopes they would keep the rodents under control.

Anna donned a wrinkled cotton housedress and shivered in the cold of the house. The cookstove would warm the kitchen until after they ate. Then Jorn could get some more wood from the lean-to and light a fire in the hearth.

Orange light streamed through the west windows. Anna wanted to see what was in the loft before the dwindling daylight faded. Maybe there was room for her trunks.

She climbed the ladder with deliberate care, then stepped into the nearly-dark attic. Only a small, rectangular window at one end admitted light. The creaky wooden floor was not thick enough to support much more than her weight, let alone that of her trunks.

She stood for a moment until her eyes adjusted to the gloom. When the shadows transformed into silhouettes of small, rough-wood crates, she inched to the closest one. Jorn would not like her snooping in his things. She considered climbing down the ladder, but instead, reached out and opened the dusty, hinged lid. Papers filled it to the brim. It was too dark to read them now, so she returned the lid to its original position.

A braided rug lay atop the next container, a cleaner version of the first. She raised the cover and found neatly-folded clothing reaching midway to the top. If all of Jorn's wardrobe fit in this crate, in the bedroom chest, and on the pegs by the door, it was scant.

She replaced the rug and stepped slowly toward the third and final box, careful to find enough open floor to avoid tripping.

"Anna!"

She stumbled backward, catching herself on the crate of clothing. Heat flooded her cheeks.

"I am up here," she called. She cleared her throat to banish the annoying tremor in her voice. "Checking to see if this would be a suitable place to store my trunks." The third crate would have to wait.

"They are too heavy. They would fall through that floor. Come down, now. I have the milk and eggs."

She crept to the ladder and climbed back to the ground floor. Jorn had left. From outside came the rhythmic clank of a pump handle hitting its stop.

She crossed to the bucket of milk and basket of eight eggs on the sideboard. He had brought enough of both for breakfast, too. She lit the lamps on the hutch and the table.

Jorn came through the door carrying two full pails of water, which he set on the floor next to the cupboard. Anna shivered as a burst of frosty air accompanied him.

"It is going to be a cold night," she observed.

He chortled. "Winters here make Denmark's seem like spring in comparison. I will get you some wool the next time I am in town. You can make yourself some warm clothes."

She took a breath. "Thank you, but I prefer to accompany you and pick out my own material."

"No." He turned and strode out the door. She stared after him.

Gritting her teeth, Anna started the fire in the cookstove. For the first time since she arrived at the house, her icy hands and chilled body began to warm. After she set the canned beef on to heat, she fetched a shawl from her trunk.

By six o'clock, the kitchen was comfortably toasty. Two steaming bowls of beef and dumpling stew waited on the table. A plate with four slices of the bakery bread and a jar of honey with a spoon served as the centerpiece. Though not fancy, it would do. The only spices she had found were salt and pepper.

She said a silent thank-you to her mother for insisting Anna learn to read recipes and prepare simple dishes, even though most of the family's meals were prepared by the cook.

A quarter-after-six came and went. At half-past, she returned her bowl of stew to the cooking pot, still warm on the stove. She stirred and dipped out a hot portion.

This was their wedding night. On her Atlantic crossing, Anna had dreamed it would be sweet and romantic as she and Jorn became reacquainted. Tonight, she had cooked their meal instead of enjoying a feast prepared by others in their honor.

The least he could do was be on time.

Alone at the table, she ate. Was Jorn late just to spite her? With each minute that ticked by, the tension in her neck and back tightened.

What would he expect of their first night as husband and wife? She felt no obligation to have marital relations with him after the lack of regard he showed for her and her child today.

Maybe the sight of her repulsed him. Did he plan to be her husband in name only? She could possibly tolerate that if he treated her with more respect.

A quarter-to-seven.

Anna rose and poured water into a fresh pot on the stove. When it was hot, she would wash her dishes and his if he arrived soon to eat his meal. She gave the stew a stir and set it off to the side, away from the direct heat so it would not taste of scorched gravy. She refused to give him a reason to find fault with her cooking.

Needing something to take her mind from Jorn's absence, she pulled her knitting needles and yarn from her trunk. On her trip into town with Peder, she had purchased fine wool to make a baby blanket. The clerk in the dry goods shop had not spoken Danish, despite what Jorn had said. The transaction would have been easier if she had not depended on Peder to translate. She must learn the language of Americans.

She tried in vain to concentrate on her knits and purls. A small flutter in her abdomen reminded her of the life inside her. Anna's mother had delayed telling her father about the pregnancy for as long as she thought she could. Both she and Anna feared his fury, but neither had imagined that he would disown Anna and send her out of Denmark. The more her mother pleaded for him to change his mind, the more steadfast he became. Moder had been able to secure only a few days to arrange transportation for Anna and her belongings to her maternal grandfather's house in Copenhagen. Fader agreed to this plan, but in the days Anna remained at home he had treated her as if she was invisible. In return for this concession, he had demanded that Moder sever all contact with Anna once she left. He had yelled and sworn at her mother, and she had acquiesced for fear he would send Anna away before preparations were complete. Anna's heart ached at the thought of never having contact with her mother again. Hopefully, over time, Moder would be able to soften Fader's heart enough to allow her to write.

Anna rubbed her aching temples. She returned the yarn and needles to her trunk and washed her dishes. Having little energy left from the weight of the day and Jorn's conspicuous absence, Anna decided to lie on the bed until he was ready for his supper. She could only guess how much longer he would be. The clock on the mantle read nearly eight.

She shifted positions, trying to find a comfortable one on the lumpy straw mattress.

Jorn had married her, giving their baby his name. He was as angry, and maybe as confused as she was, about how to behave as husband and wife. They had no real courtship to get to know each other, to build trust and respect before catapulting into married life.

Her eyelids grew heavy.

She was a married woman. It was time think of her future. She could remain angry and act like a shrew, or she could resign herself to what was and concentrate her energy on creating a proper home and family. Her choice crystalized. She had to do what was best for her baby.

The house had grown frigid. Wrapping the blanket around her shoulders, Anna heaved herself off the bed and went to feed the fire in the stove. The mantle clock's tick-tocking echoed through the cabin. She glanced up at it.

A quarter-past-ten. Where was Jorn?

Gooseflesh tightened her skin. She crossed to the window and stared out into the empty darkness.

Chapter 2

October 29, 1874

All my life I have dreamed of a marriage like Bedstefa and Bedstemor had. They always showed an obvious fondness and respect for each other. Joy at being together. They had friends. A nice house. Last summer, I expected I would have this with Jorn. No more.

He has turned out to be much like Fader. Stern. Domineering. Demanding. Fader insisted that Moder and us children meet his expectations. Now that I am in America, what he wants no longer matters, and I will not allow myself to become a carpet for Jorn to walk over. Yesterday, he was more polite than on our wedding day, but he is cold and distant.

Bedstefa offered to let me live with him. I should have accepted that offer, but marrying Jorn to give my baby his name was important. He gave me much joy and love when he was in Denmark. I do not know what to make of this change in him.

While I am with child, I cannot face another Atlantic crossing. After I give birth, I will write to Bedstefa to tell him the baby and I are coming. I will ask Peder to make the arrangements. As a married woman with a child, I will be able to hold my head high. Fader might even relent enough to let me visit Moder.

On Thursday, Jorn decreed that Anna care for the chickens. There weren't many, but enough to supply their household needs. After two egg-gatherings, she still had not resigned herself to the dreadful task.

Bucket in hand, Anna opened the door to the chicken house. The revolting stench triggered a wave of nausea. She retreated down the path and drew in several breaths of fresh air.

Closing her eyes, she berated herself for giving into Jorn's unreasonable demands that she carry out this chore. Her throat tightened, and pressure built behind her eyes.

She forced her breathing into a slow, regular pattern.

When she recovered, she trudged inside the building and spread ground corn in the trough. Now that she knew which hens would calmly allow her to take their eggs and which would peck in protest, she hoped to lure the more crotchety birds from their nests. A flock of hens ran to the food, clucking their approval. Anna set about gathering the eggs.

Jorn had been late for dinner the first three nights of their marriage, and this afternoon he rejected her request that he take her with him to town. He said he had business to handle alone, but he promised to mail her letter to her mother.

What kind of business could he be involved in that he didn't want to tell her? Seeing another woman? A prostitute? Anna cringed. They had slept in the same bed these past three nights, but she was thankful Jorn had not suggested consummating their marriage.

Before leaving for town, he said Mr. Hansen would bring milk to the house. This greenhorn lived in the little shack in the grove, and helped Jorn with milking and other chores. At least she might have a few minutes of conversation with someone other than her husband.

A pinch on the back of her hand jerked Anna from her reverie. She must remember to deflect the beaks of pecking hens. Rubbing the red welt that was forming, she reproached herself for caving to Jorn's expectations.

She finished collecting eggs and headed for the house, walking slowly and taking deep breaths of the fresh air. Since she would have to remain here for at least five months, she needed to speak with Jorn about their immediate future. Tomorrow, on the Sabbath, he might be more amenable to such a discussion.

Jorn hadn't mentioned anything about church. She had attended services on virtually every Sunday of her life, including last week with Peder. When Jorn came home, she would insist they go to church.

Anna had scarcely returned to the kitchen and removed her cloak, when a knock came at the back door. She opened it. A young man, barely older than she, stood holding a bucket. He removed his wool cap, revealing a head of thick hair, blonder even than Peder's.

"I'm Halvor Hansen," he said in Danish. His blue eyes held her gaze for a moment before he looked downward. "Mr. Stryker asked me to bring you some milk."

Anna smiled to reassure him. "My *mand* told me to expect you. Please put the bucket on the bench."

The man did so then turned to face her. His gaze darted to the cookstove then returned to Anna. "Smells like my *moder's* kitchen in here. I've missed her since I came to America."

Anna missed her mother's kitchen, too. She glanced at the table with two places already set. Though having company for dinner would be nice, it would be improper to invite a man she did not know to join her. "Why did you leave Denmark?"

"I'm from south Jutland." His eyes narrowed. "I received my notice of conscription into the Prussian army. I could never fight against the motherland. So, I had to leave. Just like Mr. Stryker."

"And your parents? How did they feel about your coming to America?"

"It is only my *moder*. She's living with my sister and her family. My brother-in-law is serving his military term for the Prussians." He sighed heavily. "But Moder is a proud Dane. She understood why I had to leave." He squared his shoulders. "In two years, when I have satisfied my debt to Mr. Stryker, I hope to find a paying position and bring her here."

Anna bit her lip. Her mother would never be able to come to Iowa, even for a visit. Her father wouldn't allow it.

"It will take me three or four years to save for her passage," he continued.

Anna took a pitcher from the sideboard.

He eased toward the door. "I best be getting back to work."

Anna recalled seeing his shack when Jorn first brought her to the farm. It was small. Mr. Hansen probably had only a fireplace for heat and cooking. "Would you like to take a slice of bread and some chicken for your supper?" She reached for a loaf she had made yesterday. "The meat will need a bit more cooking before you eat it."

Mr. Hansen looked longingly at the bread then lifted his chin. "Thanks, but no. I'm not a beggar."

Her hand flew to her mouth. She hadn't meant to insult him. An idea popped into her mind. "Do you speak English?"

His brow furrowed. "English? I'm learning. Why?"

"Because I want to learn, too, and I would be pleased to give you food in return for helping me." She smiled and told him the words she already knew. "Teach me three new words and I'll send chicken and bread with you in payment." Jorn would be furious, but he had gone to town without her. She cut a thick slice from the heel of the loaf.

A grin broke across Mr. Hansen's boyish face. He took a step toward her. "What words?"

She pursed her lips before giving him her selections. He taught her "mother," "father," and "child," before he walked out the door whistling, a bowl of food in his hands.

Anna glanced at the clock. Five before five. Quickly, she washed two potatoes and popped them into the oven beside the roaster. Dinner would be ready by six, whether Jorn was here or not.

From the peg by the door, she retrieved her cloak. She donned it, then picked up the empty water buckets. In the waning daylight, she hurried to the pump and filled them. As she passed the woodshed on her return to the house, an orange and white cat scampered across her path.

She smiled. This was the same cat that came this morning to drink from the saucer of milk she had set out. If it continued to visit the area, it might rid the house and lean-to of rodents.

After carrying the water inside, she dipped a clean, tin coffee cup into the milk. With the lantern in one hand and the mug in the other, she returned to the woodshed and re-filled the saucer. She had yet to see the feline catch a mouse, but she felt better knowing the cat was frequenting the area.

Back in the kitchen, Anna poured some water into the basin and washed her hands. She cut up four apples she had brought earlier from the root cellar, where she had also discovered a cache of spices. She set a small pot of water on the stove to boil, added cinnamon, nutmeg, sugar, and the apple slices, then stirred. The sweet aroma of spiced fruit filled the kitchen. When the fruit had softened and the syrup thickened, she slid the pot to a cooler area of the stovetop.

The kitchen door opened. She whirled around to see Jorn, setting a brown baker's box tied with a string on the table. "What's that?"

"It's for later. Do not open it." He turned and went back outside.

With narrowed eyes, Anna stared after him. Was he going to do chores? It was nearly six. If he missed dinner again, she would peek in the box.

In a few moments, he returned with a crate of groceries. Anna recognized the labels on four bottles of Peder's beer, which lay on top. He moved the half-empty water bucket to the floor and set his carton on the bench, then removed his coat and hung it on a peg.

"Dinner will be ready in a few minutes. I just have to make the gravy," Anna said, half-expecting him to grab his coat and leave.

He walked to the basin. "That will be fine."

Perhaps he'd had enough cold meals. Anna pulled the roaster from the oven and drained the drippings into a skillet.

She set the chicken aside, mixed some flour with the fresh milk, and added it to the drippings. The sauce thickened as she stirred.

Jorn sat at the table. "There's something I must tell you."

His gaze locked with hers for a moment. Returning her attention to the gravy, she straightened her spine and steeled herself. "Yes?"

He didn't speak for a long while, but she felt him watching her. Finally, he cleared his throat. "When I returned from Denmark, I began courting a woman."

Anna's chest tightened. Through another prolonged period of silence, she waited, chastising herself for being too meek to ask for the answers she deserved. Had it been his habit to seduce women wherever he went? She bit her lower lip. He had begun seeing this woman after he had been with her. Had he bedded this one, too? Was she also in a delicate condition?

"When I received your letter in September, I doubted you would really come to America, so I continued to see her."

Anna was carrying his child. How could he think she would not come?

His gaze burned into her, but she refused to look at him. She inhaled a long breath to dispel the anguish gnashing at her core.

"In early October, she left for Kimbalton to attend her sister in childbirth and to help with the other children during her recovery." Jorn paused again.

Anna ached to rebuke him, but found nothing to say. Without moving her head, Anna stole a sideways glance at him. He sat hunched over, his elbows on his knees, hands steepled.

"When Peder told me you were scheduled to arrive in Cedar Falls, I wrote her that I needed to speak with her as soon as she returned." He straightened. "I felt I should talk with her in person to explain about you. On Wednesday, before I came for you, I stopped at the post office and found her letter waiting for me. She sounded very excited, as if she expected me to propose marriage."

Did he plan to marry the harlot? Had he forgotten so easily his declarations of love last summer? She swallowed hard.

"I had no intention of proposing to her. Her family is set against drink and dance, the strictest of the Holy Danes." He paused for several long moments, shifting in his chair. "It had been a proper courtship, and since I hadn't kissed her yet, she had no reason to read marriage into my words."

If he did not plan to propose, why did he court her? Anna clenched her teeth to keep from screaming at his deceit.

"But I regretted my letter had led her to that expectation." Jorn exhaled a loud breath. "I felt duty-bound to clear things up with her. It would have been better if I could have done so before you and I were wed, but that was impossible. It is done now."

Anna lost her breath, as if he had punched her chest.

Duty-bound to talk with *her*. The woman with whom he had a "proper" courtship, unlike his seduction of Anna.

But he had not planned to marry the harlot. Was he going to bed her, too?

When he came to see Anna at Peder's home, Jorn had not behaved as if he felt duty-bound to give her and their child his name. At least, not at first.

In the end, he had done just that. She had to give him that much credit. The gravy continued to bubble, now nearly thick enough to stand the spoon in it. Anna removed the skillet from the heat and poured the sauce into a bowl on the sideboard. She set it on the table between the two plates.

Jorn grasped her arm. All the muscles in her body tensed. She clasped her hands together and slowly turned to face him.

His jaw tightened. "I should not have let this hang between us these last few days. I should have told you sooner."

Despite his earnest words, she jerked her arm free. "Yes, you should have."

Jorn hung his head. "I am sorry for it."

Tonight, he was trying to be a good husband. If she didn't

forgive him now, she might never again have a chance to make their relationship what it should be. She reached out and touched his cheek. "Thank you for telling me. I hope you will always be honest with me."

"I will." Taking her hand in both of his, he tenderly lifted it to his lips.

Warmth spread through her fingers.

He tipped his head back and fixed his intense emerald gaze on her. "The bakery box holds a wedding cake," he said softly. "I was thinking we might consider this our wedding night."

• ♥ •

A loud racket startled Anna awake. She bolted upright in bed, trying to identify the deafening noise. It sounded like a clatter of metal pots, drums, and discordant horns. A soft glow lit the window.

She grabbed Jorn's arm. "What is that?"

With an irritated groan, he rolled off the straw mattress and stood, peering into the light. He turned to Anna. "I think it is a shivaree."

Confusion replaced the last vestiges of sleep. "A what?"

"Shivaree." He pulled his pants from the bedpost. "It is a custom in these parts. Friends and relatives call on a newly married couple late at night and serenade them. Instead of music, they use whatever they can to make as much noise as possible."

"Why?"

"It is sort of a party to celebrate a wedding. Peder and I have attended several in town after friends have married."

Anna frowned. "I do not have enough food to feed a large group."

Jorn chuckled. "They do not expect that. Put on your coat. They are waiting for us to come outside and kiss. Then the din will stop."

Kiss Jorn in front of strangers? It did not seem proper, but this was America. Perhaps it was the custom here to show affection publicly. If her husband and the people outside expected her to do so, she would.

"Jorn! Anna! Jorn! Anna!" A chorus of merry voices called in singsong repetition.

She stole a few more seconds before leaving the warmth of the bed, then slipped on her shoes and coat. Swallowing against her queasy stomach, she joined Jorn at the door. He opened it, and the clamor intensified. Several gunshots rang out. Anna flinched.

"They are just firing in the air. Do not worry." Jorn took her arm and guided her outside.

Several dozen people, some in wagons and carriages, others on foot, clustered around the house, talking and laughing. Lanterns dotted the gathering. Women banged on pots with large spoons. One man blew random notes on a bugle. Another pounded an iron wagon wheel with what looked like a pump handle. Anna could not see what other makeshift instruments were being played farther back in the group.

"Kiss! Kiss! Kiss! Kiss!"

Jorn twirled her toward him and drew her close. His lips met hers. Uncomfortable heat flooded her cheeks and neck. After such a tender evening, in which they had consummated their marriage, it seemed shameful to degrade their beautiful night in this way.

As Jorn's kiss lingered, the tempo of the clatter increased.

"Three cheers for Jorn and Anna Stryker!" someone in the crowd shouted in Danish. It sounded like Peder although she could not be certain.

"Hoorah! Hoorah! Hoorah!" roared through the cold night air.

Jorn released her, turned to the assembly, and raised his hands, silencing the racket. "My wife and I are honored that so many of you would come out on such a cold night to celebrate our marriage. We thank you."

Anna forced a smile. She supposed it really was an honor, and the number of people here gave testament to Jorn's standing in the community.

From the direction of the grove, a figure ran toward the house, lantern in hand. Halvor Hansen. Was he coming to see what all the noise was about or to join the party? At least she knew someone.

A couple stepped forward. Shorter than Jorn, the man was bundled in a sheepskin coat. He shook hands with Jorn and offered his congratulations in Danish, expelling a hint of beer with his words. The woman, wearing a full cloak with a fur hood, handed Anna two jars of canned peaches.

Anna nearly dropped the unexpected gift. "*Tak.*"

"I am Greta Ringe, and this is my husband, Vilfred," the woman said. "We hope you will be very happy."

They moved on and another couple came forward. A raucous line began to form behind them.

"This is Mr. and Mrs. Holden," Jorn said. "They live down the road."

"It is nice to meet you," the wife said.

"And you." Anna was pleased that this couple also spoke Danish.

"I am Brigitte." She held out a basket of biscuits.

Anna smiled. "Thank you for taking the time to make these for us."

"Will there be services at your place tomorrow?" Jorn asked.

"Pastor Spelman will be there at ten o'clock," Mr. Holden said.

"We will have a potluck lunch after, if you would like to join us." Brigitte smiled warmly.

"That we will." Jorn put his hand on Anna's shoulder.

Thank God they would be attending worship and staying to socialize after the service. She could meet her neighbors and, maybe, make some friends. A joyful energy warmed her. So many spoke Danish! She no longer felt so isolated.

As the people in line continued to pass, offering small gifts and good wishes, Anna wondered how so many had learned of their wedding. Did they know she was with child? Surely not, or they would not be greeting her with so much enthusiasm. Tomorrow she would wear a dress that concealed her growing belly.

When the crowd had thinned, another man and woman approached. She carried a crock with fabric cover held in place by a ribbon.

Jorn spoke to the couple in English, and they responded to him in kind. His voice carried the same warm and friendly tone he had used with the Danes. Anna could pick out the words "milk" and "cheese," but no others.

After a brief conversation, he turned to Anna. "This is Graham Cook and his wife, Gabrielle. They live at the end of the section and around the corner. They have brought us a crock of goat cheese."

Anna wished she had asked Mr. Hansen the English word for "thank you," but this afternoon she had not known how badly she would need it. She turned to the couple and smiled. "*Tak!*"

These were neighbors with whom she could not communicate. She was right to learn English despite what Jorn might think.

Mrs. Cook placed the crock in Anna's hands and gave her a quick hug before stepping away.

Gabrielle was a French name. Had she come from France? Did she speak French?

Before Anna could ask, the couple moved away. She opened her mouth to call after them, but closed it without saying a word. If she was wrong, she would embarrass them and herself.

When only two more couples remained, Peder's horse drew the wagon to the front of the house. A man Anna had seen in the brewery rode in the back, holding onto a massive object hidden under a tarpaulin.

Peder secured the reins and jumped to the ground, his face beaming in the lantern light. "My sweet sister. How did you like your wedding party?"

He must have somehow arranged this odd evening as a tribute to her marriage. She had to answer carefully. "I have never seen anything like it."

"People do not normally bring gifts to shivarees," Jorn muttered, his demeanor in sharp contrast to the way he had behaved toward the neighbors.

"Usually they bring them to the wedding," Peder replied. "But since they weren't invited, they brought things they had on hand." He glared at Jorn. "They wanted to meet your bride."

Peder turned to Anna. His expression softened. "I have a present for you." He signaled the man in the wagon. The man pulled away the cover, revealing a chest of drawers topped with a large, oval mirror.

"Oh, Peder! Thank you." She threw her arms around her brother. "It is beautiful." His business was prospering, but could he afford such an extravagant gift? "Now I will not have to live out of my trunks."

"We will bring it inside." He pulled away and went to speak with the man in the wagon. Then he turned toward the corner of the house. "Halvor, we could use a hand here."

Mr. Hansen moved cautiously toward Peder.

Overjoyed, Anna turned to Jorn. He glowered at them. Her smile faded. Was he angry with Peder for bringing her the chest or at her for appreciating the gift?

"Jorn," Peder called. "Come and help us get this off the wagon."

"Hurmph." Jorn trudged toward the wagon to lend his strength to the task.

Anna swallowed. Tonight, he had been kind and gentle after telling her of the woman he had given up. Surely, a piece of furniture would not destroy the fragile start they had made to their life together.

As the men wrestled the bureau toward the house, Anna opened the door. Once inside, they set down their burden. Peder perused the rooms. His brow puckered. "The space in your bedroom is filled."

"Too bad you did not consider that before you brought the chest out here."

"I think it is lovely," Anna said quietly. "There will be room on this wall if you slide my trunks together toward the corner."

Without further comment, Jorn pitched in and helped the other men make room for the bureau then set it into place. The muscle in his jaw twitched.

"These trunks are heavier than they look." Peder's helper gave the second one a shove.

She glanced at her brother. "My *bedstefar* made them. He wanted them to be sturdy."

Peder gave her a tiny nod.

"Tak," Anna said when they had finished. "I will enjoy having a proper mirror to dress by. It will brighten the parlor by reflecting the firelight."

"Perhaps we can build you a dressing room off the bed chamber to accommodate these." Peder swept his hand, indicating Anna's items along the wall.

"This is my house," Jorn snapped. "I will determine whether or not it is to be altered."

A silence as deafening as the noise from the shivaree engulfed the cabin.

Mr. Hansen and the man from the brewery slunk toward the front door.

Anna looked from Jorn to Peder, then back again. "It would be nice to have such a room. Perhaps it could become a nursery."

Jorn held her gaze for several moments before breaking eye contact. "We shall discuss it when we are alone."

"If you decide to build on, I would be more than happy to

help." Lines of concern etched Peder's face as he crossed to Anna and gave her a hug.

"Thank you," she murmured.

"You are welcome." He released her and stepped back. "It is late. We will help bring the gifts inside, then we best be going so you can get some sleep."

Without a word, Mr. Hansen and the man who had come with Peder began carrying jars and boxes indoors. Anna, Peder, and Jorn joined in, stacking the items in the cupboard, on the sideboard, and on the floor.

After the three men left, Anna broke the silence. "That was very nice of your friends and neighbors. We will have plenty of food for months to come."

Jorn surveyed the scene before them. "They were very generous."

Anna crossed to him, took his hand in hers, and brought it to her lips.

He pulled away. "You are my wife. In the future, I expect you will support my decisions, even if it means disagreeing with Peder."

Anna's heart thudded. "I am your wife. Peder is part of your family now. What has happened between you? You used to be close friends."

Jorn hesitated. "That is between Peder and me."

Had she come between them? Anna's shoulders slumped.

Her mother had taught her a good woman leaves her family and cleaves to her husband. Of course, she must work hard to create a good marriage, but she could not just let Peder go. He was her favorite brother and her only blood relative in America. Somehow, she needed to help them overcome their animosity. She glanced at Jorn, returning his coat to its peg. If Peder would agree, she knew just how to bring them back together.

• ♥ •

Anna swallowed against the sour smell of fermentation as she considered the stairs leading to Peder's private rooms. She began her ascent. Jorn had dropped her off while he went to negotiate the sale of pork to restaurants and butchers. He was displeased that Anna wanted to visit Peder, but seemed relieved that she would not be accompanying him on his business calls.

When she reached the halfway point, the door above flew open.

"Anna!" Peder's eyes widened. An affectionate smile lit his face. "What are you doing here?"

"We are in town for supplies, and Jorn has business." Anna stopped to rest for a moment. "I wanted to see you."

Peder bounded down to where she stood. "Let me help you."

She took his arm and leaned on it. "I love the bureau you gave me. It is much more convenient to keep my clothes in it than the trunks."

He grinned. "Glad you like it."

When they reached the landing, Peder led her into his kitchen. A fire burned in the cookstove, making the room toasty. A coffee pot sat on top, the enticing, nutty aroma permeated the air. He picked it up and held it toward her. "Would you like some?"

"Yes, that would be lovely." She removed her cloak and hung it on a peg. "The ride into town was cold."

They sat at the table, and he poured coffee into two mugs. Lines of concern etched Peder's forehead.

"Is Jorn treating you well?"

The straightforwardness of his question startled her. "Yes." She took a long drink then placed her mug on the table, enjoying the warm path the liquid made inside her. Thoughts of Jorn's disparaging behavior on their wedding day mingled with more recent images. "Since the night of the shivaree, he has been much kinder."

He patted her hand. "I am glad to hear it."

"Peder," she began, then paused. Perhaps she should be as direct as he had been. "What has come between you and Jorn?"

He studied her for a few moments. "You should ask your husband."

"I did." Her lower lip trembled as she returned his gaze. She clasped her hands together. "He said it was between you and him."

A wry smile appeared on his lips. "But you cannot leave it at that."

"No," she said firmly. "I need to know."

"It might be best—"

"Please, tell me."

He took a loud breath, then released it. "When we got a new pastor at our church here in town, many of our parishioners left. Most did not like being admonished every Sunday about the evils of drink, dance, and other enjoyable activities."

"Is that when the Holdens began hosting services?" Anna asked.

"Yes." Peder sipped his coffee. "Frederik and Jorn convinced Pastor Spelman, who had the reputation of being liberal on issues like dance and drink, to preach there in the mornings and at his little rural church in the afternoon. My beliefs are closer to Pastor Spelman's as well. For a time, I attended worship at the Holdens', but it became difficult when snow covered the trails, so I returned to the congregation here in town. Jorn told me I was being hypocritical."

"How do you tolerate having your occupation demonized at your services?"

Peder straightened his shoulders. "It is not so bad. I know what I believe, and many of my customers who attend church with me feel the same way." He winked. "We are working to either get a new minister or start a new congregation."

"Like Jorn and Frederik did."

He nodded. "Yes, but here in town."

Deep in thought, Anna raised her coffee to her lips and took a sip. Now, she understood why services were held at the Holdens'. She swallowed the warm liquid. "That does not explain your falling-out with Jorn."

Peder grimaced.

"Please tell me."

He sighed. "In June, I began courting a woman from church. Her father disapproved of my brewery and saloon, so it took much of the summer to convince him I would make an acceptable suitor." He hesitated, his face losing all expression. "When Jorn came back from Denmark late this summer, he returned to my church."

Anna leaned forward. "Why?"

He stared at the remaining coffee in his cup. After many long moments, he met her gaze. "He wanted to court a woman parishioner." Peder paused, watching Anna. "The woman I was seeing." His jaw tightened. "Her father felt Jorn, being a farmer, was more honorable than me, being a brewer."

She sat back, her body suddenly feeling heavy. "Oh, Peder. He told me about her, but not that you courted her first."

"I am surprised he mentioned her at all." A scornful smile curved the corners of Peder's mouth. "When he began seeing her, I called him a hypocrite for coming back to the church to pursue a woman whose beliefs were so different from his. He laughed and said he didn't plan to marry her, but Lottie was so pretty he wanted to see her for awhile."

Anna swallowed. Since she had arrived in Cedar Falls, Jorn had not once told her she was pretty although the compliment had come easily from him last summer.

"When I learned that you were with child, I told Jorn he should break off with her."

"You were right." Her chest ached.

"Jorn became angry and accused me of fabricating your baby so I could have Lottie again." Peder took a drink of his coffee, as if giving himself time to consider how much more to tell her.

"Then he received Fader's letter, telling him he could no longer use our farmstead and to stay off Jorgesen land. Next your note to him arrived, but he did not believe you would come to America. I assured him you would come, and you would expect him to marry you."

Peder turned his cup around and around on the table. "When Bedstafa's letter came, Jorn accused me of conspiring with our family to ruin his enterprise in Denmark as a way to get back at him for stealing Lottie away from me."

She laid her hand on her chest. "But you had nothing to do with their decisions."

"His allegation enraged me. I told him his obligation was to give your child his name. He would not commit to marrying you, so I told him he could no longer use my identity to cross into Prussian-occupied Jutland."

Her stomach roiled. "You have more reason to be angry with him than he does with you. Yet, you are polite and friendly toward him."

Peder reached across the table and patted her hand. "He is your husband, part of our family. The three of us are the only relatives we have in America. We need to bury our grudges. I have told him he can use my name and papers to return to South Jutland."

"And now that he has wed me, Bedstefa will allow him to use his gathering point in Copenhagen. But why is Jorn still so angry with you?"

"He has no place near the border in Jutland to gather his immigrants. He blames me for not convincing Fader to change his mind." Peder leaned back in his chair.

A lump grew in her throat. "Can you find another site for him? He pays well."

"I know." The blue twinkle returned to Peder's eyes. "I have written to several friends, whom I know could use the money. So far, I have not heard back."

"You have already done all I could ask. Hopefully, someone

will agree to help." Anna managed a small smile. "I would love to have you join us for *Jul*."

Peder grinned. "I will be there. If I can arrange for a meeting place in Jutland by then, it will be my gift to Jorn."

Chapter 3

November 28, 1874

More and more, I feel the baby moving within me. I long for my mother, her comforting hugs, her assurances that everything will be all right. There are so many things I do not know about delivering a child, and she is not here to answer my questions. Although I have written her several letters, I have received none from her. My heart breaks when I think that I may never see her again. I am lucky to have Peder close by. He has been very good to me, but is no help in realm of female questions.

I have been working hard to make the best of my life with Jorn. He still seems to be a very different man from the tender, romantic lover he was last summer. I am nearly certain his behavior was just an act to seduce me, and he never intended to propose. We are getting along pleasantly most of the time now, but we will probably never have a wonderful marriage like Bedstefa and Bedstemor had.

Jul will be here soon. I have been working on gifts for Jorn, mostly clothing, useful items. Tomorrow's church service will mark the beginning of Advent. It is a bittersweet time. I will sorely miss joining in the annual festivities with Bedstefa, my aunts, uncles, and cousins as my family has done for as long as I can remember. But this year, Jorn, Peder, and I will have to begin our own American Jul traditions. Hopefully, they will be able to put aside their differences long enough to celebrate what should be a joyous season.

Anna watched the dreary late-November landscape pass by. Multiple freezes had turned the vegetation to browns and grays. She drew her cloak closer. Even in the buggy, the biting wind cut right through her. At least Jorn had agreed not to take the open wagon to Sunday services.

He drove the horse at a slow pace, so as not to disturb the rice pudding or topple the loaves of bread she had made yesterday for the after-worship social.

"Graham Cook stopped by yesterday when I was cutting saplings to mend the north fence."

Jorn's voice yanked Anna from her musings. He did not usually speak on the ride to the Holdens'.

"He asked if I want to butcher hogs this week. Said he was going to ask the Holdens, too."

Anna drew in a freezing breath. "But today is the fourth Sunday before *Jul*." Her father and his hired men always cleaned the barnyard, the dairy, and the stables in preparation for Christmas. Her parents would never bloody the ground by killing a hog during December. She shivered. "It is bad luck to kill a farm animal during the holiday season."

"That is an old superstition," Jorn scoffed. "We have slaughtered hogs each December since I came to this country, and my farm has grown each year."

She stared at him. Jorn insisted they observe Danish customs, insisted they would soon return to their homeland, and believed Anna need not learn English. She bit her lower lip. It was impossible to figure out which parts of their heritage he chose to maintain and which he thought it best to discard.

"Have the Holdens participated in the past?" Anna had developed great respect for them over the past few Sundays. If they did not see anything wrong with the practice, it might be all right.

"Yes." Jorn urged the horse to pick up its pace as they reached the final hill. "They and the Cooks each bring a hog to my woodyard. I shall choose several swine, as I have sold the meat of two in town, and I give pork to the hired men and greenhorns each *Juleaften*."

"That is nice of you." Perhaps the fact that Jorn gave some of the meat as gifts to those less fortunate had prevented him from suffering disaster on his farm, but she still did not like the idea of tempting fate.

He turned the horse into the Holdens' dooryard. The familiar two-story white house, with the parlor large enough to hold all the regular worshipers, seemed to welcome them as heartily as the Holdens did each week. Someday she and Jorn would have a fine home like this.

The Ringes' carriage stood under a tall tree. Pastor Spelman's horse was tethered to the hitching post.

After securing the mare, Jorn helped Anna out of the buggy. He reached behind the seat for the two large baskets of food. Brigitte waited on the porch. Her straw-blond hair was fastened in a knot at the base of her neck. Her blue-gray eyes shone as brilliantly as her smile. Embroidered flowers decorated the dark indigo velvet bodice of her dress. A sky-blue skirt flowed from gathers at the waist. Next to her, Anna assessed her dowdy, well-worn brown satin traveling dress. She had let the seams out as far as she could without compromising the security of the stitching. The full skirt still concealed her growing abdomen.

"Welcome. Come in." Brigitte gave Anna a hug. "Glad you could make it."

"Thank you!" Anna enthusiastically hugged her back. This one day in seven she would have contact with other people and would not spend sun up to sun down in the drudgery of housework. If only this reprieve from her growing sense of isolation could last more than a few hours.

Brigitte pulled away and turned to her daughter. "Marie, take Mrs. Stryker's cloak upstairs and lay it on my bed."

"Yes, Moder," the five-year-old said sweetly.

Anna smiled and folded it into a small bundle before handing it to the little girl. "*Tak.*"

"*Velkommst,*" Marie whispered. She turned and hurried up the stairs.

Anna glanced out the door. The Thomsens approached in

their wagon. Halvor Hansen followed on foot, far enough behind to avoid the dust. He carried what appeared to be a lumpy pillow, probably his usual contribution of apples picked earlier this fall from the Stryker orchard. Anna had suggested to Jorn that Mr. Hansen ride with them so he would not have to walk in the cold. Her husband had refused, saying it was inappropriate for them to ride with the help. His un-Christian response was hard to understand since he seemed not to mind worshipping with them.

"Wait here," Jorn said. "I'll take the baskets to the kitchen and come right back." He followed Brigitte down the hall.

"Hurry up and get that squash in the house." Ole Thomsen's angry shout startled Anna. Her pulse raced. "Then get in your seats and keep your traps shut." The children scurried around their mother as she lifted a basket from the back of the wagon.

Karyn walked about three steps behind her husband, half-running to keep his pace. Anna retreated to the stairway as the family blustered into the house. Without a word, the children took their usual seats. Just as Karyn started toward the kitchen, Jorn returned. They shifted one way then the other trying to pass.

"Are you daft, woman?" Ole snarled. "Stand aside and let Jorn by."

She shrank back against the wall to her right.

"Sorry." Karyn's murmur was barely audible. Her head hung down, eyes focused on the floor. Anna blushed, feeling humiliated for her.

"Good morning, Karyn," Jorn said as he moved past and joined Anna.

She stood on the second step. They were eye-to-eye as they exchanged a glance. He offered his hand and she took it. Anna silently thanked God that unlike Ole, her husband behaved quite gallantly in public. Her whole being ached for Karyn.

"My wife has no sense," Ole sneered. He spoke in a low voice, but Anna was certain Karyn could hear him.

Anna wanted to scold the rogue, but it might further provoke him. She held her tongue. As usual, Jorn ignored Ole's unbecoming conduct, escorting Anna to the parlor.

Assorted greenhorns and hired men were clustered in conversations. Anna took a chair next to Greta Ringe near the fireplace. When everyone was finally seated, services began with a familiar hymn. Pastor Spelman delivered the Bible lesson and sermon, interspersed with more singing.

He then led the worshipers to the dining room, where a wreath of evergreens with four tall candles lay in the center of the table. After saying a prayer for a joyous Advent season for all present, the minister lit one candle, as had been the custom in the Jorgesens' church in Velje.

Happy memories of past Christmases flooded Anna. Her grandfather lighting the Advent wreath with her grandmother at his side. Her mother's delicious rice pudding. Visiting friends and family, and having them return the favor.

Beneath the layers of fabric, the baby inside her moved. She closed her eyes and prayed silently that he or she would be healthy, and that her parents would come to accept their grandchild. Even if they did not, she promised God that she would do her best to give her children festive celebrations of His Son's birth.

When Pastor Spelman concluded the service, he asked Marie to blow out the candle. It had to last three more Sundays, so they could not let it burn for long. While the women readied the food, the Thomsen children helped Marie set dishes on the table. Everyone feasted on the plentiful fare and rejoiced in the good company.

After the dishes were washed and put away, Brigitte invited Anna upstairs to see the quilt she had made for her daughters. In the doorway to girls' bed chamber, Anna praised the pretty coverlet, with its appliquéd pink roses, that covered the large bed the two little girls shared.

"I made it for Christmas last year," Brigitte said. Suddenly she took Anna's arm, pulled her into the room and closed the door behind them. Anna stole a wary glance at her hostess.

"There is something I have been wanting to ask you," Brigitte whispered. "I do not wish to be indelicate, but are you with child?"

Heat rushed to Anna's cheeks. She had been careful to wear dresses with skirts fully gathered in front and back, expecting them to disguise her growing belly. "Is it obvious?"

Contrition tightened Brigitte's face. "I apologize. But the other women and I have been speculating." She slipped her arm around Anna's shoulders. "You need not hide it."

Her throat tightened. "But I have only been married—"

"It does not matter."

"But it is a sin."

"None of us are without sin. There may be some who will condemn you, but you must ignore them." Brigitte hugged Anna then released her. "When we butcher on Wednesday, I will introduce you to Gabrielle Cook. She is the midwife who delivered my youngest."

"I met her at the—" Anna searched her mind for the word Jorn had used for the midnight clamor that had awakened them weeks ago.

"Shivaree," Brigitte supplied. She sat on the bed and patted the space beside her.

"Yes, shivaree," Anna repeated, hoping it would stick in her mind. She seated herself in the designate space. "She does not speak *Danske* and I do not speak English."

"I can translate."

"*Tak*." Anna lay her hand on Brigitte's arm. "Do you not think killing swine is bad luck in the *Jul* season?"

Brigitte placed her had on top of Anna's. "The weather in December is usually right for putting up meat. Cold enough to preserve it, but not so cold that it freezes too fast. And it is good to have pork for the winter."

"But I fear something dire could happen next year." Anna

swallowed. "My baby is to be born."

"I worried about it, too, the first time. No bad luck has befallen us. And Jorn has done very well for himself." Brigette patted Anna's hand. "I will ask Greta if she will keep my children. Then I can come early and help you get ready for the canning and the noon meal."

Anna flinched. Feeding the workers had not occurred to her. "I would appreciate that."

"I want you to know that you can call on me if ever you should need anything."

Anna's heart fluttered. "I am glad you are my neighbor."

Brigitte smiled. "And friend."

"And friend," Anna echoed.

• ♥ •

The cloying stench of raw meat and cooking goose hung heavy in the air. Determined to do her part in preserving the pork, Anna swallowed back the bile rising in her throat and set another row of clean canning jars on the table.

Steam from Gabrielle's boiler wafted through the small house and collected on the windows. Anna pulled a handkerchief from her apron pocket and mopped her brow.

Brigitte stood at the counter, skillfully wielding the large knife, reducing slabs of meat to chunks that would fit through the mouths of the jars.

The door opened. Fresh, crisp air and a swirl of snowflakes rushed into the hot kitchen. Frederik Holden entered, carrying two bloody buckets filled with hunks of meat. He set them on the dirt floor, unmindful of the dark red liquid spilling over the sides.

Turning away from the sight, Anna moved into the path of the cold air and inhaled deeply.

"We'll be ready to eat soon," he said. "We just have to hang two more carcasses to bleed out." He headed back outside. Anna gulped in one last cleansing breath before the door closed behind him.

She cleared the jars from the table and began setting out her mismatched plates and silverware. If only she had nice china and silver like Brigitte's, but it would seem out of place in this house. She sliced the bread Gabrielle had brought and laid out a dish of butter.

"I'm sorry I'll have to leave shortly after we eat." Brigitte packed another row of cooled preserves into her wooden crate.

She had kept the conversation going, translating from Danish to English and back again the discussions of household matters and life in America. Anna had learned a few more English words today, but not enough for conversing with Gabrielle.

"Thanks for coming early." Anna sighed. "I could not have gotten ready without you." Brigitte had prepared the goose Jorn shot yesterday while Anna selected vegetables from the root cellar. They had combined everything in a roasting pan in the oven, leaving the stovetop clear for the boiler.

"Before I leave, we'll talk with Gabrielle about delivering your baby," Brigitte said.

At the mention of her name, Gabrielle looked up. With the back of her hand she brushed away a stray strand that had escaped from the clip holding her chestnut hair. Brigitte said something to her in English, and she smiled.

Brigitte opened the oven door, lifted the roaster out and set it on the table. Anna stepped back from the escaping heat to stand near Gabrielle. Ever since the shivaree, her French name had intrigued Anna.

"*Parlez-vous français?*" she ventured.

Gabrielle dropped her knife and turned to Anna, grinning. "*Oui.*"

Anna smiled back.

Brigitte set the lid from the roaster under the table and turned to them.

"Gabrielle speaks French!" Anna exclaimed in Danish.

Brigitte's blue-gray eyes were wide. "I knew she did, but I didn't know you did."

"Do you speak French?" Anna asked, hoping they could all converse together.

Brigitte shook her head. "Sadly, no."

The clank of the pump handle and muffled conversation signaled the men were outside washing up. Jorn brought two milking stools inside then returned to join them. A few minutes later, he led Graham, Frederik, and Halvor Hansen into the kitchen.

"Smells good in here!" Frederik bellowed. Anna wasn't sure she concurred after the nauseating work of the morning.

Jorn asked the Lord's blessings on their food, work, and health. When he finished, the men filled their plates and headed to the parlor, since the dining table was too small for everyone to sit around. Heat flowed through Anna, making her neck and cheeks uncomfortably warm. Hoping no one noticed, she served the men coffee while the other women seated themselves. Maybe after the baby was born, she could convince Jorn they needed a larger house.

Anna nibbled on a piece of bread. The women took turns hopping up to check the boiler, to make sure the jars were sealing, or to add a fresh batch to the water bath.

After everyone had eaten and the dishes were washed, Brigitte packed up the rest of her pork and the Holdens left. The remaining men returned to the wood yard.

"Are you from France?" Anna asked in French.

"Canada." Gabrielle returned to cutting meat while Anna tended the boiler and supplied more jars. "My father was a trapper. He met my mother when he was trading furs in New Orleans and took her back north with him. She was English and didn't like living in the wilderness." She paused. "When I was nine, she died."

"I am sorry." Anna had to listen carefully to understand what Gabrielle was saying, as her dialect varied somewhat from the one Anna had learned.

"My father spoke French, as it was the language of the few friends he had in Canada. Trapping was a hard life. He had to be away for days at a time in winter." Her voice had turned wistful. The sound of the knife slicing through to the cutting board punctuated her words. "So, when I was eleven, he took me to live with my aunt in New Orleans."

"Is that where you became a midwife?"

Gabrielle chuckled. "You could say that. I successfully delivered two of my aunt's children. Word spread, and many women asked me to help them give birth."

Anna cleared her throat and glanced down at her belly, hidden beneath gathers of stained cotton fabric. "As you have probably noticed, I... I am with child. It is humiliating to talk about, because the child was conceived without benefit of marriage, when Jorn was in Denmark last summer." Warmth rose to her face. "I'm so ashamed."

"Don't be." The force of the older woman's words jerked Anna's gaze to her. "It happens far more often than you think, even to the holier-than-thou society folks." Gabrielle's velvet-brown eyes flashed. She wielded her knife with increasing force. "Hold your head high, and don't place so much stock in the opinions of others."

Not as easy a task as the words made it sound. Anna sighed.

"The only opinion that matters is Jorn's, as it will affect the type of father he'll become," Gabrielle continued. "What does he say?"

"At first, he was resentful," Anna confided. "But lately, he seems to be happier about it. He wants a son." Anna carefully lifted a sealed jar from the boiler. "I don't know how he will react if the baby is a girl."

"Don't worry about it." Gabrielle slipped her arm around Anna's shoulders and gave her a brief hug. "Just try to be as happy as you can about the miracle inside you."

Miracle. Gabrielle was right. At baptisms, Anna's minister

had said every child was a gift from God. The Lord must have found her worthy of such a precious gift. Her body released the tension that had kept it wound tight all day. "I will."

They worked without speaking for awhile.

"How far away is New Orleans?" Anna asked.

"Very far. I think more than five hundred miles." Gabrielle paused. "But I am not sure."

"How did you end up in Iowa?"

"Graham was in the army of the North. When war broke out between the states, my aunt and cousins fled to England. My uncle claimed he did not have the finances to send me with them. What little money I made from midwifery, I had given over to my aunt to pay for my room and board."

On the trip to America, Anna had felt alone and abandoned. Gabrielle must have suffered the same pain after her family left her behind.

"By that time, my uncle had enlisted to fight for the Confederacy. He introduced me to a woman who said she would take me in." Several moments passed before Gabrielle continued. "It was only after he left that I learned she ran a brothel," she said, her voice tight.

Anna's mouth dropped open. "A brothel?"

"During the war, there were few ways for unmarried women without property to earn a living." Gabrielle's words carried an unexpected intensity in her lowered voice. "The men were gone. Few children were being born. My income wouldn't have been enough to support myself. Servicing men was the only way I could survive." Red color filled her cheeks. "Whether from the North or the South, soldiers were good customers." Her dark gaze met and held Anna's. "We all do what we must do."

Anna struggled to overcome the shock that had stolen her voice. "How did you meet Graham?"

"It was Christmas of 1864. The Union had taken New Orleans. Graham had recently escaped from a Confederate prison camp and made his way into the city. He was looking for a woman to spend the holiday with." Her face softened, and a wan smile curled her lips. "He found me."

Although curious about the details of their first Christmas together, Anna refrained from asking. "How did you get to Black Hawk County?"

"Graham grew up here. His parents died during the war and they left the farm to him." Gabrielle pointed to the empty jars on the table. Anna moved a supply to the counter. "When he was discharged, he brought me here. The buildings had fallen into disrepair, and the fields were overgrown with weeds. But it was ours, free and clear. Each year we have worked to improve it."

Anna scanned the room, her gaze falling to the blood pooled on the dirt floor where buckets of meat still stood. "After my baby is born, I want to make improvements here, too."

"When are you due?"

"In March." It still seemed like a long time.

"We usually go to town on Thursdays if the weather permits. I will stop in and check on you each week," Gabrielle offered. "And today, you must give me a detailed account of how you have been feeling thus far."

The door burst open. Both husbands entered carrying buckets.

"This is the last of it," Jorn said in Danish.

Anna studied the load of meat the men had deposited in the kitchen. Several hours' work remained.

"I will stay until we finish all of it," Gabrielle said, as if she had read Anna's thoughts.

"*Merci,*" Anna replied. She resisted the urge to hug her new friend. Most of the remaining pork belonged to the Strykers. "That's very generous of you."

Both men stared wide-eyed at the women.

"Does your husband speak French?" Gabrielle asked.

Anna shook her head. "Does yours?"

"No."

The women smiled at each other. They shared a private language, almost like sisters. When the time came for Anna to deliver her baby, Gabrielle would be there to help. For the first time since Anna arrived in America, she was truly glad to be here.

• ♥ •

After Sunday's services at the Holdens, the children gave each guest red and white checked hearts, woven from heavy paper, inspiring the *Jul* spirit in Anna. With less than three weeks before Christmas, she set to work baking sweets for the other families who worshipped with them, and for Pastor Spelman.

True to her word, Gabrielle dropped in on her way to town the following Thursday. She chased the men from the house and examined Anna's belly.

"All seems well," Gabrielle pronounced in French when she finished gently poking to determine the baby's position.

"That's good." Anna sat up on the bed and readjusted her clothing. "I feel movement every day now."

"Many advocate for a woman to give up activity in these last months so all her energy can go to growing her child." Gabrielle settled on the bed beside her. "But I don't agree. I believe normal activity is good for you and your baby, as long as you don't over-tire yourself or strain yourself lifting heavy objects."

Anna's mother hadn't told her what to expect as her time drew near. She eas lucky to have Gabrielle. "I'm glad, since I have no choice but to do my chores and care for my household." She smiled. "I'll be more careful about lifting, though."

"Are you and Jorn still having relations?"

Heat rushed to Anna's neck and face. She nodded, unable to acknowledge the act aloud.

Gabrielle patted her arm. "It's time to stop until after the birth. You don't want to risk hurting your baby."

Anna sighed. They would be giving up the most pleasurable activity she and Jorn shared, the times she felt closest to her husband. How could she tell him?

"I've asked Graham to speak to Jorn about this, since I didn't know if he understands the danger." Gabrielle glanced toward the door. "If his father didn't tell him, hearing this information from a man might be best."

Anna grasped Gabrielle's hand. "Thank you. I can't imagine—"

The door scraped open. She and Gabrielle stood and walked to the kitchen as their husbands entered.

"Will you take your noon meal with us?" Anna asked. If she opened a jar of fruit, the stew in the oven could stretch to feed four. There was plenty of bread.

"Thank you, no." Gabrielle shook her head. "We best be heading to town so we can get home in time for chores. I'll check on you again next week."

Anna hugged her farewell. In the spirit of the *Jul* season, she sent a fresh-baked kringle with Gabrielle.

When the Cooks were gone, Jorn pulled Anna into an embrace. "Did she talk with you about the baby?"

She knew just what he meant. "Yes."

"We wouldn't want to harm our son. He must grow big and strong."

Our son. Jorn never spoke of their baby as a daughter. He often mentioned how much he wanted a boy to carry on the family name. How disappointed he would be if the baby was a girl. He might even hold Anna responsible.

She shuddered and burrowed her head into Jorn's shoulder. Although she had been wishing for a daughter, she closed her eyes and silently prayed their child would be a son.

Chapter 4

December 23, 1874

I am so excited! Peder is coming tomorrow to spend Juleaften and Jul with us. I wish I had a proper bedroom for him to sleep in. When I stayed with him, he slept on the floor, and he will be sleeping on the floor when he stays with us. Thankfully, he says he does not mind.

From my earliest childhood memories, I have loved Jul. All Moder's relatives gathered at Bedstefa and Bedstemor's house for Juleaften dinner, gifts, and dancing around the tree. I had planned to make at least a part of our traditional family meal, but the congregation decided to have a potluck after the Juleaften services. Maybe that will become our new custom. I have made many sweets and pastries, which Jorn delivered to friends and neighbors. I even baked kringles for the greenhorns and hired hands. I've saved one to serve when Peder is here and one to send home with him.

Through December, I have given the house a thorough cleaning in anticipation of tomorrow's festivities. Unlike my father, who always had the hired men clean the farm buildings and the stables, Jorn ignores the custom. I did not expect my husband, who demands we live as Danes and speak only Danish in our home, to abandon such a long-standing practice. In many ways, he remains a mystery to me.

In this joyous season, I am thankful for Peder, for our friends, for the child I carry inside me, for Jorn, and that we are able to share our bounty with neighbors and those who work here on our farm. The Lord has truly blessed us.

On Christmas Eve morning, Anna woke early. Yesterday, she had hung a sheaf of oats in the tree for the birds. She checked to see if any grain remained, but the seeds appeared nearly untouched. Apparently, the birds didn't like oats.

She couldn't worry about that now. Pastor Spelman had scheduled the holiday service for two o'clock. There was much to do before leaving for the Holdens'. The Thomsens would not be attending, but the rest of the congregation planned to enjoy their Christmas Eve feast together then return to their homes for private celebrations.

Best of all, Peder was coming! Although she had exchanged notes with him, she hadn't seen him since they had spoken of helping Jorn find a new meeting place in Jutland. Hopefully, her husband would behave more civilly than he had at the shivaree.

While Jorn delivered gifts of meat to the hired men and greenhorns, she peeled potatoes and dropped them into a pot of water. The fluttering in her stomach grew as she worked. As soon as she arrived at the Holdens', she would put the kettle on the stove to boil while the pastor preached. The rum pudding sat cooling on the bench.

Although they had no tree in the cabin, Anna had made a few red and white paper decorations and hung them around the mirror of the dresser in the parlor. Jorn brought from town the candles and red ribbon she'd requested. She cut evergreen boughs for the mantel, strung the ribbon through them, and attached the decorations from the Holden children. Flames crackled in the fireplace. Scents of pine and coffee mingled in the air.

Sleigh bells jingled. Anna rushed to the window. Without snow on the ground, the sound seemed out of place.

Wearing a red cap, Peder sat atop his wagon, driving his team toward the dooryard. Bells were attached to the harnesses on his two horses. Heat radiated through her chest. She smiled.

Anna hurried to set cups and plates on the small kitchen table and lit the candle in its center before he finished hitching the horses to the post. Hearing his knock, she crossed the room and threw open the door. *"Glaedelig Jul!"*

Peder stood on the step, hands on his hips, a shaggy wool beard attached to his chin with a string, and the red cap topping his head. He looked like a rough impression of an overgrown *nisse*. She burst into laughter.

"Where is my porridge?" he demanded gruffly.

"Will coffee and pastry do?" She forced out the words between giggles.

"I suppose." He sounded disgusted, but his blue eyes twinkled.

"Come in." Anna stepped back to let him pass. "It's good to see you."

He reached down and picked up a crate filled with bottles of beer and wine before stepping inside. "I brought spirits for the holiday toast. I have some for the Holdens, too. They crossed to America with Jorn and me, you know."

"Yes." Anna closed the door as he set his burden on the floor next to the bench. "Brigitte told me you were nearly as sick as I was."

"Not meant to be a sea-faring man, I know." He inhaled a deep sniff from the pan on the bench then straightened, beaming. "Rum pudding?"

Anna nodded. "I'm to provide potatoes and dessert. I have no raspberries for sauce, but Brigitte said she would supply them."

Peder pulled off the wool and his cap and dropped them on top of the crate. "Come here. Let me look at you."

She crossed to him. He took her shoulders, held her at arms' length, and studied her face. "Is he making you happy?"

She nodded. "I can't complain. Although, I confess, I long for a better house."

"If that's all you want for, I won't worry about you anymore." Peder's gaze dropped to her belly. "Are you feeling well?"

"Most of the time."

"Wonderful."

She chewed her lower lip. "But I haven't had a letter from Moder since I left Copenhagen. I expected to hear from her during *Jul*."

Peder's cheerful expression faded. "I don't expect we'll hear from her for some time. Since your visit, I received a note from Bedstefa." He slid his arm around her shoulders. "He said Fader has forbidden her to write to us since he considers us dead to him. And he only allows her to write to Bedstefa once a month. He's not even certain that Fader gives her our letters."

Anna's throat constricted, and a heaviness settled in her chest. "Oh, Peder."

"Bedstefa will send us all the information he receives and will pass our information to Moder in letters, or when he visits her in Velje."

"Fader is so hard-hearted." Anna choked out the words. Hope of reconciliation evaporated.

"We are far away from him, and we have each other, and Jorn." He hugged her close. "And soon we will have my niece or nephew. We have our own family here in America, and Bedstefa in Denmark."

He released her. "And it's the *Jul* season. Time for a new beginning." His lips curled into a smile. "Be joyous, and don't let Fader spoil it." He lifted her chin with his finger. "Promise."

How could she promise the impossible? "I will try."

He brushed a kiss across her cheek. "That's my favorite sister."

She gazed at his benevolent face. "Your only sister."

"A minor detail. And now, it's time to celebrate." He stepped toward the door. "I have more to bring in while you set out that pastry you promised. Bedstefa sent us both presents, and he sent a large trunk of your things. I placed it in my warehouse, as you don't have room. You can sort through it next time you come to town."

Peder went outside. Anna set mugs on the table, and placed

prune strips and slices of kringle on a plate. Since her condition was now obvious, she would not find out what her grandfather had sent until after her baby came, more than two months yet. She needed a proper house so she could have all her things with her.

The door opened and Jorn strode in. "Peder wants you to turn your back until he gets your presents inside." He grinned. "I'm to keep watch so you don't peek."

Anna complied. Such a wonderful season, with all its happy secrecy and surprises. She had made scarves, socks, and handkerchiefs for her brother and husband. The gifts were hidden in the bottom drawer of her dresser, along with a sweater, shirt, and pants for Jorn.

She vowed to put her anger toward Fader aside and enjoy the festivities. *Jul* had apparently worked its magic on Jorn and Peder as well.

While she poured coffee, bustling and scraping sounded behind her. Footfalls padded back and forth on the packed-earth floor.

"All right," Peder called. "I'm ready for coffee now."

A massive lump, covered by two quilts and a woven rug, claimed the middle of the parlor floor. She gasped. The house might be too small to find a place for whatever hid under there.

Peder and Jorn shrugged off their coats and took seats at the table. They joked and laughed as if nothing had come between them. Her worry faded.

"I'll enjoy listening to Pastor Spelman preach again," Peder said, reaching for a slice of kringle. "I'm tired of hearing about the evils of drink, and that I will be damned on judgment day."

Jorn leaned his elbows on the table and wrapped his hands around his mug. "We were outnumbered by those who wanted an Inner Mission pastor. I still cannot believe how many who frequented your saloon and danced at the socials condemned those behaviors as sinful." He scowled. "Hypocrites."

"Some have lived to regret it, but most aren't ready to split off and form a second church," Peder said. "If all who left to join other congregations had stayed, we might have been able to reach a majority. But I don't blame you or anyone else for leaving."

Anna frowned. "You could return to services at the Holdens'."

"I have many friends in the congregation on both sides of the issue. And I hate the idea of religion dividing the Danes in our community."

"The chasm is less pronounced among our neighbors," Jorn said. "But we're all careful to steer conversations outside of church away from the topic."

There were Danish neighbors who didn't worship at the Holdens'. Anna had not met them yet. If they passed so harsh a judgement on those who danced and drank spirits, they would surely condemn her for conceiving a child out of wedlock.

• ♥ •

As Peder drove the horses toward home, Anna sat next to him on the wagon seat and listened to the bells jingle. Behind her, Jorn steadied the crate of gifts and the pan with the remaining rum pudding. She had reveled in the joyous celebration and sumptuous holiday meal. Her father never allowed his children to display such excitement as the Holden youngsters had shown. Though glad to be far from Fader, she couldn't help missing her mother.

"Tether your horses in the barn," Jorn said, standing as Peder turned into the dooryard. When the wagon stopped in front of the house, Jorn hopped out.

Anna leaned close to her brother. "Make sure Jorn gives the animals extra rations of grain tonight," she whispered. "And your horses, too. I want us all to have good luck in the new year."

"I will." A chuckle rippled through Peder's words.

Inside the cabin, Jorn stoked the fire. Then, he went to help

Peder tend the horses.

Anna picked up the crate of gifts. Brigitte had made socks for all the men in the congregation, including a pair for Peder. Greta Ringe had also given socks to Frederik and Jorn. Anna sighed. She had also knitted socks for her husband and brother. Hopefully, one could never have too many socks.

Greta had given Anna a knitted hat, which she put with her cloak. She hung the apron Brigitte had stitched for her on a peg by itself. The useful gifts pleased her.

For the women, Anna had embroidered dresser scarves, and for the men, she'd monogrammed handkerchiefs. Jorn had built a toboggan for the Holden children, and another for the Thomsens.

Resisting the temptation to peek at the lump under the quilts, Anna placed her gifts for Peder and Jorn on the bench. She lit the cookstove and started a pot of coffee. Try as she would, she couldn't keep her gaze from straying to the makeshift cover.

The banging pump handle signaled the men were washing up. She lit the lamp in the parlor and the candles throughout the room. A faint pine scent from the boughs on the mantel added to the holiday spirit.

After the men shed their coats and boots, Peder turned to Anna. "I think it's time we cleared your parlor floor. Jorn, would you like to go first?"

"After you," he replied, leading Anna to one of the parlor chairs then sitting in the other.

Peder strode to the edge of the quilt. Anna's hands quivered, and her heart raced. He lifted two wooden boxes, the size of cookie tins, and handed one to Jorn and the other to Anna. "These are from Bedstefa. I've already opened mine."

The box was extraordinarily heavy for its size. Anna could guess why. She lifted the lid. Inside was an envelope, closed with wax pressed with her grandfather's seal. She glanced at Jorn. He had an envelope, too.

She broke the seal and opened the letter.

Dearest Anna,

I was glad to receive you letter telling me you made it safely to Cedar Falls, and that you married Jorn. I hope all is going well with him.

But if it is not, I am sending the means for you to return to Denmark. I did not realize how much I would miss you, dear girl, after having you with me nearly a month.

Still, I wish the best for you in your life with Jorn and the baby.

Love,

Bedstefa

Anna's throat tightened. She missed her grandfather, too. Only two months ago, she had planned to return to him in the spring.

"What does your letter say?" Jorn asked. He held an open sheet in his hand.

Unable to speak, Anna handed him the note. He read it then returned his gaze to her.

"I don't want you to go back." His earnest words warmed her.

She took a breath and held it for a few moments before releasing it. "I won't."

He took her hand in his. "Good."

She lifted his hand to her lips and kissed it.

"What does your letter say, Jorn?" Peder asked.

Jorn looked from Anna to her brother. "That I have fulfilled my obligation by marrying Anna. He hopes I will make her happy." He hesitated. "And that I may continue to use his compound as a gathering place."

Peder smiled. "I knew he would relent."

"But our parents won't. Ever," Anna said. Whether helping Danes who wanted to escape the tyranny of the Germans, or assisting those who wanted to find a better life in America, Jorn's work was noble. It pleased her to know he would be able to resume his efforts in a few years.

"We may have found a new meeting spot," Jorn told her, his eyes bright.

"Remember Frode Rasmussen? I worked with him at the brewery," Peder said. "His family has agreed to let Jorn use their farm since he is willing to pay them."

No wonder her two men had put aside their differences. "That will be good."

She turned her attention to her box. It looked like a small, black treasure chest. On the top, her name was painted in flowing letters with flowers intertwined. The mechanism to release the hidden object in the bottom differed from those her grandfather usually made, this one being much more obvious.

She grasped the false panel on one end, pulled it out, and tilted that side of the box down. The false floor slipped out of its slot, revealing a gold bar. She tipped the box for Peder and Jorn to see. "I guess this was for my ticket home."

Peder showed Jorn how to release the bottom, exposing a silver bar. Jorn looked up at Anna. "Your grandfather's letter says I am to use this to buy something that will make you happy."

"A house." Anna smiled. If they put both their gifts together, it would be a good start toward building a proper one.

Jorn frowned. "We will talk about that later."

He was right. This wasn't a topic to discuss during their *Jul* celebration.

"And now." Peder bent down ceremoniously and threw back a corner of the woven rug. "My gift for you, Anna." From under the cover he pulled an oak rocker, which had been lying on its side.

"Oh, Peder!" Her heart swelled with love for her brother. She stood and stepped with care around the remaining lump to examine it. The chair was large, smooth, and solid, with her name carved into the top panel. "It's beautiful." She hugged him and gave him a peck on the cheek. "Thank you."

"Your turn, Jorn," Peder said.

Jorn bent down and pulled the quilt off the remaining lump. On the floor stood an oak cradle.

Tears welled in Anna's eyes. She reached over and caressed the corner of the cradle, rocking it gently.

"Oh, Jorn. Thank you." She flung herself into his arms. He'd pleased her without benefit of her grandfather's silver. She kissed him deep and long. Without risking harm to her baby, she would find ways of pleasing her husband tonight.

• ♥ •

As weeks passed and Anna's belly continued to grow, she became more and more weary. On a chilly March Monday, Anna hopped out of bed, wide awake and eager to start her day. She attacked the laundry with unusual exuberance, completing it before the noon meal. In mid-afternoon, she regretted it. Her back ached, and her abdominal muscles were contracting and releasing in a succession of cramps.

By suppertime, the spasms were so severe she had no appetite. She heated some ham and potatoes left from dinner and dished them directly onto Jorn's plate.

As he sat to eat, a cramp doubled her over.

"Anna!"

She forced in a breath. "I think the baby's coming."

"I will get Gabrielle," he said.

"What if the baby comes while you're gone?" She couldn't deliver their child alone.

"I will send Halvor to the Cooks. I'm going to tell him now and come right back!"

She grabbed the back of a chair as the pain intensified. "Hurry."

Jorn ran out the door without stopping to put on a coat.

Minutes later, a warm liquid bathed her in sticky wetness from her groin to her feet. She screamed. The baby was coming, and she had no one to help.

Gabrielle had said to stay calm and breathe deeply, no

matter what happened. Anna forced air into her lungs then expelled it. Again. Again. The pain began to subside.

Gabrielle had said Anna's body would release this fluid. It was normal. The birth could be some time away yet. Nothing was wrong. Anna closed her eyes and exhaled slowly.

She opened her eyes and stepped away from the disgusting puddle forming on the dirt floor. The damp bottom half of her body was becoming chilled. She had to get her wet clothing off before the next cramp. She pulled some linens from the cupboard.

The door burst open. Jorn rushed inside then froze, staring at the wet spot. "What happened?"

"It's part of the birthing. Close the door." Anna walked to the dresser and took out a clean nightdress.

As she moved to the bed, her abdomen clenched. She dropped the gown, grabbed a handful of quilt, and squeezed. A groan rose from deep in her throat.

"Oh, Anna." Jorn came and wrapped his arms around her. His touch intensified the pain. "Let's get you out of these wet clothes."

He released her, and she grasped the quilt with her other hand.

Gently, he eased off her clothing and dried her skin. She gasped in a breath. He helped her with her nightdress, then lifted her onto the bed, tucking the quilt around her.

Anna lost track of time. She waited for Gabrielle to come. She waited for the baby to be born. She waited for the pain to end.

Sometime in the night, Gabrielle arrived. Through the contractions, Anna realized Jorn was bathing her face with a cold cloth. Gabrielle directed her to breathe, to push, to relax. Thank God she was here.

Gabrielle ordered Anna to bear down and keep pushing. Searing pain ripped through her. Had the baby grown too big to come out? Anna feared her skin might tear wide open.

Suddenly, the agony faded. Anna fell back against the pillows.

An infant cried. Relief swelled in her heart.

Gabrielle placed the baby in Anna's arms. A warm love bathed her whole being.

Jorn kissed her forehead and whispered hoarsely, "We have a beautiful baby boy."

Chapter 5

June 3, 1875

Baby Erik nurses vigorously and seems to grow larger every day. He is a perfect little boy. I love him more viscerally than I ever thought possible. On Sunday, he will be baptized.

I am glad I agreed to name him after Jorn's father, even though I wanted to name him after Bedstefa. Erik has brought Jorn and me closer. Although planting keeps him in the fields for long hours, he makes time in the evenings to spend with the baby and me. While I wash the dishes, he holds his son and speaks quietly to him. Erik often falls asleep in his arms.

Jorn has assigned Halvor Hansen to continue caring for the chickens, gather the eggs, replenish the stove wood, carry water, and plant the garden according to my direction. I thought he might balk at such womanly tasks, but he volunteers to assist with the laundry, churn the butter, and make the soap. This has given me much more time with Erik. While he sleeps, Mr. Hansen teaches me more English. If Jorn knows of these lessons, he does not speak of them. Neither do I.

Gabrielle said to wait at least ten weeks, so I could heal properly, and not once has Jorn suggested that we engage in marital relations. I appreciate his consideration, and have found other ways to please him, but I miss sharing in our special closeness. Over the weeks, I have looked forward to resuming our private pleasure. Tonight, our waiting period ends.

Anna awakened as dawn glowed pink through the bedroom window. Recalling last night, warmth flooded through her. Jorn had been a careful, tender lover, fearing he might hurt her. She assured him she was fine, and later, he repeated the act more vigorously. Both had been worth the wait.

A sated calm mellowed her mood as she rose to check the baby. Jorn's light snore continued, and she smiled at the peaceful expression on her sleeping husband's face.

Erik cooed. His blue eyes fixed on Anna as she stooped to pick him up, carried him to the counter, and changed his diaper. When he was clean and dry, she took him to the rocker and nursed him. Her heart swelled with love.

After a quarter-hour, Jorn roused. Still in his nightshirt, he padded into the parlor, crossed to her side, and kissed her forehead. "I'll fire up the cookstove."

She stroked his arm. "Thank you."

Wood thunked against iron, and soon the muffled crackling and popping of a fire broke the silence. The crunch of the coffee grinder echoed through the house.

When the baby finished the second nipple, his eyelids hung heavy. A faint aroma of coffee greeted her as she joined Jorn in the kitchen. He held Erik while she made fried eggs and toast. When breakfast was ready, Anna placed the sleeping baby in the cradle. Jorn took his place at the table. She joined him.

"The planting is nearly done." He spread a dollop of butter on his toast. "If you make a list, I will pick up what you need in town on Wednesday."

"I'd like to go with you." Anna hadn't been to Cedar Falls since before Erik was born. She missed shopping and stopping in to see Peder.

His head jerked up. "You would?"

"I want to pick out some fabric to make summer gowns for Erik."

"But he's so little," Jorn protested. "It will be a difficult trip for him."

"He's nearly ten weeks old, and he does fine on Sunday trips to the Holdens'." She smiled. "Besides, the weather is warm, and if we take the buggy it will keep the sun or the rain off him."

Staring down at his plate, Jorn chewed his toast.

"We cannot hide Erik here on the farm forever," she said. "And he's such a beautiful baby, I would be proud to show him off."

Jorn took a drink of coffee. Finally, he looked up. "If you're sure you're ready."

"I am."

"We will see what Wednesday brings."

Over the next few days, Anna took Erik with her every time she went outdoors. This would help him acclimate to the temperatures and the wind.

On Sunday, Reverend Spelman baptized Erik at the worship service. Peder delighted Anna by attending. If only Bedstefa and Moder could have been present. Anna had written nearly a dozen letters to her mother, but she hadn't received one response. Not even to the announcement of Erik's birth. Although her grandfather had not yet acknowledged the announcement, either, he most certainly would. But Moder?

On the ride back to their farm in the afternoon, Jorn patted the baby bundled in Anna's arms. "We have a fine son. He is the envy of the congregation."

The exaggeration of a proud father. Anna smiled. "They might not have admired his wailing when the Reverend sprinkled water on his forehead."

Jorn laughed. "He was just showing the strength of his lungs."

Anna hugged the sleeping infant closer.

Maybe she and Jorn could have a marriage like Bedstefa and Bedstemor's after all.

• ♥ •

For the next two days, Anna worried over how to dress Erik, what to take along for his first trip to town, and what she would wear. Her traveling dress was still tight, and would be terribly inconvenient for nursing, but in the end, she again let out the side seams and wore it.

After a long, bumpy ride, they reached town. Anna shopped for fabric for Erik's clothes, and selected material to make curtains for the parlor and a matching drape for the bedroom doorway. Jorn stopped at the post office and retrieved their mail.

When they reached Jorgesen's Saloon, Peder escorted them upstairs. The yeasty aroma from the brewery was not nearly as revolting as before Erik's birth.

"I hired a man to tend bar so I can concentrate on the brewing and distribution," Peder said. "But he's new, and I cannot leave him for long."

"That's wonderful!" Anna exclaimed. "You will be able to visit us more often."

"Yes," Jorn agreed. "You can get to know your nephew."

Peder grinned and tickled Erik's chin. "I would like that." Then he moved to the door leading to the warehouse. "The trunk Bedstefa sent is in here if you want to sort through your things." He disappeared into the barrel-filled room and returned carrying a small box and a letter which he set on the kitchen table. "He sent these to you, Anna, along with some things for me. I'm sorry I cannot stay and visit, but I should check on my bartender."

After he left, Anna picked up the letter. She took it and the baby to the bed so she could nurse him.

"Open the package," she called to Jorn once she had Erik settled at her breast.

"But it's for you."

"Bring it here and open it so I can watch."

Jorn sat at the foot of the mattress and opened the package, withdrawing a fabric bag with something the size of a fist inside. He loosened the drawstring and pulled out an infant's silver drinking cup.

"It's beautiful," Anna said quietly. Her heart swelled with

love for her grandfather. "It looks almost like the one Bedstefa gave me when I was born." Still packed in one of her trunks, the cup was one of the treasures she brought from Denmark. How sweet of him to extend the tradition to her son.

"Erik's name is engraved on it." Jorn held the vessel close so she could see. "Do you want me to read his letter to you?"

"I will read it when the baby finishes." She loved Bedstefa's letters, with news of family members and Denmark.

Jorn stood. "I'm going down to the saloon for a beer. When I come back, we will get our provisions and head for home."

Anna smiled. "Don't be long."

After his footfalls on the steps had faded, Anna finished nursing Erik and placed the sleeping baby in the middle of the bed. She opened the letter.

Dearest Anna

Congratulations on the birth of your fine son. I am sure you will be a good mother. I am sending a gift to commemorate his birth. May he grow healthy and strong. I hope you have recovered fully.

In your mother's last letter, she said she was pleased to know you are married. When I write to her that you and your son are both doing well, it will take a great weight off her heart.

When I offered in my Jul letter to let Jorn use my place again to organize groups he will lead to America, I did not realize he would be returning to Denmark this summer to assist more emigrants in reaching America.

What? Anna shot off the bed. Jorn hadn't mentioned a word about it. She reread the line. There must be some misunderstanding.

I never expected he would be coming back so soon. Perhaps he will bring you and the baby along so I may see you. His letter did not say.

Whatever the case, I hope you are accepting of his plan.

Anna had not expected it either, and certainly had not accepted it. Her stomach clenched. He couldn't be leaving her so soon after Erik's birth.

She forced in a deep breath. And another.

Perhaps he planned to surprise her with a trip to see Bedstefa. Jorn knew how much she missed her grandfather.

I will look forward to your next letter, and hopefully will see you soon.

My best to you and the baby.

Love,

Bedstefa

Anna checked to be sure the baby was still sleeping in the middle of the bed then dropped into a chair.

She needed answers. Summer was almost here. Preparing for an Atlantic crossing with the baby would require some time.

She sprang up and paced, debating whether to wait for Jorn to return or carry the baby downstairs and confront him in the saloon.

Finally, footsteps thudded on the stairs. Anna inhaled and tried to rein in her annoyance.

A grinning Jorn burst through the door. "Ready to go?"

She stood in front of him, one hand on her hip, the other still clutching her grandfather's missive. "No."

His grin faded.

"What is the meaning of this?" She thrust the letter toward him.

He took it and began to read. His face fell. "Anna—"

"Why didn't you tell me?" She drew a quick breath to relieve the tension in her jaw. "Instead, I had to find out from Bedstefa."

After many moments, Jorn looked up, his mossy eyes fixed on her gaze. "I should have told you."

"Told me what?" She clasped her hands together. If only he would say he was taking her and the baby with him. She wasn't sure she wanted to make the trip, but it should be her decision.

"That I'm going to Denmark this summer to bring back a group of emigrants."

"Are you taking Erik and me along?"

He ran a hand through his light brown hair, already

bleached from his time in the spring sun. "The trip is hard. You know that. The baby is too little."

"So you are leaving us here. Alone." Her voice shook.

He reached for her. She ducked away.

"Anna, you won't be alone. Halvor Hansen will take care of you. The Holdens and Cooks will check on you to make sure all is well."

She crossed her arms in front of her. "All will not be well. You will be away. There's no need to go this summer, since you went last year. In the past it's been every other—"

"But, I must. Svend Christiansen is selling his two hundred forty acres to take a job at the Hurlbut Mill this fall. I need the money to buy his farm. Then, I will own the whole section."

Money to buy more land. Not to build a decent house for his family. "You already have five hundred sixty acres. You don't need a whole section. You have not even built the nursery you promised."

"I didn't promise. Your brother—"

"Well, I don't want an addition to that old shack. I want a proper home like the Holdens have! You can use the silver bar Bedstefa gave—"

He laughed derisively. "That wouldn't even cover the cost of the foundation."

"The silver bar, my gold one and—and—" She cleared her throat. "And the money you make going to Denmark this summer. That should be enough for a fine house."

"I told you. That money is for the Christensen farm." The vein in his temple bulged. "A house is not wealth. Land is wealth. When we return to Denmark, we can sell this land and buy a large estate. I have a fine son. I want to leave him a fine legacy. To do so, I must set up arrangements with the Rasmussens for the meeting place in Jutland before they change their minds."

Erik wailed.

"And we are to live like paupers. It might be years before we return." She whirled around, hurried into the bedroom, and picked up her baby. She and Erik should move back to Bedstefa's home permanently.

Footsteps clattered up the stairs. She turned to see Peder entering the room. "If you two don't want the whole town to learn your business, keep your voices down or take your row home."

"Acquiring land is more important to my husband than his wife and son." Anna burst into tears.

Peder shot Jorn a scorching glare then moved to her side. "Oh, Anna." His tone was soothing. "I didn't mean to further upset you."

Jorn moved to Anna's other side and enveloped her and the baby in his strong arms. Soon, he would be gone. As much as she wished he would stay home, she didn't want him to leave with a rift between them. Not after the loving and tender spring they had shared. She allowed him to pull her closer.

"Sweet Anna," he whispered. "I'm sorry. I should have told you, but I knew you would not like it. Our life is so good, I became a coward."

She sniffed, trying to stop her tears. "When do you leave?"

"In two weeks. I will engage a carpenter to build the nursery while I'm away." He kissed the top of her head. "Let's get our provisions and go home."

Home. To the house she hated. The house made bearable only by Jorn's presence. The house where she and her baby would spend the summer. Alone.

• ♥ •

Anna mustered the charity to forgive Jorn enough to see him off at the train station. Although her heart felt too heavy for her chest, she shed no tears as they said their farewells. She didn't want her husband's parting vision of her to be one of a tear-sodden crone.

Once again, she had given in. She promised she would not

return to Bedstefa's this summer. She forgave Jorn for planning his trip to Denmark without telling her, and for not taking her and Erik along. The onus always fell on her to forgive. Just like her mother, Anna had no spine when it came to dealing with her husband. She must grow stronger before Jorn returned home.

On the ride back to the farm Erik fell asleep, giving Anna an excuse to avoid conversation for fear of waking him. Speaking might break the fragile control she had maintained throughout the day. She didn't want Mr. Hansen to see her cry.

Over the next few weeks, Anna busied herself putting up strawberry jam and rhubarb sauce for winter. She refused to pine for Jorn. Mr. Hansen offered to help, so she set him to picking the fruit. She invited him to share midday meals so he could continue teaching her English. He accepted the invitation enthusiastically, and Anna realized for the first time how lonely his existence in the small shack must be. As lonely as her house was without Jorn, at least she had Erik.

This morning her first brood of chicks hatched, and some of the hens attacked them as they approached the ground corn. Since the farm had no brooder house, Mr. Hansen devised a crude shelter for them and enclosed a small wooden pen around it. Anna transferred the tiny balls of yellow fluff to their new home, hoping a brisk breeze wouldn't topple it.

She placed pans of food and water in the makeshift structure, then turned to find an unfamiliar man watching her. His eyes were sunken, his hair was shaggy, and his worn clothes looked as if he had rolled in dirt. He wore no shoes.

Her pulse raced.

She dashed to the nearby tree where Erik lay on a blanket in the shade and snatched him up. Holding him to her chest, she looked back at the stranger, who had not moved.

He smiled slightly, then spoke words she did not understand. She clutched Erik closer and cast her gaze toward the house then back to the man.

"No English," she croaked through her tightened throat.

The man pointed to his mouth. "Food."

She expelled a breath. He must be a beggar. Brigitte had told her they often stopped by. Most were harmless, leaving without incident if they were given a few rolls or some soup.

Mr. Hansen rounded the corner of the house, shotgun in hand. He spoke to the man in English. The stranger's eyes darkened, and he took a step back as he answered.

"He says he's just passing through on his way to Waterloo in search of work," Mr. Hansen explained in Danish.

"He wants food," Anna replied. "I will get him a slice of bread and some jam. Then, please ask him to be on his way."

She waited until Mr. Hansen had spoken to the stranger, then carried Erik into the house and placed him in his cradle.

She found a clean square of cotton fabric, left over from the summer baby blanket she had made. In the center of the cloth, she placed a half-full pint jar of jam, a large hunk of bread, and a sealed pint jar of rhubarb sauce. Queasiness swept through her as she carried the bundle outside and handed it to the man.

After staring at the gift for a few moments, he looked up, his tired eyes watery. "Thank you."

Mr. Hansen pointed the gun at the stranger and spoke to him again. The man nodded, bowed slightly toward Anna, then headed for the wagon path.

"That was nice of you," Mr. Hansen said, lowering the gun so the barrel pointed to the ground. A shy smile tugged at the corners of his mouth.

Her heart skipped a beat. Probably just relief that the stranger was gone. "I felt sorry for him."

Mr. Hanson's blue eyes twinkled. "He'll tell other beggars, and they'll all stop by to take advantage of your kindness."

"I hope you're wrong." Giving him food might have been a mistake, but if Jorn or Peder were hungry, Anna would want someone to help them.

A buggy approached from the opposite direction. Anna

lifted her hand to shade her eyes and studied the driver. A lone woman was at the reins. Gabrielle!

Anna hurried to meet her. Gabrielle hitched her horse to the post, and they went inside to check on Erik.

"I see I'm too late to warn you about that beggar," Gabrielle said in French. "He stopped at our house, too."

"Did you give him food?" Anna asked, wondering if Mr. Hansen was right.

"Yes." Gabrielle smiled. "My husband says I'm too soft-hearted, but I've been hungry. I can't help feeling sorry for them." Her smile faded. "There are stories of some tramps who get mean or steal more than food, so if Graham isn't home, I sometimes lock the door and hide where they cannot see me from the windows."

Anna's gaze swept the small rooms. Concern nipped at her. "That would be hard to do in this house. If only Jorn was here."

"I still cannot believe he went abroad this year." Gabrielle sat in the chair Anna indicated.

"He said he would be home before the harvest." Anna frowned, still hurt that he hadn't taken her and Erik along. She sighed and returned her attention to her visitor. "I am gla-*glaeder* you come." Anna tried to show off the English she had learned, and to change the subject.

Gabrielle raised a brow. "*Glaeder*? Glad?"

Anna had already forgotten the word Mr. Hansen taught her yesterday. Heat flamed in her cheeks. "Glad. I am glad you come."

"Has someone been giving you English lessons?" Gabrielle asked in French.

"Yes," Anna said in English. "Halvor Hansen. Jorn assigned him to help me with chores around the house ever since Erik was born," she explained in French. "He's been teaching me English all this time—mostly single words. Now that Jorn is gone, Mr. Hansen joins me for the midday meal, and we try to speak entirely in English. I haven't yet mastered the grammar, but I can understand much more now."

Gabrielle smiled. "That's a good way to learn."

"I think so, too," Anna said. "But I mentioned it after Sunday worship, and Greta Ringe said I should not dine with him while Jorn is away." Greta's insinuation of infidelity still stung.

"Who is she to judge?" Gabrielle's eyes narrowed. "Her husband did not leave her to return to Denmark the first summer she was here."

"So, you think it is acceptable?"

"As long as he is nothing more than your teacher." Gabrielle patted Anna's arm.

Uncomfortable warmth spread through her. She enjoyed Halvor's company during the lessons, but nothing improper had happened between them.

Gabrielle studied Anna's face. "Is everything well with you? I meant to stop by to check on you before this."

"Mostly things are fine." She paused. "But I've been queasy upon awakening. I fear I'm with child again, and I wanted to wait longer before carrying another baby." Guilt engulfed her for not happily accepting God's gift of this new life. She swallowed a sob. "I didn't think it possible to conceive while I'm nursing Erik."

The baby whimpered.

Gabrielle stood, gesturing for Anna to remain seated. "I should have advised you to wait longer before resuming marital relations. I will not counsel new mothers on preventing conception anymore. Every method I know of, save abstinence, has failed for someone."

She picked up the baby and returned to the rocker, cuddling and cooing to him as a grandmother would. Anna's chest tightened. Luckily, she and Erik had Gabrielle to care about them. Her affection eased some of Anna's sadness that her own mother didn't know her grandson.

"If Jorn does not agree to build a larger house after this child is born, I will be ready to abstain for the rest of our marriage,"

Anna declared.

"When I turned in to your dooryard, I saw the foundation laid out for your new nursery. Is someone building it while Jorn is away?" Gabrielle asked.

"Mr. Dahl. I have to rely on Mr. Hansen to translate." Anna grinned. "It is twice the size that Jorn is expecting. I need a storeroom for my trunks, so that has been added, too."

Gabrielle chuckled. "Well, he should have stayed home if he wanted it his way."

Anna heart filled with appreciation.

"There wasn't adequate space between the bedroom wall and the kitchen door, so the addition is on the end of the house." She paused. "It will look out of place, so I expect Jorn will be furious." That didn't matter. The larger addition made Jorn's refusal to build a proper house more palatable.

"He will get over it." Gabrielle's gaze swept to the clock. "Especially if you have another child."

"He has the son he wanted." She stole a glance at Erik, sleeping peacefully in Gabrielle's arms. "I do not know how he will respond to becoming a father again."

Gabrielle winked. "Most men like proving their virility with children."

"How have you learned so much?" Anna asked with a wide smile. "Since you and Graham are not parents."

The animation left Gabrielle's face. She bit her lower lip. "When we were in New Orleans, we were both quite ill." Tears shimmered in her eyes. "The physician cured us, but we will never be able to conceive."

Anna lost her breath.

Gabrielle hugged Erik to her.

"That must have been hard to hear." Anna forced the words from her tight throat. "Especially when you had helped so many women to give birth.

"Yes." Gabrielle straightened to her full height. "But at least Graham and I both survived. And we have each other."

Warmth spread through Anna's cheeks. She went to her friend and slipped an arm around her shoulder. "I am sorry. I should not have pried with such a personal question."

"It is all right. Close friends do not have secrets." Gabrielle handed Erik to Anna. "I must be getting home, but I would like to visit again soon. Will you be home next Tuesday?"

"I will be canning beans." Anna couldn't hide her loathing for work that made her kitchen even hotter on sweltering summer days.

"I could help."

The offer brought tears to Anna's eyes. She had missed her weekly visits with Gabrielle. "And I could help you on another day. Perhaps, while we work, you could teach me more English."

"I would be happy to. Between Mr. Hansen and me, you will be speaking like a true American before Jorn gets home." Gabrielle smiled and left.

Anna watched absently as the buggy disappeared down the trail. How would her husband react if she greeted him in English and told him that she was again with child?

Chapter 6

July 10, 1875

Thanks to Halvor, my English is improving every day. I do not know what I would have done without him this summer. He has worked so hard on the garden, and it is producing a bounty that will keep my family abundantly fed through the coming winter. He has taken over all of my outdoor chores and helps me with laundry, or butter churning, or whatever else he can, and he always does so with his charming, boyish smile.

Yesterday, he brought me a bouquet of wildflowers when he came for the noon meal. It was a sweet gesture, and gave us a topic for new words as we practiced our English. At night, he speaks with some of the greenhorns who have been here longer to learn more words to teach me. I have grown fond of him and will miss his help and his company when Jorn returns.

Erik is thriving. He rolls over and over, sometimes off the edge of his blanket. I hate when he reaches the dirt floor, and look forward to completion of the nursery with its wood floor. He has a most fetching smile that enchants everyone who sees him. I hope he will be in a happy mood when Gabrielle comes this week. I am eager to spend time with her again, and I will offer to return her visit so that we can continue to see each other regularly.

On Tuesday, Anna rose early, ate some dry toast to settle her stomach, and completed her ironing before Gabrielle arrived. With Jorn gone, there were fewer garments to iron. This saved her more than an hour in the dreaded weekly drudgery with the heavy flatirons. She would gladly bake bread and pastries all day long if she did not have to spend two hours ironing.

Yesterday, she asked Halvor to pick the ripe beans. She sorted them into the smaller thin ones for canning whole, and the larger ones to cut before processing. The chicken for the noon meal was roasting in the oven. The boiler, jars, lids, and water were ready. She was washing string beans when Gabrielle knocked on the door a little after ten o'clock.

"Good morning," Anna called in English. "Come in." She had practiced these words with Halvor when he brought the eggs so she would be certain of the correct pronunciation.

"Thank you," Gabrielle answered. She peeked at Erik, asleep in the cradle, then came to the kitchen and started cutting beans. Throughout the morning, they spoke in English, with much laughter, and Gabrielle supplying words and pronunciations. Time flew, and before Anna realized it, Halvor appeared for the noon meal.

"Whew, it's hot in here," he said.

"Yes." Anna tucked a stray lock behind her ear and swiped at her damp forehead with the back of her hand.

Gabrielle mopped her face with her apron. "Please take the table and chairs out under the tree, Halvor."

Anna wilted some lettuce and stirred together vinegar, sugar, and water for a dressing, while Gabrielle sliced the bread and opened the last jar of pears left from the shivaree.

"I need pears for can," Anna said, trying out her English. "Where get them?"

"Order the number of crates you want from one of the grocers in town," Gabrielle replied, then translated into French. She removed the roaster from the oven.

They dished food onto their plates. Halvor pumped fresh, cool water into glasses and put them on the table, wobbly on the uneven ground under the oak. Then he carried the cradle outside, with still-sleeping Erik, and set it in the shade near

Anna's chair.

When they were seated and had begun to eat, Gabrielle turned to Halvor. "How much longer do you plan to work for the Strykers?"

He swallowed a sip of water. "My first year is up in August, and I'll have one more to complete my obligation, but Mr. Stryker asked me to stay on as a hired hand. When he gets the Christensen farm, Morton Andreasen will move to that house."

Anna stared at Halvor. He hadn't mentioned this. Perhaps he assumed Jorn had told her, which he hadn't. Just as he hadn't told her of plans to leave her and Erik alone all summer. If not for Bedstefa's letter, when would her husband have confided in her?

Gabrielle's eyes widened. Apparently, the Cooks didn't know about Jorn's plan to purchase the additional land.

Erik whimpered and began to stir. Anna ate faster, thankful the nausea she had suffered earlier was gone.

"He wanted me to move to the house down the road," Halvor continued. "But I'd rather stay in my cabin and get higher wages. I want to save up to bring my mother to America."

Jorn would have the money to buy the Christensen farm so he wouldn't have to go back next summer. He didn't need more land. Much of what he owned now stood idle or in pasture.

"That would be nice," Gabrielle said.

Erik's whimper escalated into a cry. Anna took him inside to nurse.

By the time she finished, Gabrielle had cleared the table. Anna fixed her clothing and picked up Erik. The women walked outside to look at the foundation for the nursery.

"Did you know about Jorn's plan to buy the Christensen farm?" Gabrielle asked in French.

"Not until the day he told me he was going to Denmark," Anna replied. "I was so angry about finding out from my grandfather's letter, I really didn't think much about the land, except that the money could be used to build a new house."

"So, you get a new room instead of a house."

Rocking from side to side to soothe her baby, Anna nodded. "Since he was just there last year, I did not expect him to go this summer."

"He does like making those trips." Gabrielle scanned the area. "Your carpenter is not working today?"

"Mr. Dahl order more wood," Anna explained switching back to English. "Since nursery bigger."

They walked to the front of the house.

"Window here." Anna pointed to the middle of the low rock wall. She walked around the corner and pointed again. "Window here."

At the back of the new space there were two foundations about five feet apart. She pointed to the area between them. "Trunk storage."

"It'll be very nice." Gabrielle smiled. "Jorn will be surprised."

Yes, and he would not be pleased. Anna kissed Erik's forehead, trying to quell her anger toward his father.

When they returned to the kitchen, Gabrielle reached for Erik. He smiled his toothless grin. "What a good boy you are." She patted his cloth-covered bottom. "Are you ready to play?"

Anna put a quilt on the floor and laid Erik in the center of it. She and Gabrielle went back to canning. By the end of the day, they had worked through all the beans. Anna thanked her friend for her help.

"My house next Tuesday?" Gabrielle asked.

"Yes." Anna grinned, pleased that she would see her again so soon.

If time passed as quickly as it had today, Jorn would be back before Anna knew it. She could only hope the carpenter would finish before he arrived.

• ♥ •

Over the next few weeks, the nursery took shape. Anna insisted on a door to close it off from the bedroom. She'd also been adamant about having a wood floor so Erik wouldn't have to play on dirt.

Halvor painted the walls the cornflower color she selected. When the paint had dried, he helped her transfer the trunks to the storage area. Peder brought the third trunk from his warehouse and helped Halvor move it, the cradle, and the rocker into the new room.

Gabrielle and Anna had spent two of their Tuesdays together making blue and white gingham curtains for the windows. On one of her trips to town with Halvor, Anna had purchased a woven blue rug for the floor. She stepped back to admire the new room. The nursery had turned out better than she expected, even though it looked like it belonged in a different house.

Under her bed, the fabric from her last shopping trip to town with Jorn lay untouched. She resented the way she learned of his plan to travel to Denmark, and had transferred a part of that bitterness to the material. A drape from that fabric would constantly remind her of Jorn's betrayal. As she dressed for worship services on the first Sunday of August, she decided to offer the tainted cloth to Gabrielle.

Anna reached under the bed and pulled out the crate containing her old picnic quilt. Throughout the summer, Reverend Spelman held services outside, under the huge maple tree, in the Holdens' backyard. On this hot, sticky day, they hopefully would catch a cool breeze.

A knock sounded at the kitchen door.

"Are you ready?" Halvor called in English.

"Almost," she shouted back. "Come in."

Except for Sunday services, Anna now spoke almost

exclusively in English. Jorn would be surprised, and none too pleased, at how much she had learned since he left. No matter what he thought, speaking English was necessary for life in America.

Halvor walked into the kitchen and flashed her his big grin. "Baskets ready?"

He looked so handsome dressed in his Sunday best, with his blond hair neatly combed, his youthful face cleanly shaved.

She smiled. "Yes."

On the way home from the Holdens' last week, he asked if she would make rice pudding. The batch she made this morning was cooling in one of the baskets. He had been so helpful since Erik was born and so nice to her this summer, it was the least she could do. She had also made the butter rolls Brigitte loved.

Anna gathered Erik's things into her satchel and picked him up. "Time to go, big boy."

He smiled at her and cooed. She hugged him close. Although he had caused her much illness before his birth, he was a very good baby. Sadly, by the end of the summer, Halvor would have spent more time with Erik than Jorn had.

Halvor took the quilt and satchel from the bed. "Let's go."

She followed him to the buggy. Jorn would be appalled that she was riding to Sunday services with the greenhorn. She gritted her teeth and tried not to care what Jorn would think.

Halvor stowed the quilt and satchel next to her baskets and the bucket of tomatoes he was contributing to the meal. He held out his hands and lifted Erik from her arms. She climbed into the front seat.

"Ready for a ride?" Halvor asked the baby, tickling his chin. Erik grinned at him.

Anna smiled. Gentle and good-humored, Halvor was good with Erik. He handed the baby to her, then took his place on the seat.

"The sweet corn is nearly over," he said, as he drove the horse out of the dooryard.

"We have plenty." The harvest had been bountiful, and she had put up many quarts. "Would you like more?" She had given him a few jars of every fruit and vegetable she'd canned.

"Thanks, but I have enough." He turned onto the trail to the Holdens'. "The apples are starting to set."

Anna sighed. Many more hours of canning lay ahead. This year there would be no shivaree, and she had an additional mouth to feed.

When they reached the Holdens', Halvor dropped the baskets off in the kitchen before joining the other greenhorns. Anna settled Erik and herself on the quilt beside Brigitte and her children. After the services, Anna helped organize the food and stayed to help with the dishes. Halvor visited with Frederik while he waited.

When the last pan was put away, Anna and Halvor loaded her baskets and the baby things into the buggy. They bid the Holdens farewell and headed down the trail.

Back home, Erik drifted off to sleep. Anna headed for the kitchen. The baskets lay on the counter, her quilt and satchel on the bench. She hadn't even heard Halvor come or go.

"Is he asleep?"

Anna jumped. She turned to see Halvor sitting in Jorn's favorite chair. "Yes." He looked so much at home it unnerved her. She crossed to the basket and pulled out the pan. "Pudding is left. You want?"

Halvor rose and moved to her side, taking the pan she offered. "It was delicious. Thanks for making it."

"You welcome. You helped me much." She didn't think her English grammar was quite right.

"I've enjoyed it." He smiled shyly.

"Me, too."

He held her gaze for a moment then looked down at the

leftovers in the pan he held. "I like you."

"And I like you." It would have been a lonely summer if not for him.

He set the pan on the counter, and took a tentative step toward her. His brow furrowed. "If you were my wife, I wouldn't leave you alone like your husband did."

Her stomach clenched. She pulled back. "I wish he not gone."

Halvor lifted his hand, hesitated, then gently touched his fingertips to her cheek. His blue eyes widened and the color darkened. His face drew nearer. "You're a beautiful woman." His fingers trembled. "I love you."

His lips took hers, timidly at first, then firm and warm. Her heart raced.

Love. Is that what he felt? What she felt? Maybe it was just loneliness that compelled him to touch her and drove her to look forward to his company.

He slipped an arm around her waist. Her knees quivered as warmth flooded her. She shouldn't feel like this with Halvor. It was wrong.

Tightness squeezed her chest. She jerked away. "Stop it." She reverted to Danish to be certain she was saying what she intended. "I'm a married woman."

"That doesn't change how I feel." His indigo gaze nailed hers. "And I believe you love me, too."

"I won't be unfaithful to Jorn." Anna shouted, taking several steps back.

Halvor lifted his chin. His jaw tightened.

"And you think he isn't betraying you while he's in Denmark?" He hurled the words with a derisive tone.

He might as well have kicked her in the stomach. That same thought had crossed her mind from time to time, and it didn't help that Jorn hadn't sent one letter since he left. But she wanted to believe her doubts were unfounded.

"I will not have you saying such horrible things about my husband. The father of my son." She stalked to the kitchen door and threw it open. "Get out of my house!"

• ❤ •

All night Anna lay awake, listening in case Halvor returned. She was not sure she could be steadfast in her resistance to his advances if he did.

It would serve Jorn right if she had a fling, but she couldn't bring herself to break her marriage vows. Though she and Jorn committed a sin when they conceived Erik, since their marriage she had strived to live a worthy life. To set a good example for her son.

Had Jorn made the same commitment or was he having relations with women in Denmark? After all, he had done just that with her last summer, and then taken up with Lottie only a month later. There might have been others. She had to find out.

When dawn broke, she checked to see that Erik was asleep, then climbed the ladder to the loft. Dust floated in the air as she opened the first box. One by one, she sorted through the musty-smelling papers and ledgers. Many, she believed, were in English. Although she understood the spoken language pretty well, she could not read it.

She couldn't ask Gabrielle to read them for her, and, after what happened last night, she must no longer rely on Halvor. He might misinterpret her actions. She pulled more of the contents from the box.

Other documents were in Danish. Jorn had kept a ledger for each of his trips to Denmark, documenting those emigrants who had paid him in full to escort them to America, and those who had not. For each with balances remaining, she found among the papers a handwritten contract for how the debt would be repaid. Some promised to pay in cash, a bit each month until they were free and clear. Others had agreed to work for Jorn, with time periods ranging from six months to three years. In these agreements, Jorn often promised to provide a house and a cow to the greenhorn while he worked off his debt. When the obligation was met, both parties signed to that effect.

Halvor Hansen had promised to work for Jorn for two years, to end September 1, 1876. Jorn promised him milk, vegetables, fruit, and the tiny cabin in the grove. Now, Jorn apparently planned to hire him. Anna wished Halvor would take the little house across the road. He would be farther away, and she dreaded encountering him in the dooryard and barnyard. One by one, she put the items back into the crate.

In the next one, she found Jorn's winter clothes, which he had put away after she washed them. She rifled quickly through. Nothing.

Inside the third crate, she found a crude drawing of an older man and woman, a book on farming practices, and a school primer with Jorn's name printed on the front. With her finger, she traced the crooked block letters. She picked two toy horses, whittled smoothly from a hard wood, and wondered if Jorn would offer them to Erik when he was older. She uncovered a letter from his mother, written shortly after he first came to America, filled with family news. Jorn's treasures.

He'd brought far less with him than Anna had. It was no wonder he resented her trunks. She returned the items to their box. Nothing indicated Jorn would be visiting other women. Ever since he'd told her about Lottie, Anna hadn't been able to shake the worry that he had others. A twinge of guilt pinched her. She should trust her husband.

She went down to the kitchen to make some coffee. On the floor next to the door lay a sheet of paper. She picked it up.

Anna,

Please forgive me for last night. I am ashamed of my behavior. It will never happen again. Please do not tell your husband, and forget all about it. I would like to continue being friends.

Halvor

Anna swallowed. No matter how he felt, they could no

longer remain friends. Not like they had been.

Moving toward the stove, she grabbed some wood splits, flung them in the firebox, and lit them. She dropped the note on top of the fire. As it burned, the tension in her muscles melted away. There would be no reminder of last night's events. If only she could erase the memory so easily.

• ♥ •

On Friday morning, Anna put Erik down for a nap and picked up the dress she was hemming.

A knock sounded at the front door. She opened it, and found Peder standing on the step. His blond hair had been trimmed to just below his ears.

"What a nice surprise," she said in English. "Come in."

He stepped inside. "Every time I see you, your English has improved. Jorn will be pleased."

"Maybe." She didn't think so.

"Speaking of Jorn." Peder held out an envelope. "He sent this."

The writing on the front said: *Please give this to Anna.*

It was her first letter from him. Her fingers trembled as she broke his seal.

"He also sent one for Morton Andreasen, which I dropped off on the way here." Peder said. "Jorn is coming home on August twenty-third. He wants Morton and Halvor to bring wagons to pick up the greenhorns and their things."

Anna removed her letter and opened it.

Dear Anna,

I am sorry not to have written sooner. I ran into some unexpected complications, but all is well now.

I greatly miss you and Erik. Please come with Halvor to the station on August 23. I cannot wait a moment longer than necessary to see you and my son.

Love,

Jorn

Warmth flowed through Anna. She smiled. He had signed it 'love,' a word he rarely said to her. He'd be home in less than two weeks. Her heart fluttered. She had been right to resist Halvor's temptation. She looked up at Peder. "What complications?"

"I don't know," he said. "But fewer of the people who cross with him will be coming to Cedar Falls. Maybe he had difficulties with some of the arrangements for transport to other destinations."

The explanation was more than she could process and, though it rankled her, she had to ask for the Danish translation. The rationale seemed reasonable.

"You want coffee?" she asked, reverting to English.

"And some of that puff?" He pointed to the pastry she had earlier set on the counter.

"Of course."

He sat at the table while she served. "Don't suppose you'd like to sell some of your eggs and chickens."

She rubbed her temples as she considered the question. "Eggs, maybe. But I have only a small surplus of chickens."

"One of the restaurants that buys my beer is looking for another supplier. His old one lost most of his chickens to a fox." Peder forked a bite of pastry to his mouth.

"I send some eggs and chicken to town with Halvor." She seated herself across from Peder. "And I start raising more chickens."

"You could make a little pin money for yourself." He set his fork down and his blue gaze met hers. "I have more news. I bought a house."

"You moving from brewery?"

He laughed. "I can't live above the saloon forever."

"Why not?"

He shifted in his chair. "No woman would want to be courted by a man who—"

"Are you courting someone?" Anna grinned at his

discomfort.

"Not yet. But, perhaps after I move."

"What your house like?"

"It has two stories with four bedrooms upstairs, and a basement. There's a carriage house in back and a chicken coop and a small garden."

A flicker of jealousy spoiled the happiness Anna felt for her brother. "Sounds nice." Her curiosity got the better of her. "You have woman in mind?"

"Anna!" he protested, although an amused smile softened his angular face.

"Do you?"

"There is a woman."

"She accepts that you a brewer and saloon owner?" she asked, concerned that he might end up disappointed.

"That remains to be seen."

Chapter 7

August 22, 1875

Jorn will be home tomorrow. I look forward to seeing him, but I am uneasy about how he will react to the nursery. It is finished and looks beautiful. I love it, but I am certain he will not. Will he pay the difference in cost, or will he make me spend my Christmas gold bar? I am hopeful that he will accept the size of the addition when he learns I am again carrying his child, although I worry that he might be angry about that, as well.

Peder has kindly agreed to go with me to meet Jorn tomorrow, and drive us home so that he can deflect Jorn's wrath.

Mr. Hansen drove Erik and me to the Holdens' for church today. It was an uncomfortable ride. Although we still speak to each other in English, we have returned to addressing each other formally. He no longer joins me for noon meals, and I try to minimize contact with him when we must discuss work to be done. Thankfully, Jorn will assume that role when he returns. I pray that neither I nor Mr. Hansen will betray our indiscretion.

At three o'clock, Anna held Erik close as she waited on the platform of the Cedar Falls depot. Her stomach quivered as the train screeched to a halt. Peder stood to her left, Halvor to her right. Morton Andreasen tended the horses, harnessed to the wagons.

Conductors emerged from the exits and helped passengers disembark. In the distance, Jorn gave directions in Danish. Her pulse raced. She located the back of his head, his light brown hair curling slightly at his shoulders, and shivered despite the day's unbearable heat. With Peder and Halvor in tow, she pushed toward him, picking her way through the crowd.

Halvor stopped short. "Land's sakes!" He raced toward Jorn's group. "Moder!"

Anna shot Peder a glance. "His mother?"

He shrugged.

What a nice thing for Jorn to do. He must have known Halvor wanted to bring her to America.

Jorn hurried toward Anna. He'd grown a mustache that made him look older, more distinguished, but just as handsome as ever. His green eyes glistened. "Anna!" He threw his arms around her and the baby, then released the embrace and reached for his son. "He has grown big."

As soon as Erik was in his father's hands, his tiny face crumpled and he let out a loud, angry wail. Jorn handed him back to Anna. He quieted.

"He doesn't know you. He will get used to you again," she said in Danish.

The greenhorns, their belongings, and Jorn's trunk were loaded onto the wagons. Halvor and Mr. Andreasen started for the farm. Peder drove Anna and her family in his carriage to his home so the baby could nurse. Anna hoped seeing Peder's new house might inspire Jorn to build one.

The front door opened to an entrance hall. To the right was a large, empty parlor with tall windows and an oak floor.

"I've ordered a sofa and chairs, but they haven't arrived yet." Peder spoke in Danish, his tone apologetic. "And the cabinet maker is fashioning tables for me."

"It's a beautiful house," Anna said in English, trying not to sound too envious.

Jorn's eyes widened. "Where did you learn English?"

Anna grinned. "From Gabrielle and Mr. Hansen."

He shot her a hard look but said nothing. Dread stole over her happy mood. He would likely have plenty to say when they were alone.

"Would you like a beer?" Peder asked Jorn. He led them to the dining room, where his old table and chairs appeared very small. "Anna, you can nurse Erik in here." He closed the paneled oak pocket doors to the hallway and escorted Jorn into the kitchen, pulling the door shut after them.

From the kitchen came the clanking of glass bottles bumping together, the scrape of chair or stool legs on the wooden floor, and the sound of muffled voices.

When the other noises ceased, Anna could just make out what her brother and Jorn were saying.

"I didn't know you planned to bring Mrs. Hansen," Peder said.

"When I arrived at your grandfather's, he showed me a letter he had received from her."

"How did she know about him?"

"She had saved his name and address from Halvor's crossing."

A bottle clunked on some surface. "...letter say?"

"The German Army was transferring her daughter's husband to Munich, and Mrs. Hansen didn't want to live among Germans. She wanted to know how to make arrangements to go to America."

"Couldn't she stay in South Jutland?" Peder asked.

"She had no way to support herself. She offered to work as a housekeeper for your grandfather to earn money for her passage. Or for me."

Anna would love to have help with the housework and the baby, but Mrs. Hansen would need a place live. Her son's cabin was very small. There was room for a bed in the nursery, but Anna and Jorn would have no privacy. Maybe the Hansens could move to Morton Andreasen's place.

"I feared the mail would be too slow, so I arranged for Frode Rasmussen's sister to cross the border, pretending to be Mrs. Hansen's second cousin, and take a message to her. A week after the other emigrants had gathered at Frode's place, his sister hadn't returned, and I couldn't find out what was happening. If we waited more than another three days, we wouldn't make it to Copenhagen in time to meet the ship. I assumed Mrs. Hansen decided not to come."

Anna moved the baby to her other breast.

"The next day, a wagon arrived with Frode's sister, Adelaide Hansen, and her daughter. Turned out the Rasmussen horse had broken his leg. The border guards wouldn't let Mrs. Hansen's son-in-law cross, so his wife had to drive the wagon. She told the guards that her mother was moving in with her cousin."

"Halvor was thrilled. How is he going to repay you?"

"I don't know, but he is a good man. We will work something out." Jorn cleared his throat. "Frode asked if you need help in your brewery."

"He would come to America?" Peder asked.

"Next summer, if you need a brewmaster."

Next summer. On his own or with Jorn? A lump grew in Anna's throat.

"I could use help. With so many accounts in Waterloo, delivery keeps me from spending much time brewing." After a few moments of silence, Peder continued. "Are you going back to Denmark next year?"

Anna held her breath.

"I was not planning to, but so many men inquired, I expect to have a full group without any recruiting. They are eager to leave, but reluctant to strike out on their own. Most need time to scrape together at least part of the money for the trip, but if I don't make arrangements for the coming summer, they won't wait."

Anna suppressed a scream. He would be leaving her alone again. With two babies.

She forced in a deep breath. Of course, he didn't know of the second child. She must tell him, but not today. When he got home, the new nursery would be enough for his first day back.

Besides, she wanted to resume their marital relations to prove to herself that Halvor's kiss had really been a mistake. Jorn was already annoyed that she'd learned English. He might not want to be intimate if she added the news that she was carrying another baby.

"You don't want to pass up the money," Peder said.

"That, and I'll need hands to help work my additional land."

Land bought with money that should have been spent on a proper house. Anna clenched her teeth. She had saved the cash she earned from the sale of eggs, but it was so meager that it would take her a decade to collect enough for even the basement.

She could use some of the gift from Bedstefa, but it was best to keep that for unforeseen necessities, like food and clothes in a bad year. Or if something happened to Jorn. She sighed and adjusted the baby into a more comfortable position.

Perhaps next year, she could raise more pullets and expand the garden. In addition to her eggs, she could sell chickens, produce, and canned goods.

When the baby finished nursing, they returned to the carriage and Peder drove them home. As the trail to the Cooks' came into sight, Anna tensed.

They passed the Ringe's house. Her heart began to pound.

Morton Andreasen's place. She worried her lower lip.

When the house came in sight, Jorn's jaw tightened.

"It's a very nice nursery," Peder said as he turned the team into the dooryard. "It's large, well-built, and there's room for Anna's trunks."

She could have kissed her brother.

Jorn grunted. "We will see."

When Peder stopped the carriage and hopped out to secure the horses, Jorn helped Anna and Erik down.

"I don't believe that is the plan I gave the carpenter," he muttered, tilting his head in the direction of the new addition.

Anna squared her shoulders. "It's not. There was not enough

room between the bedroom wall and the kitchen door for a proper nursery."

She led him into the house and straight to the new room.

Silently, he studied the walls, the floor, and the storage area.

Peder brought in the satchel of baby things and set it on Anna's bed.

Finally, Jorn turned to her. "I thought I might need to add a room to Halvor's cottage, but we can put a bed in here for Mrs. Hansen. She can work off her debt as our housekeeper. I will tell her tomorrow."

Jorn wasn't mad. He seemed almost pleased. Thank God Mrs. Hansen crossed this year. Anna released the breath she had been holding. "It will be nice to have help."

Jorn obviously had not thought how having Mrs. Hansen in the next room would infringe upon their privacy, but they would cross that bridge later.

Mrs. Hansen would not be here tonight. After Peder left, Anna and Jorn would be alone.

She couldn't wait to get to know her husband again.

• ♥ •

Jorn and Anna took advantage of the night to rekindle their passion. She didn't reveal that she was again with child. She didn't want him to be hesitant in the way he touched her, loved her. He wasn't.

She'd shown Jorn how much she loved him. Halvor's kiss had been a mistake. Now, if Jorn heard talk in the congregation of Halvor driving her to church, Jorn would understand nothing improper had occurred.

In the morning, he didn't question why she stayed in bed instead of getting up to prepare his breakfast. Her queasy stomach reminded her she couldn't keep her condition secret from him for long, nor did she want to. She had to tell him at their noon meal.

Shortly after sunrise, he returned to the bedroom and kissed her cheek. "I'm sorry I tired you out last night."

"I'm not sorry." She kneaded her aching temples, then gave him a small smile.

Jorn tugged the covers up around her neck. "Rest, now. I will speak to Mrs. Hansen about her debt after I assess the condition of the fields. I'll be back by noon."

Anna closed her eyes, happy Jorn was home. She turned over, hoping for more sleep before she needed to nurse the baby.

Soon, the apples would be ready. It would be time to can them and make cider. Maybe Mrs. Hansen could help…

After another hour of sleep, Anna fed the baby, completed her morning chores, and began preparations for the midday meal.

Jorn arrived a few minutes before noon. "Mrs. Hansen will work off her indebtedness as our housekeeper for two years," Jorn said as Anna poured him a cup of coffee. "Halvor likes the arrangement, since they'll both be here on the farm."

"That's good," Anna said, wondering if Halvor would be around the house more. She pushed the thought away. "When will she start?"

"She will move into the nursery this afternoon. You can give her instructions for tomorrow."

Good thing Anna had last night alone with Jorn. Tonight would likely be much different. Anna wasn't pleased to have another adult living in their small house, but she looked forward to help with the housework and cooking now that Halvor would be assigned more of the farm chores. "How are the fields?"

"The crops look good," he said, after swallowing a large bite of beef and gravy. "The hay could use cutting, and the stack could stand to grow before winter. But there is still time."

They ate in silence. Anna didn't know why telling him of her condition unsettled her so. He was her husband, after all. She laid down her fork and clasped her hands tightly together in her lap to keep them from shaking. "I have news to tell you."

Jorn looked up from his plate, his green eyes fixed on her.

"Not long after you left, I discovered I'm again with child." She rushed on before he could digest the meaning of her words. "I didn't believe it possible while Erik is still nursing, but Gabrielle said it can happen. She has seen it before."

He blinked. His face went slack. "Is that why you changed the plan for the nursery?"

"In part." Mostly she had wanted the trunk storage. "I thought it might need to accommodate more children, but with Mrs. Hansen—"

He smiled and clasped her hand. "When is the baby due?"

"It's hard to know, but I estimate late January to early February."

"Erik is a fine boy." Jorn's grin broadened. "It will be good to have another son like him to help with the farming."

• ♥ •

Jorn threw himself into the harvest. Throughout the autumn, he, the hired men, and the greenhorns worked from sun up to sun down, stopping only briefly for a noon meal and an afternoon lunch that Mrs. Hansen sent out with one of the hands.

Anna appreciated having Adelaide Hansen in the house, for her help and for her company. She was near Anna's mother's age. A few gray hairs mingled with the predominantly dark blond ones especially around Adelaide's round face. She had a gentle air, much like Halvor's.

Anna spent more time attending to Erik, reading to him and playing with him. While he slept, she planned her chicken-and-egg business and next spring's garden, complete with extra vegetables to sell in town. She continued her Tuesdays with Gabrielle, relying on Adelaide to fix the noon meal for Jorn.

On the first Tuesday of November, Anna and Gabrielle began working on Christmas gifts in the Cook's sitting room as they caught up on each other's news from the past week. Anna was sewing a wool shirt for Jorn, and Gabrielle was knitting socks for Graham. Erik sat on a blanket, playing with a flannel dog and a ball.

"I'm not as ill with this child," Anna said, practicing her English as she always did with Gabrielle. Since Jorn's return, they spoke only Danish in their home.

"Maybe because you haven't had to cross an ocean or set up housekeeping."

"I hope it means I'm going to have a daughter." Anna thought about it often and prayed silently for it each night.

Gabrielle laughed. "Some women can tell by their body's reaction whether the child will be male or female, but that's usually after they've had at least one of each."

They stitched on in silence, except for Erik's babbling.

"Graham and I would like you and Jorn to join us for Thanksgiving dinner," Gabrielle said. "We'll invite Brigitte, Frederik, and their family, too."

"Thanksgiving?" Anna puzzled over the meaning of the word. "Is that something to do with your church? Jorn and the Holdens are strict Lutherans."

Gabrielle chuckled. "It has nothing to do with a specific religion. During the war, President Lincoln proclaimed a national holiday to give thanks to God for the successes of the North, and the blessings enjoyed in spite of the horrors of the battlefields. I believe President Grant has proclaimed November twenty-fifth as this year's holiday."

"We have a Great Prayer Day in Denmark," Anna said. "The fourth Friday after Easter. But it is for all prayers, not just those of thanks."

"You may say whatever prayers you want," Gabrielle said. "Will you come?"

"I'd like that very much, but I'll have to ask Jorn," Anna said. "And, I'd better go now. I want to be home before dark."

She drove the horse as fast as she dared without risking

upsetting her buggy in the trail's ruts. The aroma of roasting ham greeted her when she carried Erik into their house. The kitchen's warmth melted the chill that had penetrated her cloak.

Adelaide put a pot of potatoes on to boil. She'd grown slightly plump in the few months since she arrived. "Did you have a nice visit?"

"Very." Anna reverted to Danish, the only language Adelaide spoke. Jorn permitted Anna to use English only when they needed to have a few private words in front of their housekeeper. "I started working on a Christmas gift for Jorn."

"I would like to make a warm shirt for Halvor, but I have no fabric."

"Perhaps he could take you to town, or you could ride along with my husband when he goes on Saturday." Anna had stocked up on materials and provisions when she accompanied Jorn to Cedar Falls last week. She had little desire to make the trip again now that the weather had turned colder.

The corners of Adelaide's mouth drooped. She combed a hand through her curly hair. "That would be nice, but I have no money."

Anna didn't know what to say. Tonight, she would count the coins left in her reticule. Perhaps she could spare some, or draw from her chicken-and-egg earnings. She would speak to Jorn about giving Adelaide a gift of money this Christmas. She didn't need the pork he gave to the farm hands as she took most meals with the family.

Jorn arrived, lantern in hand and Halvor in tow, for dinner at six o'clock. Since Adelaide moved in, Jorn had relaxed his restriction against fraternizing with the help. Several times a week, when Jorn had more work planned, Halvor joined them for their evening meal. Anna fidgeted. She tried to resist looking at Halvor, and he avoided eye contact with her. Throughout the meal, she remained silent.

Anna wondered if Jorn sensed her uneasiness in Halvor's presence, and if so, what he made of it. She waited until they were in bed to tell him of the Cooks' invitation.

"Gabrielle and Graham have invited us to their house on Thanksgiving for dinner," she said into the darkness, after they'd both hunkered down under the covers.

"You see her every week," Jorn growled. "Isn't that enough?"

Her stomach clenched. She hadn't sensed his foul mood before now. She should have waited until morning.

"Gabrielle is my best friend." Anna knew she sounded defensive, so she tried to soften her tone. "We share our work when we are together, and I enjoy her company."

"Why couldn't you choose one of the Danish women? They are closer to your age, and you would have more in common."

"Gabrielle is like a mother to me." It meant so much to Anna since she had not heard from Moder.

He expelled an audible breath.

"I really like Brigitte," she started uncertainly. "But she is busy with her children and the weekly worship services put a large burden on her time."

"What about Greta?" Jorn asked.

Greta was opinionated and judgmental, but Anna didn't dare say that to Jorn. "She has never accepted that I was with child when we married. She treats me as if I'm beneath her."

"And Karyn Thomsen?"

She had always puzzled Anna. "She's missed quite a few Sundays since Erik was born. I hardly know her."

Jorn grunted. "We should pay her and Ole a visit. He still owes me fifty dollars from their passage."

"From the look of their clothes, I would guess they don't have the money. And as cold as it is, the children don't have proper shoes."

"Their land has plenty of trees." The scorn in Jorn's voice took Anna aback. "If he cannot afford leather shoes, he could carve some from wood. Mine and Halvor's perform very well, and he could add some height to the heel so they would not slip in the mud and snow."

The question of the Cook's invitation still hung unanswered. Although her insides quivered, Anna plunged ahead. "Gabrielle said they are also inviting the Holdens for Thanksgiving."

"I suppose it would make for a chance to plan the hog butchering," Jorn conceded.

Anna smiled into the darkness and the tension drained from her. "Thank you."

She snuggled against him and felt the length of his manhood hard against her thigh, the source of his frustration. She knew just how to put him in better spirits.

Chapter 8

November 21, 1875

Having Adelaide as our housekeeper has been a real blessing. I enjoy her company and, although she is my servant, we are becoming friends. I love having time every day with Erik, and she will be able to help with preparation of my contributions to Gabrielle's Thanksgiving dinner and with the Jul baking. It is hard to believe Jul is coming so soon.

Thursday will be the first time since last year's hog butchering that Gabrielle, Brigitte, and I will all be together, and now we can converse in English. It will be good practice for me. I wish Jorn would speak English with me at home.

When Jorn, Erik, and I go to the Cook's, Adelaide will prepare a special meal for Halvor. They will eat their noon meal here, and then take the leftovers to his cabin, where she will stay the night. It will be the first time Jorn and I will be alone in the house since she moved in with us. I am looking forward to the privacy.

"Vilfred and Greta are going back to Denmark," Frederik announced between bites of bread.

Anna looked up. Erik squirmed in her lap. She held him firmly and offered a piece of biscuit, hoping to settle him.

Gabrielle passed the platter of turkey around for seconds.

"Greta has never been happy here, and her father's becoming too feeble to farm," said Brigitte who, like Anna, was expecting another child. "They're going to take over for him."

Six months ago, Anna would have been jealous. Now, her closest friends were seated around the table in this beautiful dining room, with its oak wainscoting and green floral wallpaper. Her husband and son were here. Her favorite brother had a successful business in the closest town. Although she missed her mother and grandfather, she no longer ached to return Denmark.

"Times are hard back home." Jorn dished a second helping of mashed potatoes onto his plate. "Doesn't make sense to move back now."

"I don't think it's a business decision." Frederik winked.

He and Jorn often joked that Vilfred was cowed by Greta.

"When will they leave?" Anna asked.

"They want to sell their farm before planting season and leave in the spring," Frederik replied. "I'm thinking of buying it."

Her eyes widened. Could the Holdens afford more land? Better them than Jorn. She wanted him to save his money for a proper house. The Ringes' cabin was similar to the Stryker's.

"If I come to agreement with Vilfred on the price," Frederik continued, "I'll want you to bring a greenhorn for me next summer, Jorn. Preferably one with a wife who can serve as a housekeeper to help Brigitte. I'll cover the cost of passage." He gave his wife a tender smile.

Graham reached over and clapped him on the shoulder. "Tryin' to keep up with Jorn, eh?"

The men laughed heartily, but Anna bit her lip. A lot of truth was buried in his kidding.

"We could jointly purchase an acre or two for a church." Jorn snagged another biscuit from the plate in front of him. "As our families grow and we bring over more greenhorns, hired hands, and housekeepers, we can't expect you to host worship services anymore."

Anna's gaze flew to her husband. While she did not wish to be uncharitable, that money would make a start on a larger house for their growing family. She would discuss this with him on the way home.

"Fine idea." Frederik held out a hand to Jorn, as if to seal the contract. "It'll frost those Holy Danes in town if we have a new and larger church."

Jorn shook his hand. "And some of the country folks who travel to Cedar Falls on Sunday mornings might attend if we have a proper building."

Anna's chest clenched. She glared at him, then rubbed her temples to ease the ache arising from suppressing her anger.

"Maybe some in town with more liberal beliefs would make the trip out to hear Reverend Spelman." Brigitte turned to Anna. "People like Peder."

Anna forced a smile. "I can't speak for him, but I would love to see him every Sunday."

Jorn's generosity toward the building of a new church was admirable, but Anna's grandfather had always said that charity should begin at home. She wished, for once, her husband would follow that advice.

• ♥ •

Dressed in her sleeping gown, Anna pulled the crib to the door between the nursery and the bedroom. Anna wanted to be able to easily check on her baby if he woke in the night.

After feeding him, she rocked him and softly sang a lullaby. She planned to have Erik sound asleep before Jorn returned from checking on the cow he expected would calve soon. She hoped it wouldn't happen tonight.

Erik drifted into slumber. With a slow, gentle motion, Anna laid him in his bed. She tiptoed to the kitchen to heat some milk. When Jorn came in, she would add chocolate and sugar, just the way he liked it, and serve it with leftover bread pudding. Hopefully that would put him in a receptive mood.

A blast of cold air blew into the kitchen with Jorn.

"How is she?" Anna complied with his demand they speak Danish at home, though when she was irritated with him, like now, she reproached herself for giving in.

Jorn removed his coat and mittens. His brown hair flew askew as he pulled off his wool cap. "She is not ready tonight. She is not dilating."

"Come sit down and have a bite to eat," Anna said. "It'll warm you." She set a steaming mug next to his bowl of pudding, then filled another for herself. The tantalizing scent of warm chocolate filled the air.

Jorn took his place at the table. "That Ringe. He should have talked to me about buying his farm," he groused. "I could afford to pay him more than Frederik, but now I cannot make an offer since the Holdens are planning to."

"I'm glad you won't risk angering our friends," Anna said. If Jorn could afford to purchase the Ringes' property, he had enough money to build a proper home.

They ate in silence while Anna mustered her courage.

"This spring would be a good time to build a larger house, with Erik growing bigger every day," she said. "The new baby will be here by then." She lay her hand on her swelling belly.

He took a sip of his cocoa. His bushy brows furrowed, and his disapproving gaze swept over her. Her heart beat faster.

"The children will be small for some time," he said. "And the new nursery has plenty of room for them and Adelaide. This house will be adequate until we return to Denmark."

She cringed. "But our children should be raised in a proper home, with plenty of room for entertaining our friends and neighbors." Fighting to remain calm, she spoke in a low voice, keeping her tone even. "And we have money to build one. You said yourself that you could pay more than Frederik for the Ringes' farm."

"This house is big enough for inviting our friends. And as the children grow, they can sleep in the loft." His tone hardened. "Besides, I'm going to use that money to build a bunkhouse and a second granary. With more greenhorns, I will be able to plant more land and produce more grain. The men will need a place to stay and I'm running out of cabins and houses."

Anna gave up trying to control her anger. "A bunkhouse and a granary!" Her voice rose with each word. "You treat your cattle and greenhorns better than your wife and children!"

He slapped the table. The dishes rose then clattered back down on the wooden surface. "My herds are growing and my fields are producing splendidly! I have worked hard to make it so."

A wail came from the direction of Erik's crib.

"I need those buildings to handle the growth."

Her heart sank. He sounded just like her father. "While our babies have to play on a dirt floor."

"We will have more money to purchase a good farm in Denmark."

Erik wailed again. Anna hurried to him, glad to have an excuse to escape her unreasonable husband. She picked up the baby and held him to her, patting his back. She sat on her bed rocking slowly back and forth, trying to soothe herself as well as her son.

When he quieted, she eased back the covers, laid him in the middle of the bed, and climbed in beside him. She pulled the blankets and quilt over them and cuddled Erik to her. He cooed in contentment. Even lying beside him, she could not stop trembling. She took in deep, slow breaths in an effort to quell the ire burning within her.

Long after Erik had fallen asleep, Jorn picked him up and nestled him into his crib. He extinguished the lamp, and crawled under the covers next to Anna. She turned away from him.

He stroked her back. "You know I love you and our boy, don't you, my sweet?"

She remained silent.

"I provide well for you with food, clothes, and a housekeeper to help with your work. I don't prevent you from continuing your Tuesday hen-meetings with Gabrielle."

Anna swallowed a sob. Jorn was a good husband. "I know. But I don't understand why you so strongly oppose building a proper house."

He stopped caressing her and heaved an audible sigh. The bed rocked, and the covers tightened as he repositioned to lie on his back.

Silence hung heavy in the room.

Anna rolled to her back so she could make out his profile in the dim moonlight filtering through the curtains.

After long moments he cleared his throat. "My parents brought me up to be loyal to Denmark and our king," he began in a hoarse, quiet voice. "Fader's dairy was successful, and he built our family a fine, big house. We all loved our beautiful home."

He paused.

"When the Germans occupied South Jutland, many of their friends moved north to areas controlled by Denmark." He released a long, audible breath. "My parents were so in love with their house they refused to leave. They live under German control, even though they behave as Danes inside their home. I came here, and my brother left for Australia to avoid conscription into the German army. My brother died when his ship sank. If my parents had gone north, he would be alive."

"I'm sorry," she said. Jorn rarely spoke of his family, but his explanation didn't provide a reason for his objection to a proper house here in Black Hawk County. "I see why you're angry about your parents' house."

Jorn released a loud breath. "When Denmark recaptures South Jutland, I want to return to that area. I don't want to be prevented from doing so by love of a house."

His words shot a pang of disquiet through her. Her home was not in the occupied area, but she wouldn't be welcome if she returned to her parents' farm. Bedstefa lived in Copenhagen, far away from South Jutland. "Do you think the Danes will fight for South Jutland soon?"

"No." His tone was flat. "I don't believe the king can currently afford a military action. But someday."

Her husband expected her to pick up and move back to Denmark whenever he decided the time was right. Anna wasn't sure she wanted to, even if the alternative was to remain in this old cabin.

• ♥ •

Over the next three months, Anna's belly grew. She lay on her bed watching the snowflakes drift by the window, the gray February day providing a dreary background. Her back hurt, her legs were swollen, and the child inside her pressed against her lungs, making breathing a struggle.

When Jorn came in from morning chores, he sat on the edge of the bed and took her hand in his. "Are you feeling better, my sweet?"

"Not really," Anna answered. "I wish Gabrielle was here."

Jorn's eyes widened. "Is the baby coming today?"

"I don't know."

"The snow is knee-high, and drifting. You have Adelaide."

"She's been a great help, caring for Erik so I could rest. But she doesn't know why my legs are swollen, or why I'm so tired." Anna paused, deciding whether to tell Jorn the housekeeper's explanation. "She thinks this is happening because I conceived this second child too soon."

Jorn sat for a long time, rubbing her hand with his thumb. "She might be right."

Together, they were very fertile. To prevent another conception, they would have to abstain from marital relations, or try some of the unnatural methods Gabrielle had suggested.

Jorn touched his fingers to her chin and tipped her face toward him. "Rest, now."

She rolled to her side and a pain stabbed her abdomen. She moaned.

Jorn whipped around, his face pinched with alarm. "Are you

all right?"

She swallowed. "Yes, just a cramp."

He studied her a moment, then turned and headed for the kitchen where Adelaide was setting biscuits and coffee on the table. Erik played with pots and pans on the floor.

Another cramp stole Anna's breath. She clutched the quilt, waiting for it to pass. The baby might be ready to come.

Erik's birth began like this and the pain had only gotten worse. While she looked forward to delivering this child, she did not relish the agony of the process. "The baby is coming." Her voice trembled. "I need Gabrielle."

"I'll send Halvor in the sleigh to fetch her." Jorn hurried to the peg and donned his coat, cap, and mittens.

Adelaide stared at him as he hurried out the door. She moved a few steps toward Anna. "Is there something I can do?"

"Just take care of Erik."

It seemed like hours before Jorn returned, though the mantel clock had chimed only once.

Anna's contractions became progressively stronger and more frequent. Her water broke early in the afternoon. She feared the baby would arrive before Gabrielle did.

Sometime later, while the gray light still shone through the window, she heard Halvor's voice. "… snow is deep. Darn near got stuck in a drift."

"Halvor did a fine job driving the horses," Gabrielle said.

"I'm glad you're here. Anna wants your help when the baby comes," Jorn told her in English.

Gabrielle moved to Anna's side and grinned. "Looks like this child's cooperating with your wishes."

"Oh, Gabrielle." Tears of relief mixed with pain streamed down Anna's cheeks. "Thank God."

As the contractions became stronger, she lost track of time. Once or twice, Jorn checked on her progress.

Shortly after nine o'clock, Gabrielle exclaimed, "You have a beautiful daughter!"

She wrapped the wiggling infant in a blanket and placed her in Anna's arms. The little girl had a head full of pale blond hair and big blue eyes that stared into Anna's. Her heart felt like it might burst with love.

Jorn came from the parlor and sat on the bed. He studied the infant intently.

After a few moments, his gaze met Anna's. His soft features and small smile reassured her. "She's beautiful. She looks like a miniature you."

Touched by his compliment, she grasped his hand. Joy-filled tears spilled down her cheeks.

"I would like to name her Ingebrod after my grandmother," Anna said in Danish. "She was the sweetest, kindest woman I have ever known."

Jorn smiled then turned to Gabrielle. "Our daughter's name is Ingebrod," he said in English. "We still need to decide on a middle name."

"It's February twenty-second," Gabrielle replied. "Your little girl shares her birthday with George Washington, the father of our country and first President of the United States."

"Is that so?" Jorn's lip curled.

Gabrielle straightened to her full height. "It is."

Anna's pride swelled. Although her husband would insist on a Danish middle name, she liked knowing Ingebrod had such an auspicious birthday. Anna hoped America would give her daughter a good life.

• ❤ •

"I wish you weren't leaving us again this summer," Anna said, walking to the chair where Jorn sat. She lifted their sleeping son from his arms. Even though she'd had many months to adjust to Jorn's trip, her dread increased as June and his departure approached. She would have Adelaide and Halvor to help her, but they wouldn't make up for her husband's absence.

"I should not be gone much more than two months, since so many of the greenhorns were lined up last year." Jorn spoke softly, not looking up at her.

Adelaide emerged from the kitchen, took Erik from Anna, and carried him to the nursery where Inge was sleeping.

Anna moved to stand in front of Jorn. She wanted to memorize every feature of his face before he left. "Have you found a couple to work for the Holdens?"

"Frode Rasmussen wrote about a married man who used to work at the brewery with him. He has helped make arrangements to get the emigrants to his parents' farm." Jorn scowled. "I offered to pay extra if he would stay in Denmark and help me again next year, but he is determined to come to America."

"Peder will be happy to have him."

Jorn tilted his head, his lips pursed. His fingers were steepled before him. "If conditions change in Denmark, if South Jutland is recaptured, would you want to go back?"

She drew in a breath and squeezed her hands together. "There is nothing left there for me except Bedstefa. I miss him dearly, but he will not live forever." How hard his passing would be. She tried to smother the thought. "Here, I have Peder and close friends." She knelt beside Jorn's chair. "It would be hard to leave."

Jorn remained silent for a long moment. "If I moved back, would you come with me?"

Anna's throat tightened. She had vowed to remain with him until death, and she meant to honor her vow. Her children needed their father. As hard as leaving would be, there would be no choice. She swallowed and grasped both of his hands. "Of course. You are my husband. How could I not?"

He pulled her into his lap.

She lay her head on his shoulder and silently prayed she would never have to leave America.

• ♥ •

Anna carried her quilt toward a tall oak tree in the Cedar Falls park. The day was hot, and the fitted bodice of her new dress was constricting, compared to the loosely gathered dresses she wore around home. Beside her, Peder toted a picnic hamper with the lunch his housekeeper had prepared.

"Adelaide won't have to worry about watching Inge today. The little angel has stolen Mrs. Stensen's heart," Peder said.

Anna smiled. The older woman seemed quite enamored with the five-month-old's chubby body and wide smile. Mrs. Stensen and Adelaide had remained at Peder's house with the children. "It was nice of you to invite us to stay with you this week."

"I want to get to know my niece and nephew."

"I want them to know you, too." The sun burned into Anna's face. Lifting a free hand to shade her eyes, she wished she had worn a hat with a wider brim.

Peder stopped under the oak and set the basket down. Anna spread the quilt in the shade, thankful for the reprieve from the relentless midday heat. Although there was more than an hour before the festivities would begin, a crowd milled around the grassy lawn. Thank goodness she and Peder had come early enough to get a spot close to the speaker's platform.

Halvor waved as he and Morton Andreasen approached. Anna and Peder strolled toward them.

"Happy Independence Day," Peder greeted them, shaking hands with each man.

"Same to you." Halvor grinned. "And to you, Mrs. Stryker."

"Thank you." Anna smiled. His formal address created a proper distance, but sometimes, when they worked together in the garden, she missed the closeness they shared before last summer's kiss. "Because of you and Mrs. Cook, I'll be able to understand what is being said during the program."

Halvor's grin widened. "You learned quickly."

Morton rubbed his hand across his bristly mustache and chin whiskers. "We stopped at your saloon for a drink and met up with some men who made the crossing with me. They're up the hill. We're on our way to join them."

Anna followed his gaze to a group of men talking and laughing while they unloaded crates from a wagon. "That's nice."

"Thanks for letting us celebrate." Halvor's eyes met Anna's for a moment, his gaze intent. Unwelcome heat crept into her cheeks. He had kept his promise and made no amorous overtures toward her, but there were times when improper feelings stirred within her.

"You're welcome. Enjoy the holiday." She quickly diverted her gaze to Peder as the farm hands headed toward their friends.

He was watching a man and two women walking toward them. As they approached, Anna recognized Eluf Mortensen, a buggy driver she had met on her first night in Cedar Falls. From the apparent ages of the women, Anna surmised they were his wife and daughter.

Peder tipped his hat. "Mr. and Mrs. Mortensen." His gaze fixed on the younger woman. "Miss Mortensen."

She was slim, with long brown curls and a sweet face. She looked away demurely. "Mr. Jorgesen."

"Mr. Jorgesen." Mr. Mortensen frowned as he studied Anna. She smiled at him.

"May I present my sister, Anna Stryker?" Peder said in Danish.

"Pleased to meet you," she said to the women. "I met Mr. Mortensen on my first night in Cedar Falls. He drove me to Peder's place."

Mr. Mortensen's frown deepened. His wife's eyes narrowed. Their daugther's face crumpled, and she pressed her lips together.

Anna looked from the Mortensens to Peder.

He wore a frozen smile. "It's nice to see you. Enjoy the day."

"It was a pleasure meeting you," Anna lied as cheerfully as she could manage. She was determined to remain polite despite their unpleasant behavior.

Peder took her elbow and steered her back toward their quilt. His face slackened.

It was all Anna could do to keep silent until they were seated on the quilt. "Are those people always so ill-mannered?"

"No, they're usually quite polite," Peder said sadly.

"Then why were they so rude?" Anna threw open the hamper and snatched out the plates.

Peder hesitated, not meeting her gaze. "It might be better if you didn't know."

"Did you do something to offend them?" she persisted, continuing to set out the picnic.

Peder gave an acerbic chuckle. "I'm your brother."

Anna's eyes widened.

"Is it because I was carrying Jorn's child before we married?" Her hands shook. She could hardly say the words.

"It's because Jorn married you." Peder reached over and put his hand on her arm. "Lottie Mortensen was the woman he was courting when you came to America."

The woman Jorn had taken away from Peder. They had never mentioned Lottie's last name. Anna slid a glance toward her and swallowed hard. It had been one thing to hear about her, but quite another to see her in person. "I'm sorry."

Of course, Jorn would have told Lottie the circumstances of their marriage. It was irritating to be slighted by the woman he had taken up with just weeks after he left Anna in Denmark.

"It wasn't your fault." Peder removed his hand from her arm, picked up the knife, and began to slice the bread.

Anna handed him the hunk of cheese. She divided the cluster of grapes and placed the larger bunch on Peder's plate.

"Lottie was expecting a proposal when Jorn broke off with her. He had already married you, so Lottie blamed you," Peder said. "And because I'm your brother, she blamed me, too. Since then, she hasn't trusted any other men to court her."

"Then why did you introduce me?" It had taken Anna months to trust Jorn to be faithful. Seeing Lottie rekindled doubts.

"I hoped meeting you would put it behind her, now that it's been nearly two years," he said with a gloomy frown. "That we could all become friends."

His reaction continued to puzzle her. "Why is that so important to you?"

"Because she's a kind and caring woman, and I'd like to court her again," he said in a strong whisper. He uncorked a bottle of dandelion wine he had made and poured each of them a glass. "I was in love with her." He paused. "Still am."

Anna's throat clogged. She forced herself to swallow a sip of wine. "But she doesn't approve of spirits, and you are a brewer."

"I hoped I might be able to persuade her to accept my work, but from her reaction today, I believe she's not meant to be my wife." A resigned sigh wove through his words.

"There must be many nice women who would have the greatest respect for you and your successful business," Anna said. "Besides, you deserve someone who will love you for the wonderful man you are."

"There are few women of marriageable age in Cedar Falls."

"You'll find someone," Anna assured him.

Peder bit into a slice of bread and scanned the crowd as he chewed.

There had to be a woman somewhere in the area who would be proud to make him happy. One he could fall in love with. Anna would make it her business to help him find a suitable wife.

"How have your vegetable sales been going?" he asked.

"Very well. The restaurants are taking all I have each week." She clasped her hands together. "I've already talked to Mr.

Hansen about doubling the size of our garden next summer. It will be a lot more work for both of us, but he assures me he can handle it."

Peder grinned. "You're becoming quite a business woman."

Her chest swelled. "I guess I am."

She had told Jorn about her egg sales, but not that she was adding garden produce this summer. With his contacts in town, he would probably find out sometime. She intended to save the money she made toward building a proper house, so she hoped he wouldn't insist on using her earnings for more land or farm buildings.

From the podium, a man welcomed everyone to the celebration of the United States' centennial and announced that Mr. James Markey would read the Declaration of Independence.

It was good to hear and understand most of such an important American document. Anna wanted to learn all she could about her new country.

Mr. Markey finished to great applause. When he returned to his chair, the original speaker stood at the podium again. "Mr. S. H. Packer will now give the history of Cedar Falls."

"Have you heard from Jorn?" Peder asked.

"He sent a letter from New York, before he boarded the ship." It had been a happy surprise, since last year he hadn't written until he was ready to come home, but it made her miss him more. Now that she'd met Lottie, the worry that he might have a summer tryst would needle Anna until he returned. "I got one from Bedstefa, too. He was pleased that we named Inge after Bedstemor. I wish he would come to America to meet his great-grandchildren."

"It would be hard for him to visit in the summer, with Jorn using his place as a gathering point each year." Peder's voice carried a touch of resentment. "And our harsh winters aren't very inviting. It would be better if we accompanied Jorn to Denmark and stayed with Bedstefa while he did his work."

"I'd like that." She longed to see her grandfather again.

"Perhaps when the children are older. Do you think we could try to visit Moder?" Anna had given up writing letters to her.

Peder scowled. "Only if Fader is dead."

"What a terrible thing to say!"

"It's true." Peder took a sip of his wine. "I'm going to do something that will make him disown me, if he hasn't already."

Anna stared at him. "What are you going to do that would be so horrible?"

"Don't worry." He patted her arm. "I'm going to become a United States citizen."

She lurched forward and threw an arm around him. Then, realizing others must be staring, she released him and sat back in her place. "That's wonderful!"

"Yes, but it will mean renouncing the King." Peder paused. "Fader will consider me a traitor."

"His opinion doesn't matter." From the time they were children, they had been taught to please their father. It wasn't easy to throw that weighty cloak off the mind. "I wish Jorn would become a United States citizen, but he never will."

"Maybe in time—"

"He hopes Denmark will retake South Jutland." Anna sighed. "Then, he wants to move back."

"How do you feel about that?"

"Cedar Falls has become my home. You are here. I have friends." A picture of Gabrielle playing with Erik and Inge drifted through Anna's mind. "And I enjoy my egg and produce business."

Peder placed his hand gently on her shoulder. "I believe the Prussians will occupy South Jutland for some time."

"So does Jorn, but he still holds onto the dream."

Peder drew his lips together thoughtfully. "Jorn is a good man, but he sometimes has strange ideas."

"He demands we speak only Danish at home." They had argued repeatedly about the subject since Inge was born. "He wants to build a church with a hall large enough to start a

Danish school, so our children can learn to read and write the language as well as learning Denmark's history and customs. He fears American school will train the children to be patriotic only to America."

"As they should be. They are United States citizens." Peder refilled their wine glasses.

Anna managed a weak smile. "Maybe you can convince him."

He chuckled. "I should stay out of it."

Of course, he was right. Anna was just glad to know he agreed with her.

Despite the fact that Jorn still clung to his dream, Anna couldn't raise her children on the basis of a possibility that might never happen. They were in America, and she would do everything in her power to help her children become competent and loyal Americans. Whether Jorn liked it or not.

Chapter 9

August 19, 1880

Once again, Jorn left for Denmark with no intention of returning for our baby's birth. We had not discussed names, so I called our new son Torsten, after Bedstefa. Gabrielle and Adelaide held a party, complete with cake and lemonade, to celebrate, just as they had done when Poul was born. I am not sure whether Inge and Erik were celebrating their new brother or the chocolate cake, but we all enjoyed the party.

Several weeks ago, we had three beggars come to the house within ten days. They did no harm, but Peder is teaching me to shoot Jorn's rifle in case I need to defend myself and the children.

Jorn is to come home next week. I am already beginning to dread it. He still holds tenaciously to the dream of returning to Denmark, and this affects his decisions about our lives in America. I believe we should live as Americans as long as we are here.

Erik is old enough to attend school in September, and I want him to start with others his age. I went with Frederik and Brigitte to enroll him. Jorn expects our children to attend Danish school, not the county's public school, but the pastor he brought from Denmark last year decided he didn't like teaching after only a month. Worse, when Jorn left this summer, the man decided to move west to homestead. I think his debt for crossing to America is still unpaid. The small cabin next to the church, built for the pastor, stands empty. Reverend Spelman now leads worship twice a month for the growing congregation. I am glad to have him back. On Sundays when he does not come, the elders take turns preaching.

"I enrolled Erik for the fall school term that starts next week." Anna steeled herself for Jorn's reaction. She had sent the children outside after the noon meal, and told Adelaide to keep the little boys, two-year-old Poul, and two-month-old Torsten, with her in the shade. Inge and Erik were instructed to complete their chore of feeding the pullets. "I went with Brigitte and Frederik when they signed up their children."

"There is no need for him to go to the county's school." The muscle in Jorn's jaw twitched, but his voice was slow and even. "Next year, I will bring a teacher back for the church's Danish instruction."

"Erik is five years old. He should start classes this year so he doesn't fall behind his friends." Anna didn't mention that he and Inge had enjoyed playing teacher and students with the older Holden children frequently throughout the summer. They both knew their numbers from one to ten and most of the English alphabet. Anna had taken her two older children to town and bought school supplies for each of them, even though Inge wouldn't need hers until next year. "Erik is very excited about starting first grade. It would be a shame to stifle his eagerness."

"That's because you filled his head with such notions." Jorn took another drink of his coffee. "One more year won't make that much difference."

"There is no reason Erik cannot go to American school with the Holden children this year and start Danish instruction next." Anna wanted him to continue in the county's educational system, but that would be a battle for a later time. "Frederik and Brigitte have been happy with what their children have learned so far."

"Erik is our son, not theirs." The familiar, stubborn expression hardened Jorn's features. "He needs to learn how to harvest."

"He's a little boy." Anna tried not to sound argumentative. Through the years, she had found that challenging her husband caused him to dig in his heels. "He already has chores. And you'll have Saturdays to teach him the tasks he's able to do."

Jorn finished the coffee and set his mug on the table. For several long moments, he sat in silence. Finally, he stood and grabbed his wide-brimmed hat from the peg by the door. He turned back to face Anna. "The school is several miles away. That's a long way for him to walk."

Her pulse raced. She couldn't stop now that she had made a modicum of progress. "Frederik asked if we want Erik to go along with his children. He drives them to and from the schoolhouse."

Jorn's green eyes narrowed. He turned his hat round and round in his hands. "So he stops harvesting in the middle of every afternoon to fetch them."

"His children's education is very important to him," Anna said. Hopefully, her appeal to Jorn's competitive side wouldn't lose the ground she had gained. "He is proud of how bright they are."

Jorn scowled. "Erik is smarter than the lot of them together."

"That's why he needs a good education."

"I suppose he can try the fall term," Jorn conceded. "And either Halvor or I can take the children to school if Frederik is going to bring them home. I will tell him next time I see him."

"Thank you." Anna smiled up at her husband.

Jorn shook his head, but the corners of his mouth curved upward ever so slightly. He walked over to Anna, pulled her up from her chair, and kissed her as if he'd been home for only one day instead of seven.

The evidence of his passion pressed hard against her stomach. She prayed he would return to his fieldwork without relieving his need, though she would submit if he insisted. Although he'd been back a week, she hadn't yet adjusted to his presence. Each summer, it took longer for her to feel like his wife again. Besides, it had been only two months since she had been with child, and she wanted her body to grow well and strong again like it had in the two years between Inge's birth and Poul's. She hoped to avoid conceiving for a least another year.

Jorn pulled back, breaking the kiss.

"I'll see you at six," he said in a hoarse whisper as he headed for the door, slapping his hat on his head.

"At six," she echoed.

Anna released a long sigh of relief as the door closed behind him. With any luck, by sunset he would be exhausted from his harvest work and chores.

• ♥ •

Anna watched Erik race the older Holden children toward the school's open door, as he had done most mornings in his first three weeks of school. Beside her on the wagon seat, Brigitte straightened her cloak.

Miss Parker, the teacher, stood on the top step, ringing the bell. Jorn and Halvor had to spend so much time instructing and supervising the greenhorns in the harvest, that the task of taking Erik and the Holden children to school often fell to Anna. She didn't mind. It gave her a chance to speak frequently with the schoolmistress about Erik's progress.

Anna checked the eggs and vegetables she and Brigitte had packed in the wagon box. She wanted to make sure they would not shift when the horses began to move again. Three years ago, her egg-and-produce business had grown too large to handle alone. Gabrielle and Brigitte had accepted her invitation to join her in the venture.

"I'm glad Miss Parker is teaching in our school this year," Brigitte said. "She's much better than the woman who was here last year."

"She's taught Erik many things already. And he's so excited about learning that he comes home and teaches Inge." Anna gave the reins a sharp shake. The horses began to move. "She's a willing student, and I fear she will have learned most of the first-grade lessons before she starts school."

Brigitte laughed. "I don't think that would be a problem."

Anna drove the team toward the Cooks' farm. The morning sun and the cloudless blue sky intensified the oranges and yellows of the maple trees on the west side of the rutted road. Gusts of crisp, cool breeze set the drying leaves to rustling.

She said wistfully, "I'll miss our trips to town when winter comes."

"Me, too," Brigitte agreed. "It's nice to have these respites from the children. Most of the money I earn goes toward paying our housekeeper, but I don't want to give up that luxury."

"Neither would I," Anna said. Jorn paid Adelaide with earnings from the farm, now that she'd worked off her passage to America. The substantial proceeds from Anna's produce sales were safely put away toward the building of a proper house. Jorn had no idea how much she had saved and, though it was wrong to keep this secret, she had no intention of telling him. He would spend the money on land or farm buildings, or to pay her housekeeper. Anna relied on having help around the house and would part with the money rather than lose Adelaide, who didn't even complain about the mountain of ironing the family generated each week.

"At least we'll still have our Tuesdays together," Brigitte said.

"Yes." Thankfully, all three husbands had come to accept the "hen parties," as Jorn called them.

Anna stopped the wagon in front of the Cooks' house. They were waiting at the hitching post, Graham with a crate of canned fruits, and Gabrielle holding a paper-wrapped bundle.

"I have some embroidered tablecloths with matching napkins today," she said, as her husband secured the crate, then carefully stowed her package. Gabrielle climbed up to the wagon seat and settled herself. "They should bring in enough money so I can restock fabric for my products and pick up some special materials for Christmas gifts."

"You sales sisters have a good day," Graham called as the wagon began to roll.

"Sales sisters?" Anna turned to Gabrielle.

She grinned. "That's what Graham calls us."

Brigitte tilted her head. "I rather like it."

"So do I." Anna agreed. It was much better than the "hen party" that Jorn called them.

She drove the team toward town. The women chatted about their families and neighborhood events. When the cluster of buildings came into view, they began planning for their sales stops, picking up mail, and accomplishing their various errands.

"I need to stock up on jars," Brigitte said. "Perhaps we can stop at the mercantile."

"And I need to order my new carriage." Excitement quivered in Gabrielle's voice. "I haven't told Graham. I'm going to surprise him with it for Christmas."

Brigitte laughed. "You're giving him the gift you want."

Gabrielle lifted her chin. "We'll be riding in it together most of the time."

A comfortable, friendly warmth settled over Anna as she listened to her their banter. How lucky she was to have such good friends.

The women distributed the goods to their customers then stopped at the post office. The Cooks had no mail. Brigitte received a letter from her sister in Denmark.

The postmaster handed Anna a small bundle of letters tied with a string. She glanced at the top one. From Denmark. It was addressed to Jorn in a feminine hand. Anna's stomach clenched.

She had a notion to open it right there, or maybe just throw it away.

As she followed her friends back outside, the cool wind slapped her face. She had no reason to distrust Jorn. Shame chilled her suspicions. The letter could be from someone who wanted to cross with him next summer. It could be from one of his relatives, telling him news of his family.

It could be. But was it?

• ♥ •

After the evening meal, Poul sat on his father's lap while he read his mail. Jorn's clean-shaven, tanned face was tired and drawn.

In front of the fireplace, Erik taught his eager sister the addition he had learned in school that day. As Anna rocked Torsten, she wondered about the letter written in the woman's hand. She couldn't suppress the uneasiness stirring within her.

She settled the younger children in their beds and turned their care over to Adelaide. Erik and Inge climbed onto their mother's lap, and she read aloud the letter she had received from her grandfather. By doing this, she hoped her children would feel a family connection with him. Unfortunately, they would never have a relationship with her parents like the one she had with Bedstefa and Bedstemor.

She was thankful that Graham and Gabrielle treated Erik, Inge, Poul, and Torsten like grandchildren, and Peder doted on his niece and nephews. Anna's sense of family in America strengthened with each passing year. Bedstefa remained her only link to Denmark.

"Moder, can I send a letter back to him?" Inge asked when Anna finished reading.

"He would like that." She smiled. Their letters consisted mostly of pictures they drew and a few words they knew. When he received them, Bedstefa always wrote a personal note to each child. "But it's time for bed." Anna still wanted to ask Jorn about his letter. "We can write it tomorrow."

"Me, too," Erik chimed in.

"Inge can work on hers while you're in school, and you can write yours when you get home." Anna hugged and kissed them. "Happy dreams."

The children slid off her lap, said their goodnights to their father, then climbed the ladder to the loft where they now slept.

"I fear that as winter approaches, the loft will be too cold for the children," Anna said, trying to start a conversation with Jorn.

"Perhaps we can make a straw mattress and they can sleep on the floor near the heating stove in the nursery," he suggested.

"That's a good idea." But if they had a proper house it would not be necessary. "I'll buy some canvas for the bottom and ticking for the top."

"I'll put aside some clean straw to be sure it's dry."

"Thank you." Anna rocked in silence, waiting to see if he initiated a change in subject. He didn't. "You received a lot of mail today. What are all those letters about?"

"Different things." Jorn's face tensed. "One was the first payment by a greenhorn who came this summer. He's working on his uncle's farm in Wisconsin."

"It's good that he is keeping his part of the contract." Anna couldn't think of a tactful way to bring up the letter with the feminine scrawl, and she was determined to address the subject. "The letter on top of the bundle was from a woman. Is she someone who wants to cross with you next summer?"

He stared into the waning fire. When he faced her again, his features were flat, his gaze dark. "It's from Silje Rasmussen. Her father's farm is where I gather the people from the south who will cross with me. Like I used to at your father's farm."

"I remember. Peder arranged it several years ago." Anna carefully kept her impatience from reaching her words. This woman had brought Adelaide through the German border crossing. "What did she have to say?"

For several long moments, Jorn did not answer. "She—her family wants more money next summer for the use of their farm."

Anna released a breath. It was business. "Can you afford that, or should we ask Peder to help find someone to take their place?"

"Peder has been in America for a long time. He no longer has the connections in Denmark he once did."

Anna nodded. "Perhaps it's time to stop bringing greenhorns over. With the costs rising, and those who don't pay their debts, is there still enough money to make it worthwhile?"

He looked away. "It is none of your concern."

"But it is. Maybe your time would be better spent staying here, managing the crops and livestock." The money could be better spent on a proper house, but now was not the time to bring that up. She was already on thin ice by questioning his business.

The muscle in his jaw twitched. "Morton and Halvor manage fine while I'm away. And you aren't lacking for food, or clothing, or help around the house."

"You're right," she conceded, not wanting to argue. She didn't need to know the specifics of his business just as he didn't need to know the specifics of hers. "We could ask Bedstefa to help you find another location in Jutland."

"That's not necessary," Jorn replied. "The Rasmussen farm works just fine."

Anna sighed. The rhythm of their lives, with Jorn going to Denmark every summer, would continue as it had since their marriage.

• ♥ •

Facing the morning sun, the nine students stood lined up from oldest to youngest in front of the audience. Anna couldn't take her gaze off Erik. Over the winter, his blond hair had darkened noticeably. His eyes were already the same green as Jorn's. Erik shifted his weight from foot to foot, peering into the small crowd. Anna smiled, hoping to reassure him.

She sat on one of the benches the Holdens had brought. Brigitte was on her left, Peder on her right. Jorn had left for Denmark earlier than usual this summer in order to recruit a new pastor. Peder was attending the program in his stead.

The warm breeze carried the sweet scent of freshly cut grass.

Erik had been furious with his father for leaving two weeks before the program. Anna felt the same way, although she hid this from her son. Erik's anger had been tempered when Peder said he was looking forward to hearing his nephew recite. Anna's had not. Jorn should have been here.

On the bench in front of her, Inge sat beside Jess Holden. As the only two children who would begin first grade next year, they seemed to be doing their best to behave as proper pupils. Both had older siblings who loved to play teacher, so Inge and Jess knew what conduct would be expected. Poul and Torsten were at home with Adelaide. Somewhere, farther back in the crowd, were Graham and Gabrielle.

At ten o'clock, Miss Parker rang the school bell and everyone fell silent.

"We'd like to thank you all for coming," the teacher began, her voice raised so everyone could hear. "It's nice to see so many family members and friends here." She introduced each child by name and grade level.

"Before we enjoy the picnic that you have so graciously provided, our younger pupils would like to present a recitation of "How doth the Little Bee," and our older ones will recite from *Macbeth*." She nodded to Erik then took her seat.

He stepped forward and focused on Inge just as he had done when he practiced at home. The breeze blew his hair across his forehead. "How doth the little busy bee improve each shining hour, and gather honey all the day from every open flower?"

Erik resumed his place in the line. The audience applauded. A wide grin broke across his round face as he caught Anna's gaze. His recitation had been perfect.

Each of the other students recited their pieces in turn. When the program concluded, Miss Parker returned to stand beside her charges. "I'm happy to announce that every one of these pupils has passed to their next level. Please help me congratulate them."

The teacher began clapping, and everyone joined in.

Erik stood straight and proud. Joyful tears welled in Anna's eyes.

"We will take a few minutes to set up the food inside the school then I'll ask our current students to escort next term's new first graders through the line. Everyone else may partake after them. I'll ring the bell when we're ready." Miss Parker picked up her bell and headed into the building.

Anna and Peder moved to where Erik stood. Inge followed.

"I'm so proud of you." Anna hugged Erik close.

"Oh, Moder. Don't hug me in front of the other boys." He didn't sound too upset nor did he pull away. Other mothers were hugging their sons, too.

When Anna released him, Peder held out his right hand. "Congratulations on passing to the second grade."

Erik shook his uncle's hand. "Thank you."

Just like a little man. Anna smiled. "I have to go help set up the lunch."

"I don't need Erik to 'scort me to the food," Inge said, a pout on her rosy lips.

"That's what the teacher wants you to do," Anna replied.

Peder placed a hand on Inge's shoulder. "You don't want to make the teacher mad before you even start school, do you?"

"No." Inge shook her head, sending her blond curls flying.

Anna went inside. Everyone had been generous, bringing two or three dishes, just as she had. When the food was ready, the teacher rang her bell. Marie led the way with Jess in tow. Inge followed, with Erik close behind. Brigitte and Anna handed their children plates and silverware from their baskets, then returned to their places behind the tables to help serve.

Gabrielle shepherded the children through the line, with the help of Peder, Frederik, and Graham. When her brother reached Anna, she introduced him to the teacher, Miss Charlotte Parker, who stood next to her.

Peder studied her then beamed approval. He bent toward her in a half bow. Interest glinted in his blue eyes. "Pleased to meet you, Miss Parker."

Pink colored the teacher's apple cheeks. "And you, Mr. Jorgesen."

He nodded to her as the movement of the line swept him forward.

Anna smiled. Maybe Miss Parker could make Peder forget the girl who had rejected him for Jorn.

• ♥ •

Spring became summer. Anna tended her vegetable garden and sold her produce, along with her chickens and eggs. Her savings were growing to a level where she might be able to build a fine house in a few years.

At times, she pondered using some of her money to buy a piano. She so missed having music in her home, but there was no room in the crowded cabin. Besides, the idea of putting such a wonderful instrument on the dirt floor distressed her. For now, it was best to save her earnings for a proper home.

As long as Jorn continued his yearly trips to Denmark, Anna refused to touch Bedstefa's legacy. So many perils could befall him. If something happened to him, she would need the money to raise her children.

Halvor's days were spent apprenticing with Morton Andreasen. He had little time to visit with his mother and Anna during the days, but four or five evenings each week, after dinner had been served in the bunkhouse that he supervised, he would stop by to complete whatever tasks needed to be done around the house and garden.

Inge and Erik, eager to prove they were "big," helped pull weeds.

"See the way these three leaves grow together at the end of the stem." Halvor held the plant so the children could see. "This is clover."

"Like the clover that grows in the pasture?" Erik asked.

"That's right." Halvor smiled. "And clover is fine in the pasture. But it doesn't belong in the garden."

Inge nodded somberly. "It's a weed."

Halvor yanked the clover out of the dirt. "Yes, and we need to pull them so the beans can grow strong."

As the vegetables grew and developed, he showed the children how to pick the beans and later, the peppers. Although Anna couldn't count on them to work for long periods, she appreciated their spurts of energy on the "grown-up" tasks. She tried to make it fun for them, singing songs, reciting verses, and speaking English to make the tasks less boring.

On Sundays, Halvor and Adelaide accompanied Anna and her children, and sometimes Peder, to church.

When the service ended one mid-August Sabbath, Anna lifted her gaze to the Holdens, sitting in the pew in front of her. Miss Parker, who would be staying in their home for the fall term, sat with them. She had returned from her parents' house two weeks early to scrub the one-room school clean, ready the desks for the students, and prepare materials for her lessons. To Anna's knowledge, Miss Parker didn't speak Danish, so she probably understood little of the service.

As parishioners began exiting the pews, Anna glanced at Peder, whose gaze was fixed on the teacher. She smiled.

The Strykers and Holdens shared a table at the after-worship potluck, a custom the congregation had brought with them to the church. In summer, they ate outside on long tables built by the men. When the weather turned cold, the feast moved to the basement.

Brigitte wrapped an arm around Anna's shoulders, and they walked together up the aisle to join the other women in organizing the dozens of potluck dishes.

As Anna worked alongside her neighbors, she thought of how she had once worried about whether they would welcome her, with Erik's birth so soon after her marriage. Most of them accepted her and her family and, if the parishioners discussed it behind her back, no one ever questioned to her face her practice of allowing the Hansens to sit in her family's pew when Jorn was away. They were a great help in keeping her children from disturbing the congregation.

While the ladies prepared the food and the men chatted, the children ran and played in the tall grass of the churchyard. Jorn and Fredrick had planned for two large open areas. One was to become the graveyard, the other the play area for students at the future Danish school. On his return from Denmark, Jorn would bring a new pastor and teacher. Anna hated to lose Pastor Spelman.

The children frolicked happily despite the unbearable heat. It had always seemed unsuitable to dress them in their Sunday best, when they would likely come home with dirt and grass stains on their garments. She did so anyway. Adelaide never complained.

Standing next to Peder, Frederik surveyed the scene. "The congregation has grown so much in five years we'll need to add on to the church. There's no way to fit all of these people into the basement this winter."

"There are so many children," Peder replied, patting an adoring Poul on the head.

"It's not only them. It's the immigrants. Quite a change from the small group that used to meet in our home." Frederik's wistful words carried a note of pride.

"I hope we'll be pleased with the pastor Jorn brings back." Brigitte spoke in English for benefit of Miss Parker, who had helped her and Anna arrange the children in a line.

The men turned at the sound of Brigitte's voice.

"Miss Parker, this is my brother, Peder Jorgesen," Anna said in English. "Peder, you remember Miss Parker, Erik's teacher."

"Mine, too," Inge chimed in. She straightened to her full height. Her blue eyes shone bright.

"Yes, I do." Peder nodded. "Nice to see you again, Miss

Parker."

"And you, Mr. Jorgesen." Pink crept into the teacher's cheeks.

"Miss Parker is nice," Erik said.

True, but Anna wasn't sure whether Erik meant to convey that fact to his uncle or to score some favor with his teacher.

"The school is becoming crowded, too." Frederik's brows knitted together. "We'll need to petition the county to build a second one in our township. Miss Parker fears there won't be enough room for all the children this winter."

"The number will drop when the Danish school opens," Peder suggested.

"It won't make much difference," Anna said. "The congregation has met several times this summer. Most parents want their children to attend the county school at least some of the time so they can become familiar with American ways." Anna did too, and was prepared to stand firm if Jorn objected.

"We have agreed that there should be a winter term of Danish school," Brigitte explained. "When the older boys are finished with harvest and not yet needed for planting. That's when the largest number of students attend Miss Parker's classes."

"And two or three days per week for a month in the summer," Anna added. "That won't conflict with county school, and will still give the children some time away from their studies."

Peder frowned. "That's not what Jorn has in mind."

The thought of having to tell him of the decision to scale back his plan made Anna queasy. She straightened her shoulders. "He'll have to bend to the will of the congregation."

"We'll convince him." Brigitte's confidence buoyed Anna's spirits. Thankfully, the Holdens completely agreed with reducing the time students would spend in the folk-school classes.

When their turn came, the adults helped themselves from

the variety of food and fixed plates for the children before returning to their table. Conversation fell to small talk.

"Are you speaking English at home, now?" Peder asked Frederik.

"Yes, but Miss Parker wants to learn Danish, so we're teaching her." Frederik scooped a helping of potatoes onto his fork. "She believes it will help her teach the children who don't speak English when they come to school."

"Danish is predominant in this community," Miss Parker said. "If I know the language, it will be easier to teach the students English."

Peder's brilliant blue eyes glowed. "That's very professional of you, Miss Parker."

Anna hoped to keep Peder coming to the country church so he could get to know Miss Parker. By the entranced look on his face, he wouldn't take much convincing.

Chapter 10

August 15, 1881

Erik wanted store-bought trousers for school this year, so I purchased two pairs when Halvor and I took Erik and Inge to town for school supplies and new shoes. Erik picked a solid blue cotton fabric for a new shirt. Inge chose a print with small pink roses for a new dress. Now I am sewing furiously to complete their garments before school starts. It is such a joy to make clothes that please them.

Jorn is to come home on the first day of school. I did not mention it to the children in case he is delayed. I wish he could arrive some other day so I would not have to cope with the extra distress his homecoming creates. I worry about how Erik will react. Without his father's demand that he help with the farm work, Erik has been much happier and more relaxed this summer. I hope he will not again become tense and fearful like he was around Jorn last spring.

At least Inge will be excited to see him. I am not sure how Poul and Torsten will react. They rarely talk about him.

I have not written to Jorn about the congregation's new plan for the Danish school. He will be furious, and I am afraid he will blame me. It was not my idea, although I agree with it. I will wait until he has been home for a few days before I tell him. Maybe he will be pleased with the new pastor he has found and take the news in stride. That is likely too much to hope for.

"Moder, can I pick some flowers for Miss Parker?" The pitch of Inge's voice rose as she danced around the room in her new dress.

"That would be very nice." Anna smiled. "I'll put some

water in a canning jar so they will stay fresh."

"It's a baby thing to do," Erik muttered, following his sister out the door.

"Is not," Inge called back to him as she ran to the zinnias and daisies at the end of the garden.

Finally, with school supplies gathered into the wagon, children on the seat, and the bouquet in Inge's hands, Anna took the reins and signaled for Halvor to release his grasp on the team's harness.

"Have a good first day." He waved as the horses pulled out of the farmyard.

Brigitte and her children didn't ride with Anna. They had to get Miss Parker to school before any students arrived. After dropping off Erik and Inge, Anna would go on to town to meet Jorn's 1:10 train. Her chest tightened. She took a deep breath and commanded herself to relax.

In addition to her older children, she had loaded eggs, summer squash, and the crate of chickens the new restaurant had ordered on her last trip, and would deliver them before going to the depot.

When they arrived at the school, Anna gave Inge a hug, then held the flowers while she climbed down from the wagon. Erik had already jumped off, rounded the team, and headed for the schoolyard.

"Mind Miss Parker," Anna called after him.

He ignored her, but Inge reached up for her bouquet. "I'll be good."

Anna smiled at her. "I know you will."

Miss Parker stepped out of the door. Anna waved, checked to see that all of the children were clear of the horses and wagon, and headed toward town.

She made her deliveries, picked up fabric for dresses to replace those Inge was quickly outgrowing, and bought sugar and spices at the grocery. It was nearly one o'clock when she arrived at the station. Halvor and Mr. Andreasen were already there.

Halvor tied her team to the back of one of the other wagons then escorted her to the platform.

"Inge was so excited to start school today." He smiled. "I hope everything goes well for her."

"So do I. Erik has already taught her much of what she is to learn this year, but I trust Miss Parker to make her lessons challenging." They fell into an easy silence.

Minutes later, the whistle sounded, and the engine came into view.

Anna's pulse raced as the clacking of the wheels vibrated in her chest.

The train came to a stop, passenger cars aligned with the platform.

People streamed toward the depot in a chaotic rush. Anna stepped closer to the building to get out of the way. A few minutes later, she spotted her husband. His gaze caught hers, and he waved. She waited for him to reach her. Gone was the urgent need to hold and touch him that had been so acute on his first return.

Jorn approached, followed by a man and woman who appeared to be in their forties. The man was slight, pale, and dressed all in black. The woman wore a green dress with a tightly-fitted bodice, ruffles at the neck, and a flowing skirt. Her light brown hair stuck out in all directions from under her frilly green hat. She was nearly a head taller than the man.

"Hello, Anna." Jorn slipped an arm around her and gave her a hug.

She stiffened, but forced a smile. "Welcome home."

He turned to the couple behind him. "Anna, this is Reverend Dag Borge and his wife, Agnete."

For a few moments, Anna corralled her scattered thoughts and mustered as much cheer as she could. "Welcome to Iowa."

"Mrs. Stryker," the pastor said in a flat voice.

Perhaps he was just tired from the trip, but Anna didn't

think he had much energy to give to their growing church.

Mrs. Borge grabbed Anna's hand with both of hers and pumped it vigorously. "We are so glad to be here."

Anna froze her smile, despite the dislike niggling away at her. She slipped her hand free and studied Jorn's gaunt, tired face. He must have had a difficult trip.

He looked back toward the train. "Anna, take Agnete to the wagon while Dag and I get the trunks."

"Even with four trunks and two crates full, we had to sell most of our things before we left," Mrs. Borge complained. "Leaving behind the accumulation from twenty years of marriage is not easy."

"Why did you decide to come to America?" Anna asked, wishing they had not.

"Times are hard in Denmark." Agnate frowned. "Even though people give what they can afford to the church, it's not enough to adequately support a pastor with a wife."

This woman must have lived in a style very different from that offered by the small cabin beside the country church. Dear Lord. How would the congregation receive Reverend Borge and his wife?

• ♥ •

Inge ran to her father and hugged his legs after she and her brother jumped down from Brigitte's wagon. Jorn grinned. Erik followed, his expression blank. Earlier in the afternoon, Poul approached Jorn timidly, as if he were a stranger. Torsten cried when Jorn took him from Adelaide. He had expressed disappointment that his young sons didn't remember him.

"Thank you for bringing them home." Anna walked toward Brigitte, who was again with child.

"You're welcome." She leaned over the edge of the wagon, her brows arched. She whispered. "Have you met the new pastor?"

"Yes."

"What did you think of him?" Brigitte's voice rose.

Anna stole a glance at Jorn over her shoulder. He was still occupied with the children. "I don't know what to think. He seemed worn out from the trip. You'll have to decide for yourself when Jorn introduces them at worship."

Brigitte opened her mouth then closed it. Her gaze skipped to Jorn for a moment, then she nodded to Anna. "See you Sunday."

Anna moved back to her family as Brigitte drove out of the farmyard. Inge was calmer now, and both children carried papers with them.

"Do you have lessons to work on before Monday?" Anna asked.

"I am to draw a picture of something fun I did during the summer." Inge bounced up and down as she spoke.

"I have to write two lines about what I did," Erik said in a bland voice.

"That won't be necessary." Jorn ruffled his son's blond hair.

Anna blinked, then stared at her husband. Of course, the children needed to complete their assignments.

"Why not?" Erik looked up at his father.

"Because you're going to help me with the harvest."

Anna's jaw dropped. Erik was still a little boy.

The color drained from his face, and his jaw tightened. "But I want to go to school."

She stepped closer to the children. "You two go change into everyday clothes. Then you can go outside and play."

The children raced each other to the door. Erik stopped and looked back, his lower lip quivering, before following his sister inside.

Trying to suppress her irritation, Anna turned to her husband. "What are you talking about? You have plenty of greenhorns and hired men to help you with the harvest. You don't need Erik in the fields."

"He has to learn farm work. He will inherit one someday,"

Jorn answered, as if stating the obvious.

She clenched her hands together. "But he's only six years old."

"Time he started—"

"Started getting a good education." Anna's volume rose. She tightened the rein on her temper. "Even Frederik doesn't take his sons out of school to help with the farming, and he has much less help than you do."

"And much less land." The muscle in Jorn's jaw twitched. "What Frederik Holden does or does not do has no bearing on this family." His voice was hard. "Besides, it's not because I need him to help, it's to teach Erik what he needs to know."

"You could begin by teaching him on Saturdays, so he won't miss out on his lessons," Anna suggested, trying to find a solution they could agree upon.

"He'll work on Saturdays, too."

Digging in his heels, Jorn sounded just like Fader, just as unreasonable. Every muscle in Anna tightened. "If you force Erik to work that much while he's so young, you'll do exactly what my father did to Peder—make him look for ways to escape the farm as soon as he is old enough."

"That won't happen." Jorn's jaw jutted out.

"You're wrong," Anna snapped. No matter what Jorn said, Erik would grow to despise farming, and his father, just as Peder had. And so would she.

• ♥ •

Anna's eyes drifted closed as Reverend Borge droned on. She forced them open. Torsten had fallen asleep in the pew, and Poul was swinging his legs and pointing to his fingers, silently singing the counting song Inge had taught him. Peder's angular face slackened as he stared at the back of Miss Parker's dark head.

Jorn must not have heard the reverend preach before choosing him for their church.

Anna stole a look at her husband. He stared straight ahead.

Relief washed through her as the service ended, and she joined Brigitte, Miss Parker, and the other women preparing the food. Mrs. Borge stood at her husband's side, making loud conversation with parishioners as they introduced themselves.

"He certainly is a change from Reverend Spelman," Brigitte whispered as she and Miss Parker spread a tablecloth over the buffet table.

"His wife is a teacher," Jorn said. "She'll be good for the Danish school."

Frederik flashed a wicked grin. "But the school will only operate during winter term, and perhaps for a month in the summer." The twinkle in Frederik's eyes belied his matter-of-fact tone. "We'll have to listen to the reverend year 'round."

"What are you talking about?" Jorn's brow furrowed. "That isn't the plan."

"Your plan," Frederik said. "The congregation had several meetings over the summer." He led Jorn away from the table as he talked.

Anna tensed as her husband walked stiffly toward the corner of the church. Red colored his face. Please God, let Frederik convince Jorn to accept the reduced time frame for the school.

Peder approached Miss Parker, watching for a moment as she bent over the tablecloth and smoothed the creases. When she straightened, he moved beside her. "Would you like to take a walk?"

Pink flowed into her cheeks, and she looked down at the fabric she had just straightened. "Thank you, but I need to help–"

"You go on," Brigitte said, hazel eyes sparkling with gold flecks. "We have plenty of hands to get the food on the table."

"I'll have her back in time to eat." Peder winked at Anna. "Save us a place."

"Of course," she said with a smile, hiding her concern about

Jorn's reaction to the congregation's plan for Danish school.

Anna and Brigitte had the children settled at the table with their plates filled before Miss Parker and Peder joined them. He wore a pleased smile. Her hair was mussed. Their lips were full and red, as if they'd kissed.

The joy Anna felt for the couple could not relieve the tense ache that had settled in her temples.

Frederik and Jorn hadn't yet returned.

• ♥ •

Jorn sat in his chair, staring out the open window at the darkness. The hour was late, and the children were asleep. Adelaide had retired to her bed. When Anna finished sorting the laundry for tomorrow's washing, she joined him in the parlor.

"I'm glad you are home." She laid a hand on Jorn's shoulder. He most likely needed some comfort after absorbing the news about the Danish school.

He stiffened. "Are you?"

She compelled herself to keep her hand where it was.

"Of course." Hopefully, she sounded as if she meant it. In reality, she wasn't sure.

"It's hard to tell. You disagree with me on how to raise Erik, and you don't tell me of the congregation's decision to weaken the Danish school."

Anna wanted to pull away, but she willed her hand muscles to remain loose. "We've had a lot to catch up on, and I didn't want to upset you so soon upon your return."

"Most of the men in that church are in America because they came with me," he spat. "Yet they are quick to throw away my plan for a Danish school in favor of a feeble one."

Anna kept her preference for the new plan to herself. Jorn had probably already guessed. She tried to remain diplomatic. "They want their children to learn what they need to know to be successful in America."

"At the expense of their Danish heritage."

"Most still speak the language, keep the customs, and tell their children stories of the homeland just as we do. But I doubt they're planning to return to Denmark," Anna said. Her younger children needed to learn English before they started school. Erik and Inge had taught them many words this summer, most of which the little boys would likely forget over the winter. "We've taught our children about their heritage. They don't need to attend Danish school full time."

The lamplight cast fearsome shadows on the planes of his face. Anna shivered.

"I allowed you to send Erik and Inge to county school because you acted as if you supported my plan. Now the time has come for them to attend Danish school." His jaw tightened, and he spoke through clenched teeth. "Sadly, they'll only have a few months to learn as they should."

"As it is, they will fall behind—"

"You will not deprive our children of this opportunity. They must be ready to return to Denmark when the time is right."

Blinking back tears, Anna fought to keep her voice low and controlled. "That will be years away. They need to know how to live in America until then."

"No more arguments. They will go to Danish school, and that's final."

• ♥ •

Anna gazed at the kitchen and parlor. The log walls and the rough-hewn mantel were decorated with red and white woven hearts, Danish flags, and holiday pictures made by the children. She wanted to placate Jorn by showing she continued to observe the Danish customs. Besides, the children loved seeing their handiwork displayed, and she had enjoyed helping with their projects.

An Advent wreath lay in the middle of the table. Despite their lack of space, the children had enjoyed this *Jul* season. The younger boys understood more than before.

The door swung open, admitting a cold gust of air, along with Jorn and Peder.

"The drifts are going to be too high to get to church tomorrow," Jorn teased Peder. "Too bad you won't be able to see that girl you have your eye on."

Peder grinned. "We can wait until tomorrow to decide."

"The snow is only going to get worse." Jorn sounded more serious now. "You can stay here in the house and sleep on the parlor floor with Erik, or you can take an empty bunk with the farmhands."

"The floor. I don't want to go outside again."

"We made presents for you, Uncle Peder." Inge's blue eyes were wide and her angelic face solemn. "You have to promise not to look for them."

"I promise." Peder grabbed her and swung her high in the air, eliciting a string of giggles. He set her back down. "And what gifts would you like to receive?"

"A doll. A new slate and chalk—"

"I want a pony!" Erik shouted.

"And what does your mother want for Christmas?" Peder asked.

Anna walked into the bedroom, where Jorn was changing into his work clothes so he would be ready to finish the chores after supper. She wanted to avoid the possibility that Peder would ask his question to her directly.

The only thing she wanted was for her menses to start. It was already a week overdue.

● ♥ ●

By the first of the year, Anna accepted that she was again with child. Jorn took the news in stride. He was busy getting the Danish school started and recruiting students from the families of the congregation.

With Inge and Erik, a total of eight children were set to begin in mid-January. Jorn volunteered to pick them up in the morning and bring them home in the afternoon. The Holdens decided to leave their older children in county school and send the younger ones to the Danish classes. Anna feared Jorn pressured them, and she hoped his behavior wouldn't hurt her friendship with Brigitte and Frederik.

Jorn gathered the children's school supplies, as well as household items he thought Mrs. Borge could use in her classroom.

Although disappointed that Erik and Inge would miss the winter term of county school, Anna tried hard to act excited for them. She made new clothes for the first day of Danish school and encouraged them to approach the experience as an adventure, but when the time came for them to dress, both put on outfits they had worn before.

"I don't want to go to Danish school!" Inge wailed in English. "I want Miss Parker for my teacher."

"Be quiet and get ready," Jorn said through clenched teeth.

"You'll have fun when you get there," Anna said in Danish. "Jess and Edvard Holden will be there."

"Why do we have to go to Danish school?" Erik whined in English. "We're 'mericans."

"That's enough!" Jorn shouted. "We speak Danish in this house. No more talking. It's time to go."

Without another word, Anna helped the children with their coats. They picked up the small crates with their school supplies and lunches, and trudged out the door behind their father.

• ♥ •

In the Cooks' pretty parlor, Anna and her two best friends ran tiny stitches in the quilt pattern. Gabrielle's handiwork graced the painted, plaster walls. The quilting frame filled the center of the room, but the women could easily move around it without the bumping into either the graceful tables or comfortable sofas and chairs. Graham had crafted all of the furniture to Gabrielle's specifications, and she had applied the upholstery. Jorn had not made any new furniture in the past few years, and while Poul and Torsten were still small, Anna was not willing to invest her own money in new pieces.

"Erik and Inge still hate Danish school." Knowing how unhappy they were, Anna loathed sending them off with Jorn each morning.

"Jessen and Edvard feel the same way." Brigitte reached down and tucked the blanket around her sleeping infant, a daughter she had delivered only three weeks ago. "Last night, Edvard said the class was down to six, the Handels decided to send their children back to county school."

"It must be especially hard for your boys, Brigitte, with Miss Parker living in your home." Gabrielle tied her thread, pulled the knot under the fabric, and snipped the end.

"That's turned out to be a blessing." Brigitte stitched as she spoke. "She encourages them to go to Danish School because the number of her students has grown very large in the winter months. Then she gives my boys their lessons in the evening. They love that."

"I bet they're learning fast with all that special attention." Gabrielle smiled.

"They are."

Anna sighed. If only she had a larger house, so she could take a turn in hosting Miss Parker. "My children are jealous. They love Miss Parker, and they come home with tales about how mean Mrs. Borge is."

Gabrielle raised her full, dark-brown eyebrows. "What do they say?"

"One time, when the older Handel boy put a snowball on the teacher's chair, Mrs. Borge slapped the hands of all the children with a measuring stick." That night, Anna read her children an extra story before bed.

"Jessen says Mrs. Borge complains constantly about the cabin they live in." Brigitte paused while she threaded her needle. "I wonder if she thinks the children will bring that story home to their parents and make them feel guilty enough to build a new house." She chuckled. "It just makes Frederik angry."

With the back of her hand, Gabrielle raked a stray strand of hair behind her ear. "How does Jorn feel about the Borges?"

Anna huffed out a breath. "He doesn't talk about them, but I know he's disappointed."

Gabrielle grinned. "Maybe the congregation could help Reverend Borge find a more suitable church. And he could accept the new calling this summer." She turned to Anna. "Unless, of course, Jorn's decided to stay home for the birth of your baby."

Anna bit down on her lip. "Have you ever known him to give up his trips to Denmark just because I am with child?" she asked in a clipped tone. "But still, I couldn't be a part of such a plot."

"Nor could we." Brigitte patted Anna's arm. "Jorn has been our friend since we crossed together."

"You wouldn't have to be involved." Gabrielle's whiskey eyes flashed. "From what you've told me, many in the congregation are unhappy. A few well-chosen, innocent words to the Handels and others would probably be enough to get the ball rolling."

"They can't come from me," Anna said, as much as she would like to let others know how she really felt. "Jorn would never forgive me."

Brigitte's full mouth was a thin, grim line. "Perhaps I can plant a seed with Frederik."

Gabrielle smiled. "I can't believe the church members would continue to suffer in silence." She stood. "Let's leave this quilting and have some coffee and cake."

She put the pot on the stove. "How's Peder's courtship of Miss Parker coming along?"

"Very slowly." Anna drew out her words to stress their

meaning.

"They only see each other at church," Brigitte said. "She doesn't want the parents of her students to think she's in an improper relationship."

"And he wants to go to Marshalltown to ask her father's permission to court," Anna added, proud that her brother was so honorable, and pleased he had found a nice woman.

Brigitte frowned. "As much as I love Peder, I'm not sure I want him to marry Miss Parker."

Gabrielle looked up from the applesauce-spice cake she was cutting. "Why not?"

"She's a wonderful teacher," Brigitte replied. "If she marries, she'll have to leave the school."

"That's a silly rule." Gabrielle lifted a piece of cake onto a plate.

"It's written into the teachers' contracts." Brigitte carried three cups to the table.

"They both deserve to find happiness." Anna hoped her brother would have a much more fulfilling marriage than hers, whether or not he chose Miss Parker for his wife. She picked up two plates of cake and carried them to the places Gabrielle had set.

Gabrielle brought the last plate of cake. Brigitte carried in the coffee pot and a trivet to set it on.

"Graham says I should hire a girl to help with the house this spring." Gabrielle's lilting voice rose an octave. "Since I make money from selling my stitched goods, he thinks I can afford to pay help for a day or two each week.

Brigitte grinned. "Are you sure he doesn't just want someone to cook for him on days we take our produce to town?"

Gabrielle laughed. "He learned to cook in the Army. He gets by."

"Do you have someone in mind?" Anna asked.

"I was thinking maybe the oldest Thomsen girl. She must be

about fourteen by now," Gabrielle replied. "Close to finishing school."

Brigitte rubbed her chin. "I don't think Lise goes to school. Marie said none of the Thomsen children came this year."

Anna set her coffee cup where Gabrielle could reach to fill it. "I stopped by to leave some pastries at *Jul*—Christmas—and Lise wouldn't invite me in. She said her mother was ill."

"The same thing happened to me." Brigitte set her fork on her plate. "And she wore no shoes. Lord knows, they need the money."

"Could one of you go with me to inquire about hiring Lise? You both know the family better than I do."

"I would be happy to," Brigitte said. "They crossed with Frederik, Jorn, and me."

Good thing Brigitte had volunteered. Although Anna was eager to know why the Thomsens stopped attending church, she had always been uncomfortable around them. Perhaps now she would learn what was going on in the little house on the creek, just down the road.

• ♥ •

With the back of her hand, Anna swiped at the perspiration droplets dampening her forehead as she sweltered in the unusual late-April heat. Her physical discomfort only compounded the strain of yet another meal taken in silence. Inge and Erik hadn't spoken a word.

Since the table was so small, Adelaide had fed Poul and Torsten earlier, then taken them outside to play in the scant breeze. As soon as the meal was over, Anna, Erik, and Inge would join the little boys while Jorn finished his chores.

After Erik expressed pleasure at returning to county school, Jorn began requiring him to miss one day a week to help with the planting. Anna's interactions with Erik and Inge had smoothed back to normal after she stopped defending, or even mentioning, Mrs. Borge. The distance between the children and

Jorn only grew.

Anna passed the plate of biscuits to Jorn, who took one but said nothing. Meals in the Stryker household were nothing like the happy family mealtimes Moder described when she mentioned her childhood. Bedstefa and Bedstemor encouraged their children to participate in discussions.

The void created by the absence of conversation grew intolerable. Anna wracked her brain for a topic that wouldn't start an argument. "Gabrielle hired Lise Thomsen to work for her two days a week," she ventured. "She'll start next Thursday."

"Couldn't she find anyone better?" Jorn sipped his coffee. "Ole's drunk most of the time."

"That's not the girl's fault."

"But it's not a good influence on the child. Warn Gabrielle to keep an eye on her."

Why did he have to be so narrow-minded? Anna studied the stewed beef and dumplings on her plate. "I will."

They fell into silence.

"I have two pages of addition problems to do for Monday." Erik ran a hand through his wavy light brown hair. "But I can get the answers by myself. Miss Parker says I really know my arithmetic."

Anna smiled at him. "Good for you."

Since they had returned to county school, neither he nor Inge had not once complained about their teacher or their homework.

"Miss Parker is a good teacher," he added.

Anna shot her son a quelling look.

Jorn's jaw tightened.

Inge flashed her brother a blue glare. "Next week, we're going to get our pieces for the year-end program." She watched her father as she spoke. "Are you going to be here to watch us, Fader?"

"I'm sorry, my little sweet," he said quietly. "But I'll be on my way to Denmark by then. Today, I received my tickets for the passage."

Anna jolted upright. "When do you leave?"

"May tenth," he said between bites.

"Why so soon?"

"The railroad wants me to recruit at least twenty people to work for them." He paused. "And I need four new greenhorns to replace those who will have worked off their obligations before this year's harvest."

"Does that mean you'll come back in time for our child's birth?"

Jorn hesitated. "That depends on how things go in Denmark."

She sighed.

"It will be good money," he said.

Anger jolted through her.

"Money! We have seen little benefit from the money you earn on your trips. We're still crowded into this little cabin, and we have another child on the way." Anna's voice shook. Her children were staring at her, but she couldn't stop herself. "Will this trip mean we can finally build a bigger house?"

Jorn dropped his fork onto his plate and stood. "Jesus, woman. Stop whining about a house."

"There is no reason we can't afford a decent home. What are you doing with all that money you make on your trips?"

"You know we will need that money for our future." He stalked out of the cabin.

Anna's teeth clenched.

Inge's complexion had paled.

Anna took a breath to calm herself. She didn't like her children seeing how upset she was. They were already tense enough.

Erik studied her with wide eyes.

"Is he taking us to Denmark soon?" He had switched to English.

"That isn't likely."

"Why is Fader so set on living in Denmark?" Erik crossed his arms over his chest.

"Doesn't he love America like we do?" Inge's tiny voice quivered.

Anna looked from Erik to Inge. "He grew up in Denmark, and he loves his home country as much as you love the United States."

"I don't want to leave America." Inge's cherubic face puckered.

Anna placed her hand on her daughter's arm. "Don't worry about it." Anna managed a weak smile. "It might never happen." She heaved herself out of her chair. "Let's clear the table and then go outside where it's cooler."

"Are we going to have lessons tonight, Moder?" Inge hopped to her feet.

Erik scowled. He had been falling behind in his studies since he had been working in the fields. Anna had started the nightly 'play school' to make sure he didn't lose any more ground. It was the only time they were allowed to speak English at home.

"Yes, but Erik will be tonight's teacher," Anna replied.

His face brightened. Inge's fell. Both loved to be the one to tell their mother and siblings what to do. Anna believed the children learned by explaining the information to others, and through the lessons, she was learning to read and write English. Poul was still too young to understand much of the information, but his little round face beamed when he was included.

The experience in Mrs. Borge's classes hadn't dampened Erik's or Inge's love of learning. Anna thanked Miss Parker for that. Hopefully, the Danish school would be disbanded before the summer session. Jorn would be gone, so he couldn't prevent it. While he was in Denmark, Anna would have a break from the arguments. When he found out, he would be furious to learn she had not fought to keep it going. She would endure his anger. This year had given her plenty of practice.

Chapter 11

May 12, 1882

Jorn left for Denmark on Wednesday. I am so relieved he is gone. The children and I are resuming our comfortable summer routine. Last night, Halvor came to dinner with us and Adelaide. In all the time since his kiss, he has been true to his promise not to make amorous advances. He and his mother have come to be part of our family.

I am still angry with Jorn for refusing to postpone his departure until after the children's end-of-the-year program. How can he show so little regard for their feelings? Erik and Inge are excited that Peder is coming. Brigitte and I are planning a picnic in the evening after the program to celebrate the start of summer vacation. More importantly, we want to give Peder and Miss Parker an excuse to be together before she leaves for her parents' home in Marshalltown.

I have garnered three additional customers for my produce, two restaurants and a grocer. Halvor has once again expanded the garden, and Brigitte has enlarged hers, too. Last fall I offered Halvor a bonus for all the work he does for me, but he says Jorn pays him adequately. I am thankful, because I have been accumulating a considerable sum of money. I once again considered purchasing a piano, so we can have music in the house, but I still cannot bear the thought of putting such a marvelous instrument on the cabin's dirt floor. I have decided it would be better to make a down payment on building a house, or maybe pay for it outright, if I do not get too extravagant.

As the last day of school approached, Erik and Inge worked hard on their recitation pieces. At the program, both children recited perfectly, and, to Anna's relief, both passed to the next grade.

"Why doesn't Fader love us?" Inge asked, as Peder turned the team toward home.

"He does," Anna insisted, hugging Inge close. "He calls you his 'little sweet.'"

"He doesn't love us," Erik said in English. "He didn't even ask to hear our pieces before he left."

"He had a lot on his mind," Peder said.

Anna mouthed a silent "thank you" to him.

"But not us." Inge's face puckered. She had also switched to English.

"He goes to Denmark so we have enough money for food and clothes, and horses and wagons." Anna wanted to ease her children's pain, but it irked her to defend Jorn.

"I wish he could have waited until after the program, though," Inge said.

Erik wrinkled his nose. "Not me. I'm glad he's gone."

Inge shrugged. Anna let the subject drop.

The sun shone hot. She was eager to change into a cooler dress. Carrying a child in the summer made the heat unbearable.

"Tonight, we'll go to the Holdens' for a picnic to celebrate the end of school," Anna reminded them. "It'll be a nice way to start our summer."

"But we have to go to Danish School in July." Inge's round face crumpled.

"Don't worry about that now." Anna kissed the top of her blond head. "That's more than a month away. A lot can happen between now and then."

Finally, they turned into the dooryard.

"I'll water the horses and tie them in the shade," Peder said in English. "We'll take the wagon to the Holdens'."

When Anna and her children walked into the house, Adelaide met them, wiping sweat from her brow with her apron. "The boys are outside under the tree. It's too hot for them to nap in here."

"Fine," Anna said. "Please get a pitcher and glasses. We will pump some cool water to drink. And I'll get a bucket and some linens so we can wipe our faces."

She went to her bedroom and shed her heavy silk outfit and petticoats. The loose calico dress she donned held no more shape than a flour sack, but with sleeves that stopped above her elbows and no need for layers of undergarments to support the skirt, it did not trap the stifling heat against her body. She left her feet bare.

After picking up some cloths and a bucket, she headed for the pump. Erik and Inge emerged from the house, now dressed in worn, around-home clothes.

The air was eerily still and heavy with moisture. Thick clouds filled the sky. Anna had never before seen them in the sickly-yellow color. When the bucket was full, Anna joined her family under the shade of the big oak.

"It's too hot for this early in the year," Adelaide told Peder. She filled a glass with water and handed it to him.

"Looks like a storm is brewing," he said. "We'll need to keep an eye on the weather."

"If it's going to rain, maybe we should go to the Holdens' now," Erik suggested.

"I doubt they're even home, yet." Peder plopped down on the blanket beside Torsten. He lifted the boy onto his lap and looked off to the south.

Torsten gazed up at his uncle, a broad smile lighting his face. Peder picked him up and swung him up and down until he giggled.

Anna dipped the cloths in the water and handed them to Adelaide, her brother, and her children. In return, she accepted the glass her housekeeper offered.

Anna lowered herself to an empty corner of the blanket. Poul scooted close and leaned against her. He seemed to understand that the bulge of the child within her made it difficult to hold him in her lap. She laid a protective hand on her belly.

Mouser rubbed her head against Anna's toes. The kittens chased each other around the yard, bouncing through the grass and pouncing on each other.

Anna surveyed the scene of her family gathered together, enjoying the shade of the oak. Erik and Inge told Adelaide about the program and the picnic. Peder congratulated them once more for passing into the next grade. Although tired from the day's activities, Anna was content.

Jorn didn't know what he missed by leaving every year—the joy and peace of times like this.

"Clouds are coming in from the west." Peder set Torsten on the blanket and stood. "Smells like rain."

The blond toddler still held a damp cloth in his chubby fists.

A strong breeze blew. Anna pushed her hair back and let the air flow over her face.

"It's cooling off," Adelaide said. "Maybe we'll be able to sleep in the house tonight after all."

Above them, the leaves rustled as the breeze became a wind. A dry cloth blew off the quilt, and Erik chased after it.

Peder pointed at the sky. "Look how fast those dark clouds are moving."

"Cold," Torsten said. He had dampened the front of his blue gingham shirt with his wet cloth. He climbed into Adelaide's lap.

Thunder rumbled. Anna startled. She hadn't seen any lightning. "Children, go into the house."

"Yes, Mother," Inge said. She rose from the quilt and started toward the door, carrying her glass of water. Erik followed close behind her.

Anna gave Poul a quick hug, then heaved herself to a standing position. She took her son's hand and walked to Peder's side.

Rolling brown and black clouds darkened the southwest. The temperature dropped. A streak of lightning flashed from the sky to the horizon. An unsettling shiver wracked through Anna.

A wind squall plastered Anna's dress against her body. Loose straw and dried grass rose into the air. A crash of thunder was followed by a loud, low growl that shook the ground beneath Anna's feet.

Mouser stood by the woodshed, gaze fixed on her kittens, meowing loudly.

"Adelaide, please take the boys in the house," Anna said, spellbound by the dynamic sky.

Poul tightened his grip on Anna's hand. "I want to stay with you, Moder."

"Come, Poul," Adelaide called. Anna turned to see her gathering the quilts in her arms, glasses scattering in the grass. Torsten clung to her dress as she started toward the house.

"He can stay," Anna said, placing a hand on the swell of her belly. "We'll be in soon, and we'll bring the buckets and glasses."

"Look at that!" Peder pointed to the south. "It looks like the wind is turning in circles. From the sky to the ground. I've never seen anything like it."

Anna's body tensed.

Another bolt of lightning flared. The yard around them darkened.

"Get inside!" Anna turned and quickly gathered the glasses into the empty bucket. Releasing her son's hand, she picked up the other bucket, still half-full of water. "Poul, help me carry this pail."

The kittens raced toward their mother.

Lips trembling, Poul clutched the handle. His knuckles turned white. He headed with Anna toward the house. Thunder boomed, shaking her insides. She hurried her steps. Poul ran to keep up.

"Come on, Peder!" She called over her shoulder as she and Poul reached the door Adelaide held open for them.

"I'm going to put the horses in the barn," he shouted, and took off at a run toward the team and wagon.

Anna's heart pounded. He could be caught in the storm with a pair of frightened horses. "Be careful!"

Erik and Inge stood at the parlor window. Anna set down the buckets and joined them. Torsten and Poul followed her.

Adelaide closed the door with a bang, then lit the parlor and kitchen lamps. "I wonder where Halvor is."

An image of him caught in the storm surged through Anna's mind. She shuddered. "Hopefully in the bunkhouse."

The wind howled. A loud crack of wood sounded from the elm tree across the lane, and an enormous limb thudded to the ground.

Huge drops plopped against the glass. Then small bits of ice mixed with the rain. Soon dumpling-sized hailstones thumped on the roof and beat against the south-facing windows with a powerful force.

"Let's move back." Anna grabbed Poul's and Torsten's hands and dragged them to the middle of the room. Erik and Inge followed.

Glass shattered and crashed to the parlor floor.

Adelaide screamed.

"Stay here!" Anna's pulse raced as she pulled the table from beneath the broken window. Adelaide and Erik moved chairs to the middle of the room.

"Moder, there's a hole in the roof." Inge pointed to a ragged opening near where the ladder met the loft.

Cursing the old cabin, Anna turned to look at the dresser. It was far enough from the window and the leak in the ceiling that it should escape any harm.

"Everyone, go into the kitchen – away from the windows!" Anna hurried to move furniture and toys in the bedroom and the nursery. When she finished, she joined the children and Adelaide. She gulped a few breaths and rubbed the cramp in her belly until it eased.

After many long minutes, the hail reverted to large liquid drops. Water splashed against the remaining windows until streams streaked from top to bottom.

The rain beat down on the house, driven by the wailing wind. Anna set a bucket to catch water pouring through the opening in the roof.

Where was Peder? She shuddered. Surely, he had remained in the barn.

Through the gray sheets of water against the night-like dark, Anna saw movement. A burst of lightning revealed Brigitte was climbing off her wagon. The Holden children jumped down from the box.

Anna ran to the front door and opened it just as Marie and Greta reached the porch. Brigitte followed, holding Edvard's hand. Behind them came Miss Parker, grasping Jessen's arm. Anna released a breath she hadn't realized she was holding.

"It was a tornado," Miss Parker said through chattering teeth. Her water-sodden dress stuck to her skin.

When everyone was inside, Anna closed the door. "Adelaide, please bring some linens. Erik, fire up the cookstove so everyone can warm themselves." Both scurried off to do as they were told.

"I'll help you, Erik," Marie said, dashing to the kitchen.

Brigitte's face was pale, and wet hair was plastered to her head.

"We got down and hid under the wagon so the ice stones wouldn't hurt us," she said in a shaky voice.

"The tornado hit the Bixby's house, and it exploded!" Miss Parker's inflection rose as if she was questioning what she had seen.

"Exploded?" The color drained from Adelaide's cheeks as she appeared with an armload of towels.

Exploded? Anna's drew in a sharp breath. "Were the Bixbys in it?"

"Meta was with Magdelone at our place," Brigitte said. "I

don't know where Jeppe and Frederik are." Tears welled in her eyes.

"I'm sure they're fine." Anna led the women to the kitchen and helped them into the chairs Marie and Erik had set near the stove. Greta sat in another. The rest of the children gathered around the warmth. "Is your house all right?"

Adelaide wrapped linens and quilts around the wet guests, then started a pot of coffee.

"I don't know," Brigitte sobbed. "It was raining too hard to see."

A low roll of thunder came from a distance. The wind no longer howled, and the rain had diminished to a gentle patter. Anna stepped to where she could see the broken parlor window. Beyond the jagged glass remaining in the frame, the world had brightened to a light gray.

She moved back into the kitchen. "The storm is letting up."

"I need to get home to my little girl." Brigitte stood.

Anna put her hands on her friend's shoulders. "Sit and get warm. I'll send a greenhorn to check on them."

If something bad had happened to Magdelone, Frederik, or the Bixbys, she did not want Brigitte to be the one to discover them.

As Anna stepped out the back door, Peder and Halvor came around the woodshed. She sent up a silent prayer of thanks. Peder took her arm and led her back into the house. Halvor followed.

"There's been a tornado," Halvor said, his concerned gaze fixed on Anna.

"I know." She looked down at the floor for a moment, then lifted her gaze to meet his.

His lips parted in a slow grin. "I'm glad you and the children are safe."

"And you, too." Heat seeped into her neck and cheeks. She turned away.

"Brigitte. Miss Parker." Peder said their names reverently.

"I'm glad you made it here."

Miss Parker turned toward him with a slight smile. "And you, too."

"Ladies, your horse and wagon are in the new granary," Halvor said.

"I need to see if Frederik and Magdelone and the Bixbys are safe!" Brigitte shot from her chair.

"Frederik and Jeppe are all right." Halvor spoke slowly, as if to let his words sink in. "I was in the south pasture, checking on the sheep, when the storm came. I saw the men running to your house. It was still standing when I started for the bunkhouse."

"Good thing you got those sheep sheared before you put them to pasture." Peder grinned. "They'd be very soggy after this rain." He gave Halvor a soft punch on his arm.

Anna's brother was trying his best to break the tension, but no one, including herself, felt like joking. "I fear the hail has ruined the gardens."

Halvor's grin faded. "There will likely be some damage. Tomorrow, we'll find out if we can salvage any of the ripe vegetables, but we must give the plants a few days to see if they'll come back. If they don't, we'll replant."

Peder laid his hand on Anna's shoulder. "Sometimes the row crops can survive pretty well. The tomatoes and peppers are more vulnerable."

"There's no way to change whatever the harm, but I can't worry about it until I know the rest of the Holdens, the Bixbys, and the Borges are safe." She turned to Halvor. "How's the church?"

"I'm not sure. I think the house was hit hard, but I don't know how badly the church was damaged," he replied.

"We should check on the Borges." As much as Anna disliked them, she didn't want them to be injured.

Greta said in a tearful voice. "Guess this means we won't have our picnic,"

"Why not?" Peder quirked an eyebrow. "It's the last day of

school, we have made it through the storm, and we have to eat. Let's take the food to your house and celebrate." He turned to Anna. "Then we can come back here, and clean up this place."

The children cheered and clapped. Inge hugged Peder. Poul took his hand.

"Adelaide, we'll take the pies and the bread in the crates. We can cook the potatoes when we get there." Despite wanting to clear away the broken glass and put a temporary patch on the roof, Anna joined in Peder's spirit for the children's sake. "We can put the coffee pot in a bucket and take it along, since we haven't gotten around to drinking it yet. You and Halvor, come with us."

"Right," Peder said to Halvor, then peered out the door. "You get the Strykers' wagon. I'll get the Holdens.' I think the rain has stopped."

When the people and food were loaded, they drove the muddy trail to the Holdens'.

As the teams turned into the dooryard, Frederik ran to meet them. He picked Brigitte from the wagon, held her close, and kissed her. "I was scared to death, not knowing where you and the children were. I'm glad you're all safe."

Brigitte burst into tears and hugged him fiercely.

How close Anna had come to losing them this afternoon. How narrowly she and the children had escaped danger. They could have been killed, and Jorn was gone. Irritation rose in her like bile. He wouldn't have known if something had happened to them. As it was, repairing the house and clearing the fallen limb would fall to her, Peder, and Halvor.

Anna studied the Holdens' house. One upstairs window appeared broken, and a few shingles lay in the lawn. Although farther from the tornado, her cabin showed far more damage. Even the bunkhouse offered better conditions and was newer than the cabin. Jorn should have built a proper home like this, to keep his family safe and comfortable.

Peder lifted Miss Parker from the wagon and walked her

toward the porch, where Mrs. Bixby held Magdelone in her arms. Her husband stood beside her.

The children jumped down and raced toward the house.

Halvor helped his mother and Anna from the wagon, and they each took a crate. When they reached the porch, Halvor stopped in front of Mr. Bixby. "I'll take this food to the kitchen then we should check on the Borges."

Mr. Bixby shook his head. "They are inside."

"Then they're safe." Warm relief spread through Anna.

"They have some scratches and bruises, but they'll heal. The good Lord looked out for them," Mrs. Bixby said, cuddling the baby to her. "I'm going to take Magdalone to her mother." She turned and went into the house.

"The south side of the church is damaged, and the house is flattened." Mr. Bixby took a step closer to Anna and Halvor and lowered his voice. "The Borges plan to leave Black Hawk County tomorrow."

"What?" Anna and Halvor asked in unison.

"They believe this afternoon's storm is a sign from God that they don't belong here." He winked. "Mr. Holden and I agreed."

It was a sign from God. They were safe and leaving of their own accord. Jorn could affix culpability to no one but the Borges themselves for their decision.

Pushing a twinge of guilt from her mind, Anna took a few steps toward the edge of the porch and lifted her eyes to the heavens. She prayed silently, *Thank you, Lord, for all you have done this afternoon.*

• ♥ •

After sending Adelaide and the children outside to play, Anna hurried into the nursery and closed the door. She squeezed into the trunk storage space and opened the lid of the first one.

Carefully, she set the baby clothes on the little boys' bed. In a matter of weeks, she would need them, so she might as well get them washed and ready.

She pulled out her work coat and pulled the basting thread holding the lining to the outer shell, then reached into the secret pockets and retrieved a handful of bills from each. Slipping them into an empty pillow case, she pulled out her best cloak and repeated the process.

Early in their business partnership, Brigitte, Anna, and Gabrielle had agreed not to tell anyone outside their little group how much money they made. Jorn had no idea how large Anna's income had grown through the years. In her bank account, she kept only a modest sum, in case Jorn insisted on using her funds to buy more land.

She returned the garments to the trunk then moved to the next one and recovered the cash from the hems of her winter dresses. When she had collected all the money from her secret hiding places, she listened to be sure that neither her children nor the housekeeper had come back inside the cabin. Then she sat down on Adelaide's bed to count her currency.

Jorn's demand that the family remain crammed into the small cabin was ridiculous, especially since he was gone for at least one-third of every year. More so now with its patched roof and replaced window. Now, she resolved to find out if she had enough money to build a larger house.

Smiling, she counted the last bills then returned all of the cash to the pillowcase, and hid it at the bottom of the trunk, under her winter dresses and the children's warm clothes. It would be best to use the funds from her bank account first.

She shivered as anticipation and trepidation warred within her. Building the house was right for her children, but it could result in an irreparable breach with her husband.

It was a risk she would have to take.

• ♥ •

"I'm not sure how much longer I'll be able to do this," Anna told Brigitte and Gabrielle. They had successfully sold their produce in town and were heading home. "My belly's grown so large it's difficult to manage the crates."

"We'll be happy to make your deliveries for you," Gabrielle volunteered.

Very generous, as always. It was only the first Tuesday in June, and Anna didn't want to take advantage of her friends for the entire summer. "Thank you, but I can send Halvor to help with the lifting."

"We'll try it ourselves," Brigitte said. "And let you know if we need help." She smiled conspiratorially. "We'd like to keep this enterprise just among us sales sisters."

Anna leaned toward her friends. "I think I have enough funds between selling my produce and the gold bars my grandfather sends each Christmas to build the house I want," she confided. "Peder told me what his home cost, and I want one similar to his. He took a guess at how much I would have to spend to build one this summer."

Brigitte gasped. "What will Jorn say?"

"He'll be furious, of course." Anna winced. "But I'm ready to stand up to him. Soon, we'll have five children. I don't want them to sleep on the floor or in the loft any longer. It's stifling in the summer and freezing in the winter."

"I understand how you feel." Brigitte slipped an arm around Anna's shoulders in an awkward hug. "But I wouldn't want to deal with Jorn's anger."

Anna clasped her hands together. "I'm going to have Halvor drive me to town tomorrow to speak to the carpenter about the house I want, and how much he'll charge to build it."

"Good for you!" Gabrielle's brown eyes glinted. "If there's anything I can do to help, just let me know."

"Me, too." Brigitte smiled.

Anna swallowed back the emotion clogging her throat. "Thank you for being such good friends."

• ♥ •

"When Jorn returns with the new greenhorns, will we need that little...sha—cottage you stayed in before the bunkhouse was built?" Anna asked Halvor, as he drove her to town. All week she had eagerly awaited her appointment with Mr. Dahl. She clutched her drawings of the room arrangements for each floor.

Halvor's brow furrowed. "No. We still have empty beds in the bunkhouse. And the south cabin and the house across the road will be available after the Holdens finish building the new cabin for the Bixbys."

A faraway look settled in his blue eyes and he fell silent.

"Will it bother you if we tear the little cabin down?" she asked.

Halvor laughed. "I never minded living there. I liked the privacy. But I won't miss it."

Perhaps he didn't like supervising the bunkhouse. "Would you rather live in one of the houses or cabins?"

"I'm fine. I have my own room, and I like having the cook prepare meals," he replied. "Mr. Andreasen will probably be leaving to buy his own farm in a year or two. Then maybe I'll move to his cabin."

Too bad Mr. Andreasen wasn't moving this summer.

Halvor's bushy, sun-bleached brows drew together. "Why do you ask?"

Anna could not suppress her smile. "I'm going to have a larger house built."

His mouth fell open. "Does Mr. Stryker know?"

Her smile faded. "Not yet."

"I don't think he'll like it."

"We will have five children. We need more space."

Halvor nodded. "True."

"And I'm not asking him to pay for it."

"For your sake, I hope he won't be too angry."

"Me, too." Anna sighed. If only Jorn was as reasonable as Halvor.

They fell into companionable silence.

He turned the horse onto muddy Main Street. The wooden sidewalks were a godsend for shopping on days like this. As they passed the brick storefronts of the Phoenix Block, her gaze traveled up the edifice of the Wise & Bryant Druggist. Standing half a story above the next-highest section, it seemed to haughtily overlook the rest of the block.

Peder's horse stood tethered to a post outside Mr. Dahl's shop in the next block. Halvor stopped the rig at the whitewashed, wood-frame storefront. A walnut-framed sign ran the width of the small building announcing: "Dahl's Carpentry and Building."

Halvor jumped down, tied the horse to the post next to Peder's, and helped Anna out of the carriage.

"We'll be going to my brother's house when we finish here," she said.

"I'll pick up the new rakes we need, then meet you there."

"Good." Anna turned toward the carpenter's shop. Peder opened the walnut, eight-paneled door. She stepped inside.

"So nice to see you again, Mrs. Stryker," Mr. Dahl greeted her. The room was about the size of the cabin's sitting room, but there were ornate moldings at the ceiling, and chair rails around the walls.

"And you, Mr. Dahl," she replied. Since he had built the nursery, a sprinkling of gray had mixed with his dark brown hair, giving him a more distinguished look.

He guided her to a chair at the large walnut table, with intricate spoon carvings around the edge. Peder sat beside her, and the carpenter across from them. After exchanging pleasantries, Anna laid out her drawings. "I realize you may have to make some changes so the house will be sound, but I'd like to follow these designs as closely as possible."

Mr. Dahl examined the drawings. "Five bedrooms, a

sleeping porch, and a maid's room upstairs." He shifted the papers. "Parlor, kitchen, cook's rooms, dining room, library, and drawing room downstairs. This'll be a large structure."

Anna smiled, laying a hand on her swollen abdomen. "I have a large family."

"It'll need a strong foundation. A basement with thick supporting walls." The carpenter again studied the papers spread before him.

"Of course," she said.

Mr. Dahl looked up at Peder. "I'll have to hire many men to excavate a hole this big. And I'll need cash up front to obtain materials."

Anna glared at the carpenter. "*I* understand that."

"My sister has a good head for business." Peder grinned.

Mr. Dahl shifted his gaze to Anna. He picked up a pencil and asked her a series of detailed questions, noting her answers. When he began to address the inside of the house, Anna sighed. "If we could visit my brother's home, I would show you more precisely."

The carpenter agreed, and they all climbed into Peder's carriage and drove to his house. Anna led them from room to room, pointing out what she did and did not want in regard to porches, windows, flooring, woodwork, fireplaces, built-ins, and every other detail she had thought so long and hard about.

After they finished, Mr. Dahl turned to Anna. "This is a tall order. I'll make some drawings and cost estimates, and bring them to you next Thursday morning. I need to evaluate the site and how much work it'll take to prepare it."

"That will be fine," Anna said, reining in the exhilaration surging through her. "When can you start?"

"I'm finishing a house north of town." He rubbed his clean-shaven chin. "If the weather holds, I can begin yours in mid-June."

"And when do you think it will be finished?"

"That'll depend on your site, the weather, and how many

capable workers I can find."

"You would rather the work be done well than fast, wouldn't you, Anna?" Peder asked.

"Of course," she replied. She hoped the house would be ready and they could move in before Jorn returned, but she wouldn't quibble over time - that was a small matter considering how long she had waited.

Her dream was finally coming true.

• ♥ •

Over the next week, Anna made repeated visits to the grove. She drove sticks into the ground to mark where she wanted the house and the yard around it. With stakes and string, she marked off a lane, curving from the trail to the front of the house, then back to the trail. Although difficult and tiring due to her swollen belly, she was exhilarated, almost giddy, as she finalized her visions.

Jorn would not be pleased to lose so many trees, but she would make certain more pines were planted to the north and west for a proper windbreak. The apple and cherry orchard she and Halvor enlarged for her produce business had grown large enough provide some protection.

When Mr. Dahl arrived, she showed him the location. He whistled low through his teeth. "It's a beautiful spot, but there's a lot of preparation. Dismantling the cabin, taking down the trees. That'll slow the start of your house."

"I have men who can begin the work while you finish your other project." Anna just had to convince Mr. Andreasen to free up some of the greenhorns to clear the site. "If you will explain to Mr. Hansen what needs to be done, they can start tomorrow. I would like to surprise my husband when he comes home from Denmark. Will we be able to move into the house later this summer?"

Mr. Dahl looked away. "I can't promise that, Mrs. Stryker."

Her shoulders slumped. "But we can try, can't we?"

The corner of Mr. Dahl's mouth curved slightly upward. "Yes, we can. And the more work that your farm hands do, the sooner we will finish."

A warm glow flowed through Anna. She sent Erik to find Halvor among the barns. When he arrived, he and Mr. Dahl walked to the site.

"When they cut down the trees, I can chop up the branches for firewood and get them out of the way for our new house!" Erik offered, as he and Anna watched the men pointing and moving around the grove.

"That would be a big help." She smiled, touched by his enthusiasm.

"Inge and Poul can pick up sticks for kindling. Then we'll have plenty for lighting the cookstove and fireplace."

"We'll see." Anna wasn't sure how his brother and sister would feel about being volunteered, but if time grew short, everyone would have to pitch in and do whatever they could.

"Me and Inge won't have to sleep on the floor in winter anymore." Erik grinned. "And we'll have room for a big table, so we can all eat together."

Anna's chest swelled. This was definitely the right thing to do for her family.

When the men returned, she took Mr. Dahl inside the house, where he laid his drawings on the table. Anna poured coffee and cut them each a slice of almond pastry.

He had made only a few changes to her original drawings, and he had sketched what each side of the house would look like from the outside. Anna became more excited with each illustration.

The final page showed the cost estimate. Her stomach tightened. It came in four hundred dollars more than she had expected. Her projected earnings from this summer's produce sales would not be enough to cover.

Jorn could make up the difference from this summer's trip to Denmark. He would be shocked to learn that she had earned almost enough from her produce business to be build such a fine home. The knot in her stomach twisted. Anna hoped he might be proud, but didn't expect it.

She could approach her banker for a small loan and pay it back with from her sales this summer and next. Jorn would be livid if she went into debt, so that was not an option. He should be embarrassed that his wife paid for their new home, since he failed to provide a satisfactory dwelling for their growing family.

She could reduce the cost by having the farmhands help with more of the work, but probably not enough. Somehow, she would have to settle the bill in full when the house was finished.

"I'll need five hundred dollars so I can order the initial materials and hire men to dig the basement," Mr. Dahl said, taking the final bite of his pastry.

Anna's lips twitched. She stood. "I'll get it." She went to the dresser and pulled out the bills she had placed there earlier this morning. Holding the money in both hands, she returned to the table. Her whole body trembled as the transaction neared finalization.

"You need to sign the plans for the basement." He handed her a pen from his portfolio. "We'll review the rest of the drawings before moving to the next stage, so you need not sign them now."

She inhaled a deep breath to still the shaking, then slipped the currency into her left hand. With her right hand she signed her name with careful strokes and gave the pen back to him. "I'll count out the down payment, then you must write me a receipt."

She counted the bills. When she reached five hundred dollars, Mr. Dahl filled in a receipt in English with neat lettering. Anna watched, spelling out the words in her mind as he wrote to make sure he noted the correct amount. Mr. Dahl scrawled his signature on the receipt. Anna handed him the money.

"We'll start in about two weeks. I'll send word the day before we arrive." He tucked the bills into his pocket and returned the papers to his portfolio. After a few pleasantries, he left.

Anna went to find Halvor. She asked him to set up a meeting with Mr. Andreasen at the house this afternoon, then went to join Adelaide and her children.

Mr. Andreasen did not appear until 5:30. Adelaide was inside preparing the evening meal, so Anna decided to talk with him under the oak tree. He ran his dirty fingers through his brown beard as he approached.

She straightened her spine. "My husband and I are building a new home this summer. The work will start in two weeks. In the meantime, the farmhands will need to take out some trees from the grove and dismantle the old cabin."

His mouth fell open, and his hazel eyes widened. "Mr. Stryker didn't mention anything about this before he left."

"It must have slipped his mind. He left early this year."

Mr. Andreasen laughed derisively. "He would not fail to mention something that important."

Flaming heat flooded Anna's cheeks. "Well, despite that, you'll need to assign some of the men to clear the site."

"The men did not hire on for house building. They hired on for farming."

Her pulse raced. Her mind went back to the documents in the loft she had read some years before. "I believe the contracts indicate the men will do whatever work Mr. Stryker assigns to them."

He nailed her with a dark stare. "Mr. Stryker. Not Mrs. Stryker."

Anna held his gaze. "How many men will you assign to this work?"

"One. Mr. Hansen. He's already required to do your bidding."

"But he cannot fell and move trees by himself."

"That is his problem." Mr. Andreasen took a step backward.

"My husband won't be happy to learn how uncooperative you've been." Anna clenched her teeth, fearing he would call her bluff.

"I will explain my reasons to him when he returns. Now, excuse me. I must get home to supper so I can complete my own chores." He turned and left before she could say another word.

She refused to call after him. Halvor had said the cranky old farm manager would leave in the near future. Anna mumbled a prayer that he was right.

Pacing between the grove and the house, she massaged her aching temples. Mr. Andreasen must not stand in the way of getting her house built. The site needed to be prepared. It was a big job, and there was no time to waste.

As she watched the men outside the bunkhouse, washing up for the evening meal, an idea formed. Anna opened the kitchen door, and called in to Adelaide. "Go ahead and start without me. I'll be in later."

• ♥ •

Waiting under the oak tree for the last of the greenhorns to enter their dining hall, Anna worked out the details. If Mr. Andreasen had stopped by earlier, she would have had time to discuss her plan with Halvor, but it was too late now. He was already inside. She had to trust him to come through for her.

Anna walked toward the bunkhouse and slipped through the dining hall door. A few men were still dishing up food, but most already had their plates full and were seated.

Little by little, as the farmhands noticed Anna's presence, silence fell over the room.

Moving to the center, where everyone could see and hear her, she cleared her throat. "There is a special job that must be done. Some trees need to be removed from the grove, and the old cabin there must be taken down."

A quiet murmur rippled through the men.

"Mr. Andreasen doesn't believe he can spare any of you during the day for this project." She nearly choked on her words as she thought about that obstinate old troll. "So, I'm prepared to pay twenty-five cents to each man for each evening he works from after supper until dark." In the planting and harvest seasons, the men were in the fields until nightfall, but summer meant less intense fieldwork and more hours of daylight.

A louder, more excited response rolled through them. From the bits of comments she could pick up, they seemed willing to help. Her confidence grew.

"If you are interested in helping with this job, please sign up with Mr. Hansen tonight." She glanced in his direction. He raised an eyebrow then a slight smile softened his face. "He will make out a schedule and assign tasks that need to be done. The first group can start tomorrow evening. Mr. Hansen will keep track of who works when." She paused for a breath as the din around her rose, then clapped her hands together for silence. "Tomorrow is Friday. Next Friday morning, Mr. Hansen will turn in his records to me. I will pay those of you who work between now and next Thursday at Friday's evening meal."

The room erupted in loud, simultaneous conversations. Anna briefly lifted her gaze heavenward. She stepped to where Halvor sat. "Please stop by the house tomorrow morning and let me know how many sign up. We can iron out any remaining details then."

"I will. When I bring the milk." His blue eyes gleamed. He ran his hand through his hair.

"That'll be fine." She left the dining hall and headed toward the house. Closing her eyes for just a moment, she prayed this was a good idea. The work had to be done, whether her men or Mr. Dahl's did it. She would rather pay her greenhorns and farm hands than men the carpenter hired.

Most importantly, Mr. Dahl had agreed to try to finish the house before Jorn returned. It would be easier to tell her husband what she had done if the children and Adelaide were moved in and settled.

Chapter 12

June 18, 1882

Once again, Halvor has come through for me. He not only accepted my surprise announcement about hiring greenhorns, but he also signed up nearly all of them, and a few of the hired men, to prepare my building site. They started work yesterday, and many worked after church today. I did not ask them to work on the Sabbath, but I appreciate their enthusiasm, because there is much work to do before building can begin.

Halvor volunteered to help with the tree-clearing, but I told him his first priority must remain the gardens and orchard. After the tornado, we had to replant nearly half the crops, but they are growing nicely now. We need to keep them up so I have plenty of produce to sell this summer. As the birth of my child approaches, I am able to do less of the work.

Thankfully, I have had less nausea with this baby than with the previous four. Perhaps my body has become accustomed to carrying children, or maybe this one will be a girl. I am hoping for another daughter, but will be thankful if the baby and I get through the birthing without difficulty. I have not had a letter from Jorn since he left last month, but before he left, he told me he did not expect to be home when our child comes into the world. It did not seem to matter to him, and I find it no longer matters to me, either.

Brigitte tied her horse to the post in front of the Cooks' house, while Gabrielle helped Anna down from the Holdens' carriage.

"The next two months cannot go fast enough," Anna said, catching her breath.

"Let's get out of the sun." Still holding Anna's elbow, Gabrielle headed toward the house. "Before we go in, I want to warn you that Lise is working today."

"On Tuesday?" Brigitte stopped walking.

"Yes. I've been teaching her how to serve coffee and sweets." Gabrielle cast a glance toward the door. "That girl didn't have much English, but she's learning. And she tries hard."

"Poor girl," Anna said. "We can translate for you."

"It's better that she and I work it out ourselves," Gabrielle said in a lowered voice. "She would have been embarrassed if a third person had to tell her to bathe when she first arrives in the morning, and to wear the clean dresses I provide."

"You're very good for her," Anna said.

When the three women were seated at Gabrielle's newest quilt, Anna told them of her meeting with Mr. Dahl, the plans for the house, and the arrangements she made with the farm hands.

"That reminds me." She reached in her pocket and pulled out twenty one-dollar bills. "Would one of you please take this money to the bank and have it changed to twenty-five cent pieces?"

"Sure." Gabrielle stood, took the money, and placed it under a paperweight before returning to her place at her quilt.

Anna turned to Brigitte. "Do you think Frederik would like some logs for rebuilding the Bixbys' house?"

She shrugged. "The newly felled trees would have to be properly cured, but he might be able to use the wood and fireplace stones from the old cabin. "I'll ask him tonight."

"I wrote my grandfather about the tornado." Anna rethreaded her needle. "I asked him to share the letter with Jorn, so he won't be shocked about the church and Borges' departure."

"But not your new house?" Gabrielle grinned.

Warmth crept up Anna's neck. "I haven't decided yet when to tell him."

With a solemn expression on her plain face, Lise Thomsen walked into the room. "'Scuse me, Mrs. Cook," Lise said in a soft voice, her gaze fixed on her feet. "The big hand on twelve. Little hand on three. You want me make coffee?"

Anna suppressed a smile. Lise sounded like Erik and Inge trying to tell time.

"It's three o'clock," Gabrielle said. "Please start the coffee, Miss Thomsen."

"Yes, ma'am." She headed back to the kitchen.

"Miss Thomsen?" Brigitte grinned at Gabrielle.

"I told her that people who don't know each other well use their surnames," Gabrielle explained. "And if we become friends, we will use first names."

Brigitte raised her pale-brown brows. "But she is your employee. Don't you want her to use your surname as a sign of respect?"

Gabrielle leaned over the quilt toward Brigitte and Anna. "She is my employee," she whispered, "But I think she could really use a friend. I don't believe she ever sees anyone but her family and me."

The motherly comment sent a flash of childish jealousy through Anna. Her cheeks grew warm.

Lise shuffled between the kitchen and dining room, laying plates and silver on the table. The women continued making small talk about Brigitte's and Anna's children until Lise came into the room again. "Table ready, Mrs. Cook."

"Thank you, Miss Thomsen," Gabrielle said. "Shall we, ladies?"

They retired to the dining room and enjoyed coffee and peach upside-down cake. When they finished, Lise began to clear away the plates. Brigitte turned to her. "You are welcome to ride home with us, Lise. Your house is right on the way to the Strykers'."

"That's nice of you, Brigitte." Gabrielle turned to Lise. "When you finish washing the dishes, you can change into your own clothes and get ready to leave. It'll save you that long walk."

The girl ran a jerky hand through her fine, pale brown hair. "Thank you, Mrs. Cook."

Gabrielle pursed her lips as she watched the girl leave the room. The women moved back to the sitting room.

"We can meet at my house next week," Brigitte said. "You're welcome to join us for lunch, if you don't mind putting up with my children."

"We love your youngsters," Gabrielle replied.

"So do I, but I still like to have a break from them now and then." Brigitte turned to Anna. "Bring your children, too. They can play while we talk and stitch some new bed linens for the Bixbys."

"They would like that."

"I'll pick you up in the wagon," Gabrielle said. "Let me write it down so I don't forget." She walked to the desk and picked up a pen. She bent to write, then pivoted. "Did one of you take those bills I put under the paperweight?"

"No." Brigitte and Anna replied. Her breath caught. She could not afford to lose twenty dollars.

"I know I put them here," Gabrielle said.

"I saw you." Brigitte walked to the desk and studied it closely.

Gabrielle sighed. "I'll have to speak to Lise."

They each took a chair. Anna's muscles tensed as she sat, waiting.

After ten long minutes, Lise entered the room wearing a dirty gray dress with several rips, her hands in her pockets. "I ready."

Gabrielle stood. "Please come into the dining room, Miss Thomsen."

The girl's mouth tightened, but she followed her employer into the next room. From her seat, Anna could see Lise's face, but not Gabrielle's.

"I am missing twenty dollars," she said calmly. "It was on the desk. Do you know what happened to it?"

Lise stared at her shoes.

"I must ask you to empty your pockets." Gabrielle's tone was even, not accusatory. Anna admired the way her friend was handling the situation.

Face crumpling, Lise pulled her hands from her pockets, a fistful of bills in each. Tears streamed down her face. She handed over the money with a sob. "I sorry."

A mix of relief and anger washed over Anna.

Gabrielle waited until the girl quieted. "Why did you take this money?"

The girl stared at her blankly.

"Don't I pay you enough?"

Still no answer.

"Anna, since it is your money, would you please come and translate?" Gabrielle called. "I'm not sure how much the girl understands."

Anna rose and walked to the dining room, taking breaths to calm herself.

"Mrs. Cook wants to know if you think she does not pay you enough," Anna said in Danish.

Lise sniffled in a noisy breath. "Her pay is fair."

Anna told Gabrielle the answer, and she asked another question.

"Then why did you steal from Mrs. Cook?" Anna translated.

"My father takes my pay." The girl sobbed again.

The planes of Gabrielle's face softened. "What does he do with it?"

"He buys whiskey," Lise replied. "I took the money so I could buy my mother the supplies we need."

Gabrielle wrapped her arms around the girl, who wept on her shoulder. "Maybe, if all goes well, you could live here? I have a spare room."

Anna's voice quavered as she repeated the offer.

Lise clung tighter to Gabrielle. "I would love it," the girl said through her sobs. "But I cannot leave my mother. She needs me."

"Sweet girl," Gabrielle whispered. "Perhaps I could pay you partly in supplies, if you tell me what you need."

Anna relayed Gabrielle's suggestion to Lise.

"Flour," Lise said in English.

Gabrielle took her into the kitchen and filled two quart jars from her bin.

Anna's eyes grew moist. The poor girl was working to provide basics for her family, and her father was denying them those necessities. How could Ole be so irresponsible and cruel?

• ♥ •

On Thursday afternoon, a cloudburst drowned out all opportunity for work on the house site. Halvor brought the records to Anna when he delivered the evening milk. She was glad to have them early. A good number of the men had helped with the site preparation, so it would take a while to figure out everyone's wages.

On Friday, Anna put the coins she would need into a canning jar. The rest she hid in a biscuit tin in the sideboard. Before the evening meal, she and Halvor sat at a table in the bunkhouse dining hall. As the farmhands entered the room, they lined up for their money.

When each man reached the pay station, Halvor read his name and the number of nights he worked. Anna counted the appropriate wages and handed over the coins, while Halvor marked off those who had been paid.

After they finished, he took the records to his room. Anna followed. "That went very well."

He grinned. "The men are already talking about a trip to town to spend their money."

"Perhaps when the work is finished, you could take them in the wagon."

"That's kind of you, but I'm not sure Cedar Falls is ready for them."

"You've done a good job. The men have made a lot of progress." She held out her hand, with two dollars in it. "Thank you."

He looked at the money then at her, the line of his mouth thin. "That's not necessary."

"Yes, it is." She could never repay him for all he had done for her, but she could do this.

He shook his blond head. "It's too much."

"No, it isn't. You're the supervisor." She thrust the money firmly into his hand. "I want you to have it."

"Thank you."

Warm affection spread through her. She smiled. "I'll see you tomorrow."

He nodded. "Good night."

She turned and walked back to the house.

The rain continued, in sprinkles and drizzle, through church on Sunday. Peder stopped by and picked up Anna and her children. Halvor drove his mother and the farm hands in the wagon. The narrow trail was so muddy they had to drive in the tall grass instead of the tracks. Still the wheels slipped and slid. Anna prayed they wouldn't get stuck before they made it back home.

"Mr. Dahl asked me to tell you he won't be able to start on your house for at least two more weeks," Peder said when they reached the church. "All this rain has put him behind."

Anna frowned. "I expected it."

The children ran down the steps to the basement where the service would be held. Peder followed them with the basket of food for the potluck. Anna stepped into the sanctuary. Water dripped through the boards, nailed haphazardly to cover the storm damage. She gazed at the altar, damp from days of moisture.

Frustration rippled through her. If the rain continued, Jorn would be back before Mr. Dahl could even start building the house.

• ♥ •

The rain stopped on Monday. She and Brigitte decided it was too muddy to get the children together, so Tuesday's meeting was held at Anna's. Frederik and Mr. Bixby dropped Brigitte off and went on to Halvor's old cabin to salvage what they could use. They planned to take the first load to the Holdens', then come back for a second one and Brigitte. The rest of the cabin could then be dismantled, completing one more step toward the site's preparation.

Brigitte brought cheese and bread for the noon meal. Anna made coffee and opened a jar of bing cherry sauce. When Gabrielle arrived, they spread the meal on the small parlor table, then arranged the two upholstered chairs and the rocker around it.

Brigitte cut each of them a slab of bread. "Hopefully, some of the mud will dry up by Thursday."

They would take produce to town a day later this week, so they could pick it when the weather was drier. Anna sighed and poured coffee into each of the cups. "I hope so. I'm eager for the men to get the site cleared."

Children's voices rang out from the kitchen, Adelaide gathered them at the table for their noon meal and hushed them.

Anna smiled. "I thought your suggestion to pay Lise partially in provisions was a good one, Gabrielle," she said. "At least that way, Karyn and the children will get some benefit from the girl's work."

"Yes." Gabrielle smiled sadly. "When I paid her on Friday, she took part of it in sugar. She said she couldn't remember the last time her family had any."

"There has to be something more we can do to help the Thomsens," Anna said. "Maybe Karyn and her children could help us pick cherries. I would pay them for their work."

"We could save scraps of fabric from our sewing projects and make some crazy quilts for them." Gabrielle smiled. "I'll talk to Lise about having her mother come with her next Tuesday. I'll bring them with me to help us can peas."

When they finished their meal, they cleared the parlor table and carried everything to the kitchen counter. Inge rushed to Gabrielle's side. "I can take your plate, Mrs. Cook."

Gabrielle handed her plate to Inge and patted her shoulder. "That's very nice. Thank you."

Inge smiled as she carefully placed the dish on the counter, then turned to Anna. "Can we go outside and play with the kittens, Moder?"

The children had been cooped up in the house for so long that Anna could not deny her request. "After your little brothers are finished eating."

She turned to go back to the parlor.

Erik whispered loudly, "Hurry up, Torsten."

Gabrielle and Brigitte helped Anna move the chairs into an arrangement that would be good for hemming the bed linens Brigitte had brought. They had just sat down to begin their work when a man outside shouted, "Halvor, come help us!"

"What's happening?" Brigitte stood and hurried out the kitchen door. "Oh, my Lord!" she cried out in Danish.

Trepidation washed through Anna. She hoped nothing had

happened to any of the men working on the old cabin. She and Gabrielle rushed to Brigitte's side.

Frederik and Mr. Bixby were carrying the toboggan Jorn had built for the Thomsens many *Juls* ago. On it sat Karyn Thomsen, her face covered with bruises, cradling her arm to her chest. Lise, her brother, and sister followed behind. Mud caked their feet and smeared their clothes.

When Halvor reached them, he put his hand on Karyn to steady her. She stared straight ahead, eyes glazed over. Blood matted the hair above her forehead.

Anna placed a hand on her swollen belly and lumbered back into the house. "Adelaide, please take the children outside through the front door right now. Give us a few minutes before they come around back to play with the cats."

Adelaide's round eyes widened. "What is happening?"

Anna just shook her head and went back outside, standing next to the closed door. She could hear her housekeeper shooing the children from the table and out the front.

When Frederik reached the door, Anna opened it.

He and Mr. Bixby brought Karyn inside and set the toboggan on the dirt floor.

Brigitte brushed by her, grabbed the fabric they had been stitching, and covered the bed with it. Gabrielle gathered the Thomsen children in her arms and hugged them to her. Lise burst into tears.

Frederik tried to help Karyn off the toboggan, but she collapsed back against the wood. "Let's carry the sled to the side of the bed," he said to Mr. Bixby. "Then Halvor, you, and Brigitte can help her straight onto the mattress."

Recovering her wits, Anna hurried to the kitchen. She picked up the bucket and poured water into a pot, which she put on the stove to heat.

Karyn groaned. Anna looked up to see Halvor and Brigitte positioning her on top of the white cloth, which was now coated with mud and blood.

Gabrielle released the children and fetched the wash basin. "We need cloths."

Anna took a handful from a dresser drawer and gave them to Gabrielle. She and Brigitte began cleaning the dirt and blood from Karyn's face.

Frederik handed the toboggan to Mr. Bixby. "Take this out to the pump and wash it. We may need it later."

Anna pulled the bench out from the wall and led the Thomsen children to it. They seemed grateful to sit.

Frederik knelt before them. "What happened?" he asked gently in Danish, as he examined the boy's arms. "Are you hurt?

Anna studied the angry red welts on the boy's thin forearms. Her gaze flew to Lise's and her little sister's arms, which looked very much like their brother's.

Lise sniffled. "It's my fault. I took some flour and sugar from Mrs. Cook in exchange for part of my wages. Fader was furious. He took the rest of the money on Friday and went somewhere. Maybe to town. He came home drunk today and whipped us and beat Moder."

"No," Karyn cried from the bed. "No."

Lise jerked her gaze to her mother. Her brother put his hand on Lise's knee. "Then, he left again. He took the horses and wagon, so we put Moder on the toboggan and pulled her here. It's the closest house where anyone lives."

Karyn sobbed, making barely a sound.

"We need more cool water," Gabrielle called.

"I'll get it," Halvor answered in English. He picked up the bucket and hurried outside.

"Why did he whip you and beat your mother?" Frederik asked softly.

The young boy folded his hands in his lap and stared down at them. "That's what he does when he's drunk."

Lise's lips trembled. "And he'll be really mad that we brought Moder here." Her face turned ashen. "We aren't supposed to tell anyone."

Halvor returned with a full pail of water and took it to Gabrielle.

Mr. Bixby came through the kitchen door. "I leaned the toboggan against the woodshed to dry."

Frederik stood. "Thank you. Will you take these children outside and ask Mrs. Hansen to help clean them up?"

"Yes, sir."

After the children left, Frederik took Anna by the elbow and guided her to the far corner of the parlor. "We'll go after Ole, but first we need to find a safe place for Karyn and her children." He spoke in English so Karyn could not understand. "They can't stay here because you're close to the Thomsen's house. This is the first place he'll look."

"And they can't go to Gabrielle's," Anna said. "He knows Lise has been working there."

"We have plenty of room, but Ole might think she would come to us since we used to host worship services." Frederik paused.

Halvor joined them. "No one's in the south cabin."

Anna worried her lower lip. "Do you think they would be safe there?"

"If we find Ole, they will be." Frederik turned to Anna. "We'll put them in the church basement tonight. They'll be less visible. In the next day or two, we'll move them to your cabin."

Halvor nodded. "Hopefully, we'll have found Ole by then."

Anna turned to him. "Tomorrow, we'll clean and prepare it for them."

He shook his head. "Not you." His gaze fell to her abdomen. "I'll take care of getting it ready."

"Thank you." Anna sighed. "Do you think Ole will come back?"

Frederik nodded. "I'm afraid so. The only thing he has is his farm. He has nowhere else to go."

• ♥ •

Over the next week, the sun shone, the mud dried, and work again progressed on clearing the home site. Anna often gazed at the opening, visualizing her new home.

Frederik, Halvor, and Mr. Bixby had not found Ole. Karyn refused to allow anyone to send for a doctor, fearing word would get back to her husband. Gabrielle determined that Karyn had a broken arm, and one or more broken ribs. Although Gabrielle did not speak Danish, she volunteered to care for Karyn and her children. Each day, Anna sent food with Halvor, and Brigitte sent Mrs. Bixby to help for an hour or two.

On Thursday, when Frederik and Brigitte stopped by for Anna's produce, they expressed concern that with all the coming and going at the south cabin, the curiosity of farmhands and neighbors might be aroused. If Ole showed up and asked questions, one of her men might mention the activity and inadvertently disclose the family's location.

Fearing for the safety of her children, Anna asked Halvor to keep an eye on the house in case Ole came by. When another week passed with no sign of him, she began to relax.

By the last Tuesday in July, Mr. Dahl's employees were working on the foundation. Anna was disheartened that the house might not be finished before winter, and each day she grew more worried about Jorn's reaction. She was glad when Brigitte and Gabrielle arrived. They had volunteered to can her tomatoes, since her feet and ankles swelled when she stood for long periods.

"Graham was in town yesterday," Gabrielle said as she washed and prepared the jars. "He heard that there was a team and wagon found two miles east of the here. There was a rifle in the box, with O.T. carved in the handle. The marshal believes it might belong to the Thomsens."

"Was there any sign of Ole?" Anna asked. She moved her rocker to the open area between the parlor and the kitchen so she could talk with her friends while they worked.

"No," Gabrielle replied.

Anna felt a twinge in her abdomen. She shifted her position.

"Have you heard from Jorn?" Brigitte peeled and cut a tomato as she spoke.

"Yes. Peder brought me a letter on Sunday." She took a breath and placed her hand on her abdomen as a pain gripped her. "He said he'll be back August thirtieth." She had prayed for something to delay his return long enough to get the basement finished and the house's outer walls put up. "I'm to send Halvor and Mr. Andreasen with wagons." Her jaw tightened. "As if he will take direction from me."

"Will two wagons be enough?" Brigitte asked.

"I guess so," Anna said, thankful that the stitch in her abdomen had released. "A lot of the greenhorns will work for the railroad west of the Missouri River. I just hope Jorn rides with Halvor. I don't want Morton to mention the house to Jorn before I can talk to him."

Gabrielle chuckled. "He'll see it for himself as soon as he gets here."

"There's nothing I can do about that." Anna sighed. "Mr. Dahl told me yesterday that the best I can hope for is that the basement will be finished by then." She got up and walked to the counter. "I can help you for awhile."

"We're doing fine," Brigitte smiled. "Sit and rest."

She and Gabrielle filled the boiler with jars and set it on the stove.

Anna's abdomen tightened again. "I think the baby is coming today. I'm having cramps."

Gabrielle ran to Anna and put an arm around her waist.

"Go to bed and relax," Brigitte ordered.

"They've just started." Anna paced around the kitchen. "But my deliveries have gone faster with each child." She grabbed the back of her rocker as the telltale liquid spilled down her legs.

• ♥ •

Two hours later, Gabrielle placed Anna's baby boy in her arms. Her heart swelled with love as she cuddled hum close.

Brigitte leaned over the bed for a closer look. "What are you going to name him?"

Anna gazed at her new son, his red face, his mouth open wide in a loud cry, his tiny hands fisted. The happy voices of her other children drifted in through the open window.

"I think I will call him Jorn."

Chapter 13

August 13, 1882

Baby Jorn is thriving. As I did with each of my older children, I am enjoying the primal bond that is developing between us as I nurse him and rock him to sleep. Erik, Inge, and Poul like to hold him and talk to him. Torsten watches his new brother, but rarely interacts with him. I'm not sure if he is jealous of the attention the baby receives, or just wary because he is so small.

Karyn and her children remain in the south cabin. She identified the rifle and the wagon as her husband's. I still worry that Ole will show up drunk and angry, but Halvor keeps a close watch on the children and me. We haven't seen anything of Ole and, to my knowledge, neither have any of the neighbors. I hope he has left Black Hawk County forever.

Jorn is not the ideal husband, but thankfully he is not like Ole. From now on, I will count that among my blessings.

Peder, Halvor, and Adelaide took the children to church today. I spent my time alone, praying that something will keep Jorn from arriving home next week. Since that appears unlikely at this point, I also prayed that he will accept our new house, and maybe assign some of the greenhorns to help with its completion. The Lord will have to work a miracle for that to happen.

As Jorn's return nears, Erik has become tense and irritable. He does not want to miss school to work in the fields. He is very competitive with Inge and fears she will pass him up, since last spring Miss Parker suggested that Inge might be able to skip a grade or two in the near future. For now, she is starting out the school term in second grade.

Anna stayed home while Halvor and Mr. Andreasen went to meet Jorn and the greenhorns, giving the excuse that the baby was too young to travel in the hot weather. She didn't want to be riding on the wagon seat with Jorn when he saw the new house's foundation.

From the time the wagons left for the depot, Anna's muscles grew tense and her head ached. Baby Jorn seemed to sense her unease, fussing more than usual and refusing to nurse. Erik and Inge had been somber since they completed their chores. Even Poul and Torsten showed little interest in their father's return. It saddened Anna that her children had grown so distant from him. Adelaide took them outdoors to play until he arrived.

At the sound of the wagons, Anna's chest tightened. She rocked the chair back and forth to soothe her infant, and herself.

A few minutes later Jorn burst through the front door.

"What have you done?" he demanded, without even a proper greeting. His dusty clothes, unshaven face, and tired eyes belied the force of his voice.

Anna lifted her chin. "I have given you another son. His name is Jorn. After you."

He stopped, as if he had forgotten she was with child when he left. Slowly, he approached her. Bending closer, he studied the tiny boy's face, running a finger gently across his cheek. "Jorn."

The baby wailed.

Jorn straightened, stalked across the room, and dropped into his chair. He had not even kissed her. Anna shrugged it off. She held the infant to her chest and rubbed his back. He quieted.

"What have you done to the grove?" Jorn's voice quavered with controlled rage.

"I'm having a house built." She hoped she sounded calm.

"Without my permission."

Permission. Anna swallowed against the anger tightening her throat. "Yes. We have spoken about a house many times. You were being unreasonable. We have five children now, and this cabin is too small."

"You had no right to spend my money this way."

Anna squared her shoulders. "I did not spend your money. I used the proceeds from my produce business."

He stared at her in disbelief.

"And I will use the *Jul* gold Bedstefa has given me as the building progresses."

Jorn's hands fisted. "The building will not progress. I'll fill that pit with the trees you ruined."

"No. My children will not sleep in that sweltering loft." Her gaze shot to the crude ladder. "Or on the cold dirt floor any longer. Mr. Dahl can finish by winter if the weather cooperates."

"They will sleep where I say they will sleep." Red blotches had appeared above the stubble on his cheeks. "Didn't you hear me, woman? There will be no more building."

Pressure built behind Anna's eyes, but she refused to cry. For the first time in her marriage, she wished he had stayed in Denmark.

She forced in a breath. "I have a contract. I've paid Mr. Dahl for the lumber he has already purchased."

"Then you are out that money." Jorn sneered. "I will speak with Dahl tomorrow about terminating your contract."

He sounded just like Fader. Anna glowered at him.

"And from now on, you will give the money from your produce business to me," he said.

"So you can buy more farmland?" The volume of her voice rose with each word.

"I'll put the money away for our return to Denmark when South Jutland is free."

"Instead of building a proper house for your family. A house we need now."

"If you want a house so bad, you can have one. But not on my land." His quiet tone held the cold of suppressed rage. "I will divorce you, and you can go wherever you want. But you will not take my children."

Anna lost her breath. His children. He considered them his property, just like everything else. He could take them from her, and would if she kept pushing him about the house. Her entire body went numb.

And divorce. A chill shivered through her. Had he wanted one from the beginning? She struggled to draw air into her lungs.

They sat in silence. Suddenly, the house didn't seem so important. She did not dare bring up completing it. The ache in her chest grew as she forced herself to squelch the dream she had held for so long. It was a small price to pay for her children, but she didn't want him to destroy the foundation.

"We need bedrooms," she said in the softest voice she could manage. "If we put a roof over the basement, the older children and Adelaide could sleep there. It would be easy enough to add an entrance, and furnish two of the rooms with beds and heating stoves."

He frowned, but did not respond.

"It would give them a warm place to sleep in winter and a cool place in summer," she continued keeping her voice quiet, her tone asking permission. Divorce and taking the children was a weapon she couldn't counter. Tears pooled in her eyes. She tried to blink them back, but one spilled down her cheek

His gaze met hers for a moment, then returned to his fingertips, which he tapped together. He leaned forward, set his elbows on his knees, and steepled his hands.

"And you and I would have more privacy than we've had since we first married." As she finished her argument, she did not think her last point was necessarily a positive one. Right now, the idea of marital relations with him disgusted her. With five children already, she wasn't eager to conceive a sixth. She glanced at her husband.

He moved his hands to his knees and stood. "I'll think about it."

She sighed. It was the best she could hope for.

• ♥ •

Over the next six days, Anna tried to keep out of Jorn's way as much as possible. Neither of them had mentioned either divorce or the house since his first day home, but images of him banishing her from the farm and her children crying for her swamped her dreams. On good nights, she slept fitfully; on bad ones, she didn't sleep at all. She plodded wearily through her work, trying to act as if nothing was wrong for the sake of her family.

Jorn had gone back to the field after the noon meal. Anna cleared the remaining dishes from the table and put a pot of clean water on the stove. She sent her children outside so Adelaide could watch them while she picked squash for the evening meal.

When the dishes, pots, and pans were washed and put away, Anna checked on Baby Jorn in his cradle, then went outside to find Torsten alseep on a quilt under the oak tree. Poul chased after a gray and white kitten. The orange and white mother cat, Mouser, and her other two offspring, watched from the shade of the woodshed.

Inge and Erik raced around the corner of the outhouse.

"Moder, Moder!" Inge shouted.

Erik moved ahead of her, his face pale despite the energy he was exerting. "There's a strange man at the edge of the grove!"

Every muscle in Anna's body tensed. This summer, more beggars than usual had come to the farm requesting food. Although she never had any trouble with them in the past, Peder always said she couldn't be too careful. She had heard many stories of whole families being killed by tramps.

"Adelaide, bring Poul. We must get the children in the house." Anna scooped up the sleeping Torsten and herded Erik and Inge inside.

"You children go into the nursery with Adelaide," Anna whispered as she closed the door behind them, then hurried to the cradle to pick up Baby Jorn. The housekeeper shot her a knowing look as she took the baby from Anna's arms, and followed the older children through the bedroom.

Carefully, Anna climbed up on the bench and lifted the gun from its rack above the kitchen door. She stepped back down on the dirt floor and moved to the side of the window.

The stranger looked from side to side as he approached the house. Anna's heart beat so hard she could hear it. She wished Jorn would come in from the fields and send the stranger away.

Many long moments passed as the man came closer. In the nursery, Poul started asking about the kitten. Adelaide tried to quiet him, but he burst into tears and began wailing about the little cat.

"Please, please be quiet, Poul," Anna's pulse raced. Finally, the housekeeper distracted him with Inge's school slate. "Adelaide, he's here. It's time."

A knock came at the kitchen door. Adelaide closed the nursery door without making a sound.

Anna's grip tightened on the rifle. "Who's there?" she called in English through the panel.

No one answered.

Anna swallowed against her fear and repeated her question in Danish.

"I'm Jesper Vibbard. I crossed with Mr. Stryker this summer," a male voice answered. "Is he here?"

Hand shaking, Anna reached for the latch and opened the door a crack. "What do you want?"

Mr. Vibbard brushed his dirty shirt sleeve across his damp forehead. "Mr. Stryker said I could pick some vegetables from your garden."

"Don't you live in the bunkhouse?" Anna asked. "Three meals are served there each day."

"No. I live in the cabin at the west side of the property."

"I'm sure there is plenty of food at the bunkhouse. You could eat there tonight," Anna said.

Mr. Vibbard's clothes hung loose on his tall, thin body. His cheeks were hollow.

"You may pick some of the remaining beans and tomatoes," she said. "Do not take the melons or squash."

"Could I have a chicken?" The man's squinted gaze beseeched her. "I haven't had meat since we arrived here a week ago."

"I'll give you two jars of canned pork." Annoyance crept into her voice. Never before had a greenhorn begged for food. "And there is plenty of game: deer, rabbit, squirrel. Do not harm my chickens."

"But I don't have a gun."

Anna hoped he wasn't lying.

"I'll get the pork." She closed the door and retrieved the jars. She opened the door to hand them to the man. Out of the corner of her eye, she saw Halvor standing at the corner of her house. "And I'll arrange for you to take your meals at the bunkhouse."

"Tak," Mr. Vibbard said as he turned to leave with his loot.

Anna closed the door and blew out a breath.

"Were you bothering my wife?" Jorn's shout came clearly through the closed door.

"I'm hungry. She gave me food," Mr. Vibbard answered. "And she said I could pick some vegetables."

Anna stood motionless.

"Don't you ever bother Mrs. Stryker for food or anything else again." Jorn's voice held a hard edge. "If you need something, you go to Mr. Andreasen or me."

The greenhorn did not answer.

"Do you hear me?" Jorn roared.

"Yes, sir."

"Now, get back to the field. You may eat with the other men in the bunkhouse."

"Yes, sir."

Moments later, Jorn burst through the door. "Are you and the children safe?"

Tension seeped from Anna's muscles. "We're fine."

"That Vibbard is nothing but a troublemaker." Jorn stopped a few steps inside the kitchen, staring first at Anna and then at the gun in her hand. "What are you doing with the rifle?"

"He was a stranger. I thought he might be a beggar." Thoughts raced through Anna's mind, faster than she could talk. "When tramps come to the door, I always send the children and Adelaide to the nursery and get the gun. Just in case I need it."

Jorn's face paled. "Do beggars stop here often?"

"Yes. Mostly in the summer. When you're not here." Anna didn't even try to soften the accusation in her voice. "We've never had any real trouble with them."

Jorn took the gun from her and put it back in its place. "From now on, I'll assign Halvor to stay near the house when I'm not here."

• ♥ •

"Mr. Dahl agreed to terminate your contract," Jorn announced when he returned from town.

Anna blinked back tears as the last threads connecting her to her dream house snapped, but she couldn't protest. She wanted to keep her children.

"I engaged him to build a roof over the basement and install a large heating stove in the central room. It should give the other three rooms enough heat."

A far cry from the home Anna had envisioned, but at least Jorn wouldn't destroy the foundation. The family would have more sleeping space. She focused on this benefit to avoid falling into despair. Still, she couldn't keep herself from wishing Jorn had stayed in Denmark.

With the rest of the lumber Anna had purchased, Jorn contracted Mr. Dahl to repair the tornado damage to the church, and build a small house for a future pastor. Another part of the compromise for dissolving her contract. For the next week,

Anna prayed for the grace to accept this forced donation to the congregation.

• ♥ •

On the first day of the new term, Anna drove her children and the Holdens to school. She had made new clothes for Erik, Inge, and Poul, who was so proud he wasn't "a baby" anymore. They all had been counting the days for classes to start.

After the evening meal on Thursday, Jorn told Erik he would be working in the fields the next day.

Erik's blue eyes narrowed. "I don't want to be a greenhorn!" he shouted in English. "I want to go to school."

"I am your father," Jorn roared. "You will do as I say, or I'll take a switch to you."

Erik's lip quivered. He turned and ran out the door.

Jorn started after him, but Anna stepped in his path. "You have upset him. Let him be."

"He needs to learn to respect his father. You're too lenient with the children when I'm away." He took a step toward her. "You don't show proper respect for me. You built a house without my permission. It's no wonder they don't learn respect."

A scream rose to Anna's throat. She inhaled a breath to keep it in check and straightened to her full height. "Respect goes two ways. Did you show respect for my wishes by breaking my contract? By leaving me alone with our children every summer? By forcing our too-young son to work in the fields?"

Anna stopped short and bit her lip to keep from saying more.

Jorn's face reddened. He fixed his cold, green gaze on her. "I need to teach him to farm."

Her heartbeat pulsed in her temples. She didn't want to push Jorn too hard, but she had to protect Erik. "You can teach him what he needs to know on Saturdays."

"If you don't stop arguing with me, I'll keep him home every day. Not just Fridays."

He would do it just to spite her. She whirled around and stomped to the nursery to check on Baby Jorn, and to keep from saying more. Her husband stalked out the back door.

"I wish you had stayed in Denmark," she muttered.

On Friday, Jorn assigned Erik to one of the hired hands, Mr. Swane. He had worked on the farm for four years, and was familiar with how Jorn wanted things done. Jorn sent them to cut the hay bordering the trees along the creek.

When Erik came in for lunch, he was already complaining of aching muscles and insect bites. Anna sympathized, but knew Jorn would just tell his son to "be a man."

"I hate farming," Erik complained as Anna washed the chaff from his arms. "When I grow up, I'll never do it again."

"You like the cows and sheep." Anna tried to point out the positive aspects, but Erik had never shown an interest in the crops.

"Not that much."

After a noon meal eaten in silence, Jorn took Erik to find Mr. Swane.

Less than an hour after he had returned to the fields, Erik ran toward the farmyard, shouting. Anna rose from the blanket under the oak, where she was playing with Torsten. Baby Jorn slept on a nearby quilt. As she moved toward Erik, she understood his words.

"Fader, come quick!"

Jorn came running from the hay wagon in the farmyard. He and Anna reached Erik at nearly the same time. He was out of breath and visibly shaken.

Jorn placed a hand on each of Erik's shoulders. "What's wrong? Where is Mr. Swane?"

"H-he sent me to f-fetch you. We found a d-dead man." Erik could hardly get the words out between his sobs.

Anna's hand flew to her mouth.

Jorn's eyes widened. He caught her gaze. "A dead man?

Where?"

Erik gulped in a breath. "In the mud by the creek. It was awful."

"Who is it?" Anna asked, reaching for her son.

He snuggled into her embrace. "I-I don't know."

"You stay here with your mother. I'll get the buckboard and go help Mr. Swane." Jorn ran toward the barn.

Anna led her son to the backyard, where she pumped him a cup of water.

"His skin was falling apart." Erik said in English. His hands shook as he took the cup from her. "And some animal had chewed on his leg and arm. He stinked."

Anna sat cross-legged on the ground and pulled him into her lap. She rocked him back and forth, stroking his hair. "Sshhh. Try not to think about it."

"I never want to work in the fields again."

Anna didn't want him to go back either, but if she brought the subject up again to Jorn, he would take Erik out of school altogether. She continued to rock her son. Soon Erik was asleep on the blanket under the oak.

More than three hours passed before Jorn returned home. When he did, his shirt and pants were covered with mud and a putrid, sticky substance. Anna ran into the house and brought him a clean set of clothes, which she carried to the bunkhouse.

"It was Ole Thomsen," he said, as they entered the dining hall. "He had been shot."

"Oh, my Lord." Anna clutched her hand to her chest. "Who do you think did it?"

"No idea. But it happened awhile ago."

"Did you take him to the marshal?"

He shook his head. "Probably should have." He walked to the cupboard at the back of the room where the bathtub was stored and pulled it out. "But after what you said happened this summer, I decided to talk to Karyn at the south cabin. She seemed genuinely surprised he'd been shot."

Anna swallowed.

"What did she say?" Anna opened the door so he could carry the tub outside.

"She said to bury him on their farm above the creek. She didn't want a funeral."

Anna put two pots on the stove and started a fire. When he came inside, he carried two buckets of water. He had removed his shirt, and his muscles rippled as he poured water into the large pot. Throughout their marriage, all his hard work on the farm had kept his body in good condition. She laid a hand on her soft stomach, reshaped by her recent childbirth, and sighed. "Just the same, I should stop by to see her and take her some food."

"Karyn thanked me for the use of the cabin." Jorn poured the second pail into the other pot. "Then she said they would move back to their own home if I would take them."

"I'll send some canned goods and staples for them."

Jorn picked up the buckets.

"Lise worked for Gabrielle for a couple weeks this summer. Now that she and her family are safe from Ole, she can go back." She paused. "We should let the Cooks know. That way, Gabrielle won't go to the cabin to check on Karyn and find them gone."

"I'll stop by their place after I take the Thomsens home." He carried the pails to the pump just outside the dining hall door.

Anna followed. "Erik was very upset," she said. "He needs some time away from working the fields."

"You coddle him too much. He'll be fine by next week. Then I'll assign him to help Swane clean up around the cabin across the road. He's going to move there tomorrow. And it's been empty the whole summer."

Arguing wouldn't help, and Anna couldn't bear to hear Jorn threaten to take her children again.

• ♥ •

As the leaves turned from green to yellow and brown, the work on the sleeping basement was finished. Mr. Dahl had repaired the storm damage on the church, and was hard at work on the new parsonage.

Jorn and Halvor used the rest of the lumber to make beds for Erik, Poul, Torsten, Inge, and Adelaide. Halvor made a door for the room his mother and Inge would sleep in, and shelves for each room. Brigitte, Gabrielle, and Anna sewed on new bed linens.

Finally, the day came for Adelaide and the children to move in. Erik and Inge were elated to have beds of their own. Neither could remember such a luxury, since they had been displaced at a young age by their little brothers.

Anna moved to Adelaide's old bed in the nursery, so she could nurse Baby Jorn in the night without waking her husband. The arrangement also assured she wouldn't again conceive while she was still nursing, as she had done with Inge. What a relief to no longer share the marriage bed with Jorn.

By mid-October, the harvest was winding down. Erik would be allowed to return to school on Fridays when it was over. If Jorn believed they needed to finish a field before rains came, he required Erik to work an additional schoolday.

Anna feared her young son might become so tired he would fall asleep in Miss Parker's classes. His dislike for farming grew each week, and so did his resentment for his father.

On Friday, Erik came in for his noon meal shivering. Anna hurried him to the fireplace to warm himself until his father arrived.

"After you finish eating, you should climb into the loft and get your winter coat," Anna said, as she returned to the kitchen to get some water for him to wash. "If you get too warm this afternoon, you can shed your union suit."

"Yes, Moder."

Adelaide and Torsten ate, then she went outside to pump fresh water. When she returned, Jorn was with her.

"Looks like rain this afternoon," he said, joining Erik at the hearth. "You and Swane finish shocking those cornstalks?"

The color drained from Erik's face. "No." He took a step away from his father. "I helped him get to his house mid-morning. He was fevered and had a red rash on his hands. Could hardly stay on his feet. Then I went back to work."

That didn't sound good. Anna shot Adelaide a quick glance. The housekeeper's brows were furrowed.

Adelaide took Torsten to the nursery and sat with him in her lap, telling him a story in Danish. Hopefully, they would not wake Baby Jorn.

"I'll stop by and see how he is after we eat." Jorn led Erik to the table. "Halvor will work with you this afternoon. It's getting cold, and if the coming rain freezes tonight, it'll ruin whatever stalks aren't yet shocked."

Erik's shoulders slumped forward over his chest. They sat down to eat.

"I warmed some milk for you," Anna told Erik, setting the mug in front of him. "It'll chase away your chill."

With the backs of his hands, Erik swiped at the tears silently falling from his blue eyes. "*Tak*."

"That sounds good," Jorn said. "Warm some for me, too."

Anna obliged, grudgingly.

Erik drank his milk and ate his mashed potatoes, but he only picked at the rest of his food. Usually, he ate ravenously after a morning in the fields.

She studied him intently. "Aren't you hungry, Erik?"

"The cold wind and corn dust has made my throat sore." He fixed his gaze on his empty mug. "Could I have more of that warm milk, please?"

"Of course, son." Anna stood. She touched her hand to Erik's cheek and forehead. His skin was warm, but he had just finished the heated milk and his chair was close to the cookstove. Although he looked tired, his face wasn't flushed.

A loud wail rose from the cradle.

Adelaide appeared in the doorway, Torsten following close behind her. "I'll get Erik's milk. You need to feed the baby."

Anna ate the last few bites of ham on her plate, then went to nurse Baby Jorn. Thanks to his healthy appetite, he had grown chubby and strong in the two and a half months since his birth.

By the time the infant finished suckling, Jorn and Erik had gone.

Brigitte brought the other children home around four o'clock. Each was filled with stories of what had happened at school. Anna listened, then instructed them to change into their around-home clothes. When they returned, she sent them outside to do their chores so she could feed the baby again.

Torsten tagged along with Inge to the chicken coup.

Just after half-past four, Halvor rushed into the house with Erik in his arms. "This boy's burning up with fever."

Anna hurried to her son. His face was flushed, his eyes drowsy, and his skin hot. Her stomach tightened. She had to get him cooled down. "Put him in the bed in the nursery."

"I'm cold," Erik said in a thready voice, as Halvor laid him gently on the mattress. "And my throat still hurts."

"Adelaide, please bring a pan of water and a cloth." Anna eased off Erik's winter coat and pulled the sheet over him. He shivered.

"Not long after we got to the field, he vomited up his lunch. I wanted to bring him home sooner, but he said his father would be angry if we didn't finish the shocking."

Jorn! He was far too harsh a taskmaster. She never should have allowed Erik to return to work after the noon meal. "I'm glad you brought him now." She looked down at Baby Jorn, sleeping peacefully. "Halvor, please take the cradle to the parlor near the fire. I don't think it will be good for the baby to be in this room with Erik."

With deliberate care, Halvor picked up the cradle, as if trying not to wake the sleeping infant. He studied Baby Jorn. "He looks a lot like Erik did when he was a wee one."

Anna nodded. "I think so, too."

After Halvor carried the cradle through the door, Adelaide brought in the wash basin, a pitcher of water, and some cloths. She gazed at Erik. "Poor boy. I'll bring him a glass of cool water."

Halvor returned with Anna's rocker and set it at the bedside. For a few moments, he stood staring at Erik.

"Thank you." Anna sat in the much-appreciated chair. "Have you seen Mr. Stryker since he went to check on Mr. Swane?"

"No." Halvor ran a hand through his hair. "But I saw him take the wagon to the Thomsen's cabin, and he returned to the house across the road with Mrs. Thomsen. After he left her there, he took off down the road. Seemed to be in a hurry."

Anna sighed and swabbed her son's forehead with the damp cloth. If only Gabrielle or Brigitte was here! They would know what else should be done.

"That's cold." Erik whimpered, and tried to pull away.

"I'm sorry, sweet one, but you are on fire." Anna dipped the cloth in water to cool it, then wrung it out. "We need to break your fever."

"I-I wa-want a b-blanket," he said, through chattering teeth.

Adelaide brought a glass of cool water.

Erik had grown so weak in only a few hours. "Take a drink of this." Anna helped him to a sitting position and put the glass to his lips. He took tiny sips and moaned as the water met his throat. "We'll ask Halvor and Mrs. Hansen to leave, then we'll shut the door and take off your clothes so we can cool your whole body."

"No." He pulled his head back from the glass and whined.

If only Jorn hadn't insisted that Erik work the fields.

Anna turned to Halvor. "Please go into Cedar Falls and fetch Dr. Wade."

He nodded. "Right away."

The Hansens left the room and closed the door behind them.

Anna removed her son's clothing gently, although he tried to fight her.

"M-my head h-hurts." Erik brought a hand to his forehead.

Anna dipped a cloth in the cool water and laid it between his eyebrows and hairline. His skin still felt as hot as when she had begun. She continued bathing him with the cool cloth and singing soft lullabies for what seemed like an eternity. He fell into a fitful sleep. Gray twilight dimmed the room.

From the parlor, Anna could hear Adelaide's and Jorn's voices, but could not make out what was being said. Then the other children started speaking at once.

"Hush," Jorn told them loudly. "Your brother is sick."

Anna didn't want Erik to awaken now that she had gotten him to sleep. After Jorn ate the meal Adelaide had prepared, he would have to sit with Erik so she could feed the baby.

The door creaked open. Jorn entered in his stockinged feet. He crossed the room, lit the lamp, and turned the wick low. Worry knitted his brow. "How's he doing?"

"His fever is very high, and his throat is so sore he can barely swallow," Anna whispered. "I sent Halvor for the doctor."

"So Adelaide said." Jorn knelt at her side.

"How is Mr. Swane?"

"Quite ill." He spoke softly, but Anna heard the worry in his voice. "Karyn Thomsen thought he might have scarlet fever. I went to the Cooks and talked with Gabrielle. She thought that sounded about right for his symptoms. She offered to care for him, but Karyn said she would look after him through the night."

"Scarlet fever." The words slipped out before their meaning dawned on Anna. Dread stole through her like a winter chill. She couldn't help thinking of the epidemics she had read about, where many had died, or had been left with weakened hearts when the disease caused rheumatic fever. "Perhaps the doctor can see him when he's finished with Erik."

"Maybe."

Anna peered at her son's sleeping face. "This never would have happened if you hadn't insisted he stay home to work."

Jorn grimaced. "He's a fine, strong boy. He'll soon be his normal self."

"You don't know that," Anna growled. "If he doesn't recover, it will be your fault."

They sat in silence, watching their son's fitful sleep. After a few long minutes, Anna rose and left to nurse the baby.

• ♥ •

Anna handed the plate with her untouched dinner to Adelaide, and resumed her vigil at Erik's bedside. Jorn sat on the marriage bed in the next room. His elbows rested on his knees, his hands steepled before his face.

Hoof beats thudded in the dooryard. A rhythmic squeak of wheels signaled someone's arrival. The doctor. Thank God!

Jorn stood.

"I got him as fast as I could." Halvor hurried through the kitchen door.

"Where's the child?" A deep, raspy voice asked.

"In the nursery." Halvor's words tumbled out in a rush.

"I'll show you." Jorn cleared his throat. "Halvor, have something to eat, then go do chores."

"Yes, sir."

Dr. Wade, carrying his medical bag, followed Jorn into the room.

"Erik was working with a farm hand who got sick," Jorn said. "We think he might have scarlet fever."

The doctor checked Erik thoroughly, then turned to Jorn. "His throat looks bad. I can't say for sure at this stage that it's scarlet fever, but it could be. Just in case, we need to quarantine him to avoid infecting your other children."

"What about my wife?" The concern in Jorn's words took Anna by surprise.

"I'm fine," she said.

"Chances are good she has developed immunity. Many adults have." Dr. Wade's gaze rested on Baby Jorn. "If she has, the baby will likely be immune, too."

"That's good," Jorn said. "Does Erik require bloodletting?"

Anna shuddered. She was not sure she could stand to watch, but she would stay by her son's side if he had to endure the horrible procedure.

"That treatment is going out of favor," the doctor said. "For now, you need to keep sponging him. And immerse him in a cold bath several times per day." He reached into his bag. "This is sweet spirits of nitre. Give him half-a-teaspoon every four hours."

Anna took the bottle Dr. Wade offered and held it reverently. "Thank you, doctor."

He nodded. "If his throat gets worse, have him gargle with equal parts of muriatic acid and honey in water."

"We don't have muriatic acid," Anna said.

"I'll send Halvor to town for some in the morning," Jorn said.

"Watch for the red rash of scarlet fever," the doctor said. "If it appears, burn the clothes the boy was wearing, and anything else he has touched."

"Mr. Hansen carried Erik in from the field." Anna thought of the way Jorn had dismissed Halvor, after all he had done to help Erik. Halvor had shown more concern for Erik's welfare than his own father. "Will he get sick?"

The doctor lifted one shoulder. "No way to know. Watch him, and if possible, keep him away from the other men for a few days. And have him give you the clothes he was wearing, as they will need to be burned, too, if the boy develops the rash." He gathered up his instruments. "Fetch me if you need me again."

Anna managed a small smile. "We will. Thank you."

Jorn told the other children they would be staying in the basement for awhile. They could play outside, but they were not to come into the house unless they had his or their mother's permission. Adelaide would stay with them, and she would carry their meals from the bunkhouse to the basement.

The children gathered their toys and school things. They came to the door and quietly told Anna and Erik goodnight, then left.

She was glad they couldn't see her tears. As soon as she heard Jorn's hand on the doorknob, she dabbed at her eyes with her handkerchief.

He entered without making a sound. "Tomorrow, I'll send Halvor for Gabrielle," he whispered. "She can help you with Erik so you can care for the baby. I'll sit with him now while you attend to little Jorn."

Anna swabbed Erik's chest softly, so as not to awaken him. She handed the damp cloth to her husband and stood. "Poor baby, I haven't fed him since before Inge and Poul arrived home."

"He's fussing in the cradle, but at least he hasn't raised enough ruckus to wake his brother."

Anna sobbed.

Jorn took her in his arms, guiding her head to his shoulder. "Don't worry so. Erik is a strong boy. He'll be well in a few days."

She pulled away and hurried to pick up the baby.

While she nursed him, Anna prayed over and over that Jorn was right.

• ♥ •

Before sunrise the next morning, Jorn brought Anna a plateful of breakfast from the bunkhouse. Then he helped Adelaide carry food to the basement.

Gabrielle arrived just as dawn was breaking. Anna stumbled into her outstretched arms as she entered the nursery.

"You look exhausted." Softness laced Gabrielle's voice. "I'll take over. You lie on the bed and rest until the baby needs to nurse."

"Thank you for coming." Anna choked back a sob. She had to be strong for Erik. "Do you want some breakfast?"

"Oh, no." Gabrielle picked up the lamp and turned up the wick. The room brightened. She studied Erik's body, and touched her fingers to his head and stomach. "So far, he doesn't have the telltale rash. His face is red, but that could be the fever."

"That's a good sign." Anna tried to convince herself it was true.

"How long has he been asleep?"

Anna sighed. "I don't know. Since before I last fed the baby. Maybe an hour, or a little more. He woke often in the night."

"Has he eaten anything?"

"No. I have given him water and milk, and the medicine the doctor left, but he hasn't had anything solid since yesterday noon, and then it wasn't much. He had a good breakfast before that, though."

Gabrielle's lips parted and she released an audible breath. "We'll try some eggnog next time he wakes. Then I'll make him some pudding or custard. Things that will go down smooth over his sore throat." She turned to Anna and pointed her toward the marriage bed. "Now, go rest."

Too weary to argue, Anna curled up under the quilt and fell asleep. She woke an hour later.

For the rest of the day, Anna and Gabrielle took turns swabbing Erik, but to little avail. Halvor arrived with the medicine and they gave Erik a dose. His fever continued to rage.

They prepared a tub of water and submerged him up to his neck. This seemed to give him some relief, but no matter what cool, smooth food they offered, he refused more than a bite or two.

By nightfall, a red rash had appeared on his body.

Chapter 14

October 21, 1882
Please God, do not let Erik die.

Throughout the next day, Anna and Gabrielle took turns cajoling Erik to drink water, milk, eggnog, and chicken broth. They helped him climb in and out of the half-barrel of water, and cooled his body with the damp cloths.

By mid-afternoon, Erik's continuing fever frustrated Anna so that she was glad to turn over the swabbing of his rough, rash-covered skin to Gabrielle.

"Erik never would have gotten sick if Jorn hadn't kept him out of school to work in the fields," Anna groused. "I told him the boy was too young, but he insisted."

"You shouldn't blame Jorn," Gabrielle said in a quiet, gentle voice. "Erik might have gotten the sore throat at school. We don't know for sure."

Anna picked up her baby and paced back and forth between the nursery and the parlor. "Maybe, but he was working with Mr. Swane when he came down with the scarlet fever, and Halvor said Erik was afraid to quit work even though he was ill, for fear his father would be angry."

"Oh, Anna. You're tired and consumed with worry." Gabrielle put an arm around her shoulders. "Don't think about this now. Go feed your baby and then try to get some sleep." She shepherded Anna out of the nursery.

Baby Jorn suckled vigorously when she first brought him to her breast, but before he finished, he had fallen fast asleep.

Anna laid him beside her on the bed, and she, too, slipped into sleep.

During the night, she and Gabrielle continued taking turns caring for Erik and sleeping. Halvor brought breakfast from the bunkhouse, leaving enough for Jorn, Gabrielle, and Anna. He left a soft-cooked egg for Erik, but all he would take was a few sips of milk and some cool water. His tongue had developed a white coating with bright red spots.

Baby Jorn fussed more than usual, cutting into Anna's sleep with his cries. She did not blame her infant. He was used to much more attention from her and the other children than he had received since Erik became ill.

As the day wore on, Anna's own throat became dry. By the evening meal, she didn't feel like eating the chicken and potatoes Jorn brought from the bunkhouse. Anna forced down the eggnog Gabrielle mixed for her, then nursed the baby.

"How's Mr. Swane?" Anna asked, when Jorn returned after evening chores.

"Karyn said his fever broke this afternoon." Jorn looked toward the nursery, where Gabrielle sat at Erik's side. "How is Erik?"

"About the same." Anna sighed. "I don't see how his body can stand being this hot for so long."

"Karyn said she had scarlet fever when she was young." Jorn grabbed the slice of bread from Anna's untouched plate. "She said her fever lasted four or five days, then her skin itched and later peeled off."

"Oh, Jorn," Anna said. "I don't think I can manage two or three more days. I don't know what I would do without Gabrielle. I hope she doesn't get sick."

"She's a strong woman like you." He kissed her forehead. "She'll be fine. Do you need more wood for the nursery stove?"

"No, we haven't used much." Anna yawned. "We're trying to keep the room cool for Erik."

Jorn glanced toward the nursery, where Gabrielle sat at

Erik's side.

"I'll sleep in the bunkhouse until Gabrielle leaves." Jorn collected a suit of clean clothes from the chest in the bedroom. "She'll probably be more comfortable sleeping on the bed if I'm not on the floor in the next room, and I'll get more sleep without you and her moving around."

Anna's jaw clenched. She envied his opportunity for escape, even though she couldn't bear to be so far away from Erik when he needed her.

The next day, Anna refused the stew Jorn brought from the bunkhouse, accepting only another of Gabrielle's eggnogs. It tasted foul in her mouth, but she forced it down.

Baby Jorn suckled her first breast. When she offered him the second one, he refused to take it. She touched the back of her hand to his forehead and his leg. His skin felt a bit warm, but not as hot as Erik's had.

As the afternoon progressed, Anna could barely keep her eyes open. When Gabrielle took her turn at Erik's bedside, Anna reclined on her bed and stared at the ceiling. Sleep enveloped her.

Shrieks pierced Anna's ears. Heat shimmered all around her. Flames rose high into the sky. She ran down the basement steps and snatched Inge from her bed, only inches away from the fire.

"Get the boys," she screamed to Adelaide, as she ran for the steps. Thick black smoke shrouded the basement. Anna focused on the shadow that was the stairway, forcing her heavy feet to stagger in that direction.

Acrid taste dried her mouth and burned her throat. She persisted on toward her only means of escape.

Her weak legs stumbled up the stairs, barely able to propel her daughter and herself out of the burning hell.

They emerged into the outdoors. The fresh air choked her. She set the crying Inge on the ground, and lurched in the direction of the basement's entrance.

"Don't go," Inge wailed. "You'll burn up."

"I have to get your brothers." Anna tried to call, but the words strangled in her throat.

"Let Fader get them."

"He's not here." Anna's heart pounded so hard she could hear its beat in her ears.

Smoke billowed from the doorway Anna took a deep breath and hurled herself into the blackness. Something gripped her elbow and pushed her backward. She lost her footing, but a strong hand kept her from falling.

Anna looked up to see Halvor, carrying Poul in one arm and steadying her with the other. Close behind him, Adelaide followed with Torsten slung over her shoulder.

"Erik! Where is Erik?" Anna whirled around, freeing herself from Halvor's grasp.

She spun in circles, then landed in the nursery. Erik lay on his bed, totally still. She reached over and touched his chest. There was no rise or fall.

Anna startled awake, panting for breath. Tears streaming down her cheeks.

After a few moments, she realized she was not in the nursery. She had been dreaming. Closing her eyes, she said a silent prayer of thanks. She rose and walked to Erik's bedside, to reassure herself that he was still breathing.

"He seems to be resting more easily," Gabrielle whispered.

"Good." Anna couldn't be certain whether he actually was, or if Gabrielle was just trying to reassure her.

The door creaked open. Jorn walked into the kitchen and set a bucket of eggs on the counter. "I'll bring some milk later."

Baby Jorn began fussing in his crib. Anna bent down and picked him up. "He's hungry. Last time I nursed him, he didn't take much milk."

"His routine is upset." Jorn ran his finger along the infant's cheek. "He'll be fine when the household returns to normal."

Anna studied her baby's face. "I hope you're right."

She sat in a parlor chair and brought the baby to her breast.

He suckled for a few moments, then stopped and fussed. He repeated this pattern long after his father had left. He appeared to have taken more milk than the last time he nursed, but still not as much as he usually did.

Refusing to take the nipple any more, he cried softly. Anna swayed side to side in an effort to quiet him. After a long while, he succumbed to sleep.

Her eyelids drifted closed. She forced them open. It was her turn to sit with Erik. After putting Baby Jorn in the cradle, she warmed the last of the morning's milk and poured it into a mug, then went to relieve Gabrielle.

Erik drank half of the milk. Anna smiled. That was the most he had taken at one time since Halvor brought him in from the field.

She gently swabbed Erik's rash-roughened skin, humming hymns and lullabies. Her throat was too sore to sing.

• ♥ •

As dawn broke, Anna awoke feeling as if she were on fire. The bed linens lay in a tangle at the foot of the straw mattress.

"Anna and the baby both have a fever. Please send Halvor for the doctor," Gabrielle's voice sounded far away.

"First thing," Jorn said from the same place. "What about you?"

"I'm fine. I've taken care of scarlet fever patients before, and never gotten sick, but I'm going to need help. Please ask Karyn if she can come, and ask Brigitte if she can spare Mrs. Bixby."

Anna forced her eyes open. Jorn and Gabrielle were at the kitchen door.

"I'll get Karyn. And speak to Brigitte." Jorn poured water into two pots on the bench. "I will get you two more buckets of water before I go." He went outside.

Gabrielle picked up Baby Jorn. He let out a weak cry. "I'm so glad you're awake." She put the baby on the bed beside Anna. "You need to try to feed him."

Jorn set the buckets just inside the door and left without a word.

Anna eased herself upright, and Gabrielle positioned the pillows behind her. Anna's head felt as if the pressure inside might push her eyes out, but she prepared her dress, then reached over and picked up her son.

"He's so hot!" Anna cried, as his tiny mouth met her breast.

"He has a fever." Gabrielle's voice was so quiet that Anna could barely hear her. "So do you. You'll need to stay in bed today."

The baby nursed for a few moments, then stopped. Anna thought he was falling asleep, but he began to suckle again. The nipple slipped out of his mouth. His lips continued to move, although he seemed to be asleep. He needed to eat. She could not recall the last time he ate well. She tried to coax him back to her breast.

"Just as I feared." Gabrielle went to the kitchen and returned to Anna's bed with a cooking pot of water and a cloth. "Swab him with this to cool him. I'll try to give him spoonfuls of the milk I warmed for Erik, and I'll try to get him to take a little cool water."

Water. Good. It would cool… Anna's temples throbbed as she tried to remember who they were talking about. Erik? The baby?

Anna's arms felt heavy. She struggled to move her son onto the mattress beside her and reclined next to him. She rolled onto her side and dipped the cloth into the water, then swabbed the baby. He emitted a pitiful cry as the cool, damp fabric met his skin.

Gabrielle brought a mug of milk, a glass of water, and a spoon. She set the water on the bedside stand.

"How is Erik?" Anna croaked.

"His fever is cooling," Gabrielle said. "I think he'll be fine."

Anna sighed her relief.

"It's little Jorn I'm worried about now." Gabrielle dripped a few drops of milk into the baby's open mouth. His face wrinkled, but he swallowed it.

Caring for the three of them was too much to expect of Gabrielle. Anna must help with her infant. She concentrated on dipping the cloth into the water, squeezing it, and stroking it over her son. She focused on every detail and willed her limbs to do her bidding. She wanted to run the damp fabric over her own arm, over her forehead, but Baby Jorn needed it more.

All the while, Gabrielle spooned liquid into his mouth.

Anna's arm fell to the mattress. She struggled to lift it. Darkness engulfed her.

• ♥ •

"Give her some muriatic acid and honey, like you did Erik," Dr. Wade instructed Gabrielle, handing her a brown bottle. "And give her one grain of quinine four times a day."

"What about my baby?" Anna asked in a hoarse whisper. Baby Jorn needed the doctor more than she did.

"He's too young for the quinine," the doctor said softly. "Mrs. Cook will make a wet pack for him three times a day. And she'll continue trying to feed him broth and eggs mixed with milk."

Dr. Wade and Gabrielle would make Baby Jorn better. Anna lay her heavy head back on the pillow.

"And I'll make some milk punch for you," Gabrielle said as she dipped a cradle sheet into a pot of water. "As soon as I wring this out and get little Jorn wrapped in it."

Dr. Wade stepped toward the kitchen. "Send for me if you need me again."

Anna's world began to spin. She closed her eyes.

• ♥ •

When she awoke later, she felt as if steam from boiling water was burning her face. She was lying on her back. She forced one eyelid open. Karyn Thomsen sat at the bedside, laying a cloth on Anna's cheek. She closed her eye.

The next thing she knew, Gabrielle held a glass of water to her lips.

"Drink this," she said. "Then we'll see if the baby will nurse."

Anna took a sip of the water. It felt cool and soothing in her mouth, but when she tried to swallow, the liquid lit her throat afire.

Gabrielle helped her roll to her side. Someone stroked Anna's back with a cool cloth. She shivered. The baby's hot, tiny mouth touched her nipple. His lips moved, but he did not suckle. Gabrielle changed his position. Still, he did not nurse.

With his bright red face, he didn't look like Baby Jorn. Rash covered his body. Gabrielle laid him on the mattress. He barely moved. So tiny. So still.

Anna tried to ease her nipple between his tiny lips. He hadn't nursed well for a long time, and he needed her milk. Still, he would not take her breast. She reached out to stroke her tiny son's cheek. His skin no longer felt soft and smooth. It was dry and rough.

Tears pooled in Anna's eyes. "He has the scarlet fever."

"Yes," Gabrielle said gently. "And so do you."

This couldn't be real. It was a nightmare Anna would wake from soon. She closed her eyes, and darkness erased her thoughts.

"...need to get Mr. Stryker." Gabrielle's voice reached some corner of Anna's foggy mind.

Moments or hours later, Anna did not know which, the kitchen door creaked open.

"I'm glad you are here. Erik's fever has broken, but Anna's is still raging," Gabrielle said. Her voice seemed closer now. "And I fear the baby may not survive. We haven't been able to cool him, and he doesn't nurse or take milk or water from a spoon."

"No." Anna tried to scream. Did the word came out of her

mouth or just echo inside her head?

A rough-skinned hand touched her forehead. It smoothed her hair back. She struggled to sit up, but she was too weak to even lift her eyelids.

"Anna, you must rest," Jorn whispered. "You must get better, like Erik."

Erik was getting better? Joy welled in Anna. But maybe it was only the wishful dreams of sleep. She forced her eyes open. "The baby is sick."

Jorn's face came into focus as he bent closer to her.

"I know."

"He's sick because Erik got sick." She had trouble finding the words she wanted, but she had to tell Jorn this was his fault. He had almost killed Erik. "Because you made Erik harvest."

His eyes closed. "I'm sorry, Anna."

"Baby must not die." She was losing her words again, then her thoughts as she closed her eyes and drifted back into the darkness.

When she next awoke, Jorn was speaking. "... better to bury him now or wait for Anna to get well?"

"She needs to be part of the burial service or she may never be able to accept his death," Gabrielle said.

Death. Who died? Not Erik. He was getting better. Baby Jorn? No. God, no. He is so little. So helpless. Was she still dreaming?

Opening her eyes, she pushed away the hand swabbing her with the wet cloth. She had to hold her infant. Pressing her leaden arms into the straw mattress, she pushed herself into a half-sitting position. "Give me my baby."

The room swam. She inhaled a long breath.

Jorn hurried to her side. He knelt down next to the bed and brushed tears from her cheeks. "He passed away, Anna. God has taken him to heaven."

"No." Anna sobbed. "I need to hold him. I need to nurse him. To help him get better." She shouldn't have let herself get so sick that she could not take care of her own child.

"He's with God now," Jorn said gently.

"No. He is in his cradle." Anna could not accept her husband's words. "He's a good baby. I want to hold him."

Gabrielle placed Baby Jorn in Anna's arms. He smelled of soap. His skin was cool.

"His fever has broken. He can't be dead." Anna looked into her friend's face.

Gabrielle's dark eyes were red and watery. "I'm sorry, Anna." Her voice cracked. "I did everything I could think of, but it wasn't enough."

"No." Anna shook her head, and the room became blurry. "I should be the one to die, not my sweet baby."

"The rest of your children need their mother," Gabrielle said softly.

So did little Jorn, and Anna was here for him now.

He couldn't be dead. His fever was gone. His eyes were closed. He was still. He was sleeping. The weight of his limp body rested heavily in her arms.

When he awoke, he would be hungry. She would nurse him.

Anna held her tiny son close and swayed back and forth.

Chapter 15

October 30, 1882

We buried little Jorn in the graveyard beside the church. Halvor made a tiny walnut coffin with wood that he had salvaged from a tree cut down for the house. He feared the wood might not be properly cured, but Jorn said it would be fine since it will be covered with dirt anyway. Jorn acts as if our child's death is nothing. He doesn't grieve at all. I hate him.

I still cannot bear the thought of my sweet, little baby lying alone and cold in the earth. It is not fair that one so young and innocent should have to die, while his cruel father still lives. I do not understand how God could do such a thing.

I feel guilty for not being able to properly care for little Jorn while I was so ill, but none of us would have gotten sick if Jorn had not required Erik to work on the harvest. It is Jorn's fault that our son died. I cannot forgive him. I cannot stand to be near him. I can barely look at him. I wish every day that he had died instead of our baby. If only wishing could make it so.

I still feel weak and wretched. I have a hard time interacting with my other children without breaking into tears. They remind me of all the things Baby Jorn will miss. Thankfully, the harvest is nearly finished. Jorn said Erik no longer has to work in the fields. I am grateful for Erik's sake.

Anna lay awake on the fresh straw mattress and clean sheets in the nursery. Through the partially open doorway, she listened as her husband's breathing became slow and even. Sometime later, he began to snore.

She lay on her side and stared out the window into the cold, clear night. Stars twinkled against the black sky. Several times she started to count them, but thoughts of her children sleeping in the basement with Adelaide kept interrupting. Anna wished she could be with them.

She rolled over and stared at the ceiling, tying to clear her mind. Christmas was coming. She needed to get fabric to make gifts for her children.

Anna pulled the quilt up close around her neck to keep out the room's chill. Her eyelids drifted closed. A vision of Baby Jorn—red face, rash covering his body, mouth open, eyes staring straight ahead, motionless—forced her eyes open. A sob clogged her throat.

Even now, two months after they buried her son, Anna could hardly look at the cheerful *Jul* decorations, share in the excitement of lighting the advent candles, or bake the special cookies and pastries that she had made a tradition in their home. Her children deserved better.

• ♥ •

On the day before Christmas Eve, Peder arrived in a windy swirl of fast-falling flakes. Anna had given him money to buy candy and gifts for the children. She couldn't face the task.

"Your order, ma'am." He greeted her with a grin when she opened the kitchen door for him. He carried two large canvas bags. "Where do you want these?"

"In the nursery, on top of the trunks." Anna looked up from peeling potatoes for the evening meal. Adelaide had taken fresh linens to the basement since Anna planned for Peder to sleep in Poul's bed. Poul and Torsten would share the younger boy's bed.

All afternoon, the children had been in the parlor, rehearsing their Christmas pieces for the church program. They taught Torsten one of the other student's lines so he wouldn't be left out when they performed for their uncle.

As soon as Peder emerged from the nursery, they surrounded him, all talking at once and grabbing for his hands to pull him into the parlor for their recital. He laughed and tickled and teased. The children giggled and shouted and hooted. Anna couldn't help but smile. Her children benefited from his joyous interactions with them. Something they rarely shared with their father.

Once dragged into the parlor, Peder called, "Come in here, Anna, and watch the program with me."

"I'm peeling potatoes." She had seen the recital. Why did she have to—

"Anna, come here!"

Her brother was right. They were her children. She loved them. She needed to be with them. She put down her knife and dried her hands, then walked into the parlor.

"Moder, sit," Poul said with a wide grin.

She took the seat he designated.

The children lined up from oldest to youngest in front of the crackling fire. Erik stepped forward. "There was no room in the inn, so Mary and Joseph had to stay in a stable, with only cattle and sheep to keep them warm."

He stepped back and Inge stepped forward. "Three wise men came from the east bringing gifts of gold, frank and cents, and mirth."

Anna slanted a glance at her brother. His jaw was clenched, but he did not smile.

Inge returned to her place in line. Torsten bounced up and down, his feet flat on the floor. "Hurry, Poul. I want my turn."

His older siblings all turned and shushed him.

Poul took a step forward. "And the angels sang him a lullaby."

Anna's throat closed. She hoped angels were singing Baby Jorn a lullaby.

The latch on the kitchen door screeched. She tensed and craned her neck around to see who came in. She relaxed when she saw it was Adelaide. Anna turned back just as Torsten jumped from the line.

"Merry Christmas to all!" he shouted at the top of his voice.

Peder burst into applause, and Anna followed suit.

"Wait for us to bow," Poul said.

Erik spoke in a stern voice. "We can bow while they clap if they don't know to wait."

"Very good. All of you," Peder said.

Anna stood and hugged each child. "I need to finish the potatoes, or we won't eat on time."

When she returned to the kitchen, Adelaide had picked up the knife and was peeling the rest of the potatoes. "Snow is really piling up," she said. "We'll have to go to the basement early tonight, or the drifts will be over Torsten's head."

"I'll clear a path for you," Peder said.

She finished preparing the meal in silence.

After dinner, Adelaide carried the lantern and Jorn led the way, shoveling and stomping down the snow for the children. Anna watched until they turned past the corner of the house, then she rejoined Peder at the table as he drank another cup of coffee.

"I would feel a lot better if I could sleep in the basement with the children," she said. "But Jorn won't let me."

Peder laid a hand on her arm. "Anna, you have to stop blaming him for Baby Jorn's passing. The scarlet fever was not his fault."

"It's not just that," Anna said. "I want to be with my children to know they are safe. I hate having them out of my sight."

"You could move them back into the house."

"I've thought of that, but they love their beds and sleeping in the warm basement." Anna paused. "If Jorn had let the building continue, I could be in the same house with them."

"I can't deny that, but Anna, you must forgive Jorn or you will lose all the happiness you have with him."

Her chest tightened. "There has been little happiness since

he returned from Denmark."

"You have wonderful children, it is the *Jul* season. There is joy all around you if you will just look for it." Peder patted her arm.

"I'll try." She made an effort to smile, but her lips felt stiff.

"I need to get my satchel from the sleigh. Then I'll go to the basement." He stood and walked to the peg where his cloak hung. "Good night."

She didn't want him to go, to leave her alone with her dark thoughts. She got out of the chair and went to hug him. "Good night."

As he opened the door, a pile of snow fell in on the dirt floor. "See you in the morning."

After he left, she felt empty and cold. She had to change how she was thinking and feeling.

She lay down on the marriage bed and drew the quilt around her—she would try to think of things that would bring her joy. Seeing her children happy. They would like a Christmas tree. Tomorrow, she would ask Peder to cut a small pine and, instead of decorating it herself as she usually did, she would ask the children to decorate it.

What else? Having her brother and Miss Parker marry. Peder loved her, and she loved him—Anna could see it in the way she looked at him. Although she understood Miss Parker's reluctance to risk her job by courting openly, Anna could invite them both to dinner several times per month. She would talk to Peder about it tomorrow.

Other things that would bring her joy? Building the house she had planned. Jorn staying home from Denmark in the summer and making a happy family life like Bedstefa and Bedstemor had. Holding Baby Jorn in her arms just once more. She shivered. Those things would never happen. She had to stop thinking about them, hoping for them.

• ♥ •

As the white of winter melted into the green of spring, Anna had settled into a comfortable routine. She and Brigitte were again sharing responsibility for getting the children to and from school. Plans were completed for planting the gardens. The Tuesday meetings were back in their familiar rotation. Anna's routine had returned to normal. The change had happened so gradually that it still frequently caught her off guard.

Rains delayed the planting, giving Jorn more time around the house. Although Anna hadn't yet succeeded in forgiving him, they'd been able to manage a more civil relationship.

One evening, after Adelaide and the children had left for the basement, Anna retreated to the nursery to change into her nightdress. As she pulled it over her head, the hinges of the door squeaked. Quickly, she drew the garment down over her body and clasped the placket tightly together as there was no time to button it closed.

Jorn filled the doorway, his features sharpened by the lamplight. "How long do you plan to keep hiding away in this room every night?"

Anna froze. Her grip on the fabric tightened. She had been dreading this conversation, and praying that it would never come. Her heart pounded.

"It is time for you to return to my bed."

"I sleep better in this room." She choked out the words, suppressing a sob.

Jorn frowned.

Anna willed her trembling fingers to work the top button through its buttonhole.

"You are my wife. You must start behaving as a wife should."

His stern tone carried an implied threat that sent a chill through Anna. She feared he was insinuating that he would impose some consequence if she didn't.

The thought of having marital relations with him repulsed

her. She bit he lower lip.

He held out his hand to her.

She took a reluctant step toward him.

He clasped her by the elbow and led her to the marriage bed.

Cold streams of silent tears ran down her cheeks.

• ♥ •

"Karyn Thomsen asked if I would like to purchase her farm," Jorn said one night in April, as he climbed into bed beside Anna. "She wants her children to continue in school and she's not strong enough to complete the planting alone."

He settled himself next to Anna, laying his arm across her waist.

Her muscles tensed. "Are you going to buy it?"

"Yes. I talked with Morton, and he thinks we have enough men and time to plant half the land in crops. We'll let the rest go to pasture."

"Where will Karyn live?"

"I don't need her house, so she can stay there as long as she wants."

Anna turned to face him. "That's nice of you."

She had not expected him to be so generous with Karyn. Perhaps he was mellowing a bit. Anna hoped she and her children would reap some benefits, too.

They lay in silence for a long while.

"I'm going to town tomorrow," he said. "Is there anything you would like me to bring you?"

She rarely accompanied him to town anymore, sending a list with him, instead. He always purchased everything she asked for, and last week, he had brought her a pretty new vase. The gift had surprised her, and she filled it with a bouquet of forget-me-nots and mertensia.

Since then, she had been mulling over the possibility of asking him for a special gift. She took a breath, drawing in courage with the air. "Could we get a piano?"

Jorn chuckled. "A piano?"

She was encouraged. "Not tomorrow, but sometime in the future. It would be good for the children to learn to play. I could teach them."

"Could you?" He sounded amused.

"I always loved playing the piano and harpsichord when I was growing up. There's not enough room here, but the large room of the basement has enough space." She was glad she had required a cement floor in the plans. They wouldn't have to put such a precious instrument on the cabin's dirt floor.

Jorn stroked her hair. "We can consider it."

That was more than she had dared hope for. She lay quietly in his arms, reveling in thoughts of having music in her household and in the unusually pleasant talk they were having.

He shifted, positioning his arm under her head.

Anna didn't want the conversation to end. "I think Peder will ask Miss Parker to marry him soon."

"It's about time." Jorn stroked her cheek. "He's been fawning over her for well over a year."

"I would wager he proposes to her before you return from Denmark this summer."

Jorn kissed her ear. "You'd be happier if he did it before I left."

"Yes, I would." She pretended to ignore his advances. "When will you be going?"

Jorn sighed. "On May seventh. I have assigned Halvor to help you again. And Kibby can work in your garden when he has time."

Anna blinked. "Can Kibby do that and cook the bunkhouse meals, too?"

"Since he uses produce from the garden, it only makes sense that he grow some of it."

"Thank you for assigning him." She and Halvor would appreciate having another hand to help with the work.

Jorn hugged her closer. "And I'll be home before you know

it. Perhaps we can consider finishing the house you wanted when I get home."

Anna jerked around to look at him. "Oh, Jorn. That would be wonderful!"

• ♥ •

In the following week, Anna's thoughts keep returning the house she had planned. Jorn didn't mention the it again.

Two nights before his scheduled departure, Anna could no longer stand his silence on the topic. As soon as they settled in bed, she asked. "Would you like to see the plans Mr. Dahl drew up for the house?"

"Not now." He reached for her waist and pulled her to him.

She could feel the evidence of his arousal against her hip. "I would like you to look at them before you leave so I know if you plan to make any changes."

He nuzzled his face into her hair. "I'll consider it when I return from Denmark."

An ache began behind her eyes and spread to her temples. She suspected he had just brought up building the house so that she would be more agreeable to having marital relations with him. He might not even remember his words when he got back.

As he lifted the hem of her nightdress and ran his rough hand over her thighs, she clenched her jaw and prepared to submit to his advances.

• ♥ •

After Anna returned from seeing Jorn off at the depot, she pulled Mr. Dahl's drawings from her trunk and studied them. There was little that she wanted to change. She returned them to her trunk, telling herself not to let her hopes rise. Jorn had made no promises.

That night, she moved out of the cabin. Halvor and Kibby, carried her small bed from the nursery to the basement where she shared the room with Inge and Adelaide. How sweet it was to sleep near her children again!

As the season progressed, her produce business grew. Anna resented Jorn's demand that she turn her earnings over to him. Hopefully, he would spend the money on a new house. Maybe he was waiting to see how much she earned this summer before he would consider building, but she couldn't be certain. She kept half of her income in her various hiding places in case he didn't.

She watched Halvor load the last crates of eggs into the back of Gabrielle's wagon, wishing the queasiness in her stomach would subside. When he finished, he helped Anna up into the seat next to Gabrielle. Brigitte sat on the other side.

"There you go, ladies." He grinned. "Looks like you'll have a good day."

"Yes," Anna said. "Is there anything you need me to pick up in town?"

"No. Kibby is going after provisions this afternoon, so he can get the rope I need."

"I guess we're ready." Gabrielle started the team moving.

"Is Peder coming to the program?" Brigitte asked.

"Yes," Anna said. "The children insisted, and he likes to have the excuse to see Miss Parker."

"She signed the contract to teach again next year." Brigitte sighed. "I was hoping Peder would propose to her."

"So was I," Anna admitted. "But he was hurt more deeply than I realized by a woman just after I came to America."

"Lottie Mortensen?"

Anna locked her gaze on Brigitte. "Did you know about that?"

"Both Peder and Jorn confided in Frederik at the time, although I don't think either knew it."

Anna bit back her questions on what each had said about that woman. She needed to change the subject.

"Peder offered to drive Miss Parker back to Marshalltown.

Maybe he'll ask her to marry him then." Anna feared that might be wishful thinking. "And he could speak to her father if she accepts."

"I'm sure she would," Brigitte said. "She loves Peder, but she also loves teaching. It will be hard for her to give it up."

The wagon jolted as the front wheels hit a rut. Sour bile rose in Anna's throat. She inhaled a breath and closed her eyes.

Gabrielle stopped the team. "You might want to check the eggs and unload them until I get the wagon through this. It didn't look so deep."

"I'll get off and you can hand the crates down to me," Brigitte told Anna.

She swallowed, swiped her hand across her face, and opened her eyes.

Gabrielle touched her arm. "Are you all right?"

"I am with child again."

"When did you find out?"

"My cycle was due two weeks ago."

Gabrielle's brow arched. "How do you feel about this?"

Anna sighed. "After Baby Jorn passed, I didn't think I would ever want another baby." She smiled. "But I'm truly pleased."

"Are you going to hand down those crates?" Brigitte called from behind the wagon.

"Would you like me to get them for you?" Gabrielle offered.

"Thank you, but I'm fine now." Anna stood.

Gabrielle took her hand and steadied her as she stepped onto the seat, then down into the box. Anna picked her way through the goods and produce to the crates. One by one, she handed them to Brigitte. When Gabrielle cleared the rut, they restacked the crates and returned to their places on the seat.

"Anna is with child again," Gabrielle told Brigitte with a smile.

"Oh, Anna." Brigitte reached across Gabrielle and grasped Anna's hand.

"I'm happy about it." Anna squeezed Brigitte's fingers. "And this time, Jorn will be home for the delivery."

• ♥ •

The weeks passed pleasantly. In early July, Anna was slicing green beans. Gabrielle filled the jars with them as fast as Anna could prepare them. Other than the sounds of canning, the cabin was still.

Erik had left right after breakfast to ride his pony to the pasture with Halvor so they could check the fences. Adelaide had taken the younger boys outside while she picked vegetables for dinner.

Inge sat at the dining table with pen in hand. "Moder, this *frikadelle* recipe is in Danish. I can't read it."

Gabrielle's gaze flew to her. "Frikade—?"

"Meatballs," Inge translated.

Anna started to recite in Danish the ingredients she knew by heart.

"Ground pork," Inge interrupted in English. She wrote on the page in front of her then looked up. "What next?"

"Are you going to make these meatballs?" Gabrielle asked.

Inge shrugged. "Probably. Someday. But I want to show this to Uncle Peder, so he can tell me if I have all the words spelled right."

"I have learned a great deal about reading and writing English from Peder's reviews of Inge's recipes." Anna smiled at her daughter. "But I am sad that you are not able to read and write Danish."

Perhaps Jorn had been right about Danish School. Anna decided to use both languages in the future when she played school with the children. Their father would be pleased if they could read some of the books Anna had brought with her from Denmark, and even more so if they could write simple notes to him.

• ♥ •

"I want to learn French," Inge said one evening a few days later, when she was drying the dishes. She and Anna had waited until sunset, when the temperature dropped and the cabin was tolerable. Tonight, Anna eagerly anticipated lying in bed in the cool basement. "Will you and Mrs. Cook teach me?"

"*Oui*. That means yes."

Inge rolled her blue eyes. "I know that."

"Then you have a start." Anna grinned. "I would love to teach you. But you'll have to ask Mrs. Cook."

Inge hugged Anna's waist. "Mercy."

"It's pronounced, '*Merci*'."

"*Merci*."

"Bravo." Anna clapped her hands. "Maybe we could do our playschool lessons in French sometimes. And in Danish."

"Oh, Moder. That would be fun!" Inge handed her mother the last pot.

"I'll let this one air dry. Go on over to the basement while there's still enough light to see your way," Anna said. "I'll be along as soon as I finish cleaning the kitchen and get my clothes for tomorrow."

"Yes, Moder." Inge ran off, leaving the door partway open so the evening breeze could continue to cool the house.

Anna dumped the wash water, tidied the room, and then went to the dresser to get a fresh dress and undergarments. She bent down and opened the bottom drawer.

The kitchen door hinges squeaked.

"Did you forget something, Inge?" Anna turned with a smile, but found Mr. Vibbard standing in her house. He had filled out since last summer, somehow seeming taller than she remembered. His greasy hair was stringy, and sweat stained his dirty clothes. Loops of twine were slung over his shoulder.

Anna's hand flew to her mouth as she inhaled a sharp breath. "You startled me." She exhaled. "Is there something you need?"

A wicked grin split his face. He took a step forward. "You."

She straightened her spine and forced herself to meet his gaze, although trepidation pulsed through her. "Get out of my house. Now!"

"That's not very polite," he growled.

Anna backed against the dresser. "Mr. Stryker would be furious if he knew you were here."

"But he doesn't know, does he?" He moved toward her.

"I'll tell him when he comes home next month."

"You do that." He grabbed her arm.

She tried to scream, but her throat constricted and only a pitiful cry came out.

Vibbard twisted her arm painfully behind her, spinning her around so her back was against his chest. A whimper escaped her.

He covered her mouth with his hand. "We can do this easy or hard. It's up to you."

The vile odor of sweat and dirt made her queasy. Breathing just made it worse. She tried to bite his hand, but it was clamped so tightly against her teeth all she could manage was a tiny nip of his flesh.

She shook her head trying to free her mouth. He tightened his grip, his rough hand pinching the soft flesh of her lips. Fear throbbed in her heart, temples, and forehead.

He jerked her toward the bedroom.

Anna tried to dig her heels into the dirt floor. He was too strong. She kicked at his feet and legs, but couldn't gain enough purchase to put force behind her kicks.

He thrust her face down on the bed and released her arm. "A feisty woman. No wonder Stryker likes you."

Anna planted her hands on the straw mattress and tried to push herself off.

He reached under her waist, maneuvered her to the center of the bed and straddled her hips.

She raised her head to scream.

He pushed it deep into the quilt.

Anna swallowed the bile rising in her throat.

He grasped her wrist and tied a length of twine around it, then did the same to the other.

He moved off her. She tried to roll away from him. He clutched her dress and slid her toward him.

Lying on her back now, her mouth was free. She screamed.

He slapped her left cheek so hard her head snapped to the right.

The salty, metallic taste of blood filled her mouth.

His face twisted into a snarl. "Don't try that again or I'll hit you harder."

He straddled her again. Pulling her left arm by the twine, he tied her wrist to the bed. His arousal pressed hard against her stomach. She tried to push him off, but he was too heavy.

Shifting his weight to her right, he tied her other arm to the opposite rail.

Again, she screamed.

He backhanded her mouth.

Once more, she tasted blood. Her lips tightened as they began to swell.

He straightened and unbuttoned his trousers. Then, he tore her cotton housedress open, exposing her to the waist. He stared with greedy eyes.

Tears spilled down her cheeks.

He bent down and suckled her breast. She shuddered in revulsion.

Through his underwear, his manhood stabbed against her abdomen, where new life was growing. She closed her eyes.

Vibbard moved to the other breast.

She opened her eyes.

He reared up, hooked his thumbs in the waist of his trousers, and pulled them down.

A blast stung her ears.

Sticky, damp matter splattered her face, and clogged her nose as she inhaled a sharp breath.

An animal-like sound erupted from Vibbard. His full weight fell forward on top of her.

The pressure on her chest forced the air from her lungs.

She parted her lips for air. Chunks of soft, sickly-sweet matter met her tongue. A metallic taste filled her mouth. She gagged.

The pungent odor overwhelmed her as she fought for breath. Nausea waved through her.

Halvor rushed forward and rolled Vibbard off her. Kibby and another greenhorn appeared.

"Get him out of here!" Halvor shouted to them as he untied her right wrist. "And send someone to fetch Mrs. Cook."

The men grasped Vibbard's feet and dragged him across the floor. Trying to cover herself with her torn dress, she focused on Halvor as he untied her other wrist.

Her body felt like lead. Her skin was sticky. Cold.

Halvor sat beside her, lifted her up, and wrapped her dress and his arms around her.

"Anna, are you all right?" His voice cracked.

She rested her head against his shoulder.

He stroked her hair. "Did he hurt you?"

His voice sounded farther away.

"I realized something was wrong when we saw your lamps still lit." Regret threaded through his words. "I'm sorry I didn't get here sooner."

His voice, and the room, faded away.

• ♥ •

Voices. Familiar voices.

A damp cloth slipped across Anna's forehead.

"Kibby and I had been watching him. He lived in the west cabin, but we saw him lurking around the granaries and barn last week, and again, a couple of nights ago."

It was Halvor's voice.

"We thought he meant to steal something. Never occurred to us he might do anything like this."

The damp cloth glided across her cheek.

"What did you do with the body?" Brigitte sounded very close. Was she the one with the cloth?

"We'll bury him tomorrow in the hay field. The alfalfa will cover the grave real fast."

"Will anyone miss him?"

That was Gabrielle.

"Just Morton Andreasen. Vibbard was a troublemaker. The rest of the men will be glad he's gone," Halvor said.

Vibbard. The vision of his head at her breast flashed in Anna's mind. He had suckled the breasts that had nourished her children.

Nausea waved through her.

He reared up. A shot. Blood everywhere. The weight of his body on her.

Bile rose to the back of her throat.

Halvor must have been the one who shot him.

"Will you tell the marshal?" Brigitte asked.

"Don't plan to." Halvor's voice was resolute. "He had it coming."

"No need to bring the law into this," Gabrielle said.

The damp cloth dabbed at Anna's burning lips. Pain shot across her face. Her eyes popped open. Where was she? In the nursery. Only the oil lamp lit the room. It must still be night.

"She's awake!" Halvor exclaimed.

Her head pounded.

"Anna," Brigitte whispered. "How do you feel?"

Anna's swollen lips made it hard to form words. "Face hurts."

"It's badly bruised." Gabrielle moved to Anna's side. "I brought a poultice for the swelling. Brigitte and I will stay with you tonight."

Anna rested her gaze on Halvor. "Thank you."

She owed him so much. She swallowed.

"He stopped that man." Her chest tightened. She couldn't say the name.

"Before he could—" She couldn't say the word. Revulsion rose in her belly.

Beneath his furrowed brow, Halvor's blue eyes studied her. He patted her arm. "I just wish I'd gotten here sooner."

"Thank you," Anna said again. She couldn't think of anything else to say.

"Now that I know you're all right, I'll go clean up the bedroom." He paused and looked at Gabrielle. "I can scrub down the wall and the bed, but I don't know about that quilt and—"

"I never want to see the bed, the quilt, any of it, ever again," Anna croaked. "Burn it all."

Chapter 16

July 22, 1883

Even though weeks have passed since the attack, this is the first time I have been able to write about it. I was so scared, and now I worry that my fright may have harmed my baby. Erik asked why my face was swollen. I told him I fell against a tree in the dark. I hate lying to my children, but I do not want them to fear the farm hands.

I am trying to convince myself that my attacker was just a rotten apple in the basket of greenhorns. However, I am uneasy around all except Halvor, Kibby, and Morton Andreasen. I spent many days and nights in the basement where I felt safe, but I avoid sleep and the nightmares my memory conjures. Halvor and Kibby carry meals to the basement, and I force myself to eat for the sake of the child I am carrying.

Until the last few days, I have felt numb in my body and my mind. I cannot allow myself to think about what might have happened if Halvor had not arrived when he did. I can never repay him for saving me from a horrible fate, and I have come to appreciate all he has done for me through the years.

I avoid entering the cabin unless it is absolutely necessary. I hate the place and all it represents. Halvor and Kibby burned the bed, the linens, and all that was tainted. I ordered a new bed with the tallest headboard I could find. It should arrive before Jorn gets home. I made new curtains and bought a new lamp in an effort to change the bedroom enough so it will not conjure bad memories when I have to go back there. I cannot bear the thought of moving out of the basement.

Halvor has taken over care of the gardens and orchard. He packs up ripe vegetables, and I take them to Gabrielle's or Brigitte's to can.

Knowing that he is keeping close watch on the house and basement gives me some measure of comfort.

"It's so beautiful," Inge said, as the delivery men lifted the massive oak headboard from the wagon.

"It's so big." Erik watched as the men carried the bed frame inside, one piece at a time.

"Can I sleep in it with you tonight?" Inge asked.

Although the day was warm, a cold shiver rippled through Anna. She could never again sleep comfortably in this cabin. Jorn would have to agree to build a new house if he wanted her to share his bed again. "No, Inge. This bed is for your father. He will sleep in it first."

After the delivery men left, Adelaide served the noon meal in the shade of the oak tree.

"Play school with us after we finish eating, Moder," Poul said.

"Yes, yes," the other children cried.

Anna scanned their faces. "Did you all finish your morning chores?"

"*Ja!*" Torsten said. He was the only one she had helped with his task of scattering cracked corn for the chickens.

"I did mine," Erik said. "But I'll need to feed the orphan lambs before supper."

"We did ours." Inge pointed to Poul and then herself.

"Please don't point," Anna admonished. "Well, since all of your work is done, we can play. Whose turn is it to pick the language?"

"Mine." Inge grinned. "I want French."

Erik and Poul frowned.

Pounding hooves on the road drew Anna's attention. She stood, excused herself, and looked around the corner of the house. The rider was tall, with dark hair flying behind his black, wide-brimmed hat. He slowed his horse as he approached. She didn't recognize him. Her pulse raced.

Was he from the marshal's office? Had someone told the law about Vibbard?

Male voices, Halvor's and the unknown man's, came from the north side of the house. Although her insides quivered, she forced herself to join them.

"Here she is," Halvor said when she stopped in front of them.

"Mrs. Jorn Stryker?" the short, stout stranger asked.

"Yes." She croaked out the word, clasping her hands together to keep them from shaking.

"I'm Martin Hensley." He brushed some dust from his sleeve. "The stationmaster sent me out here with a telegram for you."

Her brow furrowed. "Telegram? Who is it from?"

"Jorn Stryker." Mr. Hensley studied her. "Your husband?"

His scrutiny unnerved her. She inhaled a deep breath.

"Yes." She dropped her gaze to the paper in his hand. "What does it say?"

"You may read it for yourself." He held it toward her.

She took a step backward. "Thank you, but I'm just learning to read English. Please, read it for me."

The man focused on the message. "New York. Have measles. Quarantine for two weeks. Some greenhorns quarantined. One wagon August 10 for men who are not."

Even with the two-week delay, he would still be home earlier than most years. Anna caught Halvor's gaze. He raised one eyebrow, and took the page Mr. Hensley offered.

"Measles!" The children had all suffered through them three summers ago, while Jorn was in Denmark. When she told him of their bout with the illness, he said he never had them. She thought he might have been too young to remember, like Torsten, but he couldn't have gotten them a second time.

Halvor handed her the telegram.

Anna had been counting on Jorn's return on August tenth. She wanted a final answer about building a house so the work could start soon, and they could move in before her baby was born.

Jorn was causing another delay. After all he had put her through and all that had happened while he was away this summer, it was not fair for him to make her wait even longer. She rubbed her aching temples.

She couldn't rely on her husband for anything.

• ♥ •

On August twenty-fourth, Anna and Peder stood on the platform, awaiting her husband's arrival. Halvor was securing the horses and wagon.

Jorn had sent a telegram saying he would return today with the four greenhorns who had been quarantined with him, and with a special surprise for her. Since receiving the wire, her curiosity had nearly swept away all the anger she'd been harboring. She hoped he would surprise her by agreeing to build a new house. Maybe he had purchased something to put in it. She dared not let herself believe it might be a piano.

It was unlike Jorn to give her presents. He hadn't surprised her with a gift since their first *Jul* together, when he had made the cradle. She smiled at the memory.

A boy, who had been sweeping the platform when they arrived, came out of the depot and walked up to Anna. "Are you Mrs. Stryker?"

She smiled at him. "Yes, I am."

"The telegraph operator asked me to fetch you." The boy motioned for her to follow him into the station. "He's receiving a message for you."

"A message?" She stared at him. "My husband is to arrive on the next train."

"Let's go." Peder took her arm and led her inside to the telegraph office. "You can get your wire, and we'll come back here to wait."

The train whistle sounded. Through the window, Anna saw

the engine come into view. Jorn would be here in minutes.

"I'm Mrs. Stryker." Anna clasped her hands together. She glanced back at the platform.

The telegraph operator gazed up at her solemnly, holding a sheet of paper toward her. "I am so sorry, ma'am."

Peder took the note from him. As he skimmed it, his mouth twisted into a grim line and his blue eyes clouded. "Oh, God."

Anna startled. "What does it say?"

"It is from the stationmaster in Burlington." Peder cleared his throat. "Stryker and Blicksen taken off train. Others coming ahead."

"Why?" Anna worried her lower lip.

"Stryker dead. Blicksen taking next train," Peder continued.

Her knees buckled. She grasped Peder's arm for support. "It can't be."

"I'm sorry, Anna," Peder whispered in Danish, hugging her to him.

"There must be some mistake." Pressure built in her temples and behind her eyes.

"Mrs. Stryker." The portly stationmaster stood before her. "I'm sorry for your loss," he said quietly.

She turned to Peder. "Surely, the telegram is wrong. Jorn is too big and strong to die from measles."

He patted her arm. "The authorities in Burlington would know."

A loud screech sounded on the tracks. Anna looked through the open door just as the train came to a stop.

"Your husband had a box locked in the safe on the train." The stationmaster tugged at the collar of his shirt.

"A box?"

"I'll get it for you." He turned on his heel and hurried away.

Anna lost the clack of his footsteps in the conversations and bustle of the crowd of arriving passengers and those waiting to greet them.

Peder led her to an empty spot on the bench beneath the

clock.

"Wait here. I'll tell Halvor to take the greenhorns on home then I'll come back for you." He headed out the door to where the wagons were parked.

Anna nodded, still expecting Jorn and his greenhorns to appear at any minute.

When Peder returned, a middle-aged man with close-cut brown hair and a hooked nose followed him. The stranger carried his hat in his hand.

"Anna, this is Mr. Welker. He was traveling with Jorn," Peder said.

She clasped her hands together tightly in her lap. "What happened to my husband?"

"He had a horrible headache and a high fever," Mr. Welker said softly. "As the train pulled into Burlington, he fell unconscious. A doctor was called, and he ordered Mr. Stryker be taken off the train. Said he thought your husband might have encephalitis. Mr. Blicksen volunteered to stay with him." He swallowed. "I had no idea Mr. Stryker had passed away until your brother told me. I am sorry."

"Thank you," Anna said. Her temples began to throb.

"You can join Mr. Hansen and the others at the wagon, Mr. Welker," Peder said. "He'll take you to the farm."

The man tipped his chin toward Anna and left.

Moments later, the station master returned. He handed a box the size of a flat iron, but much lighter, to Anna. "This was in the safe." he said. "Mr. Stryker also had a trunk. Would you come with me to fetch it, Mr. Jorgesen?"

"Of course," Peder replied.

Anna raised a hand to stop them. "What will happen to my husband?"

"He was taken to the local undertaker," the stationmaster replied. "When the body has been preserved for travel, you'll need to wire the money for his bill. The railroad will ship the body home at no charge." He and Peder headed for the platform.

Body. Anna's mind refused to accept Jorn's death. Unlike Baby Jorn, her husband was big and strong. She couldn't imagine him as cold and stiff—lifeless—as her baby had been.

It was not fair. Without Jorn, she would have to raise their four—soon to be five—children alone. It was not fair to their children. They would grow up without their father. The child she carried inside her would never even know him.

• ♥ •

Peder, Halvor and Morton Andreason carried the coffin into the parlor. Anna shivered as she crossed the threshold behind them. This was the first time she had returned to the cabin since the bed had been delivered.

She had hated this house since she and Jorn had married. She had loathed this house since Vibbard had attacked her. Now, she despised this house for being the last resting place for her husband before the grave.

"Sit down, here," Peder said.

She sank into the chair he indicated. Everything seemed like such an effort.

The undertaker had supplied a low table, assuring Anna that it would be strong enough to support the weight of Jorn and the walnut casket. It creaked as the men carefully centered the coffin on top of it.

She studied the parlor. Adelaide had done a fine job of cleaning and preparing it.

Peder came to her side and slipped an arm around Anna's shoulders. "Are you ready for the lid to be lifted?"

The other two men stood facing the casket, their backs to Anna.

She inhaled a deep breath, and nodded.

"Open it, please," Peder said.

Halvor grasped one end of the lid, and Morton Andreasen gripped the other. Together, they raised the top and eased it to the floor, leaning it against the table legs. They straightened.

Clearing his throat, Halvor turned to face Anna and Peder. His solemn expression betrayed no emotions. "Is there anything more I can do for you, now?"

"Thank you, no," Peder replied. "I appreciate you help, but please leave my sister and me alone for awhile now."

"Should I ask Mrs. Hansen to bring the children, Mr. Jorgesen?" Mr. Andreasen asked.

Anna stiffened. "No. I will ask my brother to fetch them when I am ready."

The farm manager frowned, but said nothing more before following Halvor out of the cabin.

Thankfully, Peder waited until the door closed before them before helping her up and guiding her closer to the coffin. Gooseflesh formed on her skin as she studied her husband's clean-shaven gray face. His skin appeared rough, like canvas. Slightly wilting flowers surrounded his head.

Anna's mouth went dry. Seeing him lying in the satin bed, stiff and still, she finally comprehended that Jorn was dead.

Numb of body and void of emotion, she stared at the remains of the man who had been her husband for nearly a decade.

"Would you like me to leave you alone with him?" Peder asked.

His words startled her back to consciousness of her surroundings.

She inhaled a breath and released her brother's arm. "No, definitely not. I suppose I should have you ask Adelaide to bring the children." She sighed. "I wish they did not have to see him like this, but we won't make them stay any longer than they want to, and we won't make them come back."

"I think that is for the best." He slid an armchair close to Jorn' s head. "Sit down and rest yourself."

Gratefully, Anna collapsed into the chair. "Thank you."

Peder pulled out his pocket watch. "Brigitte and Gabrielle

are going to stop by later this afternoon to help Adelaide get food ready for tomorrow's visitors, and Morton has offered to sit with Jorn's body tonight."

Anna rubbed her temples. "That is nice of them. I don't wish to spend any more time in this cabin than I have to."

Peder patted her shoulder. "I'll get the children."

Anna gazed at Jorn's lifeless face, then out the window

Poor Jorn would never see his sons grow up or give his daughter's hand in marriage. He wouldn't be the one to pass the farm on to his boys. Anna was sad for all he would miss, but she couldn't cry for him. She couldn't cry for herself. She couldn't even cry for the life she had dreamed of having with him, but never did.

She sighed. Although she had told the children several times that their father had died, they had not understood the full meaning of death. The younger boys might not, even after seeing their father's body. But Erik and Inge would. Anna wondered how they would react.

At the sound of her children's voices, Anna rose and walked to the back door.

She held it open until everyone was inside, then closed it behind them.

Adelaide carried Torsten in her arms. Poul held Peder's hand. Inge and Erik trudged slowly toward the coffin. Anna put an arm around the shoulders of each of her older children.

"Shhh," whispered Torsten. "Fader is sleeping."

"No, Torsten," Anna said gently. "He has passed away. His soul has gone to be with the angels."

Inge sniffed. "Like Baby Jorn."

"No." Torsten shook his head vigorously. "Fader, wake up," he shouted. "Wake up, Fader."

He slapped his hand on the edge of the coffin. Anna and the other three children jumped at the sound.

Peder snagged Torsten's hand and turned to Adelaide. "I think it best that you take him back to the basement."

"Yes, sir." Adelaide hurried out the back door as Torsten started to cry.

Erik, his mouth in a tight, thin line, scrutinized Jorn's face. "I'm glad he's dead. Now, I can go to school instead of helping with the harvest."

Inge stepped forward and looked at her brother. "That's not very nice."

"Baby Jorn is dead because Fader made me work with Mr. Swane." He lifted his chin.

Inge broke into sobs.

Anna considered whether she should chastise Erik for his disrespectful comment, but she couldn't bring herself to do it.

Poul lifted his face to Peder. "Can I touch him?"

Anna cringed.

Peder glanced at her. She nodded.

"Yes."

Tentatively, Poul reached out and touched a finger to Jorn's face. After a few moments, he withdrew his hand.

"He's cold and hard." Surprise laced his tone.

Peder stroked his hair.

"That's what happens when the soul goes to be with God," Anna said softly. "It leaves the body behind."

Tears streamed down Inge's cheeks. "Is Fader with Baby Jorn, now?"

Anna hugged her closer. "I think so."

Erik pulled away. "Can I go now?"

"Yes." Anna nodded. "You may all leave whenever you are ready."

Abruptly, Erik spun around and ran out the back door.

Poul tugged Peder toward the front door. "Let's go."

Inge, her body quaking with sobs, nestled closer to Anna.

• ♥ •

Lying awake in her bed later that night, Anna's sadness gave way to anger. Jorn had promised her a surprise—the expensive necklace that lay in her dresser drawer unworn. It was nothing she had hoped for. Had he meant it to placate her when he once again refused to build a proper house?

Equally unexpected and more difficult to accept, he had left her alone to raise the children. He had left her alone to run the farm—something she knew little about, and Morton Andreasen had made it clear every summer that he would not take direction from her.

• ♥ •

Throughout the next afternoon, neighbors called to pay their respects. Gabrielle, Brigitte, and Miss Parker had brought enough pastries to feed the visitors, and many of them had brought food, too. There would be more for tomorrow's funeral feast. People would have to eat outside. Hopefully the weather would cooperate.

By evening, greeting guests and accepting sympathies had worn Anna out. She had directed Adelaide to keep the children away from the cabin. They had all been too agitated by seeing their father's body to sleep well. Anna hadn't slept at all.

She sat in the armchair, gazing at Jorn's body. He could no longer divorce her and take the children. He could no longer threaten to move the family back to Denmark. He could no longer require Erik to miss school to work on the farm.

A new energy pulsed through Anna. She could run her business, even expand it, without having to hide its success. She could avoid moving back into this old cabin. She could live wherever she wanted and, from now on, she would.

"I talked with Jorn's attorney today."

Anna startled. "Oh, Peder."

"Since I'm executor of Jorn's will, I asked if anyone besides you and I need to be present at the reading." He sat in Jorn's chair. "He said no. Everything was left to you. Apparently, there is a life insurance policy with you as beneficiary. I can bring him out here next week."

"An insurance policy?"

"He didn't tell you about it?"

Anna frowned. "No."

"The attorney will explain it."

Anna thought for a moment. "Is there any hurry about reading the will?"

"Just that the property needs to be conveyed to you and a claim filed with the insurance company."

"Perhaps when we take the squash, apples, and eggs to town next week."

Peder raised an eyebrow. "While you are in mourning? You could send Halvor."

Anna lifted her chin. "I shall wear black. But if it would embarrass you, I could have Brigitte and Gabrielle leave me at your house and make deliveries for me."

"If you do that, I'll ask the attorney to meet us there."

"I'll speak with them tomorrow when they come to help Adelaide prepare the meal."

Peder stood. "I'll walk you to the basement if you are ready to leave him."

Anna cast her gaze toward Jorn as she rose from the chair.

"Halvor said he would stay with the body tonight," Peder said.

"That's very kind of him." She turned toward the door. "I don't wish to spend any more time in this cabin than I have to. And after tomorrow, I hope never to return to it."

Peder's eyes widened. "Are you thinking of moving to town?"

"No. I'm planning to finish my house," Anna said firmly. "I would like you to meet with Mr. Dahl and arrange for him to finish building it according to the original plan."

"Are you certain you want to remain out here in the country alone?"

"Yes." Anna had not considered any other option. She liked being close to Gabrielle and Brigitte, and having her own business. "I'm not alone. I have the children and Adelaide. Halvor and the greenhorns are here. But I'll need you to teach me how to run the farm and keep the ledgers. I will not rely on Morton Andreasen."

"Perhaps you should hire an accountant."

"That isn't necessary. I can learn what I need to know. I already do simple bookkeeping for my produce business." She lifted her eyes heavenward to where she was certain Jorn now dwelt. "I want to take care of my husband's legacy."

• ♥ •

Pastor Spellman presided at the funeral and Jorn's burial in the church cemetery beside Baby Jorn.

The next day, Anna tried to return her family to its familiar routines. Adelaide moved to the cabin, giving Anna and Inge more space. At Anna's request. Halvor and Peder had moved her dresser to her basement bedroom.

Halvor picked the ripe vegetables and crated the eggs, which Anna sold on her trip to Cedar Falls with Gabrielle and Brigitte.

Jorn's attorney was unable to meet with Anna while she was in town so, a week later, Peder arrived at the basement with him.

Halvor had moved the rocker, the two parlor chairs, and the table into one corner of the big center room of the basement, but Anna invited her guests to sit the kitchen table and chairs that he and Kibby had moved to another corner.

The lawyer took several sheets of paper from his portfolio. "Your husband's will is short, Mrs. Stryker. He has stipulated that all his worldly possessions be left to you."

Anna listened carefully as the lamplight cast wavering shadows on the older man's sharply planed face.

"He asked that you not sell the full section of land. He wanted it kept intact as a legacy to your children." He paused.

"If you need money, he said you could sell the farm across the road and the Thomsen property."

Anna cleared her throat. "Are these wishes of his binding?"

The attorney frowned. "No. Once the properties are conveyed to you, you can do whatever you see fit."

"At this time, I do not intend to sell any of the land," she said.

"I will start transferring the holdings to your name tomorrow." The attorney handed Peder the will.

"Please explain to my sister the terms of the insurance policy," Peder said.

The lawyer turned to Anna. "Mr. Stryker had prepared for the possibility that he might pass on before you. The spring after you married, he purchased a life insurance policy with you as the only beneficiary. It is for seven thousand five hundred dollars."

Anna clasped her hands together. "Go on."

"You may draw the money now if you need it, or you can have the insurance company invest it for the future."

"Or you can convert it to gold bars," Peder said. "That's what Bedstefa would recommend."

"Did my husband leave any debts?" Anna asked.

"Only his accounts at the local stores," Peder replied. "I'll pay those off and convert them to your name."

"Thank you." She turned to the lawyer. "I'll take one thousand, five hundred in cash, to be put into my bank account. The rest I would like in gold."

The lawyer's bushy eyebrow knitted together.

"That sounds like a good choice to me," Peder said.

The lawyer gathered up the papers, then stood. "Thank you, Mrs. Stryker. I'm sorry to bother you at this difficult time."

"It will be good to have these matters settled, sir."

She showed him to the door then returned to the table where Peder still sat.

"I have brought the farm records for you to look over." She

lifted the ledger from the extra chair. "We'll need to plan how to proceed, as we can't afford to give hired man's pay to every greenhorn who works off his debt."

"He had a large group this year." Peder pulled the lamp closer and opened the book.

"Seven. Their terms of service range from one to three years."

They spent the rest of the morning and most of the afternoon reviewing books and discussing options.

"You seem to be handling your grief quite well," Peder said when they paused for the coffee and cake Adelaide brought from the house.

"I still can't believe he's dead," Anna admitted. "I know we buried him, but to me it feels like he's still in Denmark. That he will return home someday in the future."

"That might be better for now. It will allow you to take on the responsibility for running the farm and for getting your house built." Peder patted her arm. "Just don't get so busy that you forget to grieve."

"I didn't even have a chance to talk with him." Anna folded her hands on the stack of greenhorn contracts. "Perhaps when the house is finished and we move in, it will seem empty without him."

"Are you and the children going to move back to the cabin while your house is built?"

"No. I'm hoping we can stay here for most of the building, but if necessary, the south cabin is empty. We could use it."

Peder raised a brow. "That place is very small for five people. And that doesn't count Adelaide. You're welcome to stay with me."

"Thank you, but that would be too far to take the children to school, and besides," Anna picked up the stack of contracts. "I need to stay here at the farm if I'm going to run it."

"You're probably right."

"I'll to speak to the men after their evening meal." Anna

said. "Please let everyone know."

Peder nodded. "I'll tell them before I leave for town."

"Would you come? I don't want you to speak for me, but I would like you to be there for moral support. Mr. Andreasen can be very antagonistic."

"Of course." Peder's blue eyes twinkled. "But he may have met his match in you."

"Let's talk about something more pleasant." Anna smiled. "Did you ask Charlotte's father for her hand in marriage? Life is too short to shilly-shally around."

Peder burst out laughing. "Yes. We have agreed to marry next summer." His angular face softened with his smile. "She wants to teach one last year. And she plans to see if the Normal School might allow her to lecture when she is married."

"By your wedding, my year of mourning will be nearly up," Anna said. "Will you wed in Cedar Falls or Marshalltown?"

"Marshalltown, at her parent's house," he replied. "Perhaps you and the children can all come down on the train."

"They would love that." Anna sighed. "And so would I."

"My brother, Mr. Jorgesen, and I have reviewed all of the current contracts, pay rates, and the books." Anna stood behind the table at the front of the bunkhouse dining hall, the scent of sausage and beans still heavy in the air. Peder sat at one end, with the stack of greenhorn contracts before him.

She spoke in Danish so all of the greenhorns and hired men would understand. "Based on our findings, we have decided to butcher additional hogs and cattle this fall and winter so we can sell the meat in town."

A rumble of muttering swept through the room.

"In the spring, we will fence off six pastures, mostly along the creek so we don't have to carry water to the cattle, sheep, and hogs. Next summer, we will build a barn near the north house, so the hogs can winter there. Over the coming year, a concerted effort will be made to increase the size of all three herds, and to improve the quality of the animals so we can not only sell meat, but also breeding stock."

"That is balderdash," Morton Andreasen snarled, his mouth nearly hidden by a bush of brown whiskers. "We have all the livestock we need. It will take too much money to secure purebred breeding stock."

Her chest tightened. She clasped her hands together, and scanned the faces of the other men in the room. Halvor sat at the second table back on the left. He was watching her intently. She returned her attention to the room as a whole. "I believe the investment will be worth it."

Andreasen snickered. "What do you know about farming?"

Anna swallowed back the bile rising in her throat. "I grew up on a dairy farm. My brother worked with my father to improve the quality of the herd. It was a financial success."

"This is not a dairy farm." He smirked.

"The same principles apply. And if you wish to remain in this meeting, please hold your tongue until I am finished." She turned her attention to the rest of the greenhorns. "Now, for the fields. We will continue to plant corn, wheat, and oats. This fall's harvest will proceed as usual. Next year, the crops will be planted in different fields. We'll plant additional hay for feeding the stock next winter and additional oats for straw, as well as the grain. This will mean we'll have to plow up some ground that has heretofore been unused."

Andreasen stood and pointed to Peder. "You going to let that woman get by with this?"

Her brother shrugged, sat back in his chair, and grinned. "It is her land, she can do whatever she wants. I think her plan is a good one."

Crimson colored the visible patches of Andreasen's pock-marked face. "Well, I for one, refuse to take my orders from a woman."

Anna's insides quivered. She fought to maintain a calm, but

forceful, demeanor.

"Then you can get your belongings together and leave my farm." Anna kept her voice low and even. "I will pay you through the end of the week."

"Are you men willing to work for this strumpet?" Andreasen bellowed. "Her husband has not been dead even three weeks. Not only is she not mourning for him, she is already changing around everything he has done."

Her whole body tightened.

"Mr. Andreasen." She spoke in a loud voice, but refrained from shouting. "You no longer work on this farm. You are excused. Please leave now."

Peder stood. His smile had vanished, and his face was grim.

The former farm manager stalked out and slammed the door behind him.

Anna drew in a deep breath. The men had fallen silent.

"If any others of you can't abide taking direction from me, please stay after the meeting and we'll discuss either your contractual obligation to my husband, which has now reverted to me, or your final paycheck if you have hired on to work here."

No one said a word.

Peder sat back down.

"It appears we will need to make some personnel changes." She gazed directly at Halvor. "Mr. Hansen, do you plan to continue on or leave?"

He stood. "I will stay."

Tension drained from her muscles. "Since you have apprenticed with Mr. Andreasen, you will be the new farm manager, if you agree to accept the position."

"I would be honored." Halvor's blue eyes glowed. "Thank you, Mrs. Stryker."

"Good. I'll meet with you in the morning. We'll discuss assignments and living arrangements for you and the rest of the men." She turned to her whole audience. "Thank you all for your attention. All who are staying are free to go. Those who are not, please remain and I will discuss your circumstance with each of you."

One by one, all of the men filed out of the room. She turned to Peder in surprise. "I thought at least a few of them would want to leave."

Peder took her elbow. "The men like Halvor," he said as they headed toward the door. "They respect him enough to work for him as manager."

"I just hope our plan for the farm will be a success," Anna said. "I want the men to respect me, too."

Peder smiled. "I think you just took a firm step in that direction."

Chapter 17

October 21, 1883

The harvest has been bountiful. Halvor is embracing his new position with such zeal that all of the men seem inspired by him. The cattle and hogs to be sold for meat are fattening up in the barn. Most of the men take their meals in the bunkhouse, so I will give them money instead of meat for their Jul gift. Most of them could do with some new warm clothes, and I cannot possibly sew for all of them.

My children and I will soon have a fine, warm home. I hope we can move in before the first snow falls. Thank God Jorn did not destroy the basement. Mr. Dahl and his workers started nearly where they left off. Jorn would have hated this house—too big, too fancy— but it has plenty of room for my children, Adelaide, and a possible maid. The roof is nearly nearly complete, as are the walls, which have been painted in the creamy color I chose. Mr. Dahl and the craftsmen will work on the inside through the winter. In the spring, they will come back and apply the dark brown and dark greenish-blue to the trim. It will be perfect!

Erik and Inge are enjoying their school year. Inge was skipped ahead one grade. Erik is applying himself to his studies, hoping to skip a grade, too, so they would no longer be in the same class. He is happy he does not have to work the fields this year.

I look forward to the Jul season and to delivering my baby soon after. The new house, new year, and new child will give our family fresh start.

The bare trees stood stark against the gray sky as the chill of late October set in. Anna hated this time of year. Cold and snow would soon follow. Anna studied the façade of her new house.

Two tall chimneys stood majestically above the highest peaks of the roof. A shorter one was positioned at the end of the kitchen wing. Trim at the roofline, windows, and doors, emphasized the Italianate style of the two-story house. Bay windows in the parlor gave the side facade a dash of drama that rivaled the huge wrap-around front porch. A smaller, but equally ornate, porch that ran the length of the kitchen wing would provide the perfect play area for her children and their friends while Anna and her friends visited on the front porch on warm summer days.

Anna had made only two changes to her original plan. One was to include a bathroom, with a water closet, sink, and tub for bathing. Peder had seen one in Chicago when he traveled there to sell his beer to hotels and restaurants. He came back with several contracts and a stack of papers, drawings, and a photograph of an indoor privy, which had been installed in a home by the plumber advertising the fixtures.

Since Mr. Dahl wasn't familiar with the plumbing or septic tank these new inventions required, Peder arranged for the Chicago plumber to bring Anna's chosen fixtures on the train and install the system. When he returned to Chicago, he would deliver the kegs of beer and distilled spirits Peder had sold.

He had also convinced Anna to install a modern coal burner in the basement. It was supposed to heat air, and that warmed air would rise through a system of ducts and grates in the floors. Hopefully it would work as he described, but she had left the fireplaces in the plans, just in case.

The furnace had been installed in the boys' room in the basement. A window was converted into a chute, allowing for shoveling coal directly into the bin. They wouldn't fire up the burner until enough of the house was completed to allow the whole family to move upstairs.

"This big room is all mine?" Inge stared at the space, then

skipped across the floor and looked out the window.

"Yes." Anna cherished her daughter's pleasure. "But if the baby is a girl, you'll have to share when she's older." She didn't mention that she was hoping for another daughter.

Inge's angelic face beaming, she turned and met Anna's gaze. "I wouldn't mind sharing with a sister."

Erik had a room of his own, too. He needed some privacy in which to deal with his father's death. He didn't often show his feelings about it, but when he did, he alternated between satisfaction and hostility. The intensity of both troubled Anna.

Poul and Torsten would share, but there was an extra bedroom for Poul when he was older. If Anna's unborn child was a boy, Torsten would have to share when the baby was older, unless he wanted to move into the little storage room at the end of the hall. But that would be several years away, so there was no need to worry about it now.

Mr. Dahl promised to finish the kitchen first so Adelaide wouldn't have to prepare meals in the cabin and carry them to the house. Meanwhile, the Chicago plumber would work on the indoor privy.

For now, the boys' beds were crowded into the same basement room with Anna's and Inge's. Adelaide moved into Anna's old cabin with Halvor, and just came to the house during the day.

Frost killed the remaining plants in the gardens. Halvor cleared the debris and mulched the area with straw. After their last delivery of garden produce for the season, Brigitte, Anna, and Gabrielle stopped at the Cedar Falls post office for their mail before leaving for home.

Anna received a letter from Bedstefa. There was also an envelope addressed to Jorn in that same feminine hand she had seen several times before on envelopes from the Rasmussen girl.

"Oh, goodness," she exclaimed when she saw the writing. "I forgot to send word to the Rasmussens about Jorn's passing. He always took care of the correspondence with them. I don't know if I have their address since it isn't written on the envelope. And I didn't see a contract with them among Jorn's papers."

"Maybe you can get it from Frode," Gabrielle suggested. "She's his sister, isn't she?"

"Yes." Anna agreed. "I'll ask Peder to get it."

They climbed into the wagon, and Gabrielle headed the team out of town. Brigitte and Anna opened their letters, as they always did when they weren't driving.

Bedstefa had begun writing individual letters to each of the children in addition to a longer one to Anna. She would save the mail from him, and tonight they would open them all together and read them aloud.

She opened the letter from the Rasmussen girl, wondering if they were asking Jorn for another in increase his payments to them.

My dear Husband,

I was dismayed to learn you had taken ill and hope you have fully recovered from your measles by now.

Anna looked at the envelope. It had been addressed only to Jorn. She re-read the lines to be certain she had not missed something.

As you requested in your telegram, I waited to write to be sure you would be there to receive my letter. As always when you are not here, I miss you sorely. Your girls are both thriving, although Anesa is old enough now that she feels your absence.

We talk about you every night before bed and include you in our prayers. Karoline is learning new words each day and she chatters to herself constantly.

Anna's stomach clenched. The words blurred as she scanned a page of news about Silge's parents, their farm, and people Anna had never heard of.

In September, I discovered I am again carrying your child. If you return early in May, you might be here for the birthing. This time, I feel strongly in my heart that we will have the baby boy you want so much.

Dizzy, Anna laid a hand on her forehead.

We look forward to your return next spring and hope the months between will pass quickly.

Your loving wife,

Silge

Wife? And she called him husband. She knew about Jorn's measles. Confusion swamped Anna.

Maybe this letter was meant for one of the greenhorns who had crossed with Jorn. Several of them had been quarantined, too.

She glanced again at the greeting. Husband. Did they pretend marriage? Jorn had proved himself a rogue by courting Lottie Mortensen after he had bedded Anna. But he'd given that up after they wed. Or had he? Anna's chest felt ready to explode as she suppressed the scream rising from deep within her.

It would be an unlikely coincidence if this woman's husband had the measles this fall and that she would see him only in the summer. That would make Jorn a bigamist, with bastard children. A terrible sin.

There had to be a mistake. Anna skimmed the words again.

Anna refused to accept that her life with her husband had been a lie.

"What is it, Anna?" Gabrielle asked. "You're pale as a bleached flour sack."

Torn between sharing her quandary with her best friends and protecting her husband's honor, she decided to keep the letter to herself until she had more information. "My stomach is a bit queasy."

It was true.

Gabrielle put her arm around Anna's shoulder. "Today's trip has been too much for you. Rest when you get home."

• ♥ •

Anna paced aimlessly through the house. She could not accept that her husband had been a bigamist. She read the letter again and again, then wrote to Bedstefa, asking him if he knew anything about Jorn being married in Denmark. If her grandfather had no information about the subject, she asked that he try to find out if it was true.

After dropping off the Holden children and her own at the school the next morning, Anna proceeded to town. As Cedar Falls came into view, Anna worked out a plan. First, she would show Silge's letter to Peder, and ask him what he thought. Then she would talk with Frode.

Anna posted her letter to Bedstefa, and proceeded to the brewery. Peder and a man she didn't recognize were loading kegs into a wagon.

"Did you want to take the jug of distilled spirits with you, Mr. Jorgesen?" the stranger asked.

"I'll take two of them." Peder looked up and waved to Anna. "I'll offer samples on this trip and take orders for the next one." He hoisted the keg in his hands up to the stranger, then walked to Anna's horses and tied them to the hitching post.

"To what do I owe this pleasure?" He grinned as he reached up to help her off the wagon.

"I need to talk with you privately." She frowned.

Peder's smile vanished. He led her into the building and to his office.

She pulled the letter from her reticule and held it out to him. "This came yesterday."

His blond brows knit together. He unfolded the paper and scanned it. "Jorn and Silge?" His mouth dropped open. His wide-eyed gaze met Anna's. "That harlot. That scalawag. How could this be?"

"That's what I'm here to find out. I have to speak with Frode."

"He's in the brewery." Peder stood. "I'll bring him down here."

While he went to fetch Frode, Anna reread the letter, even though she had committed the words to memory.

"Good day, Mrs. Stryker," Frode greeted her as he arrived with Peder.

"Thank you, but it's not, Mr. Rasmussen." Anna studied his brown-whiskered face, as Peder indicated the chair he had earlier vacated. "I'm here to ask what you know of your sister, Silge, and my husband."

Frode's brow creased. "I don't know what you mean."

"Did they spend a great deal of time together when he gathered greenhorns at your farm?"

"The first year they hardly spoke, but he told me he admired Silge's courage in fetching Mrs. Hansen from the occupied area." He paused, tugging on his chin-whiskers. His hazel gaze shifted toward the window, then back to Anna. "The second year, when I crossed with him, my mother was ill, so Silge took over the cooking and housework. As far as I know, they saw each other only at meals. Why do you ask?"

"Has she or your mother written you about Jorn?"

"No. They didn't want me to leave, as I have no brothers to carry on the farm. My father threatened to leave it to Silge if I went to America." He shifted in his chair. "I told him to go ahead."

"His family hasn't written to him since he's been here, Anna," Peder said.

"I got one letter the first *Jul*," Frode corrected. "My mother asked if I planned to return when I made my fortune." His mouth tightened into a thin line. "I make more money than I did on the farm or in Velje, but I'm not rich. And I have no desire to go back. I sent that message and have not heard from my family since."

Anna sighed. "I would like to have your sister's address."

"What for?"

"Show him the letter, Anna," Peder said. "It reflects as badly on the honor of his family as it does on ours."

Anna held out the missive.

Frode stared at it for a long time. His round cheeks paled. Lifting his gaze to Anna, he held up the paper in his trembling hand. "My sister and your husband." Disgust chilled his words. "They have children together. Bastards."

Anna rubbed her aching temples. "You didn't know, either."

His lip curled. "He must have duped her. Not told her about you."

"That's why I must write your sister. There are things—"

"We would both be better off forgetting this." Frode folded the letter and started to tear it in half. "It will make us crazy to think of their sinful behavior."

"No!" Anna grabbed his hands. "Give that to me. I cannot forget, and I need to verify that her writings are true."

"Don't torture yourself," he said softly.

"There are things I need to know." Anna swallowed. "And it's only fair that I advise your family of Jorn's death. He will no longer pay for the use of their farm."

Frode looked in Peder's direction. He nodded. Frode held out the letter and Anna took it from him.

"I need the address," Anna said.

Peder handed Frode a pencil and fresh sheet of paper. He wrote the address, then stood.

"Thank you. I'm sorry to have upset you." Anna picked up the page. "Is there anything you wish me to tell your sister?"

"Nothing." Frode spit out the word. "I'm sorry Silge was involved with your husband." He walked out of the office.

Anna turned to Peder. "He didn't know."

He laid his hand on her shoulder. "You're the one I'm worried about."

"I just cannot accept that Jorn would do such a thing." She blinked back tears.

"You must write and tell her of your marriage to Jorn before he ever knew her."

"I can't believe she didn't know he was married to me." She spat out the words. "But then, I didn't know he had wed her."

Anna hated Jorn. She hated Silge Rasmussen, too.

The thought of the two of them together sickened her.

• ♥ •

Dear Miss Rasmussen,

I read your letter to my husband with great astonishment. Jorn and I have been married for nine years, so you can imagine my shock when you indicated he has fathered your children and that you called him husband. I do not know what kind of game you are playing, but it is a cruel ruse since I am now in mourning.

I ask you to advise your parents that the use of their place is no longer required. It is with great sadness that I must inform you that my husband passed away on his trip home.

I beseech you to explain yourself by return post. You claim to have two children with my husband and to be carrying another. Jorn spent only a few months in Denmark each year. How do you know they are his? Could not another man be their father?

And even if he did impregnate you, why do you claim marriage? Jorn and I were wed before the first time he collected greenhorns at your parents' farm.

With my grief still so fresh, I must implore you to tell me the truth about my late husband.

Mrs. Jorn Stryker

Anna had come to accept the possibility her husband had betrayed her, but she couldn't admit it in writing. She was not pleased with what she had written. It made her sound like a hysterical schoolgirl.

On her next trip to town, she mailed the letter before she lost her nerve. Her part was done. Now weeks, maybe months, would pass before she received an explanation.

• ♥ •

Progress on the house continued at a steady pace. The bathroom fixtures were in place and plumbed into the septic tank, so Adelaide, Anna, and the children no longer had to go outdoors to the privy. It was, however, a climb of two flights of stairs from the basement to reach the indoor convenience. The second-floor bedrooms weren't completed, but Anna decided the beds should be moved into the new spaces, since the coal furnace was now operating and the crowded conditions in the cellar fostered short tempers among the children.

Adelaide was thrilled the kitchen was nearly ready. Anna ordered a new, larger cookstove, which was to be delivered just before the start of the *Jul* season, and an ice box that would arrive later.

Thankfully, many details regarding the house and farm needed her attention. They kept her from dwelling on Jorn and Silge, but at night, alone in her large, private bedroom, she couldn't help stewing over the possibility of Jorn's infidelity. There had to be another explanation. She would just have to wait for answers to her letters.

Night also brought visions of Vibbard above her on the bed in the cabin. She owed Halvor more than she could ever repay for saving her from a terrible fate, one from which she could not have recovered.

Darkness also carried memories of Baby Jorn. Even with the new life inside her, she couldn't help weeping for her little angel.

Sometimes, loneliness overtook her, and she missed Jorn's company and the security she felt when he was home. At other times, she railed against all those summers he had left her behind. All those years she had given to him, only to find their marriage was a sham.

She despised the thought he had might have bedded another woman, and struggled to push away the feeling that Jorn had fouled Anna's body with his deceitful touch.

• ♥ •

True to his word, Mr. Dahl finished the downstairs interiors before *Juleaften*. Although the rugs and some of the furnishings had not yet arrived, Anna made do with what she had.

The joy of the *Jul* season infected her and the children. They decorated the sitting room with child-made red-and-white woven hearts, Christmas-themed artwork, and a sense of great responsibility, proud that Anna had invited them to help. The colors clashed with the melon-pinks, wheat-yellows, and dark greenish-blues of the floral wallpaper above the oak chair rail, but Anna didn't care. Evergreen swags adorned the oak mantel. Many candles added warmth and light beyond that provided by the kerosene lamps.

The sofas and chairs for the parlor had not yet arrived. Anna had the sitting-room furniture placed there. She furnished the sitting room with the worn wing-backed chairs from the cabin, Anna's rocker, and the couch she had purchased for the unused maid's quarters.

Halvor drove the Strykers to visit the Holdens, Cooks, Thomsens, and neighbors they knew from church. Those families stopped by Anna's house to share kringle, fruit strips, coffee cakes, and other sweets she and Adelaide kept on hand for callers during the holiday season.

Before leaving for the afternoon Christmas Eve service, Anna and Inge set the mahogany dining room table with their new china. A blue, turquoise, and green bouquet in the center of each plate was circled first by a blue-vine swag then by a gold filigree ring at the rim.

Inge stood back and studied the scene. Excitement flickered in her bright blue eyes. "The table is beautiful, Moder."

Anna moved to her side and hugged her. "It is. Thank you for your help."

Everything looked just as Anna had planned when she picked out the décor and china. The colors in the dishes matched the colors in the wallpaper. The ornately carved sideboard had a recessed mirror that reflected the chandelier's light, and a marble counter to hold the serving bowls and platters. Despite the beautiful trappings, what made Anna happiest was having a place to be together with her family and friends, all in the same room, at the table together.

"Halvor helped me put the goose into the oven," Adelaide said from the doorway. "And the potatoes are boiled."

Anna smiled. "Thanks. I'll caramelize half of them when we get home from church. The rest we'll have with gravy."

The rice pudding and cucumber salad were ready. At the last minute, they would heat the red cabbage they had canned last summer. Peder had brought plenty of wine.

When they returned home after the Christmas Eve service, the Cooks were already there. The Holdens arrived soon after.

With everyone gathered around the table, Peder stood at the end opposite Anna. He held up his glass of wine. "To the birth of our Lord, Jesus, to good friends, to beloved family. A *glaedelig Jul* to all."

Throughout the feasting, dancing around the Christmas tree, opening gifts, and the coffee, cookies, and cake afterward, Anna rejoiced. It was good to be in America with the people who meant the most to her.

She thanked God that Jorn had not moved her and the children back to Denmark.

• ♥ •

The last week of January, Anna's feet and legs swelled and her back ached. She took to bed to await the birth of her child. Even though she loved her large bedroom, with its Morris-designed Chrysanthemum wallpaper, she was tired of reading books, and bored with the blue, green, and cream colors surrounding her. Frequent visits from her children made the days bearable.

She welcomed Peder when he came to pick up the children

for worship service on Sunday. As he had done throughout the winter, he brought her mail and a copy of Wednesday's *Dannevirke*. She laid the newspaper aside and sifted through the envelopes.

Among the letters were one from Bedstefa and one from Silge Rasmussen. The two she had waited so long to receive had both arrived on the same day. Eagerness and apprehension whirled within her. She set these two apart from the others.

"Would you like me to stay while you read the letter from Frode's sister?" Peder eyed the envelopes.

"Yes." Anna said. "I'm so glad to have you here for this." He sat down on the bed beside her. With shaking hands, she shuffled her grandfather's letter to the top. "I think I'll read Bedstefa's first, though." She opened the envelope and unfolded the paper.

Dearest Anna,

I never suspected Jorn had taken another woman, let alone a wife. I believed that Rasmussen woman's claims sounded outlandish.

Right after Jul I took a trip to Velje to seek the truth. I hoped to be able to reassure you that your husband had not committed bigamy. To my dismay, the woman's story is factual. According to church records, they were married in 1880. They had a baby girl baptized in 1881 and another in 1882.

I asked the reverend if he was aware that he had married a man who was already married to another woman. He was quite shaken.

Anna, I am sorry to have to report this to you. I did not speak with the woman, so I do not know if she was aware that Jorn was married to you.

It was a mistake for me to offer Jorn the use of my place again. If I had not, you might have been spared the heartache and humiliation he has heaped on you. That is not to say I absolve him of his own culpability. He must be held responsible for his own behavior. As always, God will pass the final judgment. Most likely, He already has.

I am sorry I cannot be with you to help you through this difficult time, especially with the birth of your child so near. I thank God that you have Peder to sustain you. I pray for a safe delivery for you and your baby.

Love,

Bedstefa

Was this Danish family the secret Jorn was going to tell her about when he returned? Was the necklace meant to be a bribe to buy her acceptance of them? Anna closed her eyes. Back when she was carrying Baby Jorn, that strumpet was carrying her youngest girl, and her child had lived. Thanks to Jorn's decision to work Erik in the fields, Anna's son was dead. She blinked back tears. It wasn't fair. Now, they were each carrying Jorn's child again.

Anna swallowed and handed the letter to Peder. She was glad to have gotten this news from Bedstefa. He was so kind to have made the trip to Velje to find answers, although they were not the ones she had hoped for.

Peder took the letter Anna offered and read it, shaking his head. "That bastard." He handed it back to her. "I'm sorry."

Anna took a steadying breath. "Ever since I received Silge's letter, I've had to face the possibility her story was true." She forced a small smile. "Bedstefa is right about you, though. I don't know what I would have done if you weren't here to help me through this."

"I'm sure Brigitte and Gabrielle have given you support." Peder patted her hand.

"I haven't told them." Anna clasped her hands together. "I was waiting to find out if the Rasmussen woman's letter was true. Now I'm not sure I want them, or anyone, to know."

"They won't think less of you for Jorn's actions," Peder said. "You should tell them."

"I don't know if I can. It's too shameful."

Peder shrugged. "It's your choice."

"They will be here on Tuesday," Anna said. "If I decide to tell them, I can do it then."

Peder pulled the watch from his pocket and flipped open the

case. "The children were already dressed for church and in the sitting room when I arrived. I told Adelaide she and Halvor could ride with us in the sleigh. He'll drive the children back in it since Brigitte has invited me for dinner after the services."

"She's eager to learn of your wedding plans," Anna said, stalling the reading of the other letter. Now that she knew the truth, she felt no urgency to see what the Rasmussen woman had to say.

Peder glanced at his watch again. "You best be reading that other letter if you want me here."

Suddenly, Anna wanted to be alone when she read it. "Now that I know what to expect, I'll be fine." Anna managed a weak smile. "You go on."

"What if the baby comes while we're gone?" Concern etched lines around Peder's eyes. He stood.

"That's not likely." Anna chuckled. "My children haven't been that eager to come into the world."

"I'll stop in to see you when I pick up the sleigh. We'll talk then." He turned and left.

Anna fluffed the pillows and stacked them against the headboard. She leaned her back against them. After a few silent moments, she opened the envelope from Silge and began to read.

Dear Mrs. Stryker,

I write this letter with great sadness. Sadness that Jorn has passed away. And sadness that you have learned of our family here in Denmark. Jorn never wanted you to know about us. He always loved you and did not want to cause you distress.

The letter fluttered from Anna's cold fingers to her lap. Jorn had not loved her, certainly not enough to remain true to her. A lump formed in her throat. She swallowed, picked up the pages, and resumed reading.

As you probably know, Jorn loved Denmark. He always dreamed of moving back to south Jutland once the Germans were forced out. He feared that by the time the Danes reclaimed his homeland, you and your children would not be willing to return.

He was also afraid he might be too old to start a new family when he returned.

Since he had to leave his parents to avoid serving in the German army, he wanted to have family around him for the rest of his life and especially a son to carry on his name and inherit his Danish legacy. When we married, he purchased my father's farm since my brother said he did not want to take it over.

Anna pounded her fist on the bed. "But I told him I would return. And I gave him sons!" she shouted into the empty house. Thank goodness no one was there to hear her.

I have known about Jorn's marriage to you since he began using our farm in his work. At first, he seemed to pay little attention to me, but as the summers passed, we became friends. I must admit, I was growing very fond of him. When he first proposed to me, I was shocked and staunchly refused.

But the next year, in 1880, Jorn convinced me that we could marry. He said that you were married in the eyes of American law, but we would be married by a pastor in the eyes of God. He convinced me that since you were not wed in the church, yours was not a true marriage.

Furthermore, he said you would never know about me. I should have stood firm, but I could not. I loved him, and I believed he loved me. You must know how persuasive he can be.

Our oldest daughter, Anesa, was born in 1881, and our second girl, Karoline, was born in 1882. And as you know, since you received my letter meant for Jorn, I am again with child. I am due in May.

Anna glanced toward the cradle Halvor had moved into her room. Jorn had made it. All her children had used it. She had given her husband four sons, but it had not been enough to keep him from marrying that woman. More than ever, she hoped her baby would be a girl.

Anna's pulse raced in anger. She took several deep breaths.

We had much rain this autumn and our harvest was poor. I need money to buy shoes for my girls and to pay the doctor for the birth of the child I am carrying. I am ashamed that I must ask you to help support Jorn's children, but I have no other choice.

He used to send us money after his harvest and after the winter each year. Since his death was sudden and I am with child, I have had no opportunity to prepare for the loss of those funds this year. And because of the poor crops, my father cannot afford to support us.

You must think I have no morals. I beg you to find the charity in your heart to forgive me. But if you can not, please do not hold my sins against my children.

Beseechingly yours,

Silge Stryker

Anna crumpled the letter in her fist. That woman had the wedding ceremony Anna dreamed of and Jorn denied her, one more thing he had kept from her with his selfishness. Not only that, the strumpet knew Jorn was already married, and claimed he always loved Anna.

Jorn could not have loved her. He had threatened to divorce her and take her children. Was he planning to take them to live with this harlot?

He had not been home for the births of any of their children who were born in in the summer. When Torsten was born, Jorn was in Denmark for the birth of his daughter.

Anna swallowed against the bile rising in her throat. How could he have married this woman, and kept his terrible secret without Anna ever suspecting? She was too gullible, too trusting. What else had he done that she never knew about? She didn't even want to speculate.

Now, Silge expected Anna to send her money. She couldn't believe the woman's boldness. Let them carve wooden shoes for the children as Jorn had suggested the Thomsen's should do!

Besides, what happened to the money Jorn paid for the Rasmussens' farm? How dare he spend money on Silge's family when he wouldn't spend it on Anna's? He wouldn't even allow Anna's a decent house. Well, the Rasmussens could sell their land again.

Anna had been crushed. She could find no sympathy for those who trounced on her, and she refused to be responsible for the woman who committed bigamy with Jorn.

Queasiness engulfed Anna. She turned onto her side, curled up, and sobbed.

What happened couldn't be changed, and she refused to believe she was at fault.

It was better that Jorn was dead. At least, now, he could no longer make a mockery of her marriage. She and the children would no longer be living with liar and a fraud.

• ♥ •

A few hours later, Anna woke to a stabbing pain in her abdomen. On the table next to her bed sat the bell to ring for Adelaide.

Anna reached for it. Before she could ring, a knock sounded at the door.

"Come in." She groaned as the cramp worsened.

Peder strode into the room wearing a wide grin. "Charlotte and I have decided to marry in July."

"Congratulations." Despite her pain, Anna managed a smile. "Won't July be awfully hot?"

"Charlotte wants to wed in the garden of her parents' home. There are tall shade trees, and she says many of her father's flowers will be in bloom."

"It sounds lovely." Anna grimaced and closed her eyes as the contraction tightened.

Peder rushed to her side. "What's wrong?"

"The baby is ready to be born." The pain eased a bit.

He paled. "Is there something I can do? Do you need Adelaide?"

"Please send Halvor to fetch Gabrielle. I need her."

"My team is hitched to the sleigh. I'll bring her myself." Urgency tightened his voice. "But the snow is deep. It'll take awhile. Will you be all right?"

"Yes." She sighed. "Adelaide is here if I need her."

"I'll hurry." He turned and rushed out the door.

Anna slipped the letters from Bedstefa and Silje into the drawer of the lamp stand beside the bed. She chastised herself for falling asleep without hiding them.

The hour before Peder returned with Gabrielle passed in agony. Anna didn't want her water to break on her new mattress, so she spent much of the time sitting on the seat of the water closet, worrying that the baby might decide to come before her friend arrived. Still, this was much more comfortable than having to go outdoors to use the privy or rely on a chamber pot. The room didn't have the odor she had expected since the flush mechanism worked just as Peder said it would. She had added a piece of rope so the children could pull the chain to start the water flowing.

Footfalls sounded on the stairs.

"Mother has spent most of the afternoon in the indoor privy," Inge said in French. It was her habit to use French whenever she talked only to Gabrielle and Anna. "She looks miserable, but she says the baby is coming! Tonight!"

"Delivering a baby is often very difficult for the mother," Gabrielle replied.

Anna whispered a quick prayer of thanks. As if on cue, her water broke. Although she knew it would happen, the event surprised her, and she let out a little yelp.

A quiet tap sounded at the door.

"Are you all right, Anna?" Gabrielle called in English.

"I'll be out in a minute." Anna gasped.

"We'll meet you in the bedroom!" Inge called.

Anna smiled. Since Jorn's passing, she and the children had taken to using whatever language suited them when they spoke

When Anna finished cleaning herself, she joined Inge and Gabrielle, giving each of them a hug before returning to bed.

Inge spoke earnestly. "I would like to help Gabrielle help our baby be born."

She sounded so much older than a child who would turn eight on her birthday next month. Anna had come to depend on her help with her younger brothers. "That will be fine."

Another spasm bore down on her abdomen. She clenched her teeth.

"Run and get some water in a wash basin, and a cloth," Gabrielle told Inge.

Throughout the evening, Anna endured the contractions. Inge swabbed her mother's forehead and face with the cooling cloth. At last, the baby was delivered.

"You have a fine son," Gabrielle said over the baby's cry.

"A little brother!" Inge cried out. She watched as Gabrielle cut and tied the cord, cleaned off the baby, and swaddled him in a blanket.

Another boy. Anna had so hoped for a girl. Still here was her son, her last child. Because of that, he would be special.

Inge ran to the head of the bed. "What shall we call him, Moder?"

"Bring your brothers to see him, and we'll all decide."

Gabrielle placed the tiny boy on Anna's chest, then covered them with a blanket. She smiled and held him close as Gabrielle tidied up the bed and the room.

This infant looked very much like Baby Jorn had when he was born. A wave of sadness washed through Anna. It wasn't fair that her innocent child was gone.

A loud clatter of feet on steps and children's voices sounded from beyond the door. It would be quieter when the carpet was installed next week. Anna cuddled the tiny boy in her arms. Just outside the room, Inge hushed the boys and they all walked in.

"Each of you take a good look at your new brother," Anna said, returning to English. "Then think of what name would fit him."

The children studied the baby as he slept in Anna's arms. He had a shock of downy blond hair. His tiny hands were tightly fisted.

"I think he should have an American name like Graham or Pete, the name Uncle Peder uses in town." Erik paused. "Maybe, George."

Inge pressed her lips together then turned to Erik. "I would like to give him an American name, too, but I'm afraid he might not feel like part of our family, since we all have Danish names." She shifted her gaze to the baby. "I think we should call him Mads or Greggers."

"Maybe we should call him Jorn after Fader and Baby Jorn." Poul looked at Anna.

"No!" Erik shouted.

"That name hasn't been good luck in our family," Inge said, tears pooling in her round blue eyes.

"Having three Jorns to talk about might be too confusing," Anna added gently. That was the one name she was dead set against, but she didn't want her children to know. "Is there another name you like, Poul?"

He pouted. "Peder."

Anna rather liked that idea.

"But if we name him Peder," Erik said. "Uncle Peder might decide he likes the baby best of all of us." He looked at his brothers and Inge. "We wouldn't want that, would we?"

They shook their heads.

Anna didn't think her brother would do such a thing, but she also didn't want her children to worry about it.

"Torsten, what do you think?"

"Halvor." He grinned. "Because Mr. Hansen is such a nice man."

Anna was taken aback. The suggestion made sense from her sweet little boy, as Halvor had been more of a father to her children than the man who had sired them. She thought of her first summer in America, when Halvor had kissed her. For all the years since, he had kept the promise that it would never happen again, but, with the exception of marital relations, he had been a better husband to her than Jorn ever was. She valued his help with the produce business, with managing the farm, and most of all, his friendship.

She sighed. If she named her baby after Halvor, friends and neighbors would gossip that the baby was his. She didn't dare take the risk. "He is a very nice man, but I don't think we'll name our baby after him."

Torsten frowned.

"Is there another name you like?" Anna asked.

"No."

"I want Greggers." Erik's angular face brightened. "But can we drop the 's' off the end? The 's' makes it sound like there is more than one of him."

"Gregger." Anna tried out the name and looked at the baby.

"Gregger," the children repeated in unison.

"Gregger it is," Anna said.

"That's a fine name." Gabrielle, who had been sitting in a chair by the wall watching the whole process, spoke up for the first time. "Gregger."

"Now you can all get ready for bed. Tomorrow, after school, we will have our party to celebrate Gregger's birth, and you can write letters to Bedstefa about your new brother. But, right now, I must try to feed him." Anna was so tired. She hoped her new son would nurse and they could both go to sleep. "Bedstefa will be excited to learn of his new great-grandson, and the name you all helped choose for him."

When the children had left, Anna unfastened her night dress and brought the baby to her breast. She had always enjoyed the special feelings of closeness with her babies she experienced while feeding them. This time was no different.

But it was. This was the last baby she would ever have.

She wouldn't marry again. She couldn't risk another devastating betrayal.

Chapter 18

April 6, 1884

I have been unable to stop thinking about Jorn's bastard daughters. Peder said the will might entitle me to his farm in Denmark. I do not want it. The harlot and her family need some way to support those girls and the unborn child. She wrote again to say they only had meager stores of food to get through the winter, and they didn't even have flour for bread. She might be lying, but I hate the thought of innocent children going hungry. I am blessed that my family and I have always had plenty.

Gregger is thriving. The other children adore him and feel that he is their baby, too. We have started speaking only English with him. Adelaide still speaks Danish to him, which I think will be okay since he will be exposed to both languages as his sister and brothers were. He gives us a lot of joy. I appreciate that right now.

Halvor has been doing a wonderful job. He and Adelaide are living in my old cabin. I have tried to convince her to move into the quarters just off the kitchen, but she refuses. Both join us for our evening meals and sometimes for family activities afterward. Halvor is evaluating the spring planting. The livestock is parceled out to the various homesteads, with the hired men designated responsibility for caring for them. Erik has been spending more and more time with him, often assisting with the barnyard chores.

"Three greenhorns will complete their contracts before the harvest this year." Anna looked across the dining room table at Halvor. His blond hair was mussed from when he removed his cap, giving him an endearing, boyish appearance, although his face had weathered over the past decade. "How many of them will we need to keep on as paid hands?"

"That will depend on how much land we put into crops this spring," he replied. His wide blue eyes held her gaze.

She looked down at her records regarding the previous fall's harvest, then back up at him. "How many men do you *want* to keep on?"

He rubbed his clean-shaven chin. "Since we plan to raise all the heifer calves to increase the herd, we should put more ground into hay." He paused and studied his notes. They were in Danish. How interesting that he could speak English fluently, but could not write it.

He continued. "We have plenty of pasture, but we'll need to be able to feed the additional stock in winter."

"The haymows were pretty full last fall. Is there enough barn space?"

"If we go ahead and build the new barn on the Thomsen place, we'll have plenty of room."

"We should build it as soon as the planting is done, when the farm hands will have time to work on it before the fields need to be cultivated."

"While we still have the extra hands?" Halvor grinned.

Anna lifted her chin. "You make it sound like I'm exploiting them."

His grin faded. "I was just teasing. Where's your sense of humor?"

She bristled. Since the letters from Bedstefa and that Rasmussen woman, Anna had been on edge. Halvor didn't know about Jorn's betrayal, so he couldn't understand. Should she tell him? He had always been honest with her and she with him. He wouldn't judge her. She glanced out the window. "I'm sorry. I'm not in the best of moods today."

"It's all right."

She couldn't meet his gaze. Learning about Jorn's Danish family didn't excuse her testy behavior. Neither did her equivocation over the one-time money she had sent to help support his daughters so they wouldn't starve during the cold weather.

Halvor had been pleasant in all their meetings about the farm. She tried to raise her spirits. "With additional cattle and hay crops, how many of the three men will we need to keep?"

"If the weather cooperates, most of the hay can be harvested before September, when the men leave." Halvor pulled a newspaper clipping from under his page of notes. "If we purchase one of these self-binding reaping machines, we can probably do without two of them." Handing the advertisement to her, he hesitated. "Maybe without all three."

"Don't you want to at least keep Kibby?" She swallowed. "Isn't he doing a good job managing the bunkhouse?"

"He is. And he doesn't hesitate to work in the fields if we need him. He enjoys working in the gardens." Halvor smiled wryly. "But he's my best friend, so I'm biased."

"I'm biased, too." Anna managed a small smile. "In the next week or so we should make him an offer to stay on as a paid hand. That way, if he wants to leave, we can decide if should make the offer to another man."

Halvor shook his head. "I'd rather do without the other two. They're nice enough, but not very work-brittle." The corners of his full mouth tipped upward again, and cheerfulness sparkled in his eyes. "But I'm confident Kibby will stay. He's as much as said he hoped we would keep him on."

"I'm glad." She studied the drawing of the machine. "Self-binding."

"We don't need the new reaper right away, but as we lose more greenhorns, we will. Last year's harvest was good, so this might be the right time to purchase it."

"I agree." Anna met Halvor's bright gaze. "And since Peder is going to be married this summer, we'll need to plan on taking a week to go to Marshalltown."

"We?" Halvor's blue eyes widened. "Me?"

"Of course," Anna said. "We'll take the train. Your mother will be going. I need her help with the children, and we'll need your help with the trunks, and with the coach Peder is hiring for us." She smiled. "Besides, Peder considers you a friend. He wants you at his wedding."

Halvor lifted his chin. "I'm honored."

His reaction touched Anna. She gathered her papers and handed the clipping back to him. "Let me know when you're ready to make the purchase. I'll arrange for the funds."

He made no move to leave. Anna didn't blame him. The coal burner kept the house much warmer than the cabin ever was in winter.

Adelaide appeared in the doorway. "Would you like me to bring some coffee?"

"Yes, thank you," he said.

Anna raised a brow. Although it seemed presumptuous of him to answer, she was glad he felt so comfortable in her home. Besides, he was certainly used to responding to his mother since they shared the cabin. Anna turned back to Adelaide. "That would be very nice. I should have thought of it."

From the sitting room, Gregger's tiny cry alerted Anna that he was awake.

"Excuse me for a moment." She went into the next room and lifted him from the cradle. His wet diaper had leaked through his gown. She wrapped him in a dry receiving blanket and returned to the dining room.

Adelaide was setting the coffee-filled cups on the table.

"He needs to be changed," Anna said. "I'll be back in a few minutes."

"I can do that." Adelaide held out her arms for the baby. "You sit down and have your coffee while it's hot."

"Thank you." Anna handed her son to the housekeeper and took her seat.

"That little one looks a lot like Erik did when he was that small." Halvor sipped his coffee.

"Yes, he does." Anna thought back to the first summer, before Adelaide had come to America, when Halvor had helped her with Erik as well as the gardens.

After Adelaide's footfalls had faded on the stairs to the second floor, Halvor set down his cup and clasped his hands together on the table in front of him. The muscle at his strong jaw twitched, as if he wanted to say something but was holding it back. Anna waited.

"I know it's too soon to ask, and you don't have to answer now." His words rushed from him. "But I would like your permission to court you after your mourning period is up."

Anna's breath caught in her throat.

"I would have asked your brother, but I believe you should make this decision for yourself."

She clasped her hands tightly in her lap. Courting was not something she had thought about for years. She shouldn't be thinking about it now, and she didn't want to think about it, not with the hurt of Jorn's infidelity so raw.

"I know the year from Jorn's death will not be up until September, and you may need a longer period to grieve." His eyes pleaded with her. "You can let me know when you are ready."

Anna swallowed back her anger. It was directed at Jorn, not Halvor, and she had already inflicted her dour mood on him once this morning.

The memory of their long-ago kiss floated through her mind. She forced herself to meet his gaze. "I may never be ready," she said gently. She liked him very much and didn't want to hurt him, but she couldn't trust any man with her heart. "It would be best if you don't wait for me. You should find someone else to court."

"I can wait," he replied in a quiet voice. "There is no one else I want. It has always been only you."

Anna's chest tightened. "I'm flattered." She managed a small smile. "But I will never marry again. You're a fine man. You deserve a wife who will make you happy."

"I am happy, working with you to make plans for the farm. Watching your children grow. Being part of your lives." He leaned forward, hands and forearms on the table. "I'll be content to continue in this way." He unlaced his fingers and held his palms up. "But I've loved you for ten years. I hope the time will come when you can love me, too."

Loved her for ten years? Her pulse raced. Halvor's declaration humbled her. She had been so focused on herself and her family, she had not even suspected. He had hidden his feelings well, but he had always been kind to her, supported her, been there when she needed him. He had been far more faithful than Jorn, and Anna had taken him for granted.

She blinked back tears. Halvor was a wonderful man.

Still, she wasn't ready to trust even Halvor with her heart. She couldn't risk a second dose of shame and betrayal, and she couldn't explain her reasons to the man across the table.

• ♥ •

In early May, the piano Anna ordered from Chicago arrived. She loved having music in her home, and invited her closest friends and Peder to share her joy.

Charlotte sat at the piano, and the children and guests gathered around. She played a tune Anna recognized as a patriotic song she had heard years ago at the Centennial celebration.

Moving at a slow pace around the group, Peder touched Anna's arm and motioned for her to follow him. He led her through the dining room and kitchen to the empty housekeeper's quarters before he spoke. "You have a letter from Denmark."

"From whom?" she asked, taking the letter he held out.

Anna tore open the envelope and unfolded the paper. She moved so that Peder could read the writing, while tipping up the bottom of the page to see who had written it.

"It's from Magda Rasmussen?" Anna read aloud.

"Silge and Frode's mother," Peder said. "What does she want?"

Dear Mrs. Stryker,

On behalf of my daughter, I would like to thank you for the generous gift you sent her this winter. She really appreciated being able to buy shoes for her girls.

"Then why isn't she writing this herself?" Irritation tweaked Anna's mood.

Peder's jaw dropped. "You sent her money?"

Anna shot her brother a defiant glance. "I didn't want my children's half-sisters to starve."

It is my sad task to inform you that Silje became quite ill and delivered her daughter several weeks before the child was due. Although the baby survived and is growing stronger every day, the birthing was too much for poor Silge. She passed away without even seeing her little girl. We have named the baby Silje, after her mother.

Anna held back a shriek of surprise. "She's dead!"

Peder lay a hand on her shoulder. "She and Jorn met their fates in less than a year."

We will use the remainder of the money you sent to pay the wet nurse we hired to nourish our new granddaughter. She will also help care for the older girls. But this is only a temporary solution. My husband and I are getting on in years. It is not reasonable that we can raise the girls much longer.

I have written to Frode to beg him to return to Velje and take on his family duties of running the farm and taking care of his sister's children. I do not have much faith that he will assume his responsibilities. There were many hard feelings on both sides when he left. I fear that if he does not return, we will have to put the children in a foundling home. They are sweet, innocent girls. They do not deserve such a terrible fate.

Anna's stomach clenched. Near tears, she turned to her brother. "Promise that if something happens to me, you and

Charlotte will take Inge and my boys."

Peder slipped his arm around her shoulders. "Don't worry. Nothing will happen to you. But of course, we would take them. We love them."

Relieved, she patted his hand. "I'm so glad you're my brother."

"You and the children are my family." He hugged her.

She returned her attention to the letter.

I know it is presumptuous to ask, but I beseech you to raise the girls as your own.

They are half-sisters to your children, and it would be good for all of them to know each other. Please give this your utmost consideration.

Anna gasped. She felt as if she'd been kicked in the chest. "I don't believe it."

Sincerely,

Magda Rasmussen

"How could that woman ask this of you after what her daughter did?" Peder sputtered. "And the parents apparently went along with it."

"Are there no other Rassmussen relatives in Denmark who could help?" Anna huffed. "I don't plan to support them now that they can plant gardens and crops. Will you talk to Frode about going back Denmark? Someone has to take care of those girls. They are his flesh and blood, not mine." Anna couldn't raise them, but she didn't want them to go to an orphanage.

"I will." Peder hesitated. "But I can almost guarantee he won't."

"Well, he can't bring them here. Our secret would no longer be safe."

"I don't think he would," Peder said. "When he left home, he and his parents as much as disowned each other."

"That's not those girls' fault," Anna said. "They weren't even born yet."

"You've always said you wanted more daughters." Peder's

words carried the tinge of sarcasm.

Anna's jaw tightened. "Daughters of my own. Not another woman's." She turned away to hide the tears welling in her eyes at the thought of what would happen to the little girls. "I can't take them. Every time I looked at them, they would remind me of Jorn's unfaithfulness."

• ♥ •

Whenever Anna looked at her children, she thought of Jorn's little girls in Denmark, and their fate as orphans. It could have been her who died in childbirth, and her youngsters would have been without parents. They were so fortunate to have Peder. She couldn't bear to think of Erik, Inge, Poul, Torsten, and little Gregger growing up in a foundling home. If only Peder could convince Frode to take responsibility for his nieces.

On Wednesday, Anna was still scurrying around to collect the baby clothes and diapers she wanted to take with her when Gabrielle's team pulled into the yard. Adelaide brought Gabrielle to the sitting room where Anna was arranging blankets in her large basket for the baby.

Gabrielle's brow furrowed with concern. "Is something wrong, Anna? You look troubled."

"Adelaide, please go upstairs and get Gregger from his crib." Anna needed some motherly advice. She waited until she heard the housekeeper's footsteps on the stairs then moved closer to Gabrielle.

"I've learned something about Jorn which has been difficult to accept," Anna whispered before she lost her courage.

Gabrielle raised a dark brow. "So long after his death?"

Anna sighed. "I began learning last fall that Jorn had another wife and family in Denmark."

Gabrielle stared at her.

"At first I didn't believe it." Anna swallowed. "But Bedstefa verified it was true." She went on to explain the letters from Silge.

"Oh, Anna!" Gabrielle patted Anna's hand. "It must've been so hard to bear."

"Recently, I received word that the woman died in childbirth." Anna throat tightened. "Her parents want me to take Jorn's girls."

Gabrielle's face softened. "Are you going to do it?"

"I'm hoping Frode Rasmussen will take them. He's Silge's brother, so they're his flesh and blood." Anna frowned. "But he's estranged from his family, and Peder doesn't think he'll consider it." Her fingers fiddled with the collar of her dress. "If he doesn't, what do you think I should do?"

Gabrielle slipped her arm around Anna's shoulders. "The children aren't to blame for the sins of their mother."

Anna flinched. The philosophy was hard to accept when the sins in question weren't her own.

Adelaide's footfalls sounded on the stairs.

"You must do what's right for you. That will also be right for the children." Gabrielle gave Anna a quick hug.

"I'm not ready to tell Brigitte, yet," Anna whispered.

Gabrielle smiled. "It's our secret."

• ♥ •

When Peder arrived for church the following Sunday, Anna could hardly contain her impatience. "What did Frode say?"

Peder's shoulders sagged. "He adamantly refused to consider caring for the girls, either in Denmark or America. It's not a matter of money. When his parents disowned him and didn't answer his letters, the only way he could cope was to make a clean break."

Anna's hope sank. "The girls are his flesh and blood."

"Yes. But Silge sided with her parents." Peder shook his wavy blond head. "That hurt him deeply and sealed his decision not to care for her children."

"Couldn't he think of any other family members to take them?"

"He said there is no one." Peder paused. "I'm not sure if that's his answer because it's true or because of his resentment toward his sister."

Anna sighed. "We likely will never know."

She couldn't think of anyone else either. Peder and Charlotte hadn't offered to raise Jorn's daughters, and Anna couldn't ask them to undertake such a monumental charge. They were just beginning their life together. If she wanted to keep the little girls from a foundling home, she would have to care for them herself. There were no other possibilities.

All through the worship service, Anna wondered how Jorn could have sat in church Sunday after Sunday, knowing he had sinned so. She searched her soul for the strength to not only care for the girls, but love them as a mother would. She prayed for guidance.

She wondered if Jorn's Danish wife would have given her children a good home and loved them if Jorn had divorced Anna. There was no answer, but it didn't matter. Anna could make only one choice.

She asked God to help her put the past behind her and to be with her as she faced the adversities to come. Her future would include eight children instead of five, and it would be filled with scandal that would taint not only herself, but also her children.

She prayed for grace in responding to the judgments of others and that her support would see her children through the humiliation. She asked God to give her friends and neighbors the charity to accept her and her children after they learned her secret.

Lastly, she thanked God for her large house.

As soon as the benediction was finished, Anna leaned toward Peder. "Tell Frode if he goes to Denmark to pick up his nieces, I won't ask him for money to help raise them," she whispered. "If he balks, tell him I'll pay his fare and those of the girls."

"And if he refuses?" Peder folded his arms across his chest.

"Tell him it's the least he can do," Anna insisted. "You can't go because you are to be married soon. I can't leave my children, and I promised Charlotte I would help prepare for the wedding."

"I'll do my best to convince him, but he's extremely stubborn. He won't want to see his parents again."

"I'll write Bedstefa and ask him to take the girls to his house. That way, Frode won't have to see his parents." Anna paused. "And I'll ask if he can find a wet nurse willing to come to America, at least until the baby is weaned."

Concern furrowed Peder's brow. "Are you sure you want to do this?"

"I'm nervous about it, but I'm sure." She patted her brother's arm. "Thank you for your help with Frode."

Four days passed with no word from Peder. On Friday morning, he called on Anna shortly before eleven o'clock. She finished feeding Greg and laid him in the cradle in the sitting room.

"Your farm hands were busy planting when I passed your fields along the road." He handed her a newspaper, before she could ask about Frode. It was not the *Dannevirke*, it was in English. "I thought you and Halvor might find this paper useful. It's all about new methods of farming."

"*The Iowa Homestead.*" Anna read the title aloud. "I read English only as well as Erik and Inge have taught me, and I fear Halvor doesn't read it at all." She smiled. "But I'll ask the children or Gabrielle to help me with the words I can't figure out."

Peder grinned, but the mirth did not quite reach his eyes. "Then it will help with both your farming and your reading skills." He pulled a letter from his pocket and held it out to Anna. "I stopped by the post office before leaving town."

She hoped it wasn't another letter from Mrs. Rasmussen. The return address indicated it was not. She tore open the envelope and skimmed the message. "It is from the store in Chicago. My parlor furniture should arrive by train the last week of May."

A smile broke across her face. She looked around the room at the inexpensive sofa and chair she had purchased for the small housekeeper's parlor. It seemed tiny and out of place in this sitting room, with its beautiful oak fireplace and colorful wallpaper. It would be nice to finally move the furniture intended for this room from the parlor, but she couldn't keep the worry from her mind. "What did Frode say?"

"Let's sit down, Anna." Peder led her to the chair, then took a seat on the sofa. "He refuses to have any part in bringing his nieces to America."

Anna sighed. She had expected as much. "Perhaps in my letter to Bedstefa, I can ask if he'll try to find someone to escort the children and wet nurse to America."

"I had another idea." Peder winked conspiratorially.

Anna cocked her head.

"You could suggest to him that he come over for my wedding," he continued. "Then not only could he bring the girls, but we could see him again, too."

"I would so love that! Your plan is perfect."

Peder grinned. "I thought you'd like it."

"I do." She stood. "If you stay for the noon meal, I'll finish my letter to him, and you can take it to the post office yet this afternoon. The sooner he receives it, the sooner we will know."

• ♥ •

On a warm, June afternoon, Anna sat with Brigitte and Gabrielle under the huge maple tree in the Cook's back yard. A breeze blew the leaves so the shade was dappled, but Anna welcomed the warmth of the sun's rays.

Her mind had only been half-engaged as her sales sisters discussed their produce and dry goods business. She waited for a lull in the conversation.

"Brigitte, I need to tell you something about Jorn," Anna

began, hating what she was about to say.

"Jorn?" Brigitte's blond brows knit together.

"He had another wife in Denmark."

Brigitte gasped.

Anna forged ahead, telling her the story from the first letter.

"Why didn't you tell me sooner?" Brigitte shot a pointed glance in Gabrielle's direction.

She sat unmoving, her hands in her lap.

Anna hung her head. "I was embarrassed. Since they were in Denmark, I thought no one would ever know. It's so shameful."

Brigitte's lips formed a thin line. "Why are you telling us now?"

Anna told of Magda Rasmussen's letter and Frode's refusal to accept responsibility for his nieces. "So, I have decided to take them in. Bedstefa will find a wet nurse for the baby. Then he'll bring them to Cedar Falls in July."

"How can you even think of taking Jorn's bastard daughters?" Brigitte wrinkled her nose. She stared at Anna with wide, hazel eyes. "After what he did to you."

"It's not easy. But I can't bear the thought of my children's half-sisters going to an orphanage." Anna returned her friend's gaze, willing her to understand. "The little girls are innocent, and my children have a right to know them."

Brigitte shook her head. "What will people say?"

"I have lived my life worrying about what others will say. About what they'll think," Anna said softly. "I have to do what is right for me."

Gabrielle came to Anna's side and gave her a hug. "I think it's very generous of you. God will reward you for your charity."

Gabrielle would have supported whatever decision Anna made. How lucky she was to have such a good friend.

"You have a big house." Brigitte said. "But how will you and Adelaide manage with three more little ones?"

"It will be difficult. But I expect the wet nurse will help care for the children. When she is no longer needed to feed the baby girl, perhaps she'll be willing to stay on as a nanny."

"What about your children?" Brigitte asked. "Have you told them about their half-sisters?"

"Not yet, but I will have to soon." Anna sighed. "I can't figure a way that will not turn them against their father."

Brigitte frowned. "What if you do? What he has done is despicable. They have a right to know—"

"Brigitte! How can you say such a thing?" Gabrielle scolded. "It's unfair to inflict such pain on ones so young."

Brigitte's cheeks flushed bright pink. She pressed her hands to them, hard. "How else is Anna to explain the existence of their half-sisters?"

"I have to be honest with them," Anna said, trying to soothe the dispute arising between her friends. "I don't want us to continue living in lies."

Anna wished she could soften the pain the scandal would inflict on her children. She would do her best to help them cope with the shame and humiliation, but her decision was made. There was no turning back now.

• ♥ •

No excuse remained to postpone telling the Hansens of the changes that would soon occur in the household, but the thought of discussing Jorn's other family with Halvor distressed her. That first summer, Halvor had suspected Jorn of cheating on Anna. Maybe Halvor had surmised Jorn's ongoing infidelity or maybe Jorn confided in him.

Anna worried her lower lip.

"We need some rain," Halvor observed, as he picked up a hoe and attacked the small weeds between the rows of beans.

"If we don't get any, we might have to water in the next few days." Anna bent down to check the development of the green beans on the plant in front of her, and to gather her courage. She straightened.

"Since Jorn's death, I have learned that he also had a wife and children in Denmark," Anna began, amazed at how calmly she was able to say the words.

Halvor looked up. The fine lines at the corners of his narrowed eyes deepened. "What?"

"I didn't believe it at first." Anna handed him the first letter she had received from Silge.

He studied the pages for several minutes, then handed them back to Anna.

"That bastard!" Dark blue anger burned in Halvor's eyes. "It's a good thing he is dead, or I would kill him myself."

She flinched. "Halvor."

"He betrayed you! While you were faithful to him." He threw the hoe to the ground.

She stepped back in alarm. His chest rose and fell, rose and fell. His teeth clenched. His hands fisted.

She couldn't remember ever seeing him this outraged. Her heart bear fast and hard.

"He cheated us out of so many years we could have had together." He turned and paced along the furrow between the bean rows.

Anna lost her breath. Would they have gotten together that first summer if not for Jorn?

At the edge of the garden, he stopped. He combed his fingers through his wind-blown blond hair. His head tilted back for a few moments. Then he drew himself up to his full height, turned, and walked back to Anna.

"He should have stayed with his wife in Denmark." Disgust frosted his words, but he seemed more in control of himself.

"He had our family to take care of here. But that's past. I need to discuss the future with you." She explained the letter from Magda Rasmussen and Frode's refusal to accept responsibility for the girls.

Halvor's fists clenched again. He crossed his arms across his chest then uncrossed them. His gaze never left Anna. "You're going to bring them here," he said as if he could not believe it, and did not approve. "Aren't you?"

Anna swallowed, fidgeting under his scrutiny. "Yes."

The planes of his face softened. "Why?"

"My children have a right to know their half-sisters."

"You have a big heart, Anna." His voice was quieter now, but his blond brows still knit with concern. "It won't be easy."

"I know."

"What are you going to tell people about who they are?"

"The truth." Anna lifted her chin.

"Which will bring shame on your household."

"I realize that." Anna steeled herself for the words she had to say. "And if you wish to leave before the girls arrive to avoid the humiliation, I will understand." She took a breath. "But we've had enough lies in our family to last my children a lifetime. I won't heap more falsehoods on their young souls."

"But they'll have to live with the consequences. The judgments of others," Halvor argued. "Have you told them yet?"

He sounded like a concerned father, but he was not their father. Anna inhaled a deep breath. "I plan to tell them tomorrow night, after the evening meal. I hope that will give them time to accept the idea before their half-sisters arrive in July."

"If there's anything I can do to help, I'll do it. I'm very fond of your children." Halvor stepped closer. "And I love you. What your husband did is not only despicable, he robbed me of the opportunity to be with you. To marry you."

Anna stared at him. She drew in a breath. "It wasn't meant to be."

He took her hand in his. "But things are different now. We are both free. I can help you raise the children." Expectation lit his suntanned face. "Anna, please marry me."

"Marry." She closed her eyes. His affection touched her deeply, but since the kiss so many years ago, she hadn't allowed herself to think of him in any way except as a friend and her farm manager. Still, she was extremely fond of him and had great respect for him. She forced herself to open her eyes and face him. He was smiling.

"I can't," she whispered.

His smile faded. "I'll wait until you are finished mourning Jorn."

She swallowed and withdrew her hand from his. "Oh, Halvor. You're a wonderful man, but I can't."

His face fell. "Why not?"

"I have been married, and as a result I will have eight children to raise. I don't want any more." She was rambling, saying her thoughts aloud as they occurred to her, without benefit of considering before speaking.

"I'll help you raise them. I love your youngsters like my own." His voice was earnest. "We don't need to have more."

"But I am very fertile."

"There are ways to prevent conception," he argued.

"I cannot marry you." She cleared her throat. "When I was wed to Jorn, I loved and trusted him. He betrayed my trust and caused me great pain. I don't want to risk that happening again."

He flinched as if she had slapped him. "You know I would never betray you." His face tightened until it looked pinched with pain.

Her chest tightened. "I know you don't think you would, but what if we married and you changed your mind about wanting a child. I don't want to be pressured—"

"I will not change my mind."

"Most men want an heir. To carry on their name."

"I am not most men." He lifted his chin and straightened to his full height. "Besides, I already feel like a father to your children." His face hardened. "I know what it is. You're ashamed to wed your farm hand. You would feel you were marrying beneath yourself."

Her breath left her. She forced herself to inhale and laid her hand on his. "That's not true," she said. "You're a wonderful man. You would make a very fine husband and father."

"Then why won't you marry me?" He looked as confused as she felt.

"I'm not ready to think about being wed again. To anyone," she whispered, blinking back tears.

"I've already said I will wait until you're finished mourning, although I don't know why you would mourn the man who committed adultery against you and God." He clasped her hand. "When will you be ready to think about marriage?"

"I don't know. I'm sorry." She couldn't say more than the truth.

Halvor squeezed her fingers. "I can wait."

Chapter 19

June 16, 1884

I would not have believed anyone could be more furious about Jorn's infidelity than I am, but I think Halvor might be. His reaction confuses me. One time, he appears angry with me for refusing to have an affair with him after our first kiss. The next time, he seems to respect me for being faithful to my husband and to despise Jorn for his adulterous marriage.

Halvor's proposal shocked me, and I immediately rejected it. I told him I did not know when I would be ready to think of marriage, but from the time I said it, I have been able to think of little else. Thoughts of our summers spent together in the garden, our weekly drives to church, the way he watches over the children and me keep flooding my mind. Visions of our long-ago kiss return to me frequently. He was right. Had Jorn been out of the picture, we might have courted, might have married. But, it is too late. I hope we can remain friends.

I have not, and will not, tell anyone that Halvor has mentioned marriage – not even Peder or Gabriele and Brigitte. I fear they would never leave it alone, and I do not want to have to defend my decision to them.

I am trying to figure out how to tell the children about Jorn's bastard family. I do not want to turn Inge and Erik against their father as their reaction will influence their younger brothers, who are too young to fully understand. And how will they respond when I explain that they have half-sisters in Denmark and those sisters will be coming to live with us? My decision to bring Jorn's Danish daughters to America will change my children's lives forever.

All afternoon Anna fretted over how to tell her children about their stepsisters. After the evening meal, she gathered them around her in the sitting room. Her chest tightened.

"Are we going to play school?" Torsten bounced up and down on his toes. "My turn to choose. I want English!" His round face glowed with anticipation.

"I'm afraid we aren't going to play school tonight." She forced herself to smile at him. "But it will still be your turn to choose our language next time we do."

"Then what are we going to do?" Poul asked.

"I have something very important to tell you," Anna began. "And then I will need you to help me make some plans. Will you do that?"

They all nodded solemnly.

"Greg is too little to help," Torsten said.

"Yes, he is," Anna agreed. She took a deep breath and began. "You know how your father always went to Denmark in the summer?"

Again, the children nodded.

Inge scooted closer to Anna. "To bring back greenhorns."

"That was an important reason, but he had another reason, too. One I just found out about a little while ago." No matter how many times Anna had rehearsed this in her head, it was still hard. "He had another family, like us, in Denmark."

Eyes widened, confused expressions surrounded her.

"You mean another mother? Another Erik? Another Poul?" Poul asked.

"Another mother, yes, and three little girls. The girls are your half-sisters," Anna replied.

Erik pursed his lips. "How can that be? He was married to you. He was our father."

"Yes. And he always will be." She wished she could have thought an easier way, a better explanation. "He is also the father of your half-sisters."

Distress pinched Inge's face. "But that's a sin. Having two

wives. It's against the Commandments."

"Yes, it is." Sometimes, Anna wished her daughter wasn't so perceptive, but she was proud of Inge's thoughtful intelligence.

"I always knew he was a bad man," Erik muttered.

"He wasn't bad." Anna was determined not to turn her children against their father.

"Yes, he was." Defiance flashed in his round, green eyes. The same green as Jorn's. "He was mean to me. He made me get sick. You and Baby Jorn got sick. It's his fault my brother died."

"Your father was human. He made mistakes."

Erik's jaw dropped. He stared at Anna. "No man is supposed to have two wives. Two families."

"No, they aren't," Anna agreed. "He made a wrong choice. A terrible mistake." She scanned her children's faces. "Have any of you ever made a mistake?"

"Not one that big," Erik sputtered.

"That's true." How could she expect her children to accept what Jorn had done, when she, herself, could not? "But that doesn't change the fact that you have three stepsisters."

Torsten's eyes widened. "More sisters? Like Inge?"

"Yes. And now their mother has died," Anna continued.

"Like Fader," Poul said.

"Yes. And the little girls can't live without a mother or a father." She paused to give her children a chance to ponder that idea.

Inge's voice was just above a whisper. "They are all alone."

Poul looked close to bursting into tears. "Poor sisters. No *moder* or *fader*."

Anna patted the spot next to her on the sofa. He climbed up beside her. "That's why they are coming to live with us. Bedstefa is bringing them next month."

"Bedstefa is coming to America?" Excitement replaced the sadness in Inge's eyes. "To be with us?"

Anna smiled. "He's coming for a visit."

"Bedstefa?" Torsten looked as confused about this news as

he was about Jorn's other family.

"It will be very nice for all of you to finally meet him. And your sisters." Anna was glad that eagerness to see Bedstefa might soften the concern over the girls. "The oldest girl is Anesa. She is four years old. The next one is Karoline. She is three years old."

"Littler than me." Torsten sounded triumphant.

"The baby sister is even younger than Greg. She was born just before her mother died."

"Poor sisters," Poul said again. "We're lucky to still have you, Moder."

"And I'm lucky to have all of you." Anna swallowed.

"Who would take care of us if you died, Moder?" Inge's eyes brimmed with tears.

"Your uncle Peder would take care of you, so you don't need to worry about being left alone. But I am just fine." Anna assured them, not wanting them to dwell on it. She forced a smile. "Remember how you all helped me name Greg?"

"Yes," her children chorused.

"I need you to help me think of a name for the baby." Anna felt a little guilty about changing the infant's name, but it was the one weakness she had allowed herself. She couldn't bear to call the child by her given name, Silge.

"Anna," Torsten shouted.

"How can we name her without seeing her first like we did Greg?" Inge asked.

"Not Anna," Poul said. "Moder might decide she liked that sister best if the baby had her name."

"She should have a Danish name like all of us," Inge said. "Maybe Ella?"

"Ella," Anna echoed. "I like that." She turned to the others. "Your baby sister will be Ella, unless you can think of a reason why that name won't work."

They were all silent. One by one they shook their heads.

Erik rose. "I don't want the new sisters. Fader never should have had another family."

"What's done is done." Anna said firmly. "They will be here next month."

"I hope they die on the way here!" Erik shouted as he ran out of the room. "We don't need more sisters."

The other children stared after him.

Anna wanted to quickly turn their attention away from Erik's words. "When your sisters get here, everything will be new to them. All of us. The house. Between now and when they arrive, we need to think of ways to make them feel welcome in our family."

• ♥ •

In early July, Anna stood on the platform, waiting for the train as she had so many times when Jorn was coming home. To her left stood Peder, and to his left, Halvor. Her stomach fluttered in anticipation of seeing her grandfather again.

"Bringing these girls over is very generous of your sister," Halvor said, his voice formal.

Anna stiffened. Since his proposal, his interactions with her had been equally formal. Holding Greg in her arms, she forced her attention to her other four children who were lined up in front of the adults.

Peder slipped and arm around her. "She has always been compassionate, even as a child."

"I had no other choice. They are my children's stepsisters." Anna felt as if she had repeated these words a thousand times since she decided to take in the girls. "I'm grateful to Bedstefa for agreeing to bring them here."

She could hardly wait to see her grandfather. So much had happened in the ten years since she left Denmark. Although they corresponded on a regular basis, it wasn't the same as hearing the deep timbre of his voice and seeing the twinkle in his eyes. How wonderful that he and his great-grandchildren would finally meet.

She had accepted that her children would never know their grandparents. They had never retracted their decision to disown her and Peder. Sadness sliced through her.

And Jorn's girls. How much would they resemble her own children? Their father? Still, the thought of taking on the responsibility of raising three additional youngsters overwhelmed her in weaker moments.

The train whistle sounded. Torsten jumped up and down.

"Won't be long now," Peder said in English.

Inge turned to him. "We're supposed to speak Danish so the girls will know what we're saying."

"Inge." Anna caught her daughter's eye and gave her a stern look.

Peder laughed. "That's a very good idea. I should have thought of it myself."

"It was Moder's," Inge said quietly.

"And you remembered." Halvor patted her shoulder. "Good for you."

Anna shot him a glance of thanks.

The chug of the engine and clacking of the wheels on the tracks drowned out any further conversation. Coal smoke wafted across the waiting crowd. The train screeched to a halt, with the passenger cars adjacent to the platform.

Before long Anna spotted Bedstefa. His hair and beard appeared much grayer than she remembered, but he still had the weathered, leather skin of a former seaman, and the proud erect posture that made him look like a king.

A small girl clung to each of his hands. Walking beside them, a tall, chubby young woman, Anna guessed her age to be around sixteen, carried an infant. She seemed so young to have carried and lost a child, but then, Anna had only been two years older when she gave birth to Erik.

The young woman's gaze fixed on Halvor.

Peder waved his hat high in the air. "Bedstefa. Over here."

"That toddler looks just like Inge did when she was that

age," Halvor whispered.

Anna studied the smaller girl clinging to Bedstefa's hand. She must be Karoline. "Yes, she does."

A wave of nostalgia for Inge's early years mixed with anger at Jorn for creating this child. He had missed so much of Inge's childhood because of the time he spent with this girl's mother. Anna dampered down the ill feelings. The youngster was innocent, after all.

As Bedstefa came closer, Peder rushed forward and hugged him. Anna urged her children toward them. She smiled her happiness.

"Dearest Anna, it's so good to see you again." Bedstefa embraced her and held her close, careful not to crush the baby.

"I'm glad you're here." Joyful tears welled in her eyes. "Thank you for bringing the girls." She introduced her children and Halvor.

"This is Tilde Yager." Bedstefa gestured to the wet nurse. The two little girls were now clinging to her skirt. "And she is holding Silje."

"We have decided her name will be Ella," Anna said. "Silje will be her middle name."

Tilde raised a brow. "Ella. And the other girls?"

"They will remain Anesa and Karoline." Anna smiled at the girls. She knelt to look at them and held out Greg for them to see. "We have two babies. This one is Gregger, but we call him Greg. And we will call your sister Ella."

Anesa looked up at her with wide hazel eyes, but said nothing. Karoline reached out and touched Greg's hand. The girls wore pretty, matching dresses that appeared to be new. Anna wondered if their grandparents purchased them with money she had sent or if Bedstefa had given them to the girls.

They made introductions of everyone in their group.

"Erik, please take Karoline's hand," Anna said.

Scowling, Erik stepped forward and did as he was told. The toddler cocked her head to one side and looked up at him, but did not pull away.

"Talk to her, Erik," Inge said, as she took Anesa by the hand. Inge stooped over until her angelic face was at the same level as the little girl. She smiled. "We are happy you are here. My name is Inge. Can you say Inge?"

"Inge." The corners of Anesa's mouth turned slightly upward.

Inge grinned. "Very good, Anesa."

"We have been practicing all your names," Bedstefa said.

Anna had been praying she and her children would accept the girls. It was a prayer she would have to continue repeating. With their blond hair and blue eyes, the infant and Karoline at least looked as if they belonged to Anna's family, but Anesa, with her dark brown hair and hazel eyes, didn't resemble Anna's youngsters. Was she really Jorn's?"

They made their way down the platform to claim their trunks. There were three—one for Bedstefa, one for Miss Yager, and one for the children—and two large wooden boxes. The men loaded the two crates and two trunks into Peder's wagon, and the other trunk in Anna's. Hers had hinged boards on each side of the box that folded down to make seats for the children. A sturdy chair had been set behind the seat for the nanny.

"Good thing we brought two wagons," Peder said.

"One of the crates is for you and your lady." Bedstefa winked. "We could take it to your house and give these women a chance to feed the babies."

• ♥ •

After the infants finished nursing and Peder's box was unloaded, they headed for Anna's place. He had declined to open the crate until Charlotte could be with him, a romantic gesture that touched Anna's heart. Charlotte was a lucky woman to be marrying Peder.

The wagons finally arrived at Anna's house and everything was unloaded. Everyone gathered around the wooden box, which stood in the center of the sitting room.

"We will need a screwdriver or small pry bar to open it," Bedstefa said.

Halvor left the room and returned with a large screwdriver. He held it out to Anna.

She shook her head. "You open it."

With deliberate movements, he pried off the lid. Inside, wrapped in newspapers and linens, was a hand-carved walnut mantle clock. Halvor slowly lifted it out. "It's quite heavy."

"Oh, Bedstefa, it's beautiful." Anna sighed.

"It is Swiss," Bedstefa said. "I imported it especially for you, since you wrote me of your beautiful marble fireplace. It's for your housewarming."

"I love it." She hugged her grandfather. "Halvor, please take it to the parlor fireplace."

He led the way and centered the clock on the mantel.

Anna gripped Bedstefa's hand. "Perfect. Thank you."

Peder grinned. "Is this what's in my crate, too?"

"I can't tell you. That would spoil the surprise." Bedstefa returned to the crate and pulled out a carved box. He opened the lid, took out the key, and set the box next to the clock. Then he pulled his watch from his pocket and checked the time. After setting the hands, he inserted the key and wound. "You can turn the hour chimes on or off as you like. For now, they are off."

Anna nodded. "That's probably best." She cast her gaze to the little girls. "Let's get everyone settled in before Adelaide finishes the evening meal."

Peder deposited Bedstefa's trunk in the empty housekeeper's suite. Then Anna led them upstairs. Halvor and Peder carried the children's trunk to the nursery.

When they had placed it in the corner of the room, Tilde stepped to Halvor's side. "You are very strong, Mr. Hansen."

Halvor smiled at her. "Thank you, Miss Yager."

Anna's jaw tightened.

"I made the girls' trunk just like the ones I sent with you when you crossed to America," Bedstefa said as he watched the men struggle under the weight. "And the bottom is the same, too. You deserve help with their upbringing."

"Oh, Bedstefa, thank you." Anna squeezed his arm. How wonderful to have him here! She couldn't help touching him. "You're so generous. But that isn't necessary."

He smiled. "You're an angel to take Jorn's children under the circumstances."

"It wasn't an easy decision."

"But you made it," he said.

"Would you like me to help unpack the girls' clothes?" Anna asked Tilde as the girls stared at the three beds and the cradle Halvor had made.

"Thank you, no." Tilde smiled. "They have only a few garments and several toys. It will not take long."

"Tomorrow, I'll find some of Inge's old clothes," Anna said. "I've been saving them in case I had another girl." She swept her arm, indicating the Danish daughters. "Now I have three more."

She left the room and followed Bedstefa down the steps.

He scanned the parlor with its tufted, golden brocade sofas and chairs and mahogany tables, then nodded in approval. "You have a fine house. Is this how you used the gold I sent in your trunks when you came to America?"

"I have always appreciated your extravagant gift, but no." Her chest swelled and the corners of her mouth lifted. "I used the money from my egg and produce business."

His grin lit a sparkle in his blue eyes.

"But I did dip into a little of Jorn's insurance money to purchase the furniture," Anna admitted.

"You have become remarkable woman." He drew her into a brief hug. "What are your plans for the gold bars?"

"All these years, I have saved it for an emergency." She gazed up at Bedstefa, his shaggy gray brows, his head full of unruly gray hair, and his neatly trimmed gray beard. She still couldn't believe he was here. "But now I'll use it to help my children go to college or start businesses of their own. So far, only Poul has expressed an interest in farming, but he, Torsten, and, of course, Greg, are too young yet to know what they want to do."

"So my legacy to you has become your legacy to them." Bedstefa's warm smile touched her heart.

"You've been more than generous with Peder and me. He has turned his into a successful brewery and saloon."

"You are the only two in my family who have ventured beyond the shores of Denmark, save a trip or two to Paris to see the new fashions." His lips thinned and his voice tightened. "When I retired from captaining my ships, I had hoped to travel with Ingebrod, but she passed on soon after I gave up the sea, and none of my children or grandchildren have any spirit of adventure, save Peder and you."

The memory of her beloved grandmother's passing flitted through Anna's mind. She had been twelve years old, and it was the first funeral she had ever attended.

She locked her gaze on her grandfather. "I could convert the housekeeper's suite into an apartment and you could stay with us."

Bedstefa hugged her. "Now you are the generous one, and I appreciate your offer. But I'm getting old. My friends and the rest of my family are all in Denmark, so I must go back. I'll have to be content with reading your letters. At least I'll be here to see Peder married."

"Are you coming with us to Marshalltown?"

Anna whirled around at the sound of Erik's voice. He was standing in the doorway to the dining room. She motioned for him to come to her.

"Yes, he is." She smiled. "With the two of you, me, Halvor, Adelaide, the nanny, and the other seven children, we will be quite a circus."

Chapter 20

July 12, 1884

Karoline has begun calling me "Moder." Last night she climbed into my lap and fell asleep. She resembles Inge in looks and disposition. So sweet.

I have been nursing Ella occasionally. This helps me to feel motherly toward her. At times I think of Ella and Karoline as Jorn's bequest to me.

Anesa avoids my touch, seeking out Bedstefa or Tilde when she wants something or needs comforting. When another child calls me "Moder," Anesa becomes upset and shouts, "You are not my moder!" or "I want my real moder!" Often, she bursts into tears. I fear a deep chasm divides us. She does not resemble my children or Jorn. Sometimes, I wonder if she was truly his daughter, or if Silge tricked him into believing it. Other times I can't help but imagine I am looking into the face of my husband's other wife.

I pray for strength to overcome this bias, for charity toward this innocent child, and for God to soften our hearts toward each other.

Tilde has bonded with her charges and is pleasant company for my older children, especially Inge. Her family disowned her when they learned she was with child, and did not accept her back when her baby was stillborn. Although a nice and polite, Tilde is prone to laziness, and she spends as much time with Halvor as she can find an excuse for. He does not seem to mind, but I do. Even patient Adelaide becomes exasperated with her. Bedstefa says Tilde was raised in a wealthy household with servants and has not adjusted to being one. Since he hired her, he promised to talk with her. I will have a talk with her, too, before we leave for the wedding.

Having Bedstefa here has been pure joy. He will be with us several more weeks, but I hate the thought of his returning to Denmark.

Sitting next to Bedstefa on a bench in the Parker's yard, Anna waited for the wedding to begin. On her other side were Inge, Poul, and Erik. Torsten had been cranky all morning, so he stayed with Tilde, Adelaide, Greg, and the little girls at the house next door. The neighbors had offered their sitting room for small children who might disrupt the ceremony.

As a string quartet set up to the left of the rose garden, Anna leaned closer to her grandfather. She had promised herself she wouldn't nag, but she had to ask one more time, "Are you certain you won't remain with us in Black Hawk County?"

"I'm enjoying my visit very much, but I can't." He patted her hand.

The quartet began to play.

A lump formed in her throat. She looked into his weathered face. "We will miss you."

Liquid shimmered in his blue eyes. "I'll miss you and Peder and your family, too."

Sadness engulfed her. This visit would most likely be the last time she would see her grandfather. She knew he was thinking the same thought. She squeezed his hand.

"You've become a fine woman," he whispered.

"Thanks for all you have done for me."

Anna forced a smile. It wasn't a day to be dismal.

The bride and groom took their places in front of the pastor. They made a good pair. Charlotte's chestnut-hair, fawn eyes, and delicate features shown beautifully in her ivory silk gown. The beading on the fitted bodice accentuated her tiny waist, and the full, floor-length skirt floated around her. The loving way Peder gazed at his bride made him even more handsome than usual.

Anna perused the guests, locating the Holdens, the Cooks, and several of Peder's friends from Cedar Falls. She found Halvor staring at her. She tensed. He was probably thinking they should marry. She diverted her gaze.

He had been so forthcoming about his feelings. Her stomach fluttered. She doubted Jorn had ever cared as deeply for her as Halvor did. But she had spurned his proposal, and she was not certain how he felt about Tilde's attentions.

Throughout the ceremony, Anna reminded herself how lucky she was to have her brother and, from today on, Charlotte, as family who lived closed by. She had eight healthy children and a legacy for their future. She had good friends, her sales sisters. Love and joy surrounded her. She didn't want for any of the necessities of life.

Word that Anna had taken in Jorn's bastard daughters had spread through the community like a prairie fire. Many acquaintances in Cedar Falls, and even some members of her own church, had been unable to accept Jorn's infidelities. Some shunned Anna and the children. Others said unkind things, sometimes to Anna's face, more often behind her back.

The greenhorns and hired hands had remained loyal, and Adelaide had stayed to help her run the house. Now there was Tilde. Well, time would tell.

And she had Halvor to manage the farm, and to help her with the children. He admired and respected her even when she felt unworthy. He had said he would be content with their arrangement if she didn't marry him. But could he be?

It wasn't fair to expect him to, especially not with when Tilde was clearly attracted to him.

If he grew tired of her refusals, would he turn to her, or would he leave? And if he did, could she run the farm alone? Could she and her children be happy without him?

His absence would create a gaping hole in their lives and in her heart. She winced. Losing Halvor would leave a far larger void than Jorn's death had.

• ♥ •

After the marriage rites ended, Anna sought out her brother and his new wife. She took Peder's hand in one of hers and Charlotte's in the other.

"I wish you both all the joy I found in my marriage and none of the heartaches." Anna squeezed their hands.

Charlotte's brown eyes shone. "And we wish you and your family nothing but happiness."

Peder slipped his free arm around Anna's shoulder. "You've had enough trials for one lifetime."

After a magnificent buffet dinner, the Holden girls helped Adelaide and Inge amuse the children until Halvor and Frederik brought the wagons around to return them to the hotel. Tilde took the opportunity to flirt with several boys who appeared to be near her own age. Good thing she would soon be gone from their company, with Adelaide to keep an eye on her.

When the wagons arrived, Anna helped the children into the box and offered to accompany them, but Adelaide shook her head. "We'll manage just fine. You stay and celebrate your brother's marriage."

Anna smiled. "Thank you."

Tilde climbed onto the seat beside Halvor.

Anna's smile faded, and her teeth clenched.

After they left, she shook off her annoyance and exchanged pleasantries with the Parkers, complimenting them on the ceremony, the feast, and their garden. Gabrielle and Brigitte joined them, adding their praise to the conversation before the Parkers excused themselves to speak with their other guests.

"I'm so glad Bedstefa could be here," Anna said. He stood under a huge oak tree talking with Graham.

"I hope Frederik and Halvor will make it back before the music begins." Brigitte's lazy, hazel gaze drifted to the musicians standing to the left of the steps leading up to the huge open back porch.

"Speaking of Halvor." Gabrielle smiled wryly. "He hasn't been able to keep his eyes from fixing on you this afternoon."

Heat rushed to Anna's cheeks.

Gabrielle whispered, "He probably wished it was you two who were taking vows."

Anna cocked her head. "How can you say such a thing?"

Gabrielle chuckled. "He's been so attentive to you through the years and has become even more so since Jorn's death. Don't tell us you haven't noticed."

"He's my farm manager," Anna said. "We work closely together. Don't confuse that with a personal relationship. I don't want to risk another heartache."

Brigitte snorted then drew her lacy handkerchief to her round face. "Halvor's loved you for years. He would never hurt you. You two have always gotten along splendidly. You can't deny the affection between you."

Anna squared her shoulders. "I don't deny it. But I'm not certain that what I feel is love."

"Are you expecting the fluttering heart and giddiness of youthful love?" Gabrielle's dark brows knit together. "If so, you're looking in the wrong place. Mature love includes affection, trust, faithfulness, and sharing of hopes."

"And companionship," Brigitte added. "It's a comfort to be with each other. You've always had that with Halvor."

Anna looked from one friend to the other. "Yes, I have."

"He's a good man." Brigitte had said those words many times, and Anna agreed. "He would be a good father to your children."

Gabrielle's coffee gaze fixed on Anna. "He's been steadfast in his love for you, which I know he felt that first summer when we were teaching you English. He's never even courted another woman."

Anna frowned. "Has he asked you to speak on his behalf?"

Gabrielle's hand flew to her chest. "He would never do such a thing."

Brigitte slipped her arm around Anna's shoulders. "We just think you should open your heart and mind to him. It's time to put the past behind you."

Anna's frown deepened. "Everywhere I turn, I'm confronted with reminders of it."

"That's why you need to put it to rest," Gabrielle said. "By making a happy future with Halvor."

"I'll consider it," Anna promised, as warmth crept into her cheeks.

Her friends hadn't mentioned a single virtue she hadn't identified herself. He had even killed a man to protect her.

Her heart was opening to him—her heart that, even at her age, gave an occasional flutter when Halvor was near.

• ♥ •

As the musicians began to play, Peder and Charlotte joined in their first dance together as a married couple. They took several turns around the large back porch. Smiling, they gazed into each other's eyes as if they were the only two people in the world.

It was the kind of wedding Anna had dreamed of. Beautiful clothes, family and friends sharing the joy, a pastor conducting a proper ceremony. Such a wedding would not have guaranteed the kind of marriage Bedstefa and Bedstemor had, but if she and Jorn had a church wedding, he might not have become a bigamist. She shook her head to stop that line of thinking. She couldn't change the past.

The strains of "Roses from the Heartfelt Waltz" rose from the string quartet. Charlotte danced with her father, Peder with her mother.

When the parents partnered with each other, Peder came for

Anna. He waltzed her around the porch several times before they came side-by-side with Charlotte and Bedstefa. They exchanged partners.

"Charlotte is a sweet woman. Peder's a lucky man," Bedstefa said, as he and Anna glided off in the opposite direction.

"Yes." Anna smiled. "And he knows it. I hope they'll be as happy as you were with Bedstemor."

"She was very special." Bedstefa's voice grew soft. "I miss her."

Anna had fond memories of her grandmother, too. "What made the two of you so happy together?"

He patted her waist. "Love. Pleasure in each other's company. And each of us tried to keep the other's happiness above our own."

A twinge of guilt nipped her. Halvor had practiced Bedstefa's recipe for happiness for as long as she could remember. She felt selfish in comparison.

Halvor hovered at the edge of the porch. He stepped forward as Bedstefa and Anna approached.

"May I have the pleasure of this dance?" Halvor held out his hand.

Anna smiled as their fingers met. Her heart gave one of those little flutters her friends had said she was too old to expect. "I'd like that."

"Remember what I told you," Bedstefa said, allowing Halvor to take his place.

"What did he tell you?" Halvor asked.

She dropped her gaze then looked up at him through her lashes. "He was talking about his marriage to my grandmother."

The musicians began to play another waltz.

Pleasure skipped though Anna at Halvor's touch as they assumed the proper position. Dancing in his arms felt natural. Just as natural as the kiss they shared so long ago.

Still, dancing with a man was one thing; being married to him was quite another. She and Halvor had a comfortable relationship, one she didn't want to jeopardize through the change in expectations that would come with matrimony.

"You seem distracted." Halvor frowned.

She smiled to reassure him. "Just concentrating. I don't want to step on your toes."

He grinned. "I wouldn't mind."

Peder and Charlotte drifted past. When she and Halvor were back-to-back with them, Peder winked at Anna.

The tune ended and the dancers applauded. Strains of a new piece filled the air. Halvor and Anna moved in time with the notes. How would she feel if he tried to kiss her next time they were alone?

Her thoughts were taking their own liberties. There was no reason to believe they would be alone any time soon. Even when they returned to Cedar Falls, the children would nearly always be around.

"You're very quiet." Halvor's brows knit together. "Are you uncomfortable with me as your partner?"

She smiled. "Not at all." Perhaps she should confide in him. She didn't want secrets between them. There had been too many between her and Jorn. "I don't know if it's due to Peder's wedding, but I've been giving much thought to the idea of marriage today."

"To me?" Caution tightened his angular features. "Or someone else?"

She gave his hand a gentle squeeze. "Only you."

He broke into a grin, which reached his blue eyes. "I hope you'll continue to think about becoming my wife."

"We've always gotten on so well," Anna said with a heavy sigh. "I'd hate for that to change."

"It won't." Halvor pulled her closer. "It will just get better."

If only she could be that certain.

• ♥ •

After their return to the farm, Anna worked hard to get her household back into their old routines. She hoped this would reassure her own children, and provide some comfort to Anesa and Karoline once they learned what to expect. Playing school became a daily routine, with Inge, Poul, and Torsten taking turns at playing teachers to the little girls. The sessions were short, but the stepsisters enjoyed the attention. The family spoke Danish around the newcomers.

Tomorrow would be the first time Jorn's Danish daughters would accompany the family to church. Throughout the noon meal, Anna, Halvor, and Adelaide talked about how the service typically proceeded. They told of how Peder usually sat with the family, and how Halvor and Adelaide did, too.

Tilde's eyes widened. "Your servants share your pew?"

Anna nodded. "Yes. Through the years I've needed their help with the children. And we think of them as part of the family."

She smiled at Adelaide, then Halvor.

"My parents would never allow our household staff to sit at the table with them, let alone join them in church." Tilde shook her head, her brown curls swinging. It was unlike her to mention her family. "America must be very different from Denmark."

"It's not America that's different, it's Anna." Adelaide's face reddened. "I mean Mrs. Stryker."

"You may call me 'Anna' in front of Tilde and my grandfather," Anna reassured her. "We hope Tilde will come to feel she is part of the family, too."

Halvor leaned forward. "When we first joined Anna in the pew at church, there was a lot of gossip and some obvious disapproval, but we all held our heads high, and now the congregation seems to accept it."

Anna nodded. "But when we all go to church together tomorrow, people will most likely talk about us, judge us, again."

"Because Fader was a bad man," Erik said.

"It's not our place to judge him." Halvor patted Erik's shoulder. "He made mistakes, but then, we all make mistakes."

"Because he sinned?" Inge asked. "Why would they blame us for Fader's sins?"

Bedstefa, who was sitting beside her, took her dainty hand in his. "Sometimes people treat friends or family of a person who made mistakes as if they are the ones who did something wrong. It isn't fair, but you must always remember you are not to blame for your father's behavior." He looked from child to child. "These people may not know any better, so be nice to them, anyway."

"But it's hard to be nice to people who make fun of me or my family." Inge's lips pinched together as if she were holding in more that she wanted to say.

"Because Fader made these Danish sisters, people will make fun of us," Erik said in English. He pushed his chair away from the table and stood.

Tilde looked up from urging the little girls to finish eating. Her brow furrowed in confusion.

"Sit down, Erik," Anna said. "You have not been excused."

Pouting, Erik plopped back down into his chair. "Fader was always mean to us."

"I know it's hard to believe sometimes, but your father loved all of you children." Anna choked out the words she sometimes questioned herself.

Halvor leaned back and draped an arm over the back of Erik's chair. "And he was very proud of all of you."

Bedstefa nodded. "Tomorrow at church, you will have me, your Uncle Peder, and Aunt Charlotte with you. If someone says something naughty, just walk away and come to one of us."

Poul set down his fork and looked from person to person around the table. "If we all go to church, there will be thirteen of us Strykers. And that doesn't count the babies."

"Not everyone is a Stryker." Inge sighed. "We'll have Jorgesens and Hansens, too."

Red crept into Poul's cheeks.

"But we're all your relatives and friends," Bedstefa flashed Poul a smile.

His eyes narrowed and he tilted his head to one side. "How will we fit in the pew?"

"We may have to split into two groups," Halvor said. "We'll go early so we can all sit together."

"Strength in numbers," Adelaide said.

Anna sighed. "As long as we all help each other, we'll get through whatever happens."

• ♥ •

Reverend Spelman was presiding over the service. He now came to the little church only when the regular pastor was away. She had a soft spot in her heart for him, since he had always accepted Anna's decision to allow her employees to join her family in their pew.

Today, his sermon was on charity. His message began with the need to gather old clothes and dried apples for the destitute in Nebraska, who were suffering because of an agricultural depression. He ended his message talking about the need for charity of spirit toward people who have faced troubles in their lives. Despite the fact he didn't mention them directly, he seemed to be talking about Anna and her family.

She made a special point of thanking him for today's message. Whether it was the pastor's sermon or the numbers of family and friends surrounding them, no one suffered ill-intended remarks about Jorn's infidelity. Anna didn't expect the charitable behavior to continue indefinitely. She worried especially about the attitudes her children would encounter in school.

As summer wound down, the new school year began. Anna was sad that Charlotte would no longer be teaching, but Torsten's excitement about being a first grader lifted her spirits. After years of playing school, he was more than ready for the real thing.

Anna feared his and her other children's enthusiasm might be diminished by derogatory remarks about their father, Jorn's Danish daughters, or herself.

Inge and Poul persuaded Bedstefa to ride along with them as Anna picked up the Holden children and drove the wagon to school. There they met Miss Roddick. The new teacher appeared very young, but was polite and pleasant. If the children liked her, Anna would offer to house her next year. It would be good to have an ally.

When they returned home, Bedstefa went outside to help Halvor in the garden. Anna pulled Inge's old winter clothes from the clothes press. The coats and dresses were in better condition than she remembered. She placed the garments on her bed, then went to the nursery, where Tilde was amusing her charges with a game of hide the button. Anna watched the search until Karoline spotted the prize under her bed. She pulled it out and held it up, grinning.

Anesa burst into tears and reached for her sister's hand. "I want it."

"Maybe next time," Tilde told her, laughing.

Now that they had settled in, the time had come for them to begin learning English. Torsten would love the chance to play teacher, and here were the perfect pupils for him. Assuming he came home excited about school, she would have him and Poul start teaching them tonight.

Anesa's mouth drew into a pout. Anna held out her arms to

the little girl. "Come with me, and try on some new dresses! We'll see if we can find some that fit you. It will be fun!"

Anesa did not come for an embrace, but she took Anna's hand and followed her down the hall.

"You're growing into a fine, strong girl. You'll need some warm clothes for church and for playing outside in the winter." And maybe for starting school, if she began learning English and if none of the scandal surrounding her father played out in the classroom.

For the next half-hour, Anna sang Danish children's songs and, in English, the alphabet song her older children had learned in school. She was pleased to have the time alone together, but Anesa held back, still wary.

When they finished, Anna returned Anesa to the nursery and exchanged her for Karoline.

Anna repeated the process with the younger girl. Luckily, most of the dresses had a loose style because the two little girls were a bit stockier than Inge had been. Still, many of the clothes fit one or the other of them.

Karoline stood in front of the mirror, admiring herself in a lavender calico that had always been one of Inge's favorites. After several moments, Karoline turned her round little face and wide blue eyes to Anna. "Karo'ine's dress?"

Anna knelt down beside the young girl. "Yes, it's your dress."

Karoline flung her arms around Anna's neck, knocking her into a sitting position then climbed on her lap.

Anna held her close. "You look very pretty," she whispered into a small ear. "I love you, Karoline."

"Me love Mor!" The little arms tightened around Anna's neck.

For a moment, she was not sure if Karoline had used the endearing form of mother to mean her or Silge. Until now, the girl had used the formal "Moder," just as Anna's own children always had. Bedstefa had mentioned they referred to their real mother as "Mor."

Anna hugged Karoline close and kissed her cheek. Karoline planted her moist lips on Anna's cheek. The two traded kisses until they were both giggling and rolling on the floor. The chime of the clock striking 11 barely reached Anna's consciousness over the shared mirth.

"I must take you back to Tilde." Anna picked up Karoline and set her in a standing position. "I need to help Adelaide."

As soon as Anna was on her feet, Karoline grasped her hand. Anna smiled down at her.

When they reached the nursery, Tilde was nursing Ella. Anna scanned the room. "Where is Anesa?"

Tilde's head shot up. "Isn't she with you?"

"No."

"She said she was going to find her mother." Tilde's brows knitted in worry. "When I heard all that laughing, I thought she was with you."

"Keep Karoline here," Anna said. "I'll look for Anesa. Perhaps she's playing in one of the other bedrooms."

She searched the rooms, under the beds, in corners, behind furniture. No sign of Anesa. Uneasiness weighed in Anna's stomach.

She opened the door to the attic, climbed the steps, and checked all of the nooks and crannies, the trunks, the crates. Still no sign of the little girl.

She must have gone downstairs to Adelaide. Perhaps Anesa had some confusion between the housekeeper's position and Anna's.

Adelaide stood in the kitchen, beating dough for biscuits.

"Is Anesa with you?" Anna asked.

Adelaide's graying head snapped up. "Why, no."

Concern flitted through Anna's chest. "We need to find her."

"She isn't with Tilde?"

"No." Anna swallowed. "You search this floor. I'll look downstairs."

No sign of Anesa in the basement. Had the child gone outdoors? Anna hurried upstairs and found Adelaide checking under the dining room table.

"Have you finished in the parlor and sitting room?" Anna asked.

"Yes," Adelaide said. "But I still have to look in the housekeeper's quarters."

"I'll do it." Anna headed to the rooms Adelaide refused to occupy. They held Bedstefa's things but no Anesa.

After assuring herself the child wasn't hiding in the suite, Anna rushed to the back door. "You check the front yard, I'll look in back."

How had the child gotten outside without being seen? Anna hurried from tree to bush, working her way toward the vegetable gardens. Her heartbeat quickened. The child was far too young to be unsupervised in the barnyard.

Anna ran to where Bedstefa and Halvor were hoeing weeds among the tomato plants. "Anesa is missing."

Halvor dropped his hoe and hurried toward her. Bedstefa followed. Nearly breathless, Anna explained the situation.

Adelaide hastily rounded the corner of the house, alone. Anna's hopes sank.

"I checked the front and the road," Adelaide said. "I didn't see her."

Was Anesa was in the fields—lost and alone?

The four hastily discussed the directions the child might have gone. They decided to check the buildings first. Adelaide headed for the chicken coop. Bedstefa went toward the bunkhouse. Halvor said he would check the barn and stable.

If Anesa had gotten in with the horses or the livestock, she could be trampled. Pushing the terrible picture from her mind, Anna ran to the granary. Throwing open the doors to allow as much light into the dark building as possible, Anna climbed the ladder on the wall to the corn crib. She couldn't see a child on top of the pile of ears.

"Anesa!" Anna called, trying to keep the panic out of her voice. She listened for a moment. Silence. "Anesa!"

Rung by rung, Anna descended to the floor. She checked all the corners.

"Anesa!" she called again. Louder.

She stood still, hoping for a reply.

Nothing.

She walked toward the carriage, bent down, and looked beneath it. No sign of the child.

Tears streamed down Anna's cheeks as she straightened. She couldn't be more frightened for Anesa's welfare if the girl was her own.

Opening the carriage door, Anna stared into the dark interior. Her eye caught a movement under the seat.

Anna broke into sobs of relief. Fearing she would scare the child, she swallowed them back.

"Anesa," she said quietly. "I'm glad you are safe."

The little girl didn't move.

"Come here, Anesa." Anna held her arms open. "It's almost time to eat."

"No." Anesa pressed her small body into the corner.

"Aren't you hungry?" Anna coaxed, hoping the child would come to her so she wouldn't have to go into the carriage to force her out.

"I want Mor!" Anesa shouted.

"I'm here."

"You not Mor." Anesa's voice shook. "I go home to Mor."

Pressure built behind Anna's eyes and spread into her temples. She climbed into the carriage, picked up the child, and sat on the seat holding Anesa in her lap.

"Mor is not in Denmark," Anna said quietly, smoothing the

little girl's soft, brown hair. "She is with God. In heaven. We'll never see her again, but He will take good care of her."

"No!" Anesa screamed. She squirmed, kicked her feet, and pounded her fists against Anna's chest.

Anna held her closer.

"I want Mor!" Anesa wailed.

Chapter 21

September 7, 1884

Now that my year of mourning for Jorn has ended, I have happily shed my black garments. After learning of his marriage to Silge, my outward appearance of grieving for him became only a pretense. I refuse to carry it on for another year, no matter how folks judge me.

For the first time since I conceived Erik, I feel free. Not from my responsibilities as a mother. Those, I love. But free to live the life I want.

Now, I must decide if marriage to Halvor is what I want. He is a wonderful man, but I fear we will lose our friendship if we wed. I am keeping Bedstefa's advice in mind as I consider Halvor's proposal.

The children are not enjoying school as in past years. I wonder if the new teacher is not as talented as Charlotte in encouraging them to learn. Hopefully, the situation will improve as Miss Roddick gains more experience.

Bedstefa will be leaving at the end of the week. I will hate to see him go and so will my children. I especially worry about Anesa. She has lost her mother, her grandparents, her home and now she is losing the man she has grown to love and trust. The poor little thing is too young to understand it all.

Anna helped Halvor pick tomatoes and pack them into crates. Tomorrow, she, Brigitte, and Gabrielle would deliver their produce and wares in town. Anna dreaded the trip. While she had not lost any business due to the scandal, she had encountered a good share of rudeness.

"How could you bring your husband's bastard daughters

into your home?" the wife of the grocer had asked.

In the post office, two women who frequented the restaurant where Anna and her friends often took their noon meal had turned away from her when she greeted them.

"He went every summer. How could she not have suspected his infidelity?" one of the women whispered loudly to the other.

Gabrielle shot them a glare. "How can women who claim to be well-bred behave with such poor manners?"

Anna could only imagine the gossip circulating through town by people who weren't as open about their disapproval. She kept reminding herself that she could never control Jorn's behavior and she wasn't to blame for it. She would just have to bear up and behave with dignity in the face others' judgments.

On the way home, Anna had thanked her friends for their support. She hated that they might be painted with the same brush of shame because of their steadfastness. Tears filled her eyes just thinking of their loyalty.

"How much of this summer squash do you want to sell?" Halvor asked when they finished packing the tomatoes.

She blinked back her emotions and focused on his question. "Let's save enough for your mother to use in this week's meals, and crate up the rest of the ripe ones."

The back door slammed. Inge ran down the steps toward the garden. Moments later Poul followed.

Anna picked her way through the viney foliage to meet her children, eager to hear about their day at school.

Red blotches covered her daughter's usually rosy complexion, as if she had been crying. Anger darkened Poul's dirt-smudged face.

"I'm not going back to school." Breathlessness diminished Inge's shout.

"Me, either!" Poul yelled.

Anna put an arm around each child. "Let's sit on the porch steps, and you can tell me what happened."

"Abigail Bacon said we are tainted, and she doesn't want to

play with me or talk to me anymore," Inge said before they reached the house. "She's afraid she'll become dirty being around me."

Anna's chest tightened.

Poul lifted his chin. "We told her we weren't and that wasn't a nice thing to say."

"But she said it was true. Her parents said so." Inge burst into tears.

"Her brother pushed Inge away from her, so I pushed him." Poul straightened, puffing out his chest. "He pushed me back, and Jess Holden came and shoved both Bacons into the corner."

They reached the steps and Anna sat down, with a child on either side. "Force is not a good solution." She hugged them close. "What did Miss Roddick do?"

"She used a switch on Jess, then made us and the Holdens stay in from all the recesses, even though Erik and the others didn't do nothing. Miss Roddick didn't do nothing to the Bacons." The action clearly offended Poul's six-year-old sense of justice.

It offended Anna's, too. If her children's account was accurate, they were only reacting to the behavior of the Bacon children.

"That's why none of us are going back to school," Inge said in a choked voice.

Anna's muscles tensed. She drew in a deep breath.

"I'm sorry that you had to face such rude behavior, but you and Jess shouldn't have pushed the Bacons." She fought to keep her voice low and her tone even.

"But they pushed us first!" Poul glowered at her.

That part distressed Anna. Why were her children and the Holdens punished, but not the Bacons? Then she remembered. Miss Roddick was living with the Bacons this year. Heat flooded through Anna. Did the teacher feel she couldn't discipline her hosts' children?

"I understand." Anna patted her son's shoulder. "But it

would have been better if you just walked away from people as impolite as the Bacons." She turned to Inge. "Wouldn't you rather play with people that are nicer than the Bacons?"

"But Abigail was the only other girl at school today, except for Magdelone Holden." A shadow of disdain crossed Inge's face. "She's too little. Torsten's age."

Poul said, "Jess said you could play with him and Erik tomorrow."

"Unless Miss Roddick keeps us all in from recess again." Inge gave a disheartened shrug. "She should have made the Bacons stay in. That's why we decided not to go to school anymore."

"Well, you must go to school." Anna hugged her children close. "You are Strykers. You can't run away from your problems. Next time Abigail or her brother are mean to you, walk away."

Anna could not shy away from the problem, either. Tomorrow, she would talk with the teacher to get her perspective on what happened.

The next morning, when Anna stopped to pick up the Holden children, Brigitte approached the wagon with them, already dressed for their trip to town.

With flaring nostrils and bared teeth, Brigitte clambered into the seat beside her. "Did you hear about what happened yesterday? We need to talk with Miss Roddick."

Anna swallowed. She was planning to do just that, but Brigitte's frame of mind would not be helpful.

"I agree," Anna said. "But I think we need to learn her side of the story."

"I don't mind her whipping my son, if he deserves it," Brigitte said in an angry whisper. "But it isn't fair that she did not also whip the Bacon boy."

"I'm sorry that my family's scandal has spilled over to your children." Anna blinked back tears. "Perhaps I should take my children out of school and ask Charlotte to teach them."

Brigitte shook her head. "If you did that, my children would be jealous. And if we both sent our children to Charlotte, there wouldn't be enough students to keep the school open, except in winter." Mischief sparkled in her blue eyes. "Perhaps we should point that out to Miss Roddick."

Anna managed a smile. "Let's see what the teacher has to say."

When they arrived at the school, the women instructed the children to stay in the wagon while they talked with Miss Roddick.

The young teacher's explanation of what happened was remarkably similar to that of Inge and Poul.

"Then why did you whip my son and not the Bacon boy?" Brigitte asked in a tone more accusatory than Anna would have liked.

"The Bacons are only repeating the sentiments of their parents." A rosy flush colored Miss Roddick's apple cheeks. "I have to live with them. I'm sure it would not go over well if I punished the children for expressing their parents' views."

"Perhaps you should move to my house," Anna said. "I have housekeeper's quarters that aren't being used."

The teacher hesitated. "I fear if I do that the Bacons and the Leckmans might take their children out of school. That would be four fewer children, six if you count the two boys who will return to school after the harvest."

Brigitte straightened her shoulders. "Between Mrs. Stryker and me, we have seven children in school."

Color drained from Miss Roddick's face.

"Perhaps you should come and live with my husband and me," Brigitte continued. "We hosted the previous teacher, Miss Parker. She is now Mrs. Stryker's sister-in-law."

"I shall consider it," Miss Roddick promised. "And, I'll speak with the Bacons about their children's behavior tonight."

Anna smiled at the teacher. "That's all we can ask."

• ♥ •

By Saturday, Miss Ritter had moved to the Holdens'. The Bacons had taken their son and daughter out of school, although the Leckmans had not. Anna hoped the school year now would be productive and pleasant for her children.

As she, Halvor, and the children accompanied Bedstefa to the depot, she couldn't shake the sadness engulfing her. When her grandfather got on the train today, she would never see him again.

She rode on the wagon seat with Halvor. Bedstefa had insisted on sitting in a chair in the box with the children and his trunk. Now that her family had grown so large, they no longer fit comfortably in the carriage. Anna wished she could have taken him to the depot in better style, but he insisted that all his great-grandchildren see him off, and she wanted her children to have this last memory of him. They had grown to love him dearly.

As the wagon pulled up to the hitching post outside the train station, Anna noted that Peder's carriage was already there.

Anesa clung to Bedstefa. He hugged her then passed her to Inge as Halvor steadied him so he could leave the wagon. As soon as Bedstefa reached the ground, Anesa insisted on holding his hand.

Halvor lugged the trunk, and Erik carried the satchel toward the platform.

As the rest of the family trooped into the depot, Peder and Charlotte met them.

"We're sorry to be saying goodbye to you." Peder gave Bedstefa a bear hug. "It's been good to see you, again."

"And I feel fortunate that you could attend our wedding," Charlotte added.

"It is I who was fortunate to meet his lovely bride." Bedstefa smiled. "You have already made him very happy."

Pressure built behind Anna'a eyes. She blinked it away.

Bedstefa's send-off must not be a tearful one.

Bedstefa led the rest of the family to stand by his belongings. He ruffled Erik's light brown hair. "You're a good man, Erik. I hope you'll help Halvor take care of your mother."

Erik straightened. "I'm the man of the family now."

Bedstefa winked at Anna. "Yes, and as such you must look out for your new little sisters and make them feel at home."

Erik's freckled nose wrinkled, but he said nothing. His resistance to his stepsisters was as hard on Anna as Anesa's rejection of her new family.

Bedstefa said his farewells to each child in turn, planting a small kiss on Karoline's cheek before he slipped his arm around Anna. "I'm so glad I got to see you again," he whispered in her ear. "From the time you were a child, you have given me great pleasure. Through the years I've looked forward to your letters, and I'm pleased to have been able to meet your lovely family." He hugged her tighter. "You've grown into a fine, charitable woman. I'm proud you are my granddaughter."

"Oh, Bedstefa." Anna sniffed back the tears that threatened to fall. "I'm glad you came. I love you so."

"And I, you," Bedstefa said in a cracking voice.

The conductor called, "All aboard!"

Bedstefa knelt down and picked up Anesa. "I must say farewell, now, my girl. Behave. Your new mother will take good care of you."

He handed her to Halvor.

"No!" Anesa shrieked, holding her arms out to Bedstefa. "Me go with you."

Bedstefa turned his back on her and hugged Anna one last time. "She'll come around in a few weeks or a few months. Just be constant in showing your love for her."

"I'll try." Anna gave him her word.

"Goodbye, all." Bedstefa raised his hand in farewell.

"Have a safe trip," Peder called after him.

"No!" Anesa screamed. "Me go."

"We will write often," Anna promised, as the tears slipped down her cheeks.

She cast her watery gaze toward Anesa's panicked face. The poor little girl was too young to understand death, or grown-up obligations.

Anna understood these, but still felt the same pain as Anesa did about Bedstefa's leaving. To her it must seem as if all the adults she had ever loved had deserted her.

Whether or not Anesa ever accepted her as mother, Anna vowed to be a constant the child could count on in her life.

• ♥ •

After Friday evening's meal, Anna gathered the children, Adelaide, Tilde, and Halvor around the piano. She played familiar tunes, hymns, and children's songs. Everyone sang.

Erik and Inge each played a song they had mastered. Everyone clapped.

"If you don't mind, I would like to play for awhile," Tilde said. Her face glowed a soft pink. "My parents used to make me perform for their guests. I swore never to touch a piano again when they disowned me." She paused. "But you've reminded me it can be fun."

Anna raised a brow. "Of course you may have a turn."

Tilde had made great strides toward becoming part of the family, and it pleased Anna that the girl felt comfortable joining in the activities instead of just watching them.

Inge stood and Tilde took her place. She ran her fingers up and down the keys. Then she began playing a waltz.

Anna caught Halvor's eye and smiled. Dancing at Peder's wedding was the last time she had been in his arms, but she didn't want to be too obvious about her desire to be there again.

She walked over to Erik, whose head now reached her shoulder, and asked him to be her partner. He shrunk away. Was he still punishing her for bringing his stepsisters into the family?

Before she could ask, Poul raced up to her. "I'll dance with you, Moder."

Anna grinned at him, positioned his hand on her waist, and took the other in hers. Halvor took Inge for his partner and Adelaide took Torsten. They circled the parlor in a makeshift waltz, all the time chattering and laughing. Erik's chin dipped to his chest and he frowned.

When the song ended, everyone, except him, applauded.

"Let's change partners," Halvor called.

Anna lifted Karoline to her hip. Halvor reached for Anesa. She pulled away.

"Come on," he coaxed. "It'll be fun." He held out his open arms. Anesa did not move into them, but she didn't withdraw. He scooped her up.

Poul moved to Adelaide and Torsten reluctantly took his big sister's outstretched hand as Tilde started playing again.

As Anna twirled Karoline around the room, she giggled in delight. Anesa was doing the same in Halvor's arms. Such a joy to see the girls happy! To see all of her children happy.

When the music stopped, everyone clapped, even Erik.

"Change again." Halvor held Anesa toward Anna. She set Karoline on the floor and Erik stepped in to take her hands. Poul moved to Inge, leaving Halvor to dance with his mother. Torsten was the odd one out. He plopped down in a chair and pouted.

Anna felt Anesa's body stiffen, but at least the little girl wasn't fighting her. When the notes began, Anna held the little girl close. She whirled her around in exaggerated swings and dips until her daughter was giggling and holding tight, her arms around Anna's neck.

"I love you, Anesa," Anna whispered loudly into the girl's ear. Anesa laughed as if Anna's breath had tickled her.

Anna's next dance was with Erik followed by one with Torsten. For years, she had longed to have family evenings like this, filled with music and joy.

After the final notes of the song, Tilde pushed herself away from the piano. "That was fun." She grinned. "But I'm afraid I don't know any more songs."

"You can't stop now," Inge said. "Moder hasn't danced with Halvor yet."

Tilde raised an eyebrow and looked from Anna to Halvor.

"Please play one more." Halvor took Anna's hand.

"It will have to be a repeat." Tilde frowned and repositioned herself at the keyboard and began a waltz.

Halvor placed his free hand on Anna's waist. She lay hers on his shoulder. Keeping a respectable distance between them, they glided around the room. The others paired up and followed suit, but before the music ended, they had faded to the couch and chairs, watching as Anna and Halvor moved with the music.

"They're good," Inge said to Adelaide as the final notes faded.

"Yes, they are," she said. "They make a nice couple, don't they?"

"Yes," Inge replied.

Heat crept into Anna's cheeks at their conversation, loud enough to be heard by everyone in the room.

"Adelaide, please give each of the children one of those oatmeal cookies you made today and a glass of milk, while Tilde and I feed the babies," Anna said, as she reluctantly slipped from Halvor's arms when the music ended. "When I come downstairs, we'll all read bedtime stories together."

After feeding Greg and Ella, then tucking them into their beds, Anna and Tilde went downstairs to the parlor. Inge read nursery rhymes in English, while Karoline sat in Anna's lap and Anesa sat in Halvor's. Poul and Torsten recited their favorites along with their big sister.

The little girls didn't seem to understand the meaning, but they enjoyed the singsong rhythm, and occasionally said a familiar word along with the others.

When Inge finished, Anna and Tilde carried the girls toward the stairs.

"Far!" Anesa called, holding her hand out in Halvor's direction. "Say good night."

Anna stared at the little girl who had just called Halvor the familiar form of father. Had she used the term to refer to Jorn? Had she transferred her feelings for Jorn to Halvor?

Halvor's blue eyes widened. His gaze questioned Anna.

"Give us a few minutes to get the girls in bed, Far. Then come up and tell them 'good night,'" Anna said in Danish. She rather liked the idea of the little girls referring to Halvor as their *far*, especially since Karoline now regularly referred to Anna as her *mor*.

The older children looked confused.

"Can we call Halvor '*Far*,' too?" Torsten asked.

Anna smiled. "You'll have to ask him."

She followed Tilde upstairs.

After Anna and Halvor had put the girls to bed, they returned to the parlor.

"Halvor is not our father." Poul glared at Torsten. "Why should we call him that?"

"You don't have to," Halvor said. "But I love you as much as any father could love his children, so if you want to call me '*Far*,' it's fine with me."

Poul's eyes widened, then he hung his head. Inge smiled sweetly at Halvor.

Torsten grinned. "Then I'll call you '*Far*,' if I can remember it."

"Me, too," Inge said.

Halvor grinned at them. "That will be fine." He turned to Erik. "Now it's time for you to read." He pulled the volume of *Tom Sawyer* they had begun a few days ago. "Here's the book."

Erik and Inge took turns reading a chapter each evening, since they read English better than Halvor and Anna. The children did not recognize some of the words and had to look them up in the dictionary. Sometimes they could not find them and had to guess at their meaning. Poul and Torsten understood little, but enjoyed being included.

Before he was finished, the mantel clock struck ten, the children's usual bedtime on Friday nights since there was no school in the morning. He continued to the end of the chapter.

"That was very good." Anna was always amazed at how well her children recognized and understood the written word. "Now, it's time for bed. You go up and get ready. I'll be up in a few minutes to say 'good night.'"

"Can Halvor—Far—come, too?" Torsten asked, his bright blue gaze locked on Anna.

"No!" Poul shouted. "That's just for babies. Are you still a baby?"

Anna jumped. Poul had always seemed to like Halvor. Why was he so opposed to seeing Halvor in a fatherly role? Jorn's death must have affected Poul more deeply than she realized.

"No." Torsten hung his head and pouted.

"It's all right, Torsten," Anna said. "When Poul was your age, he liked to be tucked in, too."

"I'll just say 'good night' to all of you here," Halvor said gently. "Good night."

The children echoed his word in a chorus, then headed upstairs.

When they were out of sight, Halvor turned to Anna. "Does it bother you to have the little girls refer to me as their father?"

"No." She smiled at him.

His blonde eyebrows drew together. "How about your own children, should they decide to call me 'Far'?"

"I rather like the idea."

The corners of his lips turned upward, and happiness lit his eyes. "Good. Because I love your children. All of them."

"I'm glad." Anna stood as Adelaide joined them, her work in the kitchen done. "I must go upstairs and tuck my children in. Even those who think they're too old for it."

"Good night, Anna," Adelaide said.

"Good night."

Anna kissed and hugged all four of her older children, then returned to the parlor to turn out the lamps. To her surprise, Halvor still sat in the same chair where she had left him. Adelaide was gone.

"This was a wonderful night," he said quietly. "It was good to see everyone so happy."

"Yes. It's time the children had more fun in their lives."

"And their mother, too." Halvor stood and crossed the room to her. "Dance with me." He held out his hand.

Anna's cheeks warmed. "There's no music."

He took her hand in his and placed his other on her waist. "Don't you hear the music I hear when we're together?"

Her eyes moistened. It had been many years since a man said such sweet words to her.

He led her around the floor with the same ease as when Tilde played the piano.

After several minutes, he stopped and pulled her close. "I love you, Anna."

Before she realized what was happening, his warm, firm lips covered hers.

She allowed herself to be swept away by the moment.

He deepened the kiss, and she tasted the faint sweetness of oatmeal cookie. Her knees weakened, and she clung to his shoulders to steady herself.

Heat pooled in her belly. It was a sensation she hadn't felt for quite some time. She reveled in it. Memories of their long-ago kiss flitted through her mind as if it had been only yesterday.

Abruptly, he broke away. "Anna." His whisper was hoarse. "Please marry me."

She forced herself to inhale deeply.

"No." Her word sounded breathless, weak.

"Do you worry about the scandal you would cause by

marrying a farmhand?" he asked gently.

Anna chuckled. "I've been through far worse scandal than that."

Puzzlement furrowed his brow. "Then why won't you say yes?"

Warmth flooded her cheeks once more. Her reason was so childish. Could she tell him?

This was Halvor. Of course, she could tell him, and she should. They couldn't have a marriage like the one she had with Jorn, filled with secrets and lies.

In a silly moment, she put her hands on her hips like a petulant schoolgirl. Joy pounded in her heart. "Because you haven't properly courted me. You have only proposed."

He stared at her as if she'd lost her mind. Then a grin broke through. "You want me to win your hand."

"Yes. I've never been properly courted." She couldn't keep the serious note from her voice. "I always believed Jorn felt I forced him to marry me."

"Well, Mrs. Stryker—Miss Jorgesen. Prepare to be courted."

• ♥ •

Over the next few weeks, Halvor treated Anna like a queen. Every day, he did something special to show his love for her. Sometimes he took her on walks to see the progress of the harvest, holding her hand as they strolled the fields. Once, he brought her a bouquet of fall-bronzed foxtail seed-heads, tied together with a bow of woven grass. Another day he took her for a picnic in the hayloft. One evening, he produced whistles he had whittled for each child and adult in the family, and they all played them and marched through the house. After the first snowfall, he took her for a sleigh ride under the full moon.

"The snow is glisteneing like diamonds in the moonlight." Halvor pulled her close.

She shivered. Not from the cold. His embrace kept her

warm. This was the moment he would as her to marry him. She smiled. "It's beautiful."

"As are you."

His mouth claimed hers. He kissed her long and deep.

Her muscles melted. She lost the breath she would need to accept his proposal.

When he broke the kiss, he picked up the reins and urged the horses homeward. "We'd better get back so you can put your children to bed."

She slumped against the seat and inhaled deep breaths of the frosty air, struggling to regain her composure before she returned to her family.

• ♥ •

By Thanksgiving, Halvor had won Anna's whole heart, but he hadn't proposed again. She could not bring herself to propose to him. It would not be right.

Each time he went to town, he brought her candles to light for the *Jul* season. He made her an Advent wreath and insisted that each candle be lit with the whole family, even the babies, present. He told the children stories of the *Nisser*, and one evening, they all went outside to search for the mischievous elfin creatures.

He set the farmhands and remaining greenhorns to cleaning the farmyard and stable in preparation for Christmas, and throughout the season he put sheaves of grain out for the birds. There would be no butchering of animals in December as Jorn had done. The Holdens and Cooks agreed to wait until January.

On December twenty-third, Halvor cut a fir tree from the grove and stood it in a corner of the parlor, then closed the doors. After the children went to bed, he and Anna trimmed it with the paper cones, Danish hearts, and other decorations the children had made this year, and the ones Anna had saved from previous years. The pine scent and colorful ornaments ignited Anna's holiday spirit.

"Tomorrow I want you to come with me when I give the livestock extra rations." Halvor took her hand in his. "Remember when you asked me to do that the first year we met?"

"I remember." She did, although she hadn't thought about it in years. "You've made this a joyful *Jul* season for the children." She smiled. "It means a lot to me."

"I've enjoyed it." He kissed her fingertips. "But I've done it for myself, too. After these past two years, we deserve all the good luck we can get."

The mantel clock struck twelve.

"It is *Juleaften*," Anna whispered.

Halvor pulled her to him and kissed her deeply, warming her to her toes. "You had better get some sleep if we're going to feed the stock in the morning." He hugged her once more then released her. "I'll see you at sunrise."

After breakfast the next morning, Anna bundled warmly and pulled her cloak around her. Her older children had asked to join her and Halvor in feeding the livestock their special Christmas Eve meal. Although the task wouldn't be as romantic with the five young chaperones, Halvor and Anna agreed it would be fun for the children.

Since the night when the family all danced together, Anesa had made great strides in accepting Anna and her family. Poul was still a little standoffish toward Halvor, but he had shown no more outright hostility, and he participated in all the family activities with Halvor. Hopefully, it would be only a matter of time before Poul felt comfortable showing affection for Halvor like his sisters and brothers did.

The little group trooped first to the pigsty and fed corn to the swine. Then, they placed mounds of hay in the pens for the cattle and sheep. They took an extra bucket of oats to the stable for the horses. They scattered cracked corn in the chicken coup for the hens and the lone rooster.

"What about the cats?" Torsten asked, as they headed back

to the house.

Halvor grinned. "There's an extra bucket of milk in the kitchen we can feed to them."

Anna was pleased he had remembered her young son's fondness for Mouser and the other cats.

Halvor retrieved the bucket, and they all walked to the granary, where the children had fixed a home of blanket-lined crates for their furry playmates. At the creak of the door opening, the cats came running. The air filled with eager mews as the felines sniffed the sweet scent of the still-warm milk. They raced to their bowls. While the cats lapped up the liquid, Poul and Torsten had to pet each one as their Christmas gifts to the cats before the family could return to the house and prepare for the day's festivities.

Peder and Charlotte arrived shortly before three o'clock. They sent the children upstairs while they carried in presents. Then the whole family attended Christmas Eve church services.

Adelaide and Anna had prepared a traditional feast, with help from Inge and even Tilde, who still had a lot to learn about cooking. All through the meal, Anna watched her children try to contain their excitement about the gifts to come.

When Halvor and Anna finally threw open the doors to the parlor, the older children squealed in excitement. Anesa and Karoline stared in awe at the tree and the mountain of presents.

While the other children opened their gifts, Anesa sat on Anna's lap, looking with wonder at the pink flannel nightdress Charlotte had made for her. When Anesa opened the box with the doll Anna had given her, the little girl turned, one eyebrow raised in a questioning slant. She held up the toy. "Anesa's?"

Anna hugged Anesa and kissed the top of her head. "Yes. That's Anesa's baby."

Anesa hugged the doll to her and kissed the top of its head. Then, still holding her doll in one hand, she turned and threw her arms around Anna's neck, nearly choking her. The doll's small cloth body lay against her back.

Anna reveled in the spontaneous embrace as she held the little girl to her.

Halvor brought the cradle he had made for the doll, with the quilt and pillow Anna had stitched inside it. Anesa hopped to the floor, tucked her new doll in, and began rocking it.

Anna had knitted a cap and scarf for Halvor, which he opened and immediately donned. Before removing his cap, he expressed his appreciation several times. She had hidden another gift for him in the box with the clock key, but wanted to wait until they were alone to give it to him.

He gave her a small, spoon-carved side table with a drawer. "It's made of walnut from one of the trees we felled to make room for the basement." A shy smile curved his lips. "I cured the wood in the bunkhouse and moved it to the cabin, hoping to someday find a use for it."

Her stomach felt as if a flock of butterflies had taken wing in it. "It's lovely."

Anna glanced around the room. Halvor had supported her in every effort to build this house. In everything she did. Whenever she'd needed him, he had been there. He never tried to make her be anything but herself. He knew her secrets, her flaws, her history, and still he loved her. Her chest swelled with love for him.

She smiled. "I'll treasure it always."

When the gifts had all been opened, Halvor and Peder moved the Christmas tree to the middle of the room. Tilde played the piano as everyone but the babies joined hands, encircling the tree. They danced around it in various skips, shuffles, and steps, singing songs in English about decking the halls and in Danish about Christmas lasting until Easter.

As the night wound down, the children were put to bed. Youngest first, then oldest.

When only the adults were left, they drank a toast to the *Jul* with the sherry Peder had brought. Soon Adelaide left for the cabin. Then Peder and Charlotte retired to the housekeeper's quarters that served as their guest rooms.

Anna and Halvor were left alone. Silence settled on the room. The flicker of lamplight cast dancing shadows on the walls.

Still wearing the gray wool scarf she had given him over his black Sunday suit, he eased the Christmas tree back to its corner. Mussed from when he had removed the cap, his blond hair fell casually across his forehead.

She fetched the box in the velvet pouch from the key case. When she met him in the center of the room, he also held a velvet pouch. A shudder of anticipation rippled through her.

"I have one more gift for you," she said, feeling shy as a child.

"And I have one for you." He grinned.

"Open this first." She held the pouch out to him.

He slipped his gift to her into his jacket pocket. Carefully, he loosened the drawstring and pulled out the gold box. Slowly, he lifted the lid, revealing the pocket watch she had selected especially for him. He opened the case and stared at the engraving.

"To H. from A. with love." He read the words aloud then looked up at her. Love shone in his eyes. "I'll cherish it always."

She smiled.

He reached into his pocket and pulled out his gift for her. Instead of handing it to her, he held it behind his back.

"Before I give this to you, I have something to ask." He knelt on one knee. "My sweet Anna, will you marry me?"

Her chest felt as if it might burst. Tears pooled in her eyes. "Yes."

He stood and handed her the velvet bag. It held a small square box. Her hands shook as she opened it, revealing a ring, with a ruby in the center, surrounded by eight diamonds. She gasped.

Halvor took the ring out and slid it on her finger. "The ruby is my love for you. The diamonds are your children."

"It's perfect." She brought his hand to her lips. "I love you."

The clock struck twelve.

"*Glaedelig Jul.*" Halvor slipped the ring onto her finger.

"Merry Christmas," Anna answered softly. His strong arms enveloped her. She looked up into his summer-sky eyes. "And happy New Year."

"It will be." He kissed her forehead. "And may we have many happy new years together."

Acknowledgement

I would like to thank to Annabelle Irvine, Howard Lund, and the Cedar Falls Historical Society for their assistance in my research for this story. I would also like to thank Kit Wells and to my critique group (Mariah Ambersen, Mary DeSive, Jenn Thor, and Deb Hines) for their feedback and support during the writing and revising of this manuscript. Without their help, *The Legacy* would not have become the story it is today.

I am also grateful to Elizabeth Gilbert for her book, *Big Magic*, which convinced me that writing for the sheer joy of it is a worthwhile endeavor.

About the Author

Ann Markim has enjoyed a three-act career, with each act allowing her to pursue a personal passion. After graduate school, she pursued her love of people, working in and directing programs providing care and services to improve the lives of elderly people and individuals with disabilities.

In her second act, she owned and operated a retail nature store. This afforded her opportunity to share her love and knowledge of birds and nature with customers, children, and other interested people through conversations in her shop and presentations to school groups and various nature and gardening organizations.

Now, in her third act, she is devoting full time to her passion for writing. Her interest in writing historical novels began some time ago with her curiosity about her ancestors and evolved into a fascination with researching historical events and imagining what life must have been like in those earlier eras. Although the stories she writes are fictional, they are set in actual historical settings and she includes authentic details about real occurrences.

Ann lives in Omaha, Nebraska, with her two cats, Ripley and Riley. In addition to writing, she enjoys gardening, quilting, and traveling.

Follow her on Facebook at www.facebook.com/AnnMarkim
Website: AnnMarkim.com

CPSIA information can be obtained
at www.ICGtesting.com
Printed in the USA
FSHW021303070219
55539FS